Wonders of My World

U.S HIGHWAYS

Cover art licensed from Shutterstock.com
Interior photos from private collection and from Shutterstock.com

First Paperback Edition
ISBN 978-1-939275-56-1

Wonders of My World

U.S. HIGHWAYS

Aroslav

*Based on the true story of my
Erotic Journey Around America
as told to Devon Layne*

Elder Road Books
Bellevue WA

Starting the Adventure

I KEPT putting off letting this story out because I'm not the kind of guy to kiss and tell. And after I've told a story a few times, I forget what part happened and what part I made up. As I told my daughter (also a writer) some time ago, my characters are often more real to me than the real people I meet.

"Dad, Dad!" she said. "Back in the 1800s, life was hard and people worked in terrible conditions to make a pittance of a living." *Did she think I lived back then?* "But at the same time dirty urban life was sapping the will to live out of people, opium became more popular. Because people could go to the opium den and they'd live in the world in their heads for a while. That world was so much better than the reality they existed in. Dad, words are our opium."

When did my daughter become so wise?

Then Alice convinced me to write the story of my trip around the world. *Border Crossings* was a crack in the dike of my memories. Soon, everything came flooding out. When she finished reading the story, she encouraged me to write more about my time wandering around the country. And Alice can be very persuasive.

So, here are the first adventures of Aroslav—the avatar of the pseudonym of the alter ego of an author. (Parse that!) There's a lot of story and sightseeing in *U.S. Highways*—kind of a travelogue through my life—but there's sex, too, even if it's slow at times. That's what my life is like. And when I started writing about the wonders of my world, it jogged my memories of some of the incredible women I've known and loved in my life.

I get sidetracked a lot and those memories from long ago become as important to me as the story I'm living in the moment. Bear with me. It's my life. Based on the true story of my travels and memories, only the names, places, and events have been changed to protect the innocent and to keep several beautiful women and from hunting me down to call me a liar.

The problem is that I've fallen in love with each of them.

~~~

A Few Years Ago: Pushed from the Nest

TREASURE AND I hadn't slept in the same bed in a year. I spent most nights asleep in the recliner in my office. Had my pillow there and a blanket. It was a big empty house for two people now that Maddie had her own apartment. Mostly, we talked about proper editorial use of terms in the manuscripts we edited and the books I designed. Neither one was paying the bills and we were dipping further into our retirement savings. That formed the other half of our conversations.

One thing had remained constant through the years. I still got up at five. My stories are full of characters who get up early in the morning. Lately, it took me about five minutes before I could stand up straight enough to walk to the bathroom after I got out of bed. My back had been deteriorating steadily for several years, even after we bought the $10,000 bed I mistakenly thought was going to be our new playground.

I picked up the newspaper from the front steps—something I could usually do without having to get dressed. I stumbled to the kitchen and made coffee while I scanned the headlines and read the comics. I made a second pot at six-thirty, frothed hot milk for Treasure's latte, and woke her up. I left the newspaper and coffee beside the bed and went to make breakfast.

Those morning wakeup calls are still some of my fondest memories. That was when Treasure would smile and thank me for the best cup of coffee ever.

The house was expensive. The mortgage was high. The maintenance was a killer. I grumbled in the kitchen that I could work from anywhere. Why was I writing from a basement in Seattle? I should be out seeing the country while I was still young enough to enjoy it. Treasure and I had always talked about traveling more. We could live on the road cheaper than maintaining this monstrosity that I'd come to view as a prison.

"You should go do it," Treasure said.

I hadn't even realized she'd come from the bedroom. Nor that I was talking aloud. She wore a robe. I hadn't seen her naked in a long time. I detected a slight emphasis on the word 'go'.

"It's time, isn't it?" I said. "We should get the house on the market, I suppose. And see a lawyer."

She nodded.

It took six more months to get things ready. We divided up what we wanted, settled our finances, and filed for divorce. July first, I moved into my new home—a sixteen-foot travel trailer, towed by a new F150.

Then a miracle happened.

I woke up after my first night in the little trailer and made coffee. *I just got up and went to the stove and made coffee.* It took me a few minutes before I realized that I had no back pain.

I was a full time RVer and eschewed freeways. I decided to follow some of the old network of highways that cross this nation. This is based on the true story of my travel down U.S. Highways since then.

⌒⌒⌒

17 August 2013

I WAS ON my own, cutting through Montana with nothing but the road, my thoughts, and me. How'd Tony put it in *The Prodigal*? "Me, myself, and I. Which asshole would you like to speak to?" I'd been through road construction all through Montana. Interstate highways were for people who had a destination. I had only a journey. This U.S. Highway was a one-lane dirt track fifty miles long, occasionally interrupted by a stretch of pavement. I drove behind a pilot truck with a sign that said 'Follow me', and the line of cars and trucks—mostly trucks—followed in a cloud of dust. I was glad my trailer was safely in an RV park while I went exploring Glacier National Park. I couldn't have pulled it over Going to the Sun Road in the park anyway, and this construction outside the park would have been murder on it. By the time I got out of the construction zone my shiny black F150 was two-tone dust and mud.

I'm sure my throat was the same color. I needed coffee.

McDonald's serves a decent cup of Joe. I'd had it with paying $3.50 a pop for an espresso when I can make drip coffee in the trailer that is just as good. If it's decent coffee, I'll drink it. Even half-way decent. And McDonald's almost always has clean restrooms. I was bursting when I got there. My bladder's only good for thirty miles or thirty minutes—whichever comes first.

As I pulled out of the parking lot, I spotted girls in short-shorts and t-shirts jumping up and down across the street trying to attract people to their carwash to support the high school cheerleaders. Carwash? Cheerleaders? Sounds like a movie I watched once. I took my dollar-a-cup coffee and drove across the street.

"You do trucks?" I asked the woman who came out to meet me as I drove in.

"This is Montana, cowboy. Bay 2."

"How much."

"It's donation. You know, thousand bucks or whatever spare change you've got lying around." I laughed, handed her a ten and pulled into the spot she pointed to. Even if all they did was rinse the top layer off, it would be worth it. Three juvenile girls ran up, reminded me to close the windows and told me I didn't need to stay in the truck. I got out with my coffee and watched them go to work. Apparently, the upper classmen were out on the street hustling business because they were... better at hustling, I guess. These little girls were just that. Little girls.

"Is this for the freshman cheer squad?" I asked the woman who had taken my money.

"Freshmen, JV, and varsity," she responded. "The older girls get the younger ones to do as much of the work as possible."

"Are you the coach?"

"I'm the mother of one of the coaches. I don't even have a girl on the squad and I get stuck out here supervising the teenies." We laughed and talked a bit. Turns out her daughter, the coach, wasn't much older than the varsity cheerleaders.

"I'm afraid those little girls can't even reach the hood of the truck."

"They are little. We'll let them work on what they can reach and the seniors will show up eventually. You're not in a hurry, are you?"

"Hurry is a suburb of Seattle I left behind me months ago."

It was obvious when the seniors showed up. I don't know what it is, but a miracle occurs between the ages of fourteen and seventeen. I guess it's called puberty. As I looked around, I could pretty much pick out the freshmen, sophomores, and juniors. But when the seniors showed up to take over scrubbing the truck, there was a whole different game to watch. The little girls had grown into young women.

I moved to the back of the bay so I could watch without being on display to the entire community. Nobody needed to see an old dude with a cup of coffee and a hard-on watching cheerleaders getting wet. They all introduced themselves with a wave and a little cheer jump. Julie was about five-two and robust. She hadn't lost all her baby fat, but there wasn't an ounce of it I wouldn't have been willing to nibble. She was bubbly, cheerleaderly, and... well, the bouncy parts bounced... a lot. Megan was blonde, about four inches taller and thinner all over except in the boobs. *Here's the girl that screws the quarterback. And when he's not looking she does the halfback, tackle, and tight end. Correction. She has* the tight end. It was encased in skin-tight pink hot pants through which I could clearly see her bikini line. I reminded myself she was seventeen and I didn't even have Montana plates on my truck.

Then there was Alice. I looked past her at first glance and then I came back to her. *Shit, she's tall!* Black hair, smallish tits and thin, but with such a tiny waist that her hips flared out nicely. But tall. Yeah.

Close to six feet. I'd either look up at her or really get a good look at her. I've always had a thing for tall thin girls. It wasn't just her shape that drew my attention, but the almost cat-like grace with which she moved, playfully tossing a sponge to her friends or dodging the spray across the truck.

"Okay, watch out!" Megan shouted. "I'm going to spray the conditioner on."

Conditioner? My truck was going to come out shiny and silky soft. I chuckled as Alice ducked over toward me to avoid the spray.

"Hey. That's a nice truck. New?"

"Yeah. Pretty new. It was a dirty little pig, though."

"It's going to be all shiny now. Are you from around here?"

"Oh. No. I live on the road. My address is on my license plate."

"That's just a license number."

"Yep. I pull a travel trailer and just go wherever the truck points."

"I want to come."

"I'm... uh... not sure I can do anything about that."

"Oh! You have a dirty mind."

"That's how I get paid."

"How?"

"I'm a writer. I write mysteries, thrillers, and erotic romances."

"You're kidding. Those are my three favorite things to read."

"Aren't you a little young for erotic romance?"

"I'm eighteen, so I'm not jailbait if that's what you're implying."

"I just... well, I know you are in high school."

"I got a late start. Okay, I flunked seventh grade. I'd just found out about sex and was a little distracted. I got my act back together, though. I've got grades good enough to stay on the team and get into college. I got early acceptance to the University already."

"Well, even if you aren't jailbait, it wouldn't be a good idea for me to talk to you here about erotic romances."

"What if I told you there was a place you could talk to me about it?" she asked.

"What do you mean?"

"Well, I'm a year older than my friends and my folks sort of stopped supporting me when I turned eighteen. They still let me live at home and usually feed me, but they're really focused on my little sister to make sure she doesn't turn out like me."

"You seem to have turned out just fine."

Alice checked to see if anyone was watching and pulled a card out of her back pocket. She wore cut-offs that barely covered her butt-ledge. Her phone bulged out of one pocket. She handed me the card. It was a 'free admission' card for Roxie's Foxes.

"What's this?"

"The gentlemen's club where I work. I start at six. Stop by and you'll see more of this." She pulled her crop top to the side with her bra and exposed a nipple. "I want to know more about what you write and how you manage to live on the road."

"Dry time!" Julie yelled. Alice spun away from me in time to catch a chamois so she could help strip the water from my truck. Strip. Yeah. Well. I didn't need to be back at my campsite tonight. I could sleep in the truck. It was clean, after all.

~~~~~~

A Long Time Ago: Carly the Clown

NEARLY EVERY TALL thin woman I've written about has been based in some way or another on Carly the Clown. That is not disparaging.

Back when I was working with an unnamed theater group years ago... Well, the important thing was that Carly was part of that group and I thought she was heavenly. She was 6' 1" and thin. Her breasts scarcely bumped out her shirt. Her hair was black and, when I met her, she was one of those totally natural girls who didn't shave anything. *But damn!* That girl kissed with her whole body.

It was the middle of September when I gave her a lift one evening. We were talking and laughing—having a great time. When I got to her apartment, she leaned across the seat to give me a thank-you kiss. The minute our lips touched, the lights flickered. I think it sucked the electricity right out of the power lines. The little thank-you kiss turned into a you're-welcome kiss. I made sure she knew she was welcome any time. We made out in the front seat of the car for a quarter of an hour when some dude flashed his headlights at us and I realized we were parked across three spaces. I was just letting her off, after all.

"Um… see you next week," she said.

"Definitely," I answered. I was so slick back then.

When she got out of the car, I had to turn the window defogger on in order to pull into traffic.

The next week, September really arrived, complete with the rain that marked the season's change.

"Would you like to come over for dinner tomorrow night?" she asked as we finished a breath-taking kiss on Friday night in front of her apartment.

"I'd love to. Can I bring a bottle of wine?"

"That would be great. See you at six."

That was all it took. We actually did have dinner, but the lights were flickering all evening. I waited until we'd gone a step beyond kissing, holding her tiny breasts in my hand as I dipped to lick her nipples.

"I'd love a glass of wine now," I said. We hadn't opened it with dinner. "I don't object to where this is heading, but I wanted to know we were going there before we drank anything."

"As long as you're okay with this heading into my bed, then we can drink anything you want."

That first night we made love was earthshaking. I already had her shirt off and she had mine open to the waist. We sipped our wine and I 'accidentally' spilled a little on her. It ran down her chest and I lowered my head to lick it up. I had to be sure I got everything, so there wasn't much of her long, elegant torso that I didn't lick.

"I'm a little sticky. Would you like to cool off in a warm tub?" Carly asked me as she nibbled on my ear and stroked my cock through my too-tight jeans.

"That would be great."

"I use a diaphragm, so we can't make love in the tub. Okay?"

"Let's enjoy the bath and then make love," I answered. "Carly. Just so you know, I do want to make love to you."

"Oh, yeah," she answered. "Oh, yeah. Last week, after you kissed me in the car, all the windows steamed over in the apartment when I walked in. Oh god, Ari. I want you so much."

We slipped into the tub and Carly leaned back against me between my legs. Just feeling her back and butt against my cock kept me rigid. For my part, gently washing her front as she lay back was an experience I'll never forget. I'd never been with a woman who didn't shave, at least under her arms, but I shampooed all her hair and found the silky texture of her pits as erotic as the thick curls between her legs. We finally stepped out of the tub and dried each other on a single towel then went to her bed.

I can't say that making love to Carly was necessarily the best sex of my life, but I knew the instant I entered her that this was my lover. We might not always be lovers, but we would always be lovers now. There was something about this woman, taller than me, hairier than me, but as sensuous and lithe as any lover could be. We fit together.

I look back on that time with a sense of yearning. We got together periodically over the years. Even when she moved to Colorado on her way to LA, I found a way to visit one summer and coming together was as easy as it was the first time. The lights still flickered. I don't know where she is now, but somehow I know that if I ever come upon Carly the Clown, we'll still be lovers now.

~~~~~~

Back to Alice

I HUNG AROUND town and went to Cabela's to get some supplies that I needed. You can never have enough stuff from Cabela's. I'd spotted the store near the interstate and decided to just stop in. About five-thirty, I realized I was just hanging around waiting to go to Roxie's Foxes. Well, I figured I might as well try it out. I hadn't seen an eighteen-year-old pussy since I was... well, eighteen. In fact, I hadn't seen any pussy in a good long while—even while I was married. I spent the next half hour munching down a venison burger in Cabela's little café and then headed for Roxie's.

I walked into the club at six-fifteen. I'd grabbed a couple hundred from a cash machine. I knew I'd have to tip and maybe I'd buy a dance.

They charged ten bucks for a soda water once I was inside, but gave me a two-for-one dance coupon. I settled into a seat in front of the stage, one of only about four guys in the room.

The first dancer—Jewel—moved to the music pretty well and I tossed a buck on the stage for her during the first number. I sat back down and she pranced over, did a couple pseudo-sensuous moves, including turning her back to me and bending at the waist to pick up my bill and twerk a bit. She had a nice ass, but was covered with tats. I like a little ink, but I felt like I needed reading glasses for this babe. I was enjoying the show, though, and when her top came off I put another buck on the stage. She stopped me before I turned away, pulled my Stetson off, and put it on her own head. She pulled my face forward and buried it between her tits. I kept my mouth shut. I'd seen the guy on the other side of the stage licking her and didn't want to kiss him second hand. I sat back down and an elegant vision sidled up to me and asked if she could join me. I looked up into the eyes of Alice.

I'd like to tell you all about the color of her eyes and their depth, yadda yadda yadda. But if you've ever been in a strip club, you know the lighting is such that you can't see any of that detail. Just when you think you've locked in on something, a light hits you in the eyes and you can't see anything. I scooted over on my little bench and she curled up beside me.

"I'm glad you decided to stop by."

"My curiosity got the best of me. You can dance here at 18?"

"Yeah. Maybe we bend the rules a little, but I'm only here twice a week. Gotta earn my way in the world."

"Don't you get hassled by fellow students?"

"They're rigid about checking ID on guys if they look younger than 35. They can't buy booze until 21. Most of my classmates aren't 18 yet and can't get in. I'll deal with it when they start having birthdays."

I watched as Jewel lost her g-string. Her pussy was wide open when she got on her hands and knees and crawled across the stage. She got a tip and clacked the heels of her thick platforms together.

"You need to tip her now," Alice whispered. I pulled out another single and leaned toward the stage. Jewel crooked her finger for me to stay at the edge of the stage. She smiled at me and picked up the dollar bill I'd creased and laid on the stage. Her eyes never left mine as she slid the crease through her slit then shoved the bill in my mouth. She bent toward me and took the bill from my lips with her lips. Then she dragged my face down through her cleavage and onto her belly as she stood up and pushed me gently back to my seat. *Shit!* That was the closest I'd been to a pussy in… a long time.

"Doesn't she have a great ass?" Alice asked.

"Yeah. I'd have to say so," I answered.

"So what do you write?"

"Oh. Well, I like romantic stories. Plenty of sex, but more interested in the character development."

"Good. I want more than Tab A into Slot B and come. What do you want here?"

"Well, it's been a while since I actually saw Slot B, so I thought a little primary research was in order."

"Just wait till you see Dakota. She'll show you all the primary you want." We chuckled at the joke. "Of course, if you'd like your research to be a little more hands-on, we've got the special running now of seven songs for a hundred or happy hour for just two hundred. Let me know."

Two hundred for an hour? I'd already spent twenty of the two hundred I got from the cash machine. That wasn't going to happen.

"Enjoy the show. I'll be on in a bit. Save your two-fer card for me," Alice said. She left me to consider how long seven songs would be.

Three other dancers sat beside me for a song or two, but when they realized I was just tipping the stage dancer and not buying dances, they got up and moved away. Jewel did a good job of trying to get me to use my two-for-one and buy her drinks and God knows what else. I kept looking around, but didn't see Alice anywhere. I got another ten-dollar soda water from the waitress just so I could get singles to tip the dancers. The waitress was cute enough that I tipped her, too. After a while, the DJ announced Sierra coming to the stage.

Alice crawled on like a cat. I was a mouse caught in her eyes. My first single was on the stage floor before she'd finished her first circuit.

Apparently, Sierra was her stage name. She stood, looked me in the eye and scuffed the bill toward the back of the stage with her foot before turning to the other side of the stage. After other dancers who tried to shove their tits in the mouths of tippers, I wasn't expecting the brush-off. But I was still hopeful.

The second number, she lost her top. She was a little bigger up top than Carly. Her areolae weren't huge and were just a shade darker than her skin. Her nipples were hard dark points in the center. I had another dollar on the stage before I realized I'd moved. Alice turned toward me and gave me a hug, her bare tits rubbing against my shirt.

"Look close," she whispered. "This is what you came to see, isn't it?"

I looked. Little bumps rose in the soft flesh of her tits as they slid across my cheek, almost but not quite touching my lips. Alice moved away and kept dancing. I had another bill out as soon as I sat down, thinking about what would happen next. I waited until the end of the song and Alice kept making her circuit of the stage, pretending to dance—sometimes grabbing the pole and swinging herself around it. Finally, I saw her hand drop to the ties of her bikini bottoms. She pulled the cord and turned away so I could see the back of the g-string disappear down her crack as she pulled it through.

I've seen lots of girls in my life—not hundreds, but plenty—and couldn't remember lining myself up behind a woman whose pussy was as full and open when she bent over. It was better than any movie I'd seen. I don't kid myself. Dancers in a strip club are there to earn the money, not to get turned on. If there was any glistening moisture around her pussy lips, it was just sweat. But looking at that 18-year-old flower from beneath her ass-cheeks made my nostrils flare as I imagined the scent of her arousal. I knew what it would be. A little sharp, but enticing. A flavor that I'd search weeks to find a word for and still never be satisfied with—sweet, tangy, spicy—what difference did it make. I'd try to find the word after I'd tasted her. *Fantasy.*

I took her another bill and she simply pulled my face between her breasts to make sure I felt exactly how soft and smooth they were.

I didn't look at the next dancer. My eyes were closed as I sat in front of the stage. I felt the short couch shift and warm breath swept across my ears.

"A-ri," she breathed in my ear. "Are you ready for some more primary research? We can go back to the naughty room."

"Yeah," I said. "I've got a hundred, is that special still on?"

"I'm going to make it really special. In fact, you've still got a two-for-one coupon. Two specials for one low price!"

She danced. Nearly an hour of rubbing against me and pushing her breasts into my face, letting my hands hold her thighs as she ground her pussy against my hard-on. That feeling was exquisite. Her bra top came off slowly, finally letting the nip free so I could catch it between my lips as she rubbed back and forth against my face. We both moaned.

"Help me along a little, Ari. Dancing for you has me all turned on. Nobody can see," she whispered in my ear. My hands had already strayed to caress her breasts and play with her nipples in the dark room. I sucked one into my mouth and Alice pushed my hand down to my thigh. Then she straddled my thigh and began to grind on my open hand. I got the message and my fingers went to work. Somehow her g-string slipped aside and I slipped inside. "Oh, god, yes!" she moaned in my ear. She had one hand supporting herself on my shoulder and the other had managed to open the buttons on my 501s and slip inside to stroke my cock through my briefs. I was imminently going to make a mess, but what I was feeling on my hand told me Alice was about to make a mess as well. I found her little button and slid a finger on either side of it as I carefully rubbed up and down.

Alice slammed her lips against mine and her tongue into my mouth to muffle her scream as she came. Her grip on my cock tightened painfully and when she released the pressure, the relief was so great that I jerked as spurts of come filled my shorts. She panted as she collapsed against me and pulled my hand out of her teabag.

The last song of our set played and she sank onto me with her arms around my neck and her cheek rubbing against my beard.

"I want to go with you," she whispered. "Do you have room?"

"You need to finish school," I answered, nobler than I felt. I'd just spent nearly an hour with a high school girl's tits, ass, and pussy in my hands. *Now I'm getting conservative?*

"But I want to do what you're doing. And I could provide more… inspiration."

"Do you want to be in a story?"

"Yeah. Yeah."

"What kind of story?"

"A really good one. Write about tonight."

I could feel her soft pussy as it continued to push against my wet cock. I could imagine a good story all right. I hugged her to mer.

"Here's my card. If you're serious, send me an email and I'll send you the story this weekend. Keep in touch. If you still want to join me when you graduate, I'll swing back up to Montana to pick you up. We need to be clear on the rules, though. I'm not rich. I just travel."

"I'll save my money so I can pay my own way."

"It doesn't cost much, but I don't go out and party every night."

"Would you like to party in?"

"In you."

"Send me the story."

I slept the night in the cab of my nice clean pickup truck. I've got to make a more comfortable bed when I'm doing overnights away from the trailer. I'll figure that out. I've got a few months.

~~~~~~

31 August 2013

ARI,

Thank you for the story, baby. Reading it made me come again, just thinking about your fingers slipping through my wet folds. It was just right. Well, we didn't really spend a whole hour, did we? But otherwise you told it the way I want to remember it.

Exotic dancers say about anything to make a buck. Who am I kidding? Exotic dancer? Stripper? I behaved like a fucktoy. That's why I have to tell you that I don't do that kind of thing all the time. In fact, it scared me that I lost control and let you touch me there and make me come. I've had guys come in their pants before, but not me. I know a couple of

14

girls make arrangements to meet guys later and turn tricks. You could have fucked Jewel for the amount you spent on me. But I don't do that. I'm using my body to earn money to live on and for college. Jewel's selling hers for dope.

The thing is that I dream about the places you write about in your blog. Thanks for friending me. I loved the pix of the Nez Perce battleground. So desolate and yet such a deep rich beauty. I can understand why they fought to keep their land. And I just wanted to be there with you, looking out over that wild landscape.

I guess that's what I'm writing about. I still want to come with you. (Get it?)

I know I have to finish school and next year I'll be in college and I can't just abandon my own life to go live yours. But maybe you could write more about the trip. Why don't you write about your other adventures with girls along the way? I bet I'm not the only one whose pussy you've had your fingers in. You need to tell the story—the story that I want to hear, not the sanitized version you post for family and friends.

Can you do that, Ari? For me? Please?

Big wet kisses, baby.

Alice

~~~

15 August 2016

THREE YEARS ON the road now. I wrote about my adventures for Alice periodically, but I never got around to editing and publishing them. After all, I write strong, character-driven romances and coming of age stories. It's about the story, not about the sex. The story Alice wanted to hear was... well, it was the story of the sex and the characters are the people I have known through my life. Alice is a very physical girl.

This is my memoir—meaning it's my life as I remember it. It cuts back and forth a lot between my adventure on the road and my memories from before—sometimes long before. I find myself daydreaming a lot, but I call it plotting the next story. Like my time on the road, I sometimes get lost along the way.

I took the road less traveled. Now where the fuck am I?

1 Disciplinary Action

19 September 2013

THE PLACE was billed as a condo resort in the Mojave Desert, but the rooms were little more than a hotel room with a half-kitchen and living area. It was nice, though, to get out of the trailer for a week and have unlimited hot water for showers, a big bed, a swimming pool, and a hot tub. The scenery at the pool wasn't bad either. It was a spa, so there weren't that many little kids and those that were there confined their activity to the waterslide and kiddie side of the pool. It was a big pool that wound its way around a fake rock island. The entrance to the waterslide was on top, but beneath it, in a grotto complete with a waterfall, was a spa. The jets were locked in the 'on' position.

I'd put the trailer in storage for the week. I own some timeshares—one of the world's great rip-offs—and tried to use up the weeks by taking a break from the trailer periodically. It also gave me the opportunity to haul my printer out of the cubbyhole where I stored it and print out various business things, like royalty statements and first drafts of stories that I wanted to work on with a pencil. I still do that at times.

I'd made it my habit to get to the pool soon after it opened at eight in the morning and to come back in the evening between five and ten when it was 'adults only.' I was catching up on some work, some writing, and my personal finances—which were in ragged shape. I didn't like how money was running through my fingers. That's probably why I wasn't paying all that much attention as I opened the stairwell door and headed down for my evening dip in the pool.

I get a room on an upper floor—third in this case—and convince myself that I'm exercising when I use the stairs instead of the elevator. The truth is, the stairs are faster. I hate waiting for elevators as much as I hate waiting for an Internet connection on the resort's antiquated WiFi. So, I didn't even see her before I was sitting on my butt in the middle of the staircase with a blonde bikini model towering over me. The impact had jarred loose the towel she'd had wrapped around her waist and her still-wet suit outlined a luscious cleft between her legs and the distinct shape of her nipples up top.

"Oh, my god! I'm sorry. I'm so sorry. Are you all right? Oh, please be all right." She knelt on the step beside me and wrapped an arm around me, pressing those golden globes against my arm. I shook my head to clear it and shifted my weight to test my tailbone. The shift rubbed her breasts against my arm delightfully. She, on the other hand, thought my headshake was an answer to her question. "Don't move. I'll call an ambulance." She started to get up, but I caught her arm and pulled her back down beside me.

"I'm okay," I said. "Just a little shook up and impressed by your… um… charms."

A pink glow began in her cheeks and spread down over her breasts in a wave, but she didn't move them away from where they were pressed against my arm. She was quiet a moment before she spoke softly.

"May I help you up, *sir*?"

There is absolutely nothing in this world that makes me feel like an old fart as much as having a beautiful young woman call me "sir." Still, she wasn't exactly running away from me.

"My name's Aroslav," I said. "What's yours?"

"Angie, sir. Um, Mr. Aroslav."

"Well, Angie, on future trips, maybe you could lift your pretty eyes up the stairs. If you really want to land on top of me, I can think of several ways you could that would be more pleasant."

"I'm so sorry, sir. Is there *anything* I can do for you to make it better?" I'm sure she didn't have in mind what instantly sprang to my mind—and was influencing the springing of other parts as well. "Can I go get your wife or help you to her?"

"I'm alone here," I said. "No one needs to be notified that I've been bowled over by a beautiful young woman. I suppose you need to get back to your boyfriend." I was making the same assumption she was. Few people come to these resort hotels alone.

"I don't have a boyfriend. I'm here with my mother. I'm trying to plot out the next three months or the rest of my life or something. Listen to me babble. Please let me help you, Mr. Aroslav, sir. Then you can tell me what kind of punishment I should have for being so careless."

Lights, bells, and sirens went off in my head. She bowed her head as I stood up, her blush continuing all the way to her waist. This was a woman who needed to make up for her mistakes. There was just one obstacle preventing me from taking matters in hand, so to speak.

"Angie, how old are you?"

"Twenty-two, sir." She didn't hesitate or attempt to lie. She kept her head down, refusing to look me in the eye. Her hair had come loose from a knot on top and the strands were so light that they blew in the slightest breeze as a stairway door opened two floors below us.

"Angie, you are to meet me in the grotto spa in twenty minutes." She looked up at me, her eyes wide. "This is a one-time offer, Angie. Do not attempt to speak to me again if you are not there in twenty minutes." I bent to retrieve her towel and handed it to her. Her breathing had quickened. She took the towel but made no attempt to cover herself as she stood staring at me. I thought, in fact, that she straightened up a bit and pushed her pretty breasts out more. Well, maybe you can't just push those points out the way they popped. It could have been an automatic reaction to the breeze, I suppose.

"Yes, sir," she whispered. Then looking up at the last flight to the third-floor door, she ran up and through the door. Somehow, I didn't feel so old when she called me sir this time. I nodded to an overweight couple as they puffed up to the second-floor landing and I went ahead to the pool.

～～～

I DON'T KNOW what got into me. Under normal circumstances, I would have chatted her up, flirted, invited her for a drink, and been summarily dismissed. This time I'd simply given her twenty minutes to hide in her room and then by my own declaration she would never need to speak to me or acknowledge my existence again.

I'm not much of a dom. I can be just as pussy-whipped as the next guy and have always been attracted to strong, independent women. The kind who eventually get bored with me. Don't ever believe a woman when she says she'll never get tired of you being sappy and romantic. It's not true.

Still, the idea of having a twenty-two-year-old blonde bombshell submissively attending to my every whim put some lead in my pencil. I had to really think through how I would handle this situation. I wasn't even sure I could maintain a position of dominance for very long. I mean, playing a game for a night was one thing, but actually taking on a sub was serious business. First, I'm not rich. I can't just take on a dependent. So, if I'm not providing money, a home, security, a new wardrobe, an education, a house with five bedrooms in a good suburb, health insurance, and 2.3 children, what is the attraction for a woman to subjugate her beautiful body to me? And not just her body. From everything I'd read, submissiveness like Angie was showing was a psychological need. It surrendered the key thing that my life was built on: making decisions. My best hope was that she realized what a mistake it was and didn't show up.

I went over my impressions of her in my mind, kicking myself that I hadn't spent more time just looking at her.

I guessed she was about 5' 2" or near that. It was hard to tell when we were on a stairway, but I was sure she was significantly shorter than me. There was no question that she was beautiful. She had a narrow waist enhanced by a fairly flat stomach with just a hint of softness in the middle. Personally, I don't have washboard abs, but I was proud of the fact that I was one of the fitter men at the pool and didn't have the pronounced beer gut that so many had. I made a note to myself to start working out a little more. I'd like to be in damned good shape by the time I get to Florida next spring.

Of course, thinking about her stomach gave me cause to let my memories drift a little lower. Her pale blue bikini tied just below her hipbones and the tiny scrap of fabric that was tightly stretched between her legs, accented the Delta of Venus. Her labia were puffy enough to give a distinctive shape to the nearly transparent fabric that showed none of the roughness that pubic hair would cause. Her legs looked smooth and, while lightly tanned by the desert sun, looked healthy and not overcooked.

The breasts she'd so innocently—innocently??—pressed into my arms were not huge and were what sparked my fears that she was a teenager. They were soft, though, and her nipples bumped out the fabric nicely. Her face had a clear complexion with lush lips framing nearly perfect white teeth. What struck me most, though, was the electric blue of her eyes—so deep and intense. With her feathery blonde hair floating around her head, she looked like an angel.

At least in my memory.

A Long Time Ago: Spank

MY LITTLE COUSIN liked to play at 'discipline'. Of course, we didn't call it that. We called it being naughty and getting spanked. Playfully, of course. I never tried to hurt her. But when the families got together—our mothers were sisters—the kids would all scatter and Emmy and I would often get left to our own devices. She was a year younger than me and I figured I was too old to babysit her. The older kids, on the other hand, felt the same way about me.

So, Emmy and I ended up being thrown together. I would tell her to do things, hoping to get her to go back to the house and play with dolls while I became a pirate sailing my imaginary ship across the sea. She would obey my commands. Climb to the second limb in the willow tree. Swing higher than my head and jump into the sand pit. Spin around the monkey bar on one leg. I didn't think she knew that everything I told her to do showed me her panties. *Ha!*

Girls all wore skirts in those days—at least Emmy did. Climbing, swinging, and other gymnastics would show her panties to me and ever since playing doctor with the neighbor girl, I'd been fascinated by what was up there.

There was a locker room joke about the little girl who came home from school with her pockets jingling with change. 'Where did you get all that money?' her mother asked. 'The boys paid me to swing high on the swing,' the little girl said proudly. 'Honey, don't you know the boys were just trying to see your underwear?' mother asked exasperatedly. 'Yeah, but I fooled them. I took my panties off.'

Emmy had me fooled.

Eventually, she would refuse to do something or she'd sneak up behind me and push me or she'd stick her tongue out at me. What could I do but chase her down and punish her? I'd manage to drag her—not putting up much resistance—to a tree stump and pull her over my knee so I could spank her. We played the game a lot that summer.

It started out that I'd just spank her a couple swats and then she'd jump up and run away or stick out her tongue again so I'd chase her. The next time, when she accused me of just trying to see her panties, I pulled her over my lap and flipped her skirt up so I spanked the little pink panties in question. It took a little time, but before long she would simply lie on my lap and I'd not only flip up her skirt, but I'd pull down her panties so I could spank her bare bottom.

The spanks kept getting softer, the less clothing that was between my hand and her skin. But I'd give her a lot more of the gentle slaps once she was bare. Maybe my hand stayed on those innocent globes a little longer each time, too.

Emmy told her older sister what we were did, and one day as she was bending over my knee she said, "You can pull my skirt up, but you aren't supposed to pull my panties down. Okay?" Of course it was okay. For the first couple swats. Eventually, her panties ended up around her ankles and my hand ended up on her bare bottom. The difference now was that we knew, explicitly, that we weren't supposed to do that.

After that summer, when we went back to our own schools, we never played the spanking game again. We were more grown up and it wasn't proper behavior. It was my first experience in being a dom and administering punishment. I wasn't very good at it. But my first wet dream was filled with images of that bare butt beneath my hand.

Back to Angie

I SWAM SEVERAL laps, paying absolutely no attention to the time. What difference would it make? I knew she wasn't coming back. I left the pool in the full darkness and made my way into the grotto to soak in the hot water and let the jets beat my back muscles into submission.

"Hello, sir," she whispered beside me before I'd set my foot in the hot water. "Let me take your hand as you come into the water."

"Do you think that I am old and decrepit?" I asked harshly.

"Oh no, sir! I just wanted to… to help you if I could. May I?"

I looked at her. She'd changed to a different bikini, this one white. In the dim light of the grotto it was still easy to make out the exact shape and size of her nipples and areolae. She was waist deep in the water and I stepped down to join her.

"Sit with me, Angie. I want to know more about you."

We settled into the tub and I found a jet that pounded against my lower back. It hadn't felt so good in years. Angie slid right up beside me, our legs touching beneath the turbulent water.

"There's not much to know about me, si…, I mean Mr. Aroslav. I'm twenty-two, a graduate of UCLA with a teaching degree and no job."

"How did you end up here at the spa?" I noticed that she couldn't bring herself to use just my name. Respectful or frightened?

"It was my mother's idea. I've been talking about going on a road trip for a while and she suggested we come out here and talk about it. That means I dream and she convinces me not to."

"We are such stuff as dreams are made on," I quoted.

"And our little life is rounded with a sleep," she concluded. I was impressed. A Shakespeare student?

"What did you say your degree was?"

"Secondary education, technically. It's a teaching degree. I want to teach high school English someday."

"I'm afraid that would be quite a challenge. I can't imagine a high school boy who could sit through your class without getting a hard-on. And you're so young, they might try some inappropriate things."

"Sadly, that's pretty much what was said in my interviews—though they neglected to use the word hard-on." She giggled a little. Then looked at me seriously.

"Do you think I'm that pretty?"

"Absolutely. You must know that."

"Well… um… not exactly. I mean, I know I'm pretty, and I'm not insecure. But I can't identify with it. It still surprises me when someone says I'm pretty. I was always a little overweight in high school and most of college. I decided that I needed to lose the weight and shape up or I'd always regret it. The problem is that I still think of myself like I did when I was fat. And I need to lose more weight. I have this tummy."

She stood on the bench, placing all her delicious bits right at eye-level and patted her tummy. Yes, there was a little roundness to the soft flesh, but I wanted to place my lips on it and begin kissing all over her body. My hand reached of its own volition and I placed it on her soft tummy. She caught her breath, but did not move away. I pulled her back into the water and she floated over onto my lap. I kept my left hand on her stomach as my right guided her.

"What's the difference between men and women?" I asked.

"You mean the obvious, sir? Women have breasts and a vagina and men have a penis and testicles."

"Okay. Beyond the primary sex characteristics."

"Oh. Secondary. Men are hairy… sort of." She placed a hand on my chest among the sparse hairs. Genetically I just didn't come from hairy stock and what little I had on my chest I'd gladly transplant to my head. She moved her hand from my chest to my beard. "Soft," she whispered. "I mean… women are softer than men."

"Yes. Women are usually softer than men, usually not as hairy, usually have a higher voice. There are exceptions on both sides. But those secondary characteristics that make you distinct as a woman—why would you want to get rid of them?" She looked into my eyes as if trying to gauge whether I was serious. I caught the glimmer of a tear there.

"I just don't want to be fat any longer."

"I won't say you are just fine because that discounts how you feel about yourself, but think seriously about what that means before you get caught in a cycle of unending dieting and self-criticism. You are no longer the fat girl. How much thinner do you really want to be, and why? I could show you the most beautiful statues of women in the world and none of them have a flatter stomach than yours." For the first time since I'd pulled her back into the water, she began to relax. She leaned against me.

"Thank you," she whispered. "Would you really show me beautiful statues?"

"Wherever we found them. Now tell me more. Tell me about what these dreams of yours are."

～～～

A Long Time Ago: Follow the Dream
I KNOW SOMETHING of dreams. I've had a few.

And I know what it is like to put them off. As much as I despised the idea of working in technical theater instead of being a playwright, it was true that I needed to earn a living. After my master's degree, two years during which I designed and built twenty-four shows in twenty-four months in addition to writing a thesis and teaching, I was nearly burnt out. Paula's and my relationship didn't survive the struggle. It would be easy to blame my shelving of dreams on her, but it wouldn't have made a difference. I had to earn a living. I was beginning to hate theater. I struggled on through my PhD and wrote a couple of plays that got some attention, but the stress was killing me, and all relationships that I potentially had.

So, I decided to go into something low-stress. Like publishing.

It evolved slowly as I completed my PhD. I would become a great novelist. I wrote volumes. But I discovered that I could make money by writing and publishing technical materials. My first contract was to develop a massive real estate sales instruction course. Then brochures, newsletters, trade journals. I made a lot of money writing.

But my novels kept being pushed aside and, eventually, I stopped writing them.

I worked for years in high tech, mostly developing documentation and training materials for publishing technology, when what I wanted to do was write novels and have people read them. I wanted to touch people with words. I wanted to make the world a better place in a way that writing error messages for computers wasn't achieving.

I had dreams that I'd delayed for years until the day I got pushed out of my nest and went off to see the world. Or at least this little corner of it. I wasn't in the business of fulfilling other people's dreams. I was just beginning to fulfill my own.

Back to Angie

"WELL, I THOUGHT that since I didn't get a teaching job this fall, that it would be a good opportunity for me to go see the country for a while," Angie said. "Lots of people I know have taken a year off to travel sometime during or after college. I just want to take a few months. I've been accepted on a program to begin my Master's degree in January."

"How did you plan to accomplish seeing the country?"

"You sound like my mother. I was just going to get in my car and go. She's all about 'Where are you going to stay? Who will travel with you? How are you going to support yourself?' All the stuff I should have thought about. I mean, I have some money that I can use, but not enough to stay in a resort like this every week. And she keeps telling me that it's too dangerous for a girl to travel alone and my car isn't dependable and on and on."

"All valid points," I said. My head was filling with ideas and I had to keep myself in check before I said something more. She squirmed on my lap a little. At first I thought she was uncomfortable and wanted to get away, but I moved my hand from her stomach and she kept wiggling until she could feel my cock pressed against her butt. Then she sighed.

"Are you going to punish me for running into you earlier?" she whispered in my ear. Hmm. There was no one else in the grotto. Apparently, the old folks at the resort had already had their Ensure and gone to bed. Maybe the younger couples had managed to go to bed, too. There was no nightclub at this resort and it was a good twenty-minute drive or taxi ride to get to one.

"I'm reluctant to punish you severely for an unfortunate accident," I said as I let my right hand move down her body to cup her ass cheeks. She caught her breath but didn't move away from my implied "severe" punishment. I moved to the right, freeing the jet that I'd been leaning against. "No. However, a little discomfort might be in order to remind you to look before you dash upstairs." The shining in her eyes was no longer tears of frustration, but a sense of excitement exuded from her.

I pulled Angie off my lap and faced her toward the waterfall outside the hot tub. I moved her intentionally so the powerful jet hit her.

"Kneel on the bench," I said. She immediately obeyed and I tapped the inside of her knees with my hand under water. She spread them apart. She moaned. I moved my right hand up to cup her ass again, my left having never left her stomach. In this position, the jets were hitting directly against her mound. I squeezed her ass and her hips rocked forward slightly. Another moan escaped her lips.

"Sir. Mr. Aroslav. What if someone…?" Her breathing was getting shallower and more rapid.

"Then they will see a naughty girl getting what she deserves," I said. She was biting her lips and her eyes were closed as the water beat unmercifully against her sex. My hands on her tummy and her butt kept her in place and encouraged the rhythmic rocking of her hips as she moved closer and closer toward a climax, humping the water jet. When I heard a whine in her throat and felt her stomach muscles begin to clench, I pulled her away from the jets and back to my lap.

"Mmm. No. Please. So close."

"This is punishment, not a reward, Angie. I will consider reward-ing you after you decide if you are coming with me."

"With you?" She turned to face me, pushing a knee into my cock. Quickly realizing what she'd done she straightened up and placed her knees on either side of my legs facing me. I knew she could feel my cock pressed against the tender places that had just been stimulated. "Where do you want to take me?"

"I travel, Angie. When we all check out of here on Sunday, I will collect my trailer and start wandering generally east and south from here so I can enjoy warm weather during winter. Sometimes it is lonely out there and having an obedient young companion and assistant would please me. You want to see the country. Your mother doesn't want you to travel alone. I agree. It could be just what you need. In many ways."

"You would take me with you?" she asked.

"If we reach an agreement," I said. I involuntarily twitched against her. She jerked back a bit so we were no longer touching.

"Sex?"

"No." She was startled. It had appeared that she'd been ready to fuck me all afternoon, but was suddenly afraid of it if it were an obli-gation. She was surprised when I said no. "There are some rules that must be obeyed, but sex is not one of them. In fact, I haven't decided if I even *want* to have sex with you," I lied. I would have to swing the other direction not to want sex with this pert little nymph.

"What rules?"

"Well, for one, I consider my trailer, like my hotel room, to be a fabric free zone."

"What does that mean?"

"It means no clothes. I lived entirely too much of my life in uncom-fortable underwear, suits, ties, starched shirts, and tight belts. When I enter the trailer after a day of traveling, or when I stay in it on days that I'm working, I get rid of my clothes. Not only would you be expected to respect my nudity, but to join in it."

"You mean I'd have to travel with you naked?"

"No. It would be way too dangerous on many levels to have a naked twenty-two-year-old in the truck when I'm driving. Nudity is confined to time in the trailer, or in a hotel room. Or if we happen to be in a location where nudity is acceptable."

"Oh. I see. What else?"

"There is only one bed." She blinked a couple of times while she put together all the implications.

"But we wouldn't have sex?"

"Correct. That doesn't mean we wouldn't be touching each other. I love to cuddle and if something came up, you'd just have to learn to deal with it. Or rather to not deal with it. In fact, you would be forbidden to try to deal with it without my permission."

"Right. So, you'll have a hard cock pressed against my ass, but you won't fuck me with it and I can't give you relief without your permission. That is so weird."

"There is nothing *normal* about the relationship I'm proposing. You'd be expected to do your share in keeping the trailer tidy, making meals, and cleaning up."

"Well, that's fair."

"I have to buy gas, campsites, and food whether you are with me or not. You do not need to contribute to that unless you want a better grade of food than I supply or more than I can afford to feed you. Of course, your personal expenses, including your healthcare, shopping, admission to events, and meals in restaurants or snacks are your own responsibility. I tend to eat simply, but get good nourishment. If you are not an omnivore, please tell me now."

"I eat pretty much anything, but I try not to eat too much so I don't gain my weight back. And I know how to cook. I wouldn't mind helping with that."

"Good. One cooks, the other cleans up," I said. "No drugs."

"Yessir. I... well, I tried some once, but I realized that it could damage my career opportunities. I... broke up with my boyfriend over it."

"Good girl." I reached up and stroked her silky hair as I said that and she leaned into my hand, a brilliant smile lighting her face.

"Does that mean I get a reward?" she asked.

"This is your reward, my sweet." I caressed her cheek and neck and she shivered, even in the hot water.

"Thank you, sir."

We sat there for a few minutes and she slipped off my lap to cuddle under my arm. I still wasn't sure if there was any point in all this. I couldn't imagine any young woman would willingly put up with the requirements this old fart had spelled out for her. But she hadn't slapped me and run away. And I had a feeling her pussy was still tingling. That gave me one last idea.

"Well, it's time for me to get back to my room. Perhaps you'd help this poor man who was nearly run over this evening get up the stairs."

"Yessir. It would be my pleasure." We stepped out of the water and I reached for my towel. Angie snatched it out of my hand and proceeded to dry me. She was circumspect, drying up my legs to my crotch, but not overtly touching anything of interest. She held my t-shirt and slipped it over my head. I did not offer to dry her and she tucked her towel around her and took my arm as we headed back to the stairs.

When we reached my door, I inserted my keycard and stepped inside. Angie started to follow me, but I turned her back.

"Not tonight, young lady. You have until noon Saturday to decide if you want to take me up on my offer. There will be details to be worked out, but I don't care to waste mental cycles on them unless you decide you want to travel as my companion. You should know that within the rules I have stated, I expect to be obeyed. My first order to you is this. You are not to come—let me be clear and say orgasm—until you have brought me your decision. Do you understand?"

Her mouth dropped open. I'm sure she planned to jill herself off as soon as she was alone. I reached over to close her mouth and she started to speak.

"Not tonight," I said. "Go consider everything I've said and even talk it over with your mother. But no answers tonight. Think about it." I stroked her cheek one last time, honestly believing I wouldn't see her again. Then I closed the door.

If she talked it over with her mother, they'd be gone tomorrow.

I HAD PREPARED myself to never see Angie again. She was a nice young woman who would come to her senses about the time she reached her orgasm, strumming her little clit as fast as the water jets had vibrated it. It was an image I would savor the next time I stroked myself.

Nonetheless, I was disappointed that I didn't see her at all the next day. I had visions of her fleeing with her mother back to the safety of wherever home was—LA, I presumed. I spent more time by the pool that day than usual for me, wanting to be in plain sight when she sought me out. I could feel my skin beginning to heat and rushed into my room for a long cool shower.

I was a little sullen that night and passed on my usual evening hot tub. I passed on jerking off, as well. I just didn't feel up to it.

I went out to the pool the next morning and settled into a lounge chair in the shade. I had my coffee and my clipboard and was ready to do some serious work. Unfortunately, my mind kept wandering and I found myself staring vacantly into space.

"Are you staring at my boobs?" a harsh woman's voice jerked my mind back from its reverie. I focused on the woman five feet in front of me. She was attractive, no question. She packed a few extra pounds on her five-four frame, but it wasn't unsightly in a comparably modest two-piece bathing suit. I caught a glimpse of Angie standing a few feet away, watching. Ah. This must be the mother. Well, I was 'offering' to take her daughter off her hands for a few months. I figured I might as well brazen it out.

"I apologize, ma'am. I certainly would be happy to stare at your boobs, but I'm wearing my reading glasses and you would need to bring them much closer." There was an awkward moment of silence before her laugh echoed around the low-walled pool. She looked over at Angie and made a shooing gesture. Angie left and I saw her lie down on a lounger across the pool, still looking toward us.

"So, you are the dirty old man who wants my daughter naked in your travel trailer," she said.

"Well, I confess to being a dirty old man," I said. "However, being naked is simply a condition of traveling with me—not an invitation to assuage my prurient interests."

"How well-spoken," she said. "As you might have guessed, I am Angie's mother, Margaret. I take my daughter's well-being and safety very seriously."

"If Angie has told you that a condition of traveling with me was to be naked in my trailer, then I have to assume that she told you the rest of my rules and requirements."

"Right down to and including you forbidding her to come until she had answered you. Frankly, I was relieved that you are still here. If you had left before she answered you, I'm afraid my daughter would never have climaxed again."

"Oh, dear."

"Now, I want to know all about you and your intentions. I want to know what kind of man you are. I want to know if I trust you with my daughter, because Lord! she is gone on you."

We talked. Margaret was charming and witty and nearly as sexy as her daughter. I told her of the accident on the staircase and of my sudden realization that Angie craved being subserviant. I considered that a dangerous situation and thought that if I gave her a little of what she needed, it might help her to settle so she could think straight.

"That's her father's fault, the rat bastard," Margaret said. In spite of her words, there didn't seem to be any real sting behind them.

"Did he abuse her?"

"Oh heavens, no! He doted on her—adored her—and the feeling was returned. But she looked to him for everything. His approval. His instruction. His love—and not a sexual love. He genuinely loved her as a father loves a daughter. Sometimes, I admit I was jealous," Margaret said. "We lost him two years ago. It was quick. A heart attack at two in the afternoon and at two-thirty, I was a widow and she was an orphan. It left her without an anchor. I was afraid she'd go with any man who could fill his place."

"I'm sorry for your loss. Both of you."

"Thank you. That was the problem with her last boyfriend," Margaret continued. "He stepped into her father's shoes to order her around, but had none of the moral fiber of her father. He pushed her to try drugs. That was the last straw. I can't tell you how thankful I was that she had the spine to reject him when it came to that. I was worried, but I'm more pleased with her ability to make a decision."

"I found her to be an amazing girl. When we talked, which is what we spent most of our time together doing, I found she was articulate, educated, funny, and pleasant company. She is definitely a young woman I would love to spend more time with."

"Naked in your bed."

"I confess, that appeals to me as well, but I won't push her to that."

"Well, remember that your initial assessment was correct. She is an amazing *girl*. Physically, she is twenty-two years old—twenty-three in January. Emotionally, she is still a teenager, trying on life like a new pair of shoes to see what fits."

"I seem to detect that you are tending toward approving her travels with me."

"Nearly. There is one more thing, though. Could we go someplace more private to discuss this?"

CALL ME NAÏVE or an idiot. Both fit. I was seriously out of practice, to say the least. I led Margaret to my room and invited her inside. I asked if I could get her a cold water to drink and bent to the refrigerator to get a bottle. When I turned around, Margaret was standing in front of me, stark naked.

"Angie told me you considered your room to be a fabric free zone," Margaret stated. "Well, now you can bring your reading glasses over here for a closer look."

I handed Margaret her water and stripped out of my swimming trunks and t-shirt. I led her to the sofa and offered her a towel to sit on.

"I'm not really likely to leak on the sofa," she laughed, "but God knows what might already be lurking in the cushions. Thank you." We settled in and continued our discussion. There was really nothing new in what we talked about and I sensed that she was really interested in whether I could sit with a naked woman and keep my hands to myself. If I was what I said I was. I was surprised when she turned the conversation to sex, but not shocked.

"Angie tells me that you won't order her to have sex with you. Is that true?"

"The only way Angie and I will ever have sex is if she asks, and there may be conditions to that."

"So, if I *asked* you to have sex with me now, what are the conditions you would impose?"

"Margaret, when was the last time you were tested for STDs?"

"What? I've never needed to be tested. I was faithful to my husband and have done without for the past two years. Actually, for close to a year before that."

"As likely as that makes it that you are disease free, before I had unprotected intercourse with you, I would insist on a blood test."

"*Un*protected."

"I do have condoms. I even have little blue pills if they are needed, though I suspect they wouldn't be. But Margaret, there is another condition."

"What?"

"No, why? Why do you want to have sex with me? There are many reasons I can think of that are good reasons and several I can think of that are not good reasons. Because I don't expect this to go any further, I'll say that among the good reasons are that you are horny, lonely, in love, or curious. Of the not good reasons, the worst are that you want to put me in my place, you think I expect it of you, or that you want to spoil the experience for your daughter. I suspect, frankly, that it is the latter."

"Then, Mr. Aroslav, you suspect wrongly." I noted that she changed from the familiar address of Ari to the formal way her daughter referred to me. I'd have to figure that out eventually. "I've no reason to believe that you expect it of me," she continued. "I would never try to spoil an experience for my daughter, nor do I think that my having sex with you would affect her decisions in the least. I am not sure what your place is, so I am the last person who should attempt to put you there."

"Then why?"

"You covered a few of them. I am horny and lonely. I miss the days when Angelo, my husband, made love to me. I've missed them for more years than he's been gone. I won't pretend that I love you nor that I'm particularly curious. I know what sex is like and one man or another, there can't be that much difference."

"Would you like me to help with the first two of your issues?"

"You are a kind and attractive man, Ari. If you can put your reading glasses aside and not look too closely at what you are getting, I'd like very much to have sex with you."

"I've never been able to do that."

"Put your reading glasses aside?"

"Have sex. All I really know is how to make love."

I pulled Margaret toward me and softly kissed her lips. She turned her body and settled into my arms before lifting her face for me to kiss her again.

Frankly, it had been a while. Actually, a long time. Aside from my brief encounter with Alice, I'd not touched a woman sexually for close to four years before my latest divorce. I was savoring each taste of her lips, the tip of her tongue, the depths of her mouth. Margaret was an experienced kisser and joined enthusiastically. For a long time, we were content to just kiss on the sofa, my hand softly stroking her side and occasionally rising over the mound of her breast. It flattened slightly against her chest meeting gravity's demands. She had large round areolae and dark nipples that had gradually awakened to rise from the softer flesh. She sighed.

"I don't think my nipples have been erect in years," she said. "Not since menopause anyway. Everything kind of shriveled up then." I bent my head trailing kisses down her neck, shoulder, and across her breast, finally flicking the nipple lightly with my tongue. Her sigh turned to a soft moan as she pressed her breast upward into my mouth. "So long. So good."

As nice as it was to have her lying back in my lap, the position on the sofa had defined much of what I could do to bring her pleasure and it was not enough. I scooped my right arm under her butt and lifted her so I could stand and carry her to the bedroom. I've discovered that on a long lonely drive of a few hundred miles you can do several thousand stomach pulses, tightening and strengthening the abs as you watch the country go by. It doesn't reduce any layer of fat over the muscles, but it strengthens the core enough that I could stand and lift her without throwing my back out.

"Oh, no! I'm too heavy to do that," she gasped and put her arms tightly around my neck.

"Hush. If I can do it, you are not too heavy."

"Then could I ask a moment to use the toilet before you get me all the way into your lair?"

"Of course, fair maiden. The dragon awaits." I set her gently on her feet next to the bathroom door and stroked all the way up her body as I stood up. She went into the bathroom and closed the door. I continued into the bedroom and used the opportunity to straighten and turn down the bed. I heard the toilet flush and the water run. As I tightened the sheets she slipped up behind me and wrapped her arms around my waist. She caressed my chest and let her hand drift to my lower abdomen. She eventually found what she was looking for, but it was a disappointment to her.

"You're not…"

"Right now, I'm interested in you," I said. "It takes more, however, than merely being in the presence of a pretty woman for me to be ready. On the other hand, you will know when I *am* ready."

I turned in her arms and kissed her again and she felt the stirrings of what she'd been looking for. We moved onto the bed and arranged ourselves so that we could roll in whichever direction passion moved us. And passion began to move us.

Margaret was a hungry lover. She didn't kiss with her lips as much as try to swallow my mouth. I let her have her way and our tongues coupled. I explored her body with my hands as we kissed, hefting her breasts, petting her ass, reaching between her legs. She had been in a bathing suit most of the week at the spa and, while not shaved smooth like I suspected her daughter was, she was tightly trimmed and her lips opened in invitation. The pathway was moist which was as much as I expected.

A Long Time Ago: Great Skills

TREASURE WAS A gourmand of oral sex—giving and receiving.

We'd begun our relationship as professionals and then began to socialize. We'd had a couple of sweet kisses and it seemed that our dating was going along well when we went out to dinner about four weeks after we started. We were still catching up on discarding former relationships and building the lives we wanted to live. It was during a lively and funny conversation over dinner that she surprised me with a question.

"What's your greatest skill?"

Our conversation had been light and flirtatious. I hesitated, but finally decided she wasn't looking for my ability to correctly identify all twelve tenses in the English language. This was definitely going into new territory for us.

"I can peel a grape with my tongue," I said. I could tell by the way she gulped that it had the right effect. But she didn't miss a beat as she looked into my eyes.

"I don't have a gag reflex."

That started an extremely satisfactory sexual relationship that had been all I needed for the better part of twenty years—even through the dry times. Oral sex was a pleasure to both of us. Eventually, she had begun turning her back to me when I initiated intimacy.

"You can rub your cock on my ass tonight. Go ahead. I don't mind. You can owe me one this time."

Foolishly, I believed her. It wasn't long before all sex was me rubbing my cock in her crack. She didn't even like me to hold her breasts. But she kept insisting, "Go ahead. I don't mind." I ended up *owing her* for each one.

Things progress slowly and you don't realize how your relationship has changed over the course of a couple years. I became a master of a quick come so as not to inconvenience her for too long. Eventually, I realized that using my hand was more satisfying and I quit cuddling up against her ass at all. It got down to birthday cunnilingus. And then nothing.

I'd sworn that I would never be deceived about what a woman wanted again. 'Go ahead' and 'I don't mind' became big red letter words in all capitals that had signs pointing to them saying 'LIES!'

Back to Margaret

WHATEVER IT WAS that Margaret wanted from me, it wasn't being used as a dump for my pleasure.

"Ari, again. Lick me again!" Margaret called out. What was the old Woody Allen line? *I should have feeling in my lips again sometime next week.* But what the hell? I had my face buried in a very tasty and enthusiastic pussy for the first time in a very long time. I was making the most of it. And by Margaret's first orgasm, I was hard as a rock and stayed that way as I slipped a condom on.

She shuddered under me as another wave overtook her.

"Now," she whispered. "Please make love to me, Ari. I didn't know I could be so ready for a man. I'm ready. I want you."

I moved up her body sprinkling kisses as I went. As soon as she could reach it, Margaret had hold of my cock and guided it directly into her pussy. I slipped in without hindrance and buried myself deep within her.

Once I was in her, we slowed down. I slowed down because it had been so long since I'd felt the inside of a woman that I wanted to savor every moment. She slowed down because she had what she wanted right then. She affirmed that with panted words. "Yes. Good. Oh yes. So deep. Yes." From the immediate orgasms that Margaret had when I went down on her, we had progressed to a long slow build as we moved together.

We kissed and her kisses no longer held the ravenous desperation of the first few, but were calmer. Yet more intense. We'd been in the missionary position since the beginning. I think Margaret wanted to experience the submissive posture, though I somehow didn't think that was how her relationship with her husband had gone. For my part, I found this position to be one that sped my climax, so I slowed down and pulled her with me as I rolled to my back.

"Yes!" she said as she began posting on me. "I love it like this!" I thrust up into her to meet her bounces and realized this wasn't going to slow me down that much. Note to self: Work on prolonging my orgasm. I'd worked too many years on speeding it up.

Nonetheless, Margaret had become sloppy wet and we were making enough noise where we were connected to think that we were sloshing in the bathtub. She went first and the orgasm as she ground her clit against my pubic bone was double what I'd achieved with my tongue. That delicious heat and pressure combined to trigger my release and a minute after her, I filled the condom with more come than I thought I was able to produce. It had been so long. So long since I'd come in a woman.

～～～

WE LAY IN the afterglow, holding and stroking each other. I'd long since slipped out of her and she showed no inclination to restart the engine. Our kisses were light. We pulled a sheet over us to settle for the night.

"I think," Margaret sighed, "that I might be ready to start dating again. I can't expect that there are a lot of Aroslavs out there just waiting to satisfy mature women, but perhaps I can find *one* in the greater Los Angeles area. Now that I know the species exists, I know how to target my search. Thank you, Ari."

"Thank you, Margaret. Perhaps someoe is waiting for me as well."

"Will you be able to provide what Angie wants? She needs you far more than I did. But it will be a challenge to you. You have a great deal of discipline, but my daughter can be… problematic. She'll push you. She knew that her submissiveness to her father was also a way to manipulate him. He would do anything for her."

"Do you have any idea how hard it is going to be to have a beautiful, naked twenty-two-year-old blonde living in my little trailer?" I laughed. "But somebody's got to do it. I'll sacrifice myself to the cause."

"It will do her good to see exactly how hard it is," Margaret laughed, giving my cock a little stroke.

"We need to meet and go over the details. Tomorrow is Saturday and we have to leave the resort on Sunday," I said.

"Kiss me one more time, Ari. Then I'll go to my room and tell my daughter that she can bring her answer to you in the morning. Do you want her here?"

"Might as well start here and see if she hesitates over the rules."

"Fabric free? I'd like to see that."

"You should be here, too. It will show her how serious I am."

"Are you sure you don't just want to have a naked mother and daughter to assuage your lusts, old man?" she laughed.

"Hmm. The implications of that image hadn't quite hit me. But I'm not into intergenerational incest. Let's keep it calm and talk about the rules and how things will work. Okay?" I said.

"I have no complaints about that. I am sure she will want to move in with you tomorrow. Will you be okay with that?" she asked.

"A night in each other's company before we move into the limited space of the trailer will probably be a good thing. We'll play it by ear, but that's how we'll plan it."

"Then goodnight, Ari. I'll let myself out. Don't get out of bed. I want to remember you with that freshly fucked look."

Margaret left the room. There is something about watching a woman's ass walk away from me that is almost as good as watching her tits walk toward me. I drifted off to a very pleasant sleep.

I JUST HAD coffee and toast for breakfast. Condo kitchens are supposed to be fully equipped, but I found that I couldn't do without my Chemex coffee pot and my own grind from Trader Joe's. I'd have to stock up on coffee when I headed east. I didn't think there were any more TJs until I reached Florida. But the one appliance that I didn't have in my trailer and missed was a toaster. I'd picked up a loaf of crusty peasant bread and sliced it thickly to toast in the condo. I slathered butter on it and sprinkled a light coating of cinnamon and sugar over that. I guess I can be decadent when I choose to be.

I was sitting on a towel in the reading chair by the window when I heard the knock. It was precisely nine o'clock and I wondered how much Margaret had to restrain Angie to get her to wait that long.

I checked to be sure it was Angie before I opened the door. Her mother entered the room behind her.

"Good morning, Angie. Welcome. Good morning, Margaret. Please come in."

"Good morning, Mr. Aroslav," Angie began. "I've come to give you my answer and tell you…" I cut her off by placing a finger against her lips. She was startled and raised her eyebrows at me.

"You're forgetting something, Angie," I said. I glanced down at the very pretty sundress she was wearing. It left her shoulders bare and the loose skirt stopped about halfway down her thighs. It was a bright yellow plaid and it looked lovely on her. She'd taken the time to apply a light amount of makeup and her skin fairly glowed. A matching bow was in her blonde hair that otherwise hung loose around her shoulders. Very fetching. She wore flat sandals.

For the first time, Angie really focused on me and saw that I was nude. She caught her breath and reached for the bodice of her sundress. She turned quickly to look at her mother and got the shock of her life. As soon as she'd come through the door, Margaret had stripped off her shirt and shorts and was standing behind her daughter naked with her clothes dangling from one finger.

"Oh!" Angie squeaked. "You're… It's… You…" She unzipped the little dress, looking a little frightened as she held it to her and gazed into my eyes. I tried to stay relaxed and neutral and could see her eyes relax as well. Instead of fear, there was just a little shyness. She let the dress fall to the floor and stepped out of it. She wore a matching pair of yellow bikini panties, and frankly I was glad to see it wasn't a thong. She'd been dressed as if to go out shopping, not to go out hooking. I kept my eyes on hers, even though it was a struggle. I would take my time thoroughly staring at her ripe, lush body later. Right now, though, this had to stay casual and simply be accepted as the rule of the house.

She pushed her panties down and took off the sandals as she slipped the undergarment off her feet. I could see her struggling with the effort not to use her arms and hands to try to cover herself but she could see that my eyes were locked on hers.

"Mr…" she paused long enough to reach up and pull the ribbon from her hair. It joined her clothes on the floor. "Mr. Aroslav, I would like to accept your offer to travel with you for a while. I accept your rules and will be obedient in return for your protection and care."

"Angie, I'm happy to *tentatively* accept you, pending the three of us working out the details of the arrangement today. I don't think there will be any problem. You might want to pick up your pretty dress and fold it," I said. She smiled and quickly turned to pick up her clothes from where she'd let them fall. What a view. Watching that ass as she bent, would be enough to fill dreams for a month. Only I wasn't going to have to dream about it. Her mother was smirking at me. I rolled my eyes. Angie obediently folded her clothes and stacked them on her mother's clothes on the dining table.

"Thank you, sir," Angie said, rushing to me. She flung her arms around me and pressed those beautiful breasts into my chest. It was all I could do to force myself to pry her off me. She looked slightly embarrassed, but I thought the flush might have another cause. She was tense and rubbed her legs together. How far was she willing to go?

"You may come now, Angie," I said softly. I nodded toward the towel-covered sofa. She hesitated only a moment then flung herself down on the towel, spread her legs and jammed her fingers into her bare pussy. I ignored her and went to embrace Margaret. She found me responding to her naked hug and gentle kiss.

"That was brilliant," she whispered. Behind me I heard Angie squeal as she brought herself off on the sofa. I turned and saw her lying there with one hand still idly rubbing her pussy while the other twiddled a beautiful pink nipple.

"Now," I said, cheerily, "who would like a cup of coffee? I also have juice and toast. We'll sit at the table to work out the details and then all go out to lunch." I completely ignored the fact that Angie had just had a screaming orgasm a few steps away and was dripping onto the towels. "If you need to freshen up, dear, the bathroom is just in there," I said. Angie looked at herself, grabbed the towel she was sitting on, and ran to the bathroom.

2 In Ari We Trust

21 September 2013

"I T'S so small!"

Not exactly the words any man wants to hear. No matter what the subject.

"I told you."

"Yes, but it's such a surprise to actually see it. How will we fit?" Angie asked. I couldn't help myself. I wrapped my arms around her from behind and breathed in her ear.

"Closely together," I whispered. I felt her shudder with the chill in her ear, but she didn't pull away from me. She pushed back into to my embrace and rocked her head against my shoulder. I think women have a marking instinct, not unlike what a cat or dog might do. When she claims something as her own, she rubs her cheek on it. That was the feeling that I got from Angie. She started to pull her sundress up to take it off. I pushed her hands down.

"We aren't staying in the trailer right now, so keep your clothes on," I said. "We need to get the hitch on the truck and connect the trailer. Get your gear stowed and then we'll head to Costco and restock the food supplies. We'll camp at Joshua Tree tonight and for the next couple of days while we settle in and get used to each other."

"Whatever you say, sir," she sighed. "Where shall I put my things?"

"Here's an empty drawer for your toiletries, undies, and t-shirts. Anything small will fit. There are eight hangers in the closet. You can share this drawer with me for a pair of jeans and shorts," I said, going through the limited storage space in my trailer with her.

"What about the rest of my clothes?" she squeaked.

"How many clothes do you think you'll need?" I asked. "You saw the little roll aboard that I packed all my clothes in. It will take me five minutes to put everything away. The only additional things in the closet are the sports coat that I've only worn once in the past three months, and my hiking boots. Those are down here. You should have room for any shoes you need here."

"I have two suitcases."

"Be selective. If you discover that you need something that you didn't plan on, we can open the back of the truck and get at it. I'm not asking you to burn all your clothes," I laughed.

"Are you sure you don't want me to just take off my clothes and leave them off?" she asked. Oh, yeah.

<hr/>

A Long Time Ago: Going Naked

LYNN AND I saw each other for about six months until my relationship with Anabel got so tumultuous that Lynn couldn't put up with it. You might have read my very fictionalized account of our relationship in *One-Hour Do-Over* that got third place in the Halloween contest a few years ago. Anabel Lee was going by the shortened version, Belle, at the time. Things are never as neat and tidy in real life as in stories. That's why we call it fiction. I try to end my stories 'happily ever after.' Life is not so cooperative.

Lynn was certainly bewitching, but she wasn't really a witch. In my book, she was an angel. Even though we didn't live together, we spent several weekends together. I often stopped by her apartment on my way home from work.

We made love.

Lynn was always ready to make love, though she hated condoms. She said she'd rather I come in her mouth than feel latex in her vagina. Still, we both liked making love and she was highly orgasmic. She had the biggest breasts of any of my lovers up to that time and could come from me sucking on her nipples. If I had my hand in her panties, at least. So much for my theories on the concentration of nerve endings in small breasts.

So, as I was saying, we'd made love. It was Friday night and I had no plans for the weekend other than feasting on her glorious body, repeatedly. She rolled out of her narrow bed and started toward the bedroom door.

"We need food," she said. "I have some stuff ready to heat. It will be ready in about fifteen minutes." She turned and looked at me as I sat on the edge of her bed reaching for my underwear. "I don't see any reason we need to dress this weekend," she said. "Were you expecting company?" I looked at her. She turned toward me and then pirouetted. I certainly saw no reason for *her* to get dressed. She headed for the kitchen. I tossed my underwear onto the pile of clothes at the foot of the bed and went to use the bathroom. I washed things up so that I was clean when I went to the kitchen. When I found her there, she had an apron tied around her front so she wouldn't get any delicate parts spattered as she cooked. The rear view, though…

I walked up behind her and she leaned back against me. The pasta was boiling and the sauce looked hot. She rubbed back against my stiffening cock and sighed.

"No real reason to get dressed at all."

I called that my first experience with nudism, even though Lynn and I were mostly excited about being nude *together*, not just being nude. I was pretty shocked the first time I didn't get an instant erection when I saw her naked. But as soon as she sidled up to me and said, "Would you like to make love again before dinner?" I came to full attention.

Did I mention how sensitive her nipples were?

~~~~~~~~

Back to Angie

AFTER WE'D AGREED on the rules and how things would work yesterday, Angie moved her suitcases to my room at the resort and undressed. Once her mother had left the room, Angie stood in front of me nervously. She was suddenly blushing furiously. You'd think that she'd have been more embarrassed to be naked with me in front of her mother, but I believe it was the realization of the intimacy of our situation and her furtive glances at my semi-hard-on that burst in on her. We had just begun a new relationship, living with each other. Just the two of us. The nudity took on new dimensions.

A man she had known for less than a week was going to look at her naked body. Blatantly. Whenever he wanted.

For my part, I won't deny that I was a little embarrassed, too. I had never anticipated that I would leave this resort at the end of the week with a beautiful naked young woman as a companion. There was certainly some churning in my loins. I figured the best bet would be to ease into our relationship with food.

I cooked.

"We'll get comfortable with working together soon enough," I said when she asked what she should do. "I don't expect you to have to ask me for instructions on every little thing. In fact, if I need to tell you to do something obvious, I would consider that a failure to observe and be fully a part of our relationship. I'm cooking. Food will be ready in about ten minutes. You should find something helpful to do."

She stood looking at me and blushing some more before the wheels started turning at full speed. It was delightful to watch her open the cabinets and reach up to get plates and glasses out. That simple act of stretching her arms lifted her breasts into a 'winged victory' position. Standing on her tiptoes as she leaned forward sculpted her butt and legs into an ideal shape.

She saw me looking at her and, despite blushing furiously, she lifted down just one plate before slowly reaching up to get the next one. She held the pose a second longer than was necessary, but not long enough for it to become uncomfortable. She disguised her posing as simply being careful about what she was doing. She repeated the moves with the same amount of stretch to get down each glass, even though they were on a lower shelf than the plates.

She set the table and I told her that I had a bottle of wine chilling in the refrigerator. As I moved the chicken breasts and Asian broccoli from the pan to a serving platter, I watched her get the wine. She glanced my direction to be sure I was watching and then bent at the waist much farther than necessary to retrieve the wine off the bottom shelf of the fridge.

It wasn't that I didn't appreciate the display of her feminine charms. I did, and intended to appreciate them much more in the future. But I *didn't* appreciate the idea that she'd decided teasing me was okay. She was trying to get me to make a pass at her. To control me. There was going to be a contest of wills here and I needed to find a suitable means of disciplining her without making her think I didn't want to see her body.

After dinner, I picked up my glass of wine, my reader, and a cigar, and headed for the lanai. I had a robe next to the patio doors since the lanai is not a particularly private area. Angie went to grab her robe and made to follow me. I cocked an eye at her and glanced toward the table. If she had cooked dinner, I'd have immediately done the cleanup. But I cooked. She followed my look and dropped her robe. She gathered the dishes from the table and went to the kitchen to clean up. I relaxed and enjoyed my cigar while keeping one eye on what she was doing.

Okay. I didn't give a fuck what she was doing. I was just keeping an eye on her. My lust was beginning to get the better of me and I was inspired as to her punishment.

<hr />

"COME HERE, ANGIE," I said from the easy chair in the living room. The girl approached and faced me. I looked her up and down, letting her know that I was appreciating the view of her tits and pausing for quite a while as I looked at her smooth pussy. She was a little fidgety. Good. "Here," I said. "Come sit on my lap." She could clearly see that I was partially aroused and sucked in her breath. That did nice things for both her stomach and her breasts. Nonetheless, she perched her bare bottom on my lap and eventually slid back far enough to make contact with my stiffening cock.

"Yes, sir," she whispered.

"I believe you have been teasing me this afternoon," I said. "You've been making sure that I got especially good looks of you as you got dishes from the cabinet, got wine from the fridge, and did the dishes."

"We're naked," she defended herself. I scowled at her.

"You put your robe on when you joined me on the lanai, but made sure your legs were well-spread when you were facing me," I said. "If it is a compliment you are fishing for, then, yes, I think you have a very pretty pussy. I intend to look at it a lot while we are together."

"Um… Thank you?" she whispered.

"But you are not going to tease me into fucking you. I told you that I wasn't sure if I wanted to fuck you yet. I don't expect you to try to make me lose control. We are going to be naked with each other. A lot. You do not want that to mean that I can automatically start fucking you whenever I want. Sex should always be mutually agreed. I am very displeased."

"Are you going to spank me?" she asked.

"Angie, I don't like to hit people. Least of all, women. If there comes a time when you would like to play a spanking game because it turns you on, we'll discuss doing that. But I will *never* raise a hand to you to punish you," I said.

"How will you punish me, sir?" She hung her head and looked contrite.

"It seems that you wanted me to notice your pretty, smoothly shaved pussy. So, I'm going to have you show it to me."

"Um… okay?" she said hesitantly.

"But, you won't see the results." Now she looked really puzzled. "Stand up and face away from me," I directed. She was shaking as she stood and turned away. "Spread your feet apart. This is your punishment position." When I nudged the inside of her bare foot, she moved her feet about two feet apart. "Now bend over and put your hands on your knees. Keep your eyes facing forward." She complied.

I looked directly into the eye of God.

~~~~~~~

A Long Time Ago: Building Trust

MY NIECE TRUSTED me.

That was the beginning, middle, and end of the story, as far as I was concerned.

Well, she wasn't biologically my niece. I know that in *Triptych Interviews* I let people believe that Amanda's mother was my sister. But that was fiction, you know? I'm constantly twisting the truth and building on it.

Boeing, in its infinite wisdom, decided airplanes should be built by the lowest bidder and was moving its plant to the Carolinas. Allen was transferred and he and April put the house up for sale. It sold before they stopped to consider that Amanda was half way through her senior year in high school and DID NOT WANT TO MOVE! Treasure and I offered her a place to stay.

But that isn't why Amanda trusted me.

When we moved to that *Leave It to Beaver* neighborhood, we discovered more than sidewalks and white picket fences. We found a *neighborhood*. We found people who became friends. Neighbors joined us for dinner, for backyard barbecues, for birthday parties, and just to have a margarita or a martini after work. Allen was the master of margaritas. No one has ever improved on my martinis. But Allen and April weren't the only neighbors. We got together with many like-minded people. Of course, one of the things that drew us together was our children. Amanda was the frequent and preferred babysitter for our daughter, Maddie. And Maddie adored her.

When the parents were sipping martinis one night while the kids played tag in the park, some 'new' ideas in childcare came up. I say new because most of us hadn't heard about some of this stuff and many were first-time parents, but it made a lot of sense to us. We were all reeling that week because some kids from the local high school—*our* high school—had been out partying and were in a car accident. One of the kids was killed. One was crippled. When the teenage driver was charged with vehicular homicide, he committed suicide. Our whole community was devastated.

The parents agreed in principle and eventually we signed a pact that we shared with our children. The pact included a little card that had the phone numbers of every parent on the agreement. The numbers were entered in the cell phones of all the kids that had them with the prefix ICE—In Case of Emergency. If any of our children were intoxicated, stranded, or endangered in any way, that child could call any parent on the list. Said parent would immediately go to get the child. There would be no lectures, no punishments, and no recriminations. Our number one concern was to get our children home safely and alive. The child could even spend the remainder of the night with the rescuer's family and we'd just let his or her family know the kid was safe.

We all prayed that our children would never have to use the numbers.

But, of course, they did.

Amanda wasn't the first to use the safety net, but she was the first one to call me. She was precocious and had started dating in junior high. As a freshman, her boyfriend was a slimebag. Her mother did everything but forbid her to see him. We knew how that would play out. She'd just go behind everyone's back to see him. She was smart and knew how to get around just about any rule.

~~~

"Uncle Ari," she said when I answered my cell phone out of a sound sleep. I squeezed my eyes so I could focus on the digital clock. Just after midnight. "I'm scared. Can you come and get me?"

"Where are you, Amanda?" I said. I was already out of bed and pulling on my clothes. Treasure stirred and looked at me to see what was going on. I held up a finger to delay her question. The address Amanda gave me wasn't good, but I could be there in about ten minutes.

I cruised up 164th slowly, but didn't want to stop until I saw her. I just hoped she was still safe. This was an area known for late night drug trafficking and prostitution. There'd been reports of gang activity.

I heard three gunshots in rapid succession some distance away. I was about to accelerate out of the area and dial the police when Amanda raced out from behind a parked car and jumped in the passenger seat. I hit the accelerator before the door was fully closed.

"I'm sorry, Uncle Ari. I'm sorry."

"Mandy, honey, you don't have to say anything else," I said. "We promised you no questions asked and you are safe now. I need to call the police about the gunshots." I hit 911 and gave them the neighborhood. I was moving onto the main artery and away from the area. The 911 operator said a patrol was on the way to investigate.

"It was Pal," Mandy said softly. Her slimy boyfriend. "I ran away when I saw he had a gun. He said he was just going to conduct a little business. Those gunshots. He's either dead or he killed someone."

"Amanda, do I need to take you to a hospital?" I asked. She was fifteen years old. What a fucked-up world we live in. "I'm not asking to criticize you, but I need to know if you are in danger of overdose or... or a disease... or if you've been raped." She gasped. I'd already headed toward the hospital.

"No, Uncle Ari. I'm... I'm a little high. But I didn't have anything hard and nobody... used me. I think... I think Pal was going to trade me. That's why I ran."

"You did the right thing, sweetheart. You're safe now."

"Can I spend the night at your house?"

I let her parents know that she was safe and at our house. Of course, it was after curfew and they'd been up pacing. But we'd all agreed to the terms of our contract. No recriminations. Amanda had gotten herself into a stupid situation despite repeated warnings, but she'd used the safety net and got away safely. Treasure and I met with April and Allen and even with our misgivings, we decided to abide by the terms. None of us ever mentioned the event again.

Amanda, it turned out, was hard enough on herself. Pal was arrested for murder that night. He's still in prison. I'm happy to say that Amanda is a doctor.

She trusted me.

WHEN ALLEN TOOK the transfer to South Carolina, Amanda asked to stay with us until she graduated from high school. Both families agreed.

We had a large room in the lower level of the house that was supposed to be my office and den. The reality was that I occupied a corner of it and the rest of the room was filled with boxes and the general shit that people with attics put upstairs. Christmas decorations, Halloween decorations, Thanksgiving decorations, 4th of July decorations. Treasure was big into decorating for the holidays. Add to that every piece of paper that Maddie had touched from the scribbles to her most recent short story, her gymnastics awards, her collection of Harry Potter books in both the U.S. and the U.K. versions, a couple computers that we'd outgrown but I'd never gotten rid of, and so on and so forth. The room was a mess. There was a small guest room next to it and a bath across the hall.

After a lot of debate, we decided against putting Amanda in the little guest room. It had all the space I needed for an office and we devoted ourselves to clearing the detritus out of the big room so Amanda would have a space she could call her own, complete with study nook, bedroom, and huge closet. She was thrilled. I was pleased because I didn't have to wade through a bunch of crap to get to my desk. Maddie was jealous, but had already declared that when Amanda went to college, she, Maddie, would get the big room. Well, fair was fair.

Amanda became part of our family.

Treasure and I had been growing gradually apart. It seemed that we just didn't have much in common other than the well-being of our daughter and the current financial crisis—whatever it happened to be. I was spending more and more of my time in my little office where I'd moved in a reclining chair next to my desk. I had a sweet setup. I could sit beside my desk with my keyboard in my lap. My huge 24" monitor swung out from the desk and could be positioned at the perfect height for whatever I was doing. Or working on. Or watching. I'd given up on television a long time ago. That was another difference between Treasure and me. She not only watched a few hours each evening, she recorded so many shows to watch later that there was never room on the DVR for a show I wanted to watch if one happened to come on. So, I just watched Netflix on my computer when I wanted to see something. I got further and further out of touch with the things Treasure was seeing.

Ever since the days of Lynn, years ago, I'd been pretty casual about nudity in the house. Usually, I remembered to put clothes on, or at least a robe, before I walked out the front door to get the newspaper in the morning. I was often up puttering around the kitchen early in the morning in my altogether. My normal wake-up time was a couple of hours before anyone else.

I often wore my robe to my office in the morning and when I settled into my chair, let it slip off my shoulders.

I was never blatant about exposing myself to either my daughter or our new guest. I'm sure one or both caught a glimpse of my bare behind as I ran into the bathroom in the morning on occasion, but it was nothing they couldn't ignore. No one else in the family shared my joy in being fabric free.

That's why it was such a shock to me when I saw Amanda.

It was about eleven on Friday night and I was watching some anime series that was exclusive to Netflix. I had a glass of wine by my side and figured that in half an hour or so, I'd either drag myself to bed or fall asleep in my chair. It was an even chance.

That's when I heard Amanda come in from her date. My door was open and she could tell I was watching a movie. Thank god it wasn't porn and even though I was naked, I wasn't beating off.

"Hi, Uncle Ari," she said as she passed my door. She just kept going into her room as I grunted a greeting. I didn't really think anything of it.

Until she came back to my office. Naked.

"Can we talk for a minute, Uncle Ari?" she asked. She didn't really wait for an answer. She'd brought a pillow with her and threw it on the floor and settled down on it. She popped a can of sparkling water and tipped it back. I pulled off my headset and stopped the movie as I looked at her. I was reminded of a line that Mad Aunt Hattie used when describing herself as a teen in one of my first online serials, *Accidental*

Witness. 'Beauty sits on a teenage girl like the blush of dawn on a new day.' Amanda wasn't and would never be a *Playboy* model. But she was beautiful. She wasn't preening or displaying herself. I could clearly see her breasts in the low light of my computer screen, but she wasn't spreading her pussy or anything. And from her angle, I was sure she couldn't see my cock, which having recovered from the shock of seeing her was lying at about half a chub on my right thigh.

"What's on your mind, Mandy?" I asked as soon as I had taken a breath and gotten oxygen flowing to my brain again.

"I think I'm going to quit dating," she said. "I just don't have time for the games. It's not like I don't like boys or I'm a lesbian or something. They're just so demanding."

"Are boys trying to get you to do things you don't want, honey?" I could understand, but I'd still kill them.

"Oh, it's not that. Face it, all the guys I know are teenagers. The only thing they know is 'must touch tits.'" I laughed. She did a good caveman imitation, even though the tits in question were right in front of me and looked supremely touchable. She kept on with her diatribe that boys were simply too high maintenance for a girl with a future to deal with. Amanda had already decided she was going to become a doctor. I listened as she talked. That seemed to be all she really wanted.

While I listened, I looked at her.

I saw at once both the little girl she had been when we moved into the neighborhood and the beautiful young woman she had become. There was no way to keep from noticing how firmly her breasts stood out from her chest. Definitely more than a handful, I decided. Her light brown hair was cut just above her nipples. The nipples were like accents to her breasts, not something that overshadowed them. They were a few shades darker than the pale skin around them, and puffed out, though I wouldn't have said they were quite erect.

She wasn't skinny, but she didn't have rolls of fat like so many girls her age. It seemed like fat was in these days, especially if you could wear clothes that caused it to hang out. Amanda wasn't a toothpick by a long shot. She shifted and I saw her dark bush. She hadn't adopted the fad of shaving everything, so she looked like an adult woman and not like a busty twelve-year-old.

She looked, in short, like someone I'd like to cuddle in my lap and make out with until we slid together and made love.

But I didn't.

She finished her diatribe and I made some affirming comments. She stood up, came over and kissed me on the cheek, grabbed her pillow, and went to bed.

I turned off my computer, suddenly uninterested in anime. I sat there in the dark, reliving having Amanda sitting naked in front of me. My cock, which had been reasonably well-behaved while she was in the room, grew to rigidity. It didn't take too many strokes before I was scrambling for tissues to mop up the mess. I pulled a blanket over myself and went to sleep with images of the naked teen in my head.

It didn't become a habit, but twice more before she graduated, Amanda wandered into my office naked to talk about what was on her mind. Whether she should live on campus at SCU or if she should find an apartment in Seattle. Plans for her graduation party and her excitement that her parents would be here for a week before and a week after graduation. She wasn't teasing. She'd obviously seen my casual attitude about nudity and considered it safe to try it out herself.

No. Even though I had a few fantasies about her, I never touched my niece inappropriately. I never made suggestive comments to her. I didn't give her long hugs, even when she was clothed. I didn't try to kiss her.

She trusted me.

End of story.

~～～

Back to Angie

I HAD EVERY intention of just stroking off a good come while I stared up Angie's twat. Relief. God knows, I was hard enough. But there was more at stake than a quick come. In fact, there was more to Angie's teasing than trying to get me to fuck her. Angie was risking her body, being demeaned, becoming a slave, based on my promise.

Angie trusted me.

I got out of my chair and headed toward the bedroom. At the door, I looked back at the girl. She was still bent over in front of the chair, but she was looking at me. Tears were running down her cheeks.

"Angie, your punishment is over. It's time to get ready for bed now," I said.

I didn't expect her response. She ran to me and wrapped her arms around me, hugging me like her life depended on it. I was still hard and having her naked stomach pressing my erection between us didn't help.

"I'm sorry. I'm so sorry, sir. I teased you and I tried to make you break your word. I didn't believe you weren't going to use me. I'm so sorry!"

"There, there now, Angie. We've been together for less than a whole day. We both have a lot of learning to do. All is forgiven. Let's get ready for bed now. I have to find out if you snore."

"I don't!" she giggled through her tears. She snuffled and I grabbed a tissue to wipe her nose. She hugged me again. "You're... um... you still have an erection," she said. She didn't *rub* against it, but she pressed firmly.

"Yes."

"I can give you a hand job or a blowjob," she said. "It's my fault. I thought you'd come when I was bent over in front of you. I don't want you to suffer because of my teasing."

"No. I think I'll live with this for tonight. Just as a reminder."

"Of what?"

"That you trust me. Our relationship—as it develops—isn't about me using you as a sex slave. I'm going to show you the country in a way you might never have expected. I'm going to keep you safe. We'll have a lot of fun," I said. "Angie, one day, if it all works out, we might make love. But that isn't why you are here with me. You are here for adventure and to see a little corner of the world. You are here because you can trust me."

"But... You shouldn't have to suffer. I could just..." I stopped her hand reaching for my cock.

"What's more, I need to trust you, Angie. I don't want you to touch me like that or to try to get me off tonight. Leave it alone. You can't go with me tomorrow if I can't trust you," I said. She gulped and withdrew her hand. We got ready for bed.

Once we were lying down, Angie hugged the edge of the bed. I tried to give her room, but I lay down where it was comfortable. I usually sleep on my back and I don't like to have a leg hanging out of the covers. Especially in an air conditioned hotel room.

"You know the bed in the trailer is large enough to be comfortable, but it's not a king size like this one," I said.

"Is it... um... okay if we touch?" she asked.

"Of course it is, Angie. We're going to be in intimate quarters. We will often touch. It would be way too awkward if we had to avoid brushing against each other all the time." She rolled toward me. She was shaking.

"Will you... hold me?" she pled. I opened my arms to her and she flowed toward me. It wasn't long before she was in that favored position that women have, tucked under my arm with her head on my chest.

It had been a stressful day. We were asleep by ten.

My EYES FLICKED open at five o'clock. Angie had rolled away from me during the night but she still held my hand. Those beautiful breasts were uncovered and I spent a few minutes just watching her breathe. It was hypnotic. Swell and relax. Rise and fall.

I crept out of bed and into the bathroom. Knowing full well what I was about to do, I locked the bathroom door. My 'reminder' was still standing at attention in front of me. I assumed it had gone down sometime during the night, but watching Angie's nipples had it back at attention before I stepped into the shower. I cleaned the appendage extremely well. Twice. For the first time, I considered that traveling with this doll might be a painfully frustrating experience. I'd set the rules. I was the one she could trust. She'd shown me last night that I could trust her, as well.

I made coffee and wrote for an hour and a half on my first *Props Master* story before I went in to wake her and get us rolling. We had to eat, pack up, and get the trailer hooked up before we could begin our adventure together.

Angie woke up and stretched luxuriously, doing wonderful things for the shape of her torso and breasts. When she realized what she was doing, she started to cover herself. Then she looked at me, took a deep breath and kicked the covers off. I watched her pad off into the bathroom.

"Take a long, hot shower," I called after her.

"Are you suggesting I stink?" she said, sticking her head out the door.

"No. I'm suggesting that we have no idea when we'll have an unlimited supply of hot water again," I answered.

"Oh. Oh, shit!"

I heard the shower start and made another pot of coffee. In my experience (having a daughter) even a short shower would take a long time.

~~~~~

AND THAT'S WHAT brought us to the trailer and Angie's unfortunate comment about how small it was.

Margaret met us with another suitcase of Angie's clothes and an envelope of papers that she entrusted to me, including Angie's health insurance papers, checkbook, passport, and birth certificate. Margaret said that it also had all her emergency contact information—just in case she was needed. She inspected the trailer, hugged us each good-bye, and left.

Angie got her things stowed and paid careful attention as I backed the truck under the hitch. She accompanied me all the way around the rig and asked why I was doing things.

"I moved the rig forward four feet so I could get the leveling blocks out from under the tires on that side," I said as I stowed the blocks. "Now all we have to do is the walk-around."

"What's a walk-around?"

"Oddly enough, it's something I learned from reading stories by Dual Writer about characters who became pilots. Before you get in an airplane and take off, you check to make sure everything is where it should be and is functioning correctly. So, front of the trailer. The hitch is secure, the drag chains are connected, the power is connected. The post is fully retracted. The front lights are on. The shutter for the front window is closed and locked. The bicycle is locked into place and the straps are tightened so the lock doesn't flop around and scratch things up."

"I need a bicycle!" she said.

"We'll see. I don't use mine very much and have been thinking of selling it. You can try to ride it if you want, but it's a pretty big frame for such a little... frame as yours."

"Very clever. Do you write like that?" she laughed.

"Unfortunately, yes." We continued the walk around, making sure that all blocks had been picked up and stowed, all hatches were closed and locked, the slide-out was securely all the way in, no water, electric, or sewer connections were left, steps were up and hand-hold collapsed in. Awning in. All lights work. Truck lights all work and are on.

"I need to write this stuff all down."

"I had it listed once but I've done it so often now that the big thing is that I do the walk-around. I just check everything that could fail. There's a different list when we dock. You'll see this afternoon," I said. "Now, miss. It's time to roll. Mount up."

I let her run around the truck and open her own door since I was at the driver's door. I believe in opening doors for a lady, but when she is completely capable and it doesn't make sense to halt everything so that the convention can be followed, I'm fine with letting her get her own door. Besides, Angie had to get used to lifting her little body up into the cab. I wasn't her servant.

I didn't think.

We made the stop at Costco, shopped, had all-beef franks with sauerkraut for lunch, refilled our soft drinks, and hit the road.

Angie was a little disappointed. She was still tuning the radio and trying to discover all hundred XM stations when we got to the park less than two hours later. I'd made a reservation, so a quick flick of my National Parks pass had us directed to the campground. I stopped on the way to our site and filled the water tank from their potable water source. I also had six gallons of bottled water stowed in the shower with two boxes of wine. When I'm in the area, a rule I try to follow is 'Buy wine in California and gas in Arizona'.

Even the RV sites at Joshua Tree have no services. We were going to be dry camping. We'd see how Angie handled this end of the spectrum.

The site was long enough that I didn't unhitch. We were going to be here for three days and I had no intentions of driving anywhere. We went through the checklist. I ran out the slide and turned on the water heater and water pump.

"I need to charge my phone, sir," Angie said. "But there's no power in the outlet."

"No. When we are dry-camped, we don't have 110-volt service. We only have 12-volt. The solar cells keep the batteries charged up as long as we aren't wasteful. I'm running the water heater and the refrigerator on propane. You'll find a phone charger in the cab of the truck. Your phone won't run down the truck battery while it charges."

It was two o'clock in the afternoon and I was ready to do some writing. I got my computer and sat in the shade of the awning.

"Um… sir?" Angie said. I really needed to deal with that. Being called 'sir' all the time was embarrassing.

"What is it, Angie," I said. I scarcely looked up because I'd had a scene developing in my head all day today.

"What should I do?"

"Angie…" I said, looking up at her. She looked like a little lost waif. I set my computer on my side table and opened my arms for her to sit in my lap. "Pudding," I said. She looked at me.

"Is that a new nickname for me? I kind of like it."

"Well, we might arrange that. But I'm thinking of a Broadway musical called *Hello, Dolly!*"

"I've heard that song. What's his name, who plays trumpet?"

"Louis Armstrong. Well, in the musical there are two shopkeepers who decide to go have an adventure in the city. Cornelius and Bartleby have never had a day off and decide this is it. Only Bartleby doesn't really know what an adventure looks like."

"He sounds like Winnie the Pooh," Angie said. I laughed.

"Yes. You are quite right. Bartleby asks Cornelius how he will know when they are having an adventure. Cornelius promises to tell him and they agree on the code word, 'Pudding.' When the time comes, Cornelius will tell Bartleby, 'Pudding!' and Bartleby will know they are having an adventure."

"So, you're telling me 'Pudding' to let me know I'm on an adventure?" she asked. I nodded.

"The thing is, you need to discover what kind of adventure you are having," I said. "I'm a writer. I sit and write a good part of each day. But I like adventure, too. So, I usually write first thing in the morning and in the afternoon after I've been driving. On the days when I'm in one location, I head out to find my adventure for the day after I've written in the morning. Here we are in one of the most famous National Parks. There are hiking trails, exhibits, a ranger station and naturalist building. This is what you came out to see, Angie. It's your first big bit of pudding."

"Wow. I guess I just assumed that we'd do all this stuff together."

"Some of it, certainly. But I write. My pace is probably different than yours. I'm a little bit older." She snorted and I scowled at her. She looked contrite. "When I'm writing, you can hang around the trailer reading or writing or just sitting naked inside looking beautiful. Or you can go have an adventure of your own and tell me about it when we eat dinner tonight. What's it going to be?"

"I guess I'll go explore a little," she said. "I'd better put on a pair of jeans instead of my little sundress."

"That's a good idea. But, Angie? I liked the sundress while we were traveling today. You are very cute in it."

"Thank you, sir. Um… Mr. Aroslav? Could I be your pudding?"

"Puddin', you definitely are my adventure."

She went off to explore around the campground and immediate

area. I went back to writing. I was just at the point where Wayne and Judith were going out on their first date. It was a story I'd originally written years ago, but I'd decided to let the sex aspects that I kept alluding to in the original emerge in the foreground. It was turning into something fun.

~~~~

"I SAW A fox!" Angie said. When she arrived at the trailer, her clothes went flying. She stowed her hiking boots and stripped out of her jeans and t-shirt before I'd managed to get the food off the grill. Her breasts were bouncing with the same rhythm as her voice as she told about her afternoon.

We sat at the table in the trailer. I'd grilled a steak and tomatoes. I'd also tossed a couple zucchini on the grill. We'd get into a system eventually, but right now, Angie was excited about the things she'd seen while out exploring. I had my doubts about a fox being out there in the afternoon, but she was convinced. I restrained myself from telling her I could see a fox sitting right in front of me.

"We'll have more opportunity to explore tomorrow," I said. "It's one of the reasons I always stay at least two days when I camp."

"Even if there's nothing to see?" she asked.

"Pudding, if there was nothing outside to see, I could just sit in the trailer and stare at you." She blushed. I noticed that it made her nipples rosier.

"Thank you, sir. That makes me feel pretty," she said.

"We need to do something about this 'sir' business. I'm not comfortable with it. Nor with you calling me Mr. Aroslav. They are terms that make me feel old," I said.

"But I want… I need to show proper respect to you. I can't call you Father. It just isn't right. My father… well, I wouldn't have run around naked in front of him. It just sounds so disrespectful of me to call you Ari."

"Well, I have a pet name for you now. You need to come up with something that we can live with. When we're out in public, I don't want people looking at us like I've enslaved you," I said. "That means absolutely no reference to any term that could be construed to be a slave's relationship. I know I heard you mutter 'master' before we went to sleep last night. Absolutely not in public."

She ate quietly for the rest of the meal. I explained the two-two-two rule of travel. Never drive more than two hundred miles. Always arrive by two o'clock. Always stay at least two days. We wouldn't simply get in the truck and drive to Florida the next day. She cleared up the dishes, which amounted to washing our plates and silverware. I scanned through my email and looked up to find Angie standing in front of me.

"Can I cuddle with you?" she asked.

I moved to the bed and propped my pillows up against the headboard.

"Do you want the inside or the outside? I need to warn you that I often get up in the night and rise early. I'd have to be crawling over you if you take the outside." The bed in the little trailer was transverse mounted and only one side was open to get in and out of. It made it a bitch to make the bed. But I'm a guy. Realistically, how often am I going to make the bed? Angie crawled over me, which wasn't unpleasant at all.

"I'll take the inside. It will make it easier for you and I don't mind climbing over you if I have to use the bathroom." She settled in next to me and I wrapped my left arm around her. She sighed. I put the computer away and switched to my tablet. I figured I might get some reading done. I saw a new chapter of Jay Cantrell's *A Flawed Diamond* was up. His stories could keep me from working for days at a time.

"It's pretty warm, so I probably won't sleep with a blanket. If you get chilled, though, the blankets are rolled at the foot of the bed. I only use a bottom sheet. Kind of a European thing. These new microfiber blankets are warm and wash easily. All you have to do to make the bed is roll the blankets up at the foot," I said. Even though we had been together all day and had been nude for dinner, this was the first time since we left the resort that I'd held her. I liked it.

"Uncle?" she whispered.

"What?"

"Could I call you Uncle Ari?" she said. "It would sort of make sense. I mean, we're not related, but in lots of cultures an unrelated older man who is important to a person is referred to as uncle. I'd feel like I was showing you the respect that I want to and it wouldn't make you feel old or masterful would it?"

I had a brief flash of Amanda sitting in my office discussing her latest boyfriend dilemma. Uncle would do just fine.

A Long Time Ago: Wang

I WORKED IN an office once, supervising a staff that operated a Wang word processor. It was before we became socially aware of the sexist environment we'd created and was the kind of office that was constantly filled with double entendres. Most of us were either single or didn't care and the women made as many suggestive comments to the men as the other way around. Working in real estate and home building was like that. We had an afterhours bar in the break room and often sat around for an hour or more after work to drink and flirt. Cynthia was my special nemesis, teasing me unmercifully.

"Ari, does your Wang ever go down?" she jibed.

"Not if you don't fuck with it," I snapped back. There came a time when she did, but that's another story.

The point is, I like being hard. I've written about it before and I suppose it is a part of my nature. The idea of a four-hour erection is not a medical emergency to me, it's a medical miracle. So, I don't rush to orgasm. I want to feel that impending crisis for as long as I can.

Back to Angie

IT WAS OBVIOUS that it would be hard having Angie running around naked in the trailer and curled up against me to sleep.

As the week progressed and we moved camp south, our relationship got easier. Angie made a casserole in the microwave that wasn't *too* hard to clean up. We laughed about it and even though the cook isn't supposed to clean up, Angie was appalled at the mess and dug in to scrub out the microwave with me.

We got south as far as the Mexican border and turned back north. I had no real desire to cross—certainly not with the truck and trailer, nor with a beautiful young blonde—and suggested that we go visit London Bridge.

"Go to England?" Angie said.

"No. I went there a long time ago with a theater troupe," I said. "Everybody thinks Tower Bridge is London Bridge. It isn't. London Bridge is just a steel girder bridge across the Thames downriver from the Tower. What I didn't know when I visited is that the real London Bridge, built to replace the one in the nursery rhyme in the 1800s, was bought by some developer and moved to his resort on Lake Havasu. I've always wanted to see it."

"Yes!" she shouted happily. Then she went into a rendition of 'London Bridge is Falling Down', holding my hands and making a bridge. Apparently, the nursery song and dance hasn't changed since I was a toddler.

Of course, getting to Lake Havasu wasn't a one-day trip. We stopped off in Quartzite to camp out in the BLM lands for a couple of days. Quartzite is a little town of about 3,000 surrounded by Bureau of Land Management land. During the late fall and winter, snowbirds flock to the area until some have estimated that over 100,000 populate the campsites. There are no hookups. You cart your water in and your sewage out. People who don't have solar power use generators to power their humongous motor homes.

The first of October was too early in the season to see many snow-birds, so the whole territory looked empty and desolate.

"What do people do here?" Angie asked.

"From what I've heard, the two major activities are drinking and rock collecting," I said. "However, we are going to the Magic Circle. Angie, this is definitely pudding!"

There were only two other campers in the section of the park designated as the Magic Circle. There would be hundreds by January. We efficiently set up camp and I leveled and stabilized the trailer. I extended the slide-out, turned on the water pump and furnace, and made sure I had a full propane tank on standby. Nights were chilly in the desert and we might need heat.

Angie opened the back of the truck, got our tables and chairs out, set up the grill and ran the awning out so we had shade. I choose east-facing sites when possible so we can sit out in the afternoon without having the sun straight in our eyes.

Angie's eyes popped when she saw me come out of the trailer naked. She was used to seeing me naked, but not outdoors.

"Uncle Ari! You're naked!"

"Yes, Pudding. You should get your skin in the wind, too."

"But we're outside!"

"So are they," I said, gesturing toward the couple who were walking toward us. It was an older man and woman and aside from the rugged boots they wore, they had nothing else on.

"Greetings, neighbors," the man said. "John and Leah, here."

"Hi. I'm Ari and this…" I turned to introduce Angie, but she'd disappeared into the trailer. "Angie, are you going to come out and meet our neighbors?" I called.

"Yes, sir," she said. "I'm coming." The door opened and Angie stepped out in just her boots. Both John and Leah were appreciative of what they saw, but they didn't make it obvious.

"This is Angie," I said. "We're on an adventure to explore the south this winter." Angie put her arm around my waist and held on. I could feel her trembling.

"Well, there aren't many of us down here just now. Still too early in the season," Leah said. "We're the camp hosts and just wanted to welcome you. How long will you be staying?"

"Just three days, I'm afraid. We're headed up to Havasu for a couple of days before we go to the Grand Canyon."

"I saw a picture on the internet that showed snow around parts of the Grand Canyon already," John said. "Stop by for a drink later if you'd like. We've been going out rock hunting for a while each day. We can show you some good spots if you want to pick up a few specimens. Enjoy your time here!" They continued their walk around the track that served as a road in this section.

"They seemed nice," Angie said. She didn't let go of me. I wrapped her up in my arms. "We're outside naked. And they didn't even notice!"

"Oh, they noticed," I said. "There are seventy-five acres out here that have been set aside as clothing optional. So, all winter, nudists will be coming for a week or two or even all season. And believe me John and Leah noticed you. But they've been around nudists for a long time."

"How can you tell?"

"It isn't hard." I gave it a minute to sink in and then Angie sputtered in laughter. "Did you notice that he had his arm around his wife when they walked away? She's probably whispering something along the lines of 'Remember when I used to look like that?' They might not rush home and fuck like bunnies, but when they cuddle up tonight, they'll both have a fresh vision of what it was like when they were young."

"But she's… fat."

"I won't pretend to understand the individual makeup of people who have different body-types," I said. "There is no body-shame among nudists. That's the only lesson you need to learn while we're camped here this week. Now, who's cooking tonight?"

3 Pudding

5 October 2013

ONE OF the issues we needed to work out as we traveled was what Angie would be doing while I was writing. I encouraged her to be independent in her explorations but, in the evening, she was often left with nothing to do.

"Can I read what you're writing?" she asked one evening.

"I suppose so," I said. "I have to warn you, though, that my second ex-wife read the first novel I wrote and laughed all the way through the first page. The operative word there is 'ex.'"

"You write humor?"

"No."

"Oh."

I admit, it wasn't stellar writing, but she could have shown some sensitivity. It was the derogatory 'You'll never be a writer' attitude that started us on the path to divorce about a week after we were married. Unlike Treasure, who begged me to read to her in the early days. Those were good times. "Why don't you read something that's already been published? Do you want to read one of my mysteries or erotica?"

"I want to read the real you," she said. I gave her my SOL address and suggested she start with *Model Student*. We sat together on the bed, the most comfortable spot in the trailer, and I wrote while she started reading. That became our nightly ritual, just before we cuddled up to sleep.

And, yes, there was a lot more cuddling and skin-to-skin contact. I'd woken up just this morning spooned behind her as she held my hand to her breast. I stayed in that position for as long as I could stand. She wasn't making any overt sexual moves—at least not obviously.

But occasionally, my hand would twitch and squeeze her breast. That seemed to trigger a reflex of her squeezing her butt cheeks together on my rigid cock. Before I made a mess of things, I slipped out of bed and went to the bathroom for relief. Then I made coffee.

Havasu was only of interest because we carried our child-like innocence with us. London Bridge was just a stone arch bridge over a channel separating the mainland from a small resort island in the lake. We walked across it holding hands and occasionally humming parts of the nursery rhyme.

We joined up with old Route 66 in Kingman, Arizona, and went to the Historic Route 66 Museum. The Mohave Museum of History and the Arts had a section about Andy Devine that really took me back to my childhood watching Roy Rogers. What a trip! That night, I noticed she had earbuds in while she was reading.

"What are you listening to, Pudding?" I asked.

"I downloaded all the music on Tony's playlists in *Model Student* and I'm listening to them while I read," she said. "You sure have eclectic taste in music." I had to laugh.

"I suppose I do," I said. "But remember, I'm not Tony. He probably has some pieces in there that I wouldn't listen to."

"Right." I'm not sure she was convinced.

We camped at Williams, Arizona, and drove up to the Grand Canyon for a day trip. It was only about thirty-five miles. My enjoyment of the magnificence of nature was doubled by the childlike excitement of Angie. I'd been to the canyon before, but seeing it with her was something else.

And at night, we read, wrote, and cuddled together for warmth as the nights became steadily colder.

~~~~

IN MID-OCTOBER, WE camped at Navajo National Monument. The campground was empty. There was a sign that said one of the restrooms was closed for the season. The ranger station was open for limited hours during the day to accommodate tour buses that arrived and left within an hour.

I was grilling a couple of country pork ribs. I'd stocked up on about everything we could need for a week because there isn't a grocery store within two hours of the campground. We were isolated out here. I turned when Angie brought me a glass of wine.

She was naked except for her camp shoes.

"Pudding, this campground isn't really clothing optional," I said.

"Uncle Ari, look around. We're the only ones in this campground. I thought we could have a campfire tonight and cuddle in the camp chair," she said. "Please?" I nodded. How do you say no to a naked beauty who wants to cuddle in front of the campfire? I stripped off my clothes.

We spent most of the night wrapped in a blanket in front of the campfire.

The next morning, after cuddling under the blankets in bed against the cold, we got dressed and hurried out to the viewpoint to see the sunrise gradually illuminate the Betetakin cliff dwellings of the Anasazi Indians.

It was a special moment for me for reasons that had nothing to do with the pleasant company under my arm.

A Long Time Ago: Desert Musings

JOY WAS BEAUTIFUL beyond my sixteen-year-old mind to comprehend. What's more, she was friendly. I guess that comes with the territory. Her mother was a county judge. Her father commuted to Fort Wayne to teach government at IUPUFW (Indiana University/Purdue University Fort Wayne). Joy was destined to become President of the United States. Or at the very least, First Lady. I wish she was running now.

She was part of what I had always considered 'the privileged' class, of which I wasn't. My family moved the summer between freshman and sophomore year and my meeting with Joy had been arranged by our parents as a sort of get to know the area arrangement. What I got to know was that Joy was so far above me socially, I couldn't reach her with a stepladder. Try one of those fire department ladder trucks and I could maybe reach the bottom ledge of her window. But she'd been raised in our little town by parents who believed in an egalitarian society. She went to public school and tried out for the cheer squad— unsuccessfully. Even in our little school, cheerleaders were a special class of their own and simply being smart, beautiful, and rich didn't ensure that you'd get in.

Joy was one of only half a dozen girls in my class who didn't turn me down for a date. That's because I never asked her. Even after the night she let me feel her breasts and make out just before graduation. But that's a different story. This is the one when she convinced me that I needed to go to a college prep school for the summer like she did each year. It was a cinch that I wasn't going to get any playwriting instruction at the little high school I was attending, so I researched until I found a school in Colorado that had a playwriting program, applied, and miraculously was accepted on a summer scholarship between sophomore and junior years.

My sport for the summer was hiking. My summer girlfriend was Sue. That's a different story, too, but suffice it to say that even though we didn't go all the way, at the end of the summer, Sue was the only girl whose bare breasts had actually been in my hands and the only girl who had ever had an orgasm with me.

But at the end of the summer session, Sue was assigned to a different unit than I was, so we never got a chance to see what that last step would be like. Instead, I was with a group of 40 boys and girls who rafted down Lake Powell for two days, observing the effects of the Glen Canyon Dam, until we reached Rainbow Bridge National Monument. It wasn't impossible to reach the bridge via overland trail, but already most visitors were coming by boat.

Our group was to hike from the bridge over that land route to Navaho Mountain where we would be picked up by trucks to take us to Betetakin cliff dwellings and then we'd visit the Four Corners monument and head back to school for our last week of synthesizing our experiences.

In the middle of the night, while hiking under a full moon from Rainbow Bridge to Navaho Mountain, we were to pass the other group of 40 students and teachers (the group Sue was in) on their way from Betetakin to Rainbow Bridge.

But before that happened, my group's leader missed the trail turn-off that would lead to the pickup point and instead led us out into the desert. At dawn, we stumbled to a stop beside a puny watering hole as the teachers decided what went wrong.

We camped for the day by that spring but it dried up a little after noon. We slept and talked while we waited for our leader to backtrack until he found out where we'd gone wrong. Then he came to get us at moonrise and we all headed back to what proved to be too rugged a path for some of our exhausted group. I collected backpacks from a few people who couldn't carry theirs and make the ascent.

Disaster struck again with daylight. Mitzi, one of our students, was sick. She had diabetes and no medication as I understood it. So, two teachers—Fritz and my hiking coach, Leslie—stayed with Mitzi in shade and cooled her with what precious little water they had while waiting for supplies and rescue. The rest of us began the long climb out of the canyons to Navajo Mountain. Fearless leader had hiked with half a dozen of the strongest boys, out of the canyon to the trailhead, collected supplies, and started back down into the canyon. When we met up on the trail, he was nearing exhaustion. As I figured it, he hadn't slept in at least 48 hours. I volunteered to exchange packs—since I was carrying about four of them—and take the supplies back down to Mitzi, Fritz, and Leslie.

And thus, we spent another night in the canyon.

I told Fritz that I'd seen water up the trail when we came through in the night and I was going to hike back to see if I could refill canteens. He agreed. What I found wasn't just water. We'd hiked right through a park service campground with water, restrooms, picnic tables, and rustic signs with yellow lettering pointing the direction. We just hadn't seen it in the night. I returned with water.

In the heat of the afternoon, while the others slept, I absently gathered twigs from around the juniper where we rested. I started putting them together in an elaborate sculpture, balancing one twig on another and building from a small base to a large top like a tree. Fritz rolled over in his sleep and kicked it down. It didn't matter. It was temporal.

Early the next afternoon, we watched as five horses and three horsemen came down the long steep trail into the canyon. We loaded our packs on one horse and Mitzi on the other and the other three of us walked out. Fritz stayed with Mitzi. Leslie and I walked out ahead, being much faster than loaded horses going uphill. We'd been hiking together all summer and even though she was much older than me and was faculty, we'd developed a good rapport. She'd even teased me about having to separate Sue and me. Once we crested the canyon ridge, it was a downhill romp all the way to the trailhead and we decided to race the rest of the way to the trucks. I had to keep my hands in my pockets as we ran down the trail to keep my lederhosen from falling down.

We were two days late getting out of the canyon, so we never made it to the Anasazi ruins or Monument Valley or the Four Corners. We did stop at a trading post before we crossed back into Colorado and a trader offered me fifty dollars for my hat.

I've often wondered about the people I met that summer. Did Ed become a politician? Did Sue get together with Frenchy? Was Laramie really an Indian princess? I've thought of Paul's explanations of the dreams I'd had that came true. I've thought of Leslie's warnings and tempered some of my recklessness. And I've thought of emerging from the canyon yelling and screaming as we ran.

I was changed that summer. It wasn't radical—at least in my way of thinking. I still fantasized about Joy, but I figured most of the boys in my class did, too. In addition to plays, I started writing poetry that fall. Volumes and volumes of it. Well, if you don't write poetry when you're a teenager, you have no heart. And then I quit football. I'll never forget Coach Hancock's expression when I said, "Coach, I just don't think there should be a game like this." I became progressively more and more a pacifist.

Back to Angie

AND WHAT DOES all this have to do with my travels with Angie?

When we visited the Four Corners Monument and photographed each other with our feet in four different states, I got a special permit to enter Navajo territory. I gave Angie the option of staying in camp, but she wasn't about to be left behind.

I drove up Indian Road 16 in Arizona to Navajo Mountain. As soon as you first see the mountain, the speed limit drops to 45 mph. For thirty miles, we watched its incredible hulking presence fill more and more of our field of vision. I drove on up into Utah past the mountain and onto Trailhead Rd. That's a sand track and we drove out as far as I considered it safe to take the truck. Technically, that trailhead leading to Rainbow Natural Bridge is closed now. We weren't equipped for backcountry packing. We parked on a promontory overlooking what the newspaper story back then had called 'the airless canyons'.

I brought my spiritual tools with me and cast a circle. I told the wind, the fire, the rain, and the earth that I was here. It was beautiful as I sank into a trance looking out over the desert.

As I meditated in my circle, I met my younger self emerging from the canyons, whooping up a storm. I found, oddly, that I had no advice for him. It's his journey. I've already been there.

I had a small drum with me and I began to tap out a rhythm. I don't do it frequently, but I have my own meditation rhythm. Angie and I had listened to hours of Native American flute and drum music as we drove, so no doubt there was some influence on my drumbeats.

I was so caught up in my own memories that I ignored Angie. My attention was caught, however, by a scuffling beside me and her shadow crossing over me. I looked up and as I kept my drumbeats going, Angie danced. She'd been wearing shorts and a bandana top. As she danced, she stripped off the top and used it as a kind of veil to accent her dance. She captured it. The journey. The adventure. The race to freedom. Emerging from the canyons to the mountain. I watched, mesmerized, as this creature of light and sand danced my story and then settled in my lap looking out over the desert.

We camped at Navajo National Monument for nearly a week. It was amazing how little we said during that time.

OF COURSE, WE had to stand on a corner in Winslow, Arizona. I let Angie drive the truck (without the trailer) down the street and open the door for me to climb in. Then we headed for Santa Fe.

It was getting darn cold at night in the mountains. In fact, it wasn't always very warm during the day. We drove as far as Taos and camped in a nice RV park with full hookups. I got out the electric heater so I wasn't burning so much propane and we were toasty warm.

I'd been outside having a smoke and contemplating just how good life is. Not only was I getting a lot of writing done—and I had great prospects for what I was outlining for my new erotic paranormal romance western mystery, *Redtail*—but I had great company. Every night I held a small goddess in my arms. I touched her breasts and she snuggled her little butt up against my erections until I had to go relieve myself. I was glad we hadn't had sex. What we'd developed was far more than what I ever anticipated.

I finished my cigar and my last sip of wine, and took one last look up into the crystal clear night sky. The next day we planned to cross the mountain to the Capulin Volcano. A high pass lay between Taos and the northeastern New Mexican volcano but all reports were that it was clear and open. I walked into the trailer and stopped, stunned.

Angie didn't notice that I was inside as I slipped my shoes off at the door. She was sprawled out on her back on the bed. Her head was propped up on pillows enough that she could see her iPad. Her left leg was bent with the knee in the air to prop the tablet up so she could read without holding it. Her right leg was spread so far out that her foot dangled off the edge of the bed. One hand was pulling at her nipples while the other was very busy in her pussy. It was obvious that she was near to orgasm.

We tried to allow each other a bit of privacy to take care of those base urges. I knew I should go back outside and let her finish. But it was so beautiful. She was flushed, her shuddering breaths causing a small quake in her breasts. Her hand occasionally abandoned her breast to turn the page on her tablet, but her awareness was limited to the words she was reading and the stimulation of her clit. Tears ran from her eyes.

Her pitch increased and her fingers plunged into her pussy. Her nipples looked almost painfully stiff as she pinched and pulled on one and then the other. The tablet rolled off its prop onto the bed as she arched her back and cried out in orgasm. She threw her head back against the pillows and gasped for air.

I'd shed my sweats when I entered the trailer. My rigid cock was leaking lubrication as I continued to helplessly look at her recovering from climax. The tears continued to flow from her eyes.

"Are you all right?" I whispered. She turned her head toward me, making no attempt to cover herself or conceal what had just happened.

"So beautiful," she said. "So loving. Uncle Ari, touch me. Touch me, please. Make me come again."

My body moved of its own volition. I was next to her, reaching toward her, before I stopped myself.

"Angie…" My words were cut off when her hand, still drenched with her own juices, wrapped around my cock to spread my own pre-come. I groaned.

"We've been together for a month and a half," she said. "We've been hiding our fantasies from each other. If we were only dating each other a couple times a week, we'd have progressed to touching each other by now. Uncle Ari, please touch me and make me come. Please let me touch you."

She was already touching me. I stretched out on the bed beside her and began stroking her beautiful body. I'd woken up many mornings recently with one of her breasts in my hand and my hard cock lodged against her butt. This seemed more… deliberate. I kissed her. In six weeks living together and naked most of the time, I'd never kissed her lips. There was something final about that kind of intimacy. A line that once crossed couldn't be uncrossed. As I kissed her, I felt the lines dissolve. I explored her body thoroughly with my fingertips and when I found the slick passage between her legs, she arched her back against my hand encouraging me to go deeper as she stroked my cock. The round pebble of her clitoris begged for attention and when I gave it, she came, crying and weeping once again.

"You'd better stop now or I'm going to make a mess," I said as I felt my balls beginning to contract.

"I wash. Go ahead and make a mess."

I didn't need more encouragement. Another stroke and I was spraying her abdomen. We kissed some more, coming down gradually from our summit and enjoying the afterglow.

"What set you off this evening?" I asked.

"It was so beautiful," she said. "I read it over and over. Each time I read it, I got more turned on until I just couldn't contain it any longer."

"What passage had such a profound effect on you?"

"In *Triptych*, where Tony places the collar around Wendy's neck." Oh yes. I'd taken some flak for that when it was released. Some readers were offended that I'd brought in a character who was submissive and called Tony 'master'.

"That scene isn't particularly sexy," I laughed. I kissed her again. Now that we'd begun, I couldn't get enough of her lips.

"But it is," she said. "Tony wasn't a master. He wasn't particularly dominant through any of the rest of the story. Even when Wendy needed him to help her choose clothes to wear, he did it in a way that helped her make decisions. And when he put the collar on her, he accepted her. He accepted her for what and who she was, even though it was hard for him to do. It made me realize… Uncle Ari, you've done that for me."

"Hey, Pudding," I laughed softly. "You are not a slave in need of a master like Wendy."

"No. You could have made me into that, but you didn't. You might not accept the title of 'master', but you are. You made it clear from the first night that we would have a relationship built on trust. The punishment you gave me... You could have fucked me and I'd have been your slave. Instead, you used it to show me I could trust you and that you had to be able to trust me. You broke through my body issues. You got me to run around naked outdoors with other people around. You showed me a bit of your soul up on that rock overlooking the desert. You encouraged me to go off exploring by myself and made me independent. And you've shown me love. You... We *do* have a sexual relationship that you've allowed me to grow into rather than force upon me. I don't want us to have to masturbate alone in the dark any longer."

Is it still called masturbation when it's someone else's hand? Or butt. Or mouth? We didn't get quite that far that night, but my fingers seemed to stay wet in Angie's juices as we cuddled all night long.

For the first time in a long time—possibly since I started this trip—I didn't wake up early. In fact, after Angie had put me to sleep again rubbing my cock between her butt cheeks, she got up and hummed a tune as she made coffee. I came back to life with the aroma of the blessed brew.

A Long Time Ago: Milkless Latte

IN MOST OF my stories, the hero has a coffee addiction. Well, that's me. When I moved to the Pacific Northwest to work on publishing technology for a big software company, I discovered lattés. Seattle was the home of Starbucks and paying four dollars for a cup of espresso and steamed milk was the norm. So was weight gain.

I was sitting with some of my colleagues—mmm, one of my colleagues. That was during my time with Colette. Irish, about five-three, red hair. Very, very smart, but complained that no one took her seriously because she had big boobs. It wasn't that they were *really* big, but she had a pretty small frame, so they really stuck out under her sweaters. I'm getting sidetracked. I'll talk about her again sometime. We were drinking coffee and shooting the bull when I came to the sudden realization that...

"I don't like milk," I said.

"Then don't drink it," Colette answered. Colette always had a simple answer for life's dilemmas.

"But lattes are full of milk. Drinking coffee flavored milk is the same as drinking milk. It's the coffee I like." Colette went to the Starbucks coffee bar where we were sitting and a moment later returned with a tiny cup. She set it down in front of me and waited. "What?"

"It's a latte without the milk," she said simply. *Espresso! Oh yes!*

The only problem with drinking straight espresso is that a shot is only one and a half ounces. That's great for an energy boost in the middle of the day, but it makes a lousy beverage. I could remember a time in college when I would start a huge pot of coffee in the scene shop in the morning and drink cup after cup all day long. So, I set out to find the perfect brewed coffee.

It took a while, but I discovered Chemex. It wasn't just the elegant shape of the pot, like an hourglass figure. It even has a nipple. Did you know that James Bond in Ian Fleming's books used a Chemex pot to brew his coffee? *From Russia with Love*, 1956: "It consisted of very strong coffee, from De Bry in New Oxford Street, brewed in an American Chemex, of which he drank two large cups, black without sugar." I got the brewing technique down quickly, but it took a long time to find the right coffee. De Bry went out of business years ago.

$$\sim\!\!\sim\!\!\sim$$

Back to Angie

ANGIE WAS EXPERTLY copying my method for brewing a pot of coffee just like I like it. Hot, strong, and black. Just like God made it.

Or in this case, a goddess.

Just call me Bond, James Bond.

"We should probably go use the showers before we pack up this morning," I said. "You, sweet girl, are covered with dried come."

"And you smell like a pussy," she laughed as she kissed me. She grabbed her sweats, towel, and shower kit and opened the door. "Ari... I think we have a problem," she said.

"What?" I asked.

"Snow."

Oh, shit! I scrambled around and looked out the door. In fact, there was a good three inches of heavy wet snow blanketing everything. I dressed and pulled a hoodie out of my closet. I wasn't prepared for snowy weather. That's why I came south. Of course, Taos is 7,000 feet in elevation. I needed to get downhill. While Angie took her shower, I went into the park office and asked about the weather.

"The pass is closed. They got thirty inches at 9,000 feet," the manager said. "We're expecting to get hit by another storm blowing down out of the northwest within a couple of hours. If you are moving today, you should get going. This is the beginning of winter and once it hits, we won't see bare ground again until spring."

That was all it took. When I got back to the trailer, Angie was dressed and I sent her to the roof to scrape the snow off while I got us hitched. I had her batten down the inside of the trailer, filling the thermos with hot coffee and making sure everything inside was stowed and ready for travel. We disconnected the electric and water. I was amazed that my hose hadn't frozen in the night, but the temperature didn't drop as far as it was about to. The next wave was expected to bring temperatures in the teens.

In half an hour, we were slowly navigating our way south out of Taos.

~~~~~

AFTER RACING THE snow past Albuquerque, we found a more temperate climate following the Rio Grande. I'd been in touch with the author GraySapien who writes so many stories set in New Mexico and he'd given me some hints on places to stay and visit while I was there. We worked our way south to Las Cruces and then cut across a low mountain range and White Sands National Monument to Alamogordo. I left the trailer at an off-season park there and we took the truck East. On Halloween, we pulled into Ruidoso.

My timeshares had mostly gone unused for the past few years because I kept convincing myself that I didn't have time or money to travel. Amazing how a divorce can change your perspective. I exchanged a week for a nice, if rustic, two-bedroom unit. Snow hadn't reached this far south yet, even though the elevation was over 7,000 feet and everyone was looking forward to the start of ski season. Our condo even had a fireplace.

"I figure you can have this bedroom," I said, pointing to a room with two double beds in it. "It has its own bath. Mine has a bigger bed, but the bath is in the hall. We'll go out and get some groceries after we've unpacked."

I turned to Angie and found her staring at me with such a look of horror that I couldn't imagine what had happened. Tears were streaming down her face and she was shaking.

"You don't want me with you?" she cried. *Oh, my god! She thought I was sending her away.*

"No, no. That's not it, Pudding. I just thought you'd like to have a little privacy for a change. We've been cooped up in that little trailer for seven weeks. I know it has to be hard on you to never have any privacy."

"No," she said.

"You know that tomorrow is November 1," I said. She nodded. "Well, you know that is the start of NaNoWriMo?" She shook her head.

"What's that?"

"National Novel Writing Month," I explained.

"You write like a novel every month," she said.

"Well, not quite. But this is a special time when I write at the same time as about half a million others. We do a lot of chatting and sharing what we're doing. I'll probably be up late at night and/or early in the morning because they are in a lot of different time zones. Like tonight. I plan to be asleep by six, but I'll be up before midnight so I can join my group in Seattle for the kickoff. I'll probably write for a couple of hours and then crash. Then I'll get up early when my friends in the Eastern and Central Time Zones get up to start writing. My phone might be buzzing at all hours of the night with Facebook notifications."

"Are you starting a new story?"

"Yeah. It's called *Redtail*. Now with all that chaos going on this week, are you sure you don't want a private room?"

"Yes. Uncle Ari, I just want to be with you. I won't get in your way. I'll do all the cooking and cleaning this week so you can write. I'll keep a fire in the fireplace and coffee in the coffee pot. I'll be quiet. Please, just let me sleep with you. Don't send me away," she pled. *Well hell. How can I resist that?*

"What are you doing with your clothes still on?" I asked.

OUR WEEK IN the condo wasn't all focused on me writing my erotic paranormal romance western mystery. Occasionally, I would read a passage to her as she stroked my ego. Sometimes she would read while I dipped my fingers into her honeypot. And my phone buzzed with Facebook messages at all hours. I could always tell when WritingMama in Kansas City got her kids off to school in the morning. My phone would start in as she 'liked' all the posts from the previous day and started responding. She was a flirt, too, and occasionally, Angie would suggest ways that I should respond to her.

There were times when we wrote more in our Facebook posts during a session than we did in our stories. Nonetheless, having company while writing was a great thing. I was over halfway through *Redtail* before the week was over. Part of that was also meeting local writers at a coffee shop in Ruidoso. We spent a couple hours each day in front of the fireplace at the coffee shop. A few other writers joined us on an irregular basis for our daily write-ins. It was a crazy time and I was pleased to have Angie's naked butt bobbing around the apartment as I wrote my erotic scenes. She was quite an inspiration.

Of course, the condo was only ours for a week and we headed back down the mountain to retrieve the trailer. Once we were hooked up, we went back across the mountain eastward and dropped down into Roswell. We camped there a couple days and interrupted my writing with trips to take our pictures with aliens beside the road or in the museum. Then we headed generally southeastward. I stopped in several towns to meet with other NaNoWriMo writers. It's a great social event, as well as a productive one. I'd finished the first draft of *Redtail* by the seventeenth. By then we were camped near El Paso.

Angie started showing her skills as an English major and editor. She was reading everything and making solid suggestions regarding the storyline and characters.

"He needs to respond in kind when Geneive sucks him. Can't you just see them trying to get into position in the front seat of his truck?" she asked. *Oh, yeah. I could imagine that.* "We could try it if you like," she whispered. "Just for the sake of research. I want to make sure you get it right." I was thinking that I wanted the first time I licked her smooth little snatch to be in a nice comfortable bed, but in the interest of the story, we slipped out of the trailer and into the truck where we made out and got each other's clothes off. That wasn't much since we'd only slipped our sweats on to leave the trailer.

It wasn't as easy to get into position in the front seat of the truck as you might think. Fortunately, the seats in the F150 slid back to give us more room and after a good bit of giggling and one accidental horn blast, Angie settled her slick, smooth pussy on my mouth while she swallowed my cock.

And the world stood still.

I thought about the first time I'd punished her and sat staring into the eye of god a few inches from my face. Now I reached out my tongue and tasted her treasure. It was more than I could have anticipated, even after having her juices all over my fingers for the past two weeks. She was sweet and a little salty, a combination I decided I liked. I almost forgot about my cock being sucked into her mouth simply because I was so engrossed by the tiny pussy in front of my face. This was one of the rare times I was glad to be nearsighted. Without my glasses, the details of her pussy were clear to me at about six inches away. And everything I saw I wanted to touch and lick.

We probably spent a lot more time just exploring each other with our tongues than the two teens, Cole and Geneive, would have. I was having trouble holding back so I could enjoy the experience. I was sure it would be over a lot faster for two sixteen-year-olds.

It was over much too quickly as it was. Angie bathed my face in her juices while I filled her mouth with mine. The difference between using my own right hand to pound the meat and feeling the delicate fingers of a beautiful naked girl surround it was astounding. It was another order of magnitude better to feel her lips and tongue sucking me deeper into her mouth as I came.

"Towel," she said as we entered the trailer afterward. It was late at night and we'd dared running naked from the truck to the trailer.

"We have plenty of them, Pudding."

"No. Cole and Geneive. They're going to get the seat of the truck a mess. They need a towel or a blanket or something."

~~~~~

WE STOPPED IN Abilene for a couple days and I visited my editor. Old Rotorhead and I had never actually met except through our correspondence and as a volunteer editor. His help on the *Model Student* series had been invaluable. As we chatted by email, he even suggested places I should visit as I traveled. I liked him a lot and could see that we'd be working together for a long time into the future.

But I didn't tell him about Angie. This story is as much a surprise to him as it is to you.

From there, we fled the cold that had already hit as far south as Dallas and took two long driving days to get to Corpus Christi. It wasn't exactly beach weather, but the temperatures were mild even if the wind was so strong that I couldn't run out the awning. We stayed there for a week as I finished re-writing *Redtail* and launched my next project, *Pygmalion Revisited*—a continuation of my tribute to the art world.

Over the next few weeks, we slowly worked our way along the Gulf Coast. Galveston. The Houston Space Center. The Bayou.

"This is where that character in *Triptych* came from. Whitney, the athlete," she said when I pulled into a parking lot where we could see the fairly new school building, a portion of which was still under construction. In front of it, much of the rubble from the original school was still piled and awaiting removal. To our right, the land stretched smooth and uninterrupted to the water about two miles away. I could just imagine a wall of water rushing inland with the hurricane. "How did you choose this as where she was from?"

"I was doing some part time work on the docks in Seattle," I said, "processing the tickets for people going on cruises. It was an opportunity for me to have daily interaction with people so I could expand my stock of characters. I met some good ones that summer. I heard a rich accent and looked up to greet a family from Louisiana going off on an Alaska cruise. The daughter was so stunning I had to force myself to pay attention to her father. By stunning, I don't necessarily mean just teenage beautiful. She was at least an inch or two taller than me and she just looked like she was fast. Her name was Whitney and that was all I needed in terms of a character. When I started writing about her, I had to do a ton of research on this general area and came up with this location as her home. Everything else about her, I based on Carly."

"Carly the Clown. You told me about her. I can't wait until the day I end up in one of your stories."

WE CAMPED AT Lake Pontchartrain a few days before Christmas. My time with Angie was growing short. She'd booked her flight from New Orleans to Los Angeles on Christmas morning. She was going home to start her master's work at the university. We were both feeling a little sad, but we'd found a quiet and private campsite next to a sandy stretch of beach. It had been a wet winter and there was no burn ban, so we spent a lot of time cuddled in a blanket next to the fire. If anyone chanced to come by, they couldn't tell we were naked wrapped in our blanket.

I'd promised to celebrate Yule with Angie. It was a far cry from the celebrations of my favorite holiday that I'd held over the past twenty-five years. Often, there were twenty to fifty guests, enough food and champagne to last the night, and stories told by everyone. We kept our champagne bottle concealed under the camp chair that we cuddled in against the chill night air. We drank it from a shared paper cup.

Don't be too appalled. It was cheap champagne.

"We'll use this as our Yule log," I said as I pulled a stick out of the pile of firewood. "Yule is like an annual rite of passage. The price of any passage is to leave a part of yourself behind. Remember, the goddess was left in the underworld for six months each year. So, the question we answer in the ritual is 'What are you leaving behind?' Typically, it is something that we want to be rid of. Once we place it on the log, we burn it."

"Mmm. What am I leaving behind?" she mused. "It might seem strange, but I think I can leave some of my submissiveness behind. I still have a craving for approval. Maybe even discipline. If you told me to run out and swim across the lake, I'd do it."

"The lake is five miles wide."

"I'd still do it, just because you said to. But, I don't think I'll be looking for anyone to take your place when I go back to school. I hope that doesn't sound like you were so bad I've learned my lesson!"

"Maybe you need to be punished again!" I laughed.

"Oh god! Would you? Please?"

"Hmm. I'd have a lot more trouble resisting temptation this time," I said. She smiled.

"I think I was so shocked when my father died that I felt like I had to replace his love. But the only thing I could identify was seeking his approval and direction. He praised me when I did good things and disciplined me when I was bad. I mistook those for his love. I dated that crazed guy who used my submissiveness to make me do perverse things. I refused to do drugs and broke up with him. It wasn't something my father would make me do. Then you came along. You were kind. You demanded that I pull my weight. You punished me when I was disrespectful. You guided me in making some of my own decisions and in freeing me from poor body image." She snuggled close to me and whispered as she put her hand on the log. "Uncle Ari, I think you helped me mourn my father and adjust to his loss. I think I can let go now."

We sat cuddled together and shared another sip from our champagne glass. What was I leaving behind?

～～

A Long Time Ago: Price of Passage

WHEN PAULA FINALLY admitted that it was over and left, she took everything with her. What was mine was hers. What was hers was her own. The only thing she didn't dare take was my manuscripts. She considered them worthless anyway. She took the few pieces of artwork that we had, all the books, all her LPs and all mine. She took the bed but left the mattress because she didn't want to sleep where we had slept. I had a typewriter. That night I sat on the floor of my barren apartment and typed the first words of my first novel.

And I started accumulating things again. When Anabel Lee left me, she took just about everything. She swore that she would never take my music and she lived up to her word. She left me one painting and my recliner.

And I started accumulating things again.

Treasure and I parted amicably and split things evenly. We still had some things in storage that we hadn't been able to liquidate. There were family mementos as well. After all, we'd had a daughter together. You can't just throw away her kindergarten art projects.

But I had to reduce my life to less than 750 pounds. That was all I could add to my trailer and still tow it successfully with the little F150. A third of my weight allowance was paper. I needed to cull that and digitize what was of value. I'd shred the rest.

So really, what did I have left to leave behind?

Back to Angie

"I'M LEAVING THE accumulation of stuff," I finally said. "I'm leaving behind the perception that my self-worth is tied up with what I own. Stuff doesn't contribute to my self-worth. In fact, it hides it. I am laying that burden on the log. Let it burn."

Angie got up and placed the log on the fire. Darkness had fallen and we couldn't see anyone else on the beach. It was delightful, though, to see her naked form silhouetted in the firelight. She returned to my arms and I covered us with the blanket as she shivered against me. We drank more champagne.

"And what would you like to have remembered from this year?" I asked, moving on to the second part of the ritual.

"I want to remember this night, held in your arms, forever," she sighed. I could only agree.

"I'll seal that memory with a kiss," I said.

We kissed for a long time. She was on my lap and turned to straddle it. She didn't attempt to mount me, though as stiff as I was, it wouldn't have been difficult. We hadn't had much genital to genital contact aside from a few slips when we were waking in the morning and I could feel my cock slide through her wet folds. The heat from her pussy now inflamed my desires and we kissed more as she slid against me.

"What do you hope for in the future?" she whispered. "That's the last part of the ritual, isn't it?"

"Yes," I said. I reached down next to the champagne bottle and retrieved two beeswax candles we'd found in a voodoo shop in New Orleans. My lighter was in a pouch attached to the chair. "I hope to always be your friend, of whom you think fondly on occasion," I said as I lit a candle. I pressed it into the sand next to us and watched the flame flicker in the slight breeze off the lake. Angie took the other candle and lit its flame.

"I hope you will make love to me," she whispered.

"Angie?"

"Not a one-night stand. Not a goodbye fuck. I want to be your lover. And I want you to say truthfully like you still say of Carly, 'We might not always *be* lovers, but we will always be lovers *now*.' Will you say that for me, Uncle Ari?"

"Will you ask that question without using the 'uncle' in front of my name?" I whispered. She pressed her candle into the sand next to mine and kissed me.

"I love you, Ari. Make love to me, darling."

We were much too far gone to change positions. I couldn't have moved us to the trailer for anything. We had a fire on the beach and were covered by a blanket. I lifted Angie a bit and she pushed my cock to her entrance. As she settled onto me, we resumed our kiss.

What was that I said about an order of magnitude? I wanted to *live* in her pussy. It grasped my cock and she rose and fell on me as we continued to kiss. I held her breasts in my hands, but as our passion increased, I slid them around to hug her to me.

"I love you, Angie. My god, I love you." Those were my last coherent thoughts as I was lost in the sensation of making love to my companion.

~~~~~

FOR MOST OF the next three days, we stayed in the trailer making love. I didn't write anything new, but the day before Christmas Eve, I began posting *Redtail*. We celebrated together.

On Christmas morning, we made love again before I took her to the airport. We both wept as she passed through security and I lost sight of her. I hung around the area for an hour and a half until she'd boarded and had to shut off her cell phone. I finally went to a Chinese restaurant for Christmas dinner and then returned to my trailer. I opened my computer and started to type.

Maybe I'd write a coming of age story. A kid grows up in Indiana loving his next door neighbor. I don't know what all will happen, but it will have a happy ending.

~~~~~

"WE NEED TO talk," my sister growled into the phone.

"What?" I asked innocently. She'd recently decided she needed to read everything I'd written. We'd reconnected after ten years when I went on my book tour a couple of years ago. Not that we were estranged. We just lived in different states and different worlds. Well, she'd only read one of my stories at SOL. Then she'd told me she certainly didn't need to read any more of that. But my newest literary fiction, *The Volunteer*, had come out in the middle of January, and I'd just sent her a copy automatically.

"You must have had a different father than I had. Mine was nothing like the one you wrote about in this book."

"Shay, it's fiction. It's not my autobiography."

"But I recognized things! I recognized the house and the cars and the neighborhood. The housing development where all the basements sank. I even remember when you got your first stage role."

"Well, sure. Experience creeps into what I write. That's what keeps it real. But please. I'm not a homeless wino catching boxcars and wandering around the country." That was mostly true. I guess technically I was homeless. My most recent ex-wife still let me use her street address. Can't get a driver's license without a street address. But other than that... And I like to have a couple glasses of wine in the evening. But other than that... I sighed.

"It just seemed so real," she said. "It was like I even knew the neighbors."

"Well, I'm glad I was so convincing. What did you think of the book?" I asked. Yeah. I'm a glutton for praise, even if my sister's was one of the only twelve copies that would ever sell.

"It's good. I understand why Maddie thinks it's your best. But it's a hard book to read. That's not exactly what I mean. It's a hard book to *have read*. It was so sad. Couldn't you have given him a home at the end?" she asked plaintively.

The book had even upset the Unitarians at the church I sometimes attended. They believed they could put an end to homelessness. They weren't happy that I challenged that idea and told them that their ten-year plan to end homelessness in King County wasn't working. I wasn't complaining about what they were doing. It was good work. It was helping a lot of people. But it wasn't ending homelessness.

"I write books with happy endings," I laughed. "I think you called them smut."

"Not that kind of happy ending. Maybe we're not related at all!"

We were back on an even footing and I promised that I'd stop and visit her again when I went through Missouri.

Her complaint wasn't all that unusual. A woman in my neighborhood had read *For Blood or Money* and nodded knowingly at me. "I could see this was you," she said. Really? I'm a fifty-seven-year-old computer forensics detective waiting for a heart transplant? Another friend had said, "Did you have heart surgery? What you described was exactly like what it was like for me before I had my quadruple bypass surgery. I felt like I never got my lungs completely full of air. Walking from one room to another left me needing to sit down and rest. Why didn't I know you had heart problems?" *Um... because I don't?*

"Only you could have written this book," a former co-worker of mine had said on my book tour for *The Gutenberg Rubric*. "This was you all the way. I could just see you working on those manuscripts." Yeah. I wish. That was twenty years of research that made that book realistic. I'd never touched a manuscript over a hundred years old.

But my experiences crept into what I wrote. Someone once said that we should write what we know. I had my own interpretation. Write what you wish you knew.

4 Baseball and Bikinis

21 February 2014

I FOUND a nice place to camp on Mississippi's Gulf Coast. Unbelievably beautiful. I looked out at the white sand and blue water. The beach was empty. It was February and Mississippi's spring break bonanza wouldn't start for a few weeks.

I'd received a flood of love after the final chapter of *The Prodigal* posted in September. That was cool. I got good response from *The Props Master 1: Ritual Reality*. *Redtail* was getting a good response and would end this week. I'd released the eBook and paperback in January. A lot of people were grabbing it so they didn't have to wait for each installment on SOL. Clever, but there was something about teasing readers to buy the book before it finished posting that I wasn't enthused about. My readers on SOL had been good to me.

They'd saved my life.

A Few Years Ago: Words Are Opium

I GOT HOME from my 2011 book tour determined to save my marriage. It wasn't just for Maddie's sake. She was an adult now and while I would always give her whatever help I could, she was doing well at making her own way. But Treasure was the love of my life. The second book I'd published, *Steven George & The Dragon*, was a collection of fairy tales that led a hapless dragon slayer from adventure to adventure as he sought his dragon. Not a kids' book, I kept reminding people who bought it. Think *Grimms' Fairy Tales*, not Disney's. I'd dedicated it to my wife, without whom there would be no happy endings.

Writing gets under my skin. Deep under it. I'd just finished writing *For Money or Mayhem* and was depressed over the way I'd once again treated perfectly fine people who were near happiness. Mystery solved, life wrecked. I needed some TLC. That's when Treasure told me she just wasn't interested and we needed to figure out what our next steps would be.

Fuck!

Dad, words are our opium.

I went digging through my files and found a locked and password protected story that I'd written fifteen years earlier. I'd abandoned the story because 'I don't write that kind of stuff!' Miraculously, I remembered the password.

It wasn't bad. Not finished, by a long shot, but it had the makings for the one thing that I desperately wanted. I wanted to have a happy ending. I did some rewriting, cleanup, and editing. Five days after my wife's announcement, I posted the first chapter of *The Art and Science of Love*. I'd been reading stories on SOL for a couple of years, but had never considered posting a story there. It seemed like a good thing at the time. I kept writing more chapters of ASL and when the second chapter posted, email started coming in. My first fan mail was from the ubiquitous 'Anonymous' who wrote, "An excellent start. I find the characters believable and the plot interesting. I hope to read much more like this from you in future. Thank you for making your efforts available." I framed it and put it on a wall like the first dollar bill earned by a new restaurant.

But the notes kept coming. Several authors that I'd read responded to the story. InvidFan. Crumbly Writer. GentleButFirm. They were all encouraging. By the eleventh chapter, the email was all over the map, but mostly positive. If you can call this positive: "Fah-h-h-h-k! The sex in this chapter is so-o-o-o hot! I would give my right nut to be the man meat in that sandwich just once. Thanks for sharing." One even wrote to thank me for correcting his technique for a particular sex act! Aroslav: sex therapist.

After the story finished posting, I got a raft of messages. In general, it seemed that people appreciated my style, my understanding of art, and believable sex scenes. Imagine that. I seriously considered letting Treasure see what she was missing out on. "Wow. A piece of erudite, brain-seducing erotica. What a treat. Thanks so much. I trust more of your finely-crafted and believable erotica will grace this site before too long."

I was determined that it would. No one had ever responded to my mysteries and thrillers so enthusiastically. I started in on a sequel to *The Art and Science of Love* based on the book I'd originally planned to write twenty years ago. But it was going to take a long time to get the story written—or rewritten so it would make sense. I figured I should write a piece just to keep my name in the market. The ill-fated *Art School* was the result. I realized as soon as I posted and reread it that I'd made a huge mistake. The very reason I'd started writing erotica in the first place was to have a happy ending. I'd betrayed the promise in *Art School*. Even though I quickly changed the ending so it wasn't as miserable as my 'reality-based' mysteries, the damage was done and scores were poor.

In the meantime, I was bogged down in details of my intended story and decided once again that I needed to get my name out there with another story. Since people seemed to really like stories set in the art world, I thought maybe I could jot off a quick story about an art student who found love on the other side of the easel when a classmate asks him to pose for her. It would be a simple couple of chapters. I posted the first chapter of *Model Student* before I'd even begun writing the second.

"I'm looking forward to the next chapter. I hope there are many more. Thank you!" Well, there would be a second chapter, because having a slightly older supermodel athlete as the third part of a three-some would be hot. But the notes kept coming asking for 'the next chapter.' I was writing as fast as I could and posting as soon as the chapter was finished. They were long (7,000-word) chapters and I was getting one a week out. It wasn't until the fifth one posted and Tony had just painted the mural that I realized I was in this for the long haul. And I'd just introduced the enigmatic Kate. Funny how I'd started thinking about her just then. It wasn't even going to be enough to end the story at the end of Tony's freshman year in college. I was going to have to take this all the way through to graduation.

"My God. I have just read 5 and 6. Now I understand your blog and the forum when you talk about the feedback you've been getting. Your work is amazing! You have a gift. You really don't need hints on where the story should go next, because these characters inside you will tell you exactly what you need to do, and which step to take next. That they are so alive on paper (well, on the screen), means they are living and breathing inside you, and there is no skin between them and the words you write. Oh, my god. Thank you for daring to do this, to open your heart like this. I don't know whether these people exist in real life or not, but they for sure exist inside you, and now they live for us. Incredible, and thank you."

The black depression that had descended on me at the end of November when Treasure told me we were through was gradually lifting. It took a while. It took figuring out how to divide the property, when to put the house on the market, where we would each live. But throughout that year, I wrote chapter after chapter and posted them. Black Irish read and reviewed the story and volunteered to help me with some editing. He could only help temporarily because Jay Cantrell was his first priority and a new tome was coming out from the master. But close on his heels, Old Rotorhead volunteered to help with the editing and proofreading. My work was benefiting from the added eyes before it was posted.

And email kept coming in, thanking me—thanking me!—for writing this story. A publisher expressed interest in taking on the book, but wanted me to stop posting it on SOL. I delayed the second half of *Triptych* two months while I negotiated with the publisher and eventually withdrew the manuscript from consideration. I'd committed to the readers to put this story out on SOL for free. I'd publish the books as eBooks so people could buy them, but SOL readers had saved my life.

I was going to be okay.

~~~~~

Back to Alabama
EVEN THOUGH I was alone and traveling the country in a truck and sixteen-foot trailer, I was trying to figure out how I could thank my readers. The answer was obvious.

Write a story for them.

I had the trailer parked somewhere near Foley, Alabama and 'Lambert's Café, The Only Home of the Throwed Rolls.' I needed to take a few days to edit and design a book for one of my clients and having the famous restaurant so close was a big bonus. I was also near a white sand beach on the edge of the Gulf. I drove out onto the beach, which was packed solid enough to support the truck. In fact, several trucks parked or cruised along the shore. Popular place. I went wading.

I like to be by the water. I'm not so wild about being *in* the water. My ideal homestead would be camped next to a small river where I could hear the water and sit next to it. But I'd determined that I would dip my feet in the waters of all four U.S. coasts. I'd waded in the Pacific at Malibu. Now the Gulf. Eventually I would get to the Atlantic and the Great Lakes. Today was South Coast Day.

After I'd fulfilled my objective, I sat in the truck watching the sun go down and listening to 'The 70s on 7' on my satellite radio. Smokie (originally Smokey) came on. I've looked this group up and I think they only ever had one song hit the charts. It was 'Living Next Door to Alice.' Sweet song about a guy who grows up next door to the love of his life, but never tells her. The song ends with the words, 'Now I'll just have to get used to not living next door to Alice.' My ears tend to pick and choose what they hear and how they hear it. What I heard was 'Living Next Door to Heaven.'

I had the title for my new story.

Now I just needed a location and a cast of characters.

A Long Time Ago: Our Gang

I WAS THREE years younger than Jessica. She was the second oldest of the kids on our section of Mosquito Road. Mitch was the oldest. His sister, Betts, was a year younger than Jessica. Jessica's brother Drew was next. Despite the character I turned him into, he wasn't a bad guy and I was happy to count him among my friends. All the rest of us on that stretch of road were in the same grade except Geoff's brother, John, who was a year younger. That meant my best friend Carl, Geoff, Liz, Cassie, and I were in the same class. Our section of Mosquito Road was about half a mile long. We represented every family that lived along it. The next person in our school lived nearly half a mile farther on in either direction. So, of course, the ten of us did stuff together. Mitch and Jessica were both considerably more advanced, but Betts and Drew were just young enough that they considered it okay to hang out with the rest of us.

One of our favorite pastimes was to play softball in Geoff's pasture or mine. Mine had the 'advantage' of not having horses or ponies in it like Geoff's and Carl's. If they weren't busy doing older kid stuff— Mitch had to help his Grandpa with the farming and Jessica… well, who knows?—then we could field two full teams of five for softball. If everybody couldn't play, we had a rotation game. It was hard to keep score, but we all got to play all positions. We had to keep skipping up so the rotation didn't stay exactly the same. Nobody wanted me to pitch to them because I pitched on the church team. Nobody wanted Carl to play first base because he was so tall he could stretch halfway to second. If he ever made contact with the ball, you could about guarantee we'd have to chase it into the next field. Fortunately, he didn't hit it very often.

Anyway, there was this lake a few miles away. We'd all been to it on occasion, but for whatever reason, the parents got together one summer when we all thought we'd die of the heat and told all of us to get our bathing suits on because we were going swimming. It took half the parents to drive us all to the lake and the other half brought food a little later.

Any of this sound familiar? Yeah. This was pretty much the cast that started shaping up for *Living Next Door to Heaven*.

At fifteen, Jessica was the most well-developed of our group and I'd observed her from afar as she sprouted a nice pair of breasts. I thought she was beautiful. Of course, it was Betts who was the first girl who had let me look and touch between her legs in the infamous horse barn hayloft. She was just as fascinated when she played with the bell on top of my ding-dong, as she called it, and I got my first ever erection. Neither of us knew what to do with it, but we had fun. Her brother, my best friend Carl, told on us and that put a quick end to the explorations.

Suffice it to say, Jessica had the tightest swimsuit that day. She might have been trying to fit into last year's. I've never understood what drew us together, but Jessica wanted to play with me. Really play. We swam together and when we were out deep enough, she kept brushing against me. I mean brushing really interesting parts against me. We played 'toss' where I'd put my hands on her waist and throw her up into the air. Then she'd swim up to me and while we were getting ready for the next toss, she'd make sure that my hands got a chance to explore her burgeoning breasts before they slid down to her waist. I was totally lost in the moment. She did a good amount of groping as well until Betts put a stop to it.

"You guys!" she hissed at us. "You're going to get caught doing that stuff. Quit it!" I think that she was a little jealous that I was getting to feel Jessica up so thoroughly and wasn't touching Betts. Well, Betts hadn't really developed quite the handholds that Jessica had.

As things go, though, that was the extent of my relationship with Jessica. We never got a chance to do anything else. Well, she was a sophomore in high school and could date *real* guys.

After my freshman year, my family moved to a new school district. I got my first ever yearbook and the big thing was to have as many kids as possible sign it. Because I was approaching a reunion year, I had my daughter bring me my yearbooks from the store room when she came down to visit me in Florida. I was leafing through that first one and looking at all the pictures. Cassie had written a very nice little note wishing me luck and signed it 'Love, Cassie.' I had to think back fondly on those times we met in the woods that joined our two properties.

But when I turned to the last page of the yearbook, I saw a note that just brought back a flood of memories. The longest note anyone had written. Jessica had graduated and was headed for Purdue. She admonished me to think of her sometimes as she was slaving away. "And always remember the crazy times we had, like that time at the lake," she concluded. There was a little heart drawn next to her name. Three years after the event, she was remembering us playing in the lake and exploring the mysteries of our young bodies. And she was asking me to always remember it, too. Well, I did. That became the basis for the story I was about to write.

~~~~~~

Back to Florida

THE GROUPER SANDWICHES that Dual Writer talks about in his *Florida Friends* series are not the only reason to go to Florida. They *are* a sufficient reason, though. Nor are the 'Tampa Twins' at the Harley store, though I'm glad to say I got to see them.

No, there are only two reasons to be in Florida in March. Spring Training and Spring Break. Baseball and Bikinis.

I'd managed to stake out a prime slot for my trailer in Fort Myers Beach for the month. It was high season and I paid as much for that month as I had for all the camping sites I'd stayed at so far in the eight months of this trip. And what did I get for it? When I say a 'slot' that's exactly what I mean. My trailer was parked on a cement slab twelve feet wide. With the slide-out extended, the trailer is a little over eleven feet wide. On either side of the slab is a strip of grass, four feet wide, separating my slab from my neighbor's. I couldn't fully extend my awning without hitting the next trailer.

And the awning was necessary if I wanted any shade. There were four trees in the RV park and they bordered the mostly unused play area.

When I was young, I had a tendency toward religious fervor. I'd fortunately outgrown it by the time I finished my degrees. It is humorous to me in retrospect that all the classmates who scorned me in grade school because of my firmly held religious beliefs and 'goodie-two-shoes' attitude have now become hyper-religious bigots who are willing to condemn anyone for anything that is different than what they happen to believe. I know that's harsh. Most of them are still good people. Some of those who weren't are now. We all tend to remember our childhood as miserable and blame everyone else for it. In my bliss-ful state as a born-again pagan, I've become both socially and morally liberal. Kind of wish I could get my hands on some of those girls the way they were when we were growing up.

Some of those people live in Florida. At least part of the year. They have condos, trailers, winter homes, or for all I know, tents on the beach. Winter can be hard in northern Indiana, so why not retire to warm and sunny Florida?

I'll tell you why not.

I cannot understand why old people want to flock to a state where the State Bird is a vulture! These huge black birds are everywhere. Including on the unused playground equipment in the center of the RV park. There are no children living in the RV park and when one comes to visit a grandparent, he avoids the playground. The vultures perch on the jungle gym watching the benches around the edge. Old folks go out for their daily walks—usually with some yappy little dog—and take a break to sit on the benches around the playground where the four trees provide a little shade. The vultures eye them the entire time they sit there, as if to say, 'Are you dead yet?' If a vulture hops down from the bars to the ground, you've sat still too long. There are warning signs at the entrance to the park that admonish caution because the vultures will eat the rubber on your car. Door seals, tires, bumper guards. Camping World does a brisk business in covers for tires to protect them from the sun while you are parked. We know it is really to protect them from vultures.

Maddie visited me in Florida, anxious to get her own bikini time in on the beach. I sat and watched the scenery while she went wading and swimming in the salt water. Then we'd sit in the evening and go over the plots for our newest book projects. She loved the concept of *Redtail* and was happy that it had done so well on SOL. We have an agreement that she doesn't read her father's porn, though I found out later that she cheated and read *Redtail*. She said she liked it.

She spotted the potential business in the park immediately. With the same enthusiasm that she plots a novel, she plotted a business strategy: Pimp My Golf Cart. Everyone in the park, it seemed, had a golf cart. Aside from the required twice-a-day walk around the park with the dog, no one walked anyplace. Walmart was half a mile away. They had a special parking area for golf carts. Maddie had the idea of doing custom paint jobs on carts. She even went so far as to suggest kits to put a Rolls Royce grill and ornament on the front of them like they used to do with customization kits for Volkswagen Beetles. (Back in the old days, she said. *Grr!*) She could do custom canopies to keep the sun off delicate skin. She even suggested a tattoo parlor where customers could get decorated to match the paint job on the cart. She pulled up so many designs for 1950s and 60s muscle cars on her computer to manipulate onto pictures of golf carts that she exceeded my data allowance for the month.

Then she flew back to Seattle.

If you are around Fort Myers, watch for a new business coming soon. The last I heard, she planned to promote it with a television show like 'Chop Shop' or something. Get the cart, the tattoo, and the video. Creative kid. She'll get to that after she finishes her next novel.

When we weren't plotting stories and business pipe dreams, we went to the beach—where she took great delight in pointing out the best bikini butts—or to the baseball game. I'd lived in Minnesota years ago, and since the Seattle Mariners were in the Cactus League for spring training, I contented myself with going to Twins games, starting with the opener against the University of Minnesota Gophers. The Gophers gave the Twins a good run for the money and a close game. Mostly the players were the same age. Some of the pros were younger than the college kids. There wasn't a name on the roster for either team that I recognized. Early training games are a testing ground for those who have been invited to spring training, but will probably end up on

Double-A or Triple-A teams. You don't really see the top players much until the last week of training.

~~~~~

YOU MIGHT HAVE noticed that there isn't much here about me getting laid. Well, since Angie left to go back to school, I really hadn't felt like pursuing any opportunities. I was pouring all my energy into writing *Living Next Door to Heaven* and was churning out 4-5,000 words a day when I was camped. My characters were carrying on non-stop conversations in my head when I was traveling.

Pixel the Cat had joined my editorial team and he and Old Rotorhead were sending the chapters back to me almost as quickly as I wrote them. I was determined that I would not start posting until I had completed a full sub-arc of the story. It would be one long—very long—serial, but within it, there would be ten parts (later reduced to nine) that each had a distinct end-point. I'd start posting the first one while I wrote the second one, but I planned to be way ahead of the game before the chapters ever hit SOL. I absolutely hated stories that I followed only to have them fade away to nothing and eventually turn yellow with a note that says, 'unfinished and inactive.' That was not going to happen to one of my stories if I could help it.

It's hard to develop a relationship when you are only camped for two or three days. People come and go. I've never been all that good at pickup lines or identifying the fast movers. But I would be in Florida for two months. I had my eye peeled for opportunity. I never expected where it would come from.

I'd been accumulating more and more Facebook followers as I wrote about my travels. More relatives. Some old friends from my years in high school. Some relatives went to school with me in the early years and knew people on their friends lists with whom I'd grown up.

"Ari, are you coming to Indiana for the reunion this summer?" my third cousin twice removed asked in a post.

"Reunion? What reunion?" I responded.

It turned out that I would be just in time this summer to go to a class reunion for St. Joe Valley High, the school I'd left after my freshman year. The school where all the people I'd been making up stories about in LNDtH had gone. *Well, shit. Why not?* I wrote to the reunion organizer and asked if it was okay to attend, even though I didn't graduate with the class. I'd gone through ten years of school with many of them. I was registered.

"Ari? Is that really you?" read the email note. "Are you really coming home for the party?" There was no signature. All I had was the return email address. Cassie Clinton Jones. My one-time next door neighbor and playmate in the woods between our houses. I still considered Cassie to be my first girlfriend, back before I understood what a girlfriend was.

A Long Time Ago: A Walk in the Woods

ENTERTAINMENT OUT IN the country was whatever we could make of it. Like following Cassie's father as he plowed the fields and breaking up dirt clods with our bare feet. Sometimes we'd find a worm stuck between our toes and giggle about how gross it was. It would take hours to scrub the dirt off our feet at night. At least it seemed like it. Neither of our mothers would allow us in the house until we'd been through the hose outside.

We were in kindergarten together and I was even invited to play at her house on occasion in the winter. Cassie was cool. Her mother allowed her to jump on the bed. We had our own circus with a trampoline!

The first day of first grade was a catastrophe. The teacher seated us in alphabetical order. Cassie was heartbroken and cried because she couldn't sit beside Ari. We got through it and sat next to each other at lunch. School does that to kids. In the summer, we continued to meet and go play in the woods. Sometimes we were joined by other kids from our part of Mosquito Road. Mitch and Betts often rode their horses out there. Sometimes we'd even see Geoff or John on their pony. Mostly, though, we just built tree forts, climbed for crab apples, and played hide and seek among the maple trees.

There was one instance between second and third grade where

we met a couple older kids out in the woods. They scrambled around when they saw us and I thought they must have stopped to pee because he was pulling his pants closed. She was sweet and bubbly. I thought I recognized her as one of Shay's friends.

"Look at the little boyfriend and girlfriend," she said. "Are you having fun on your date in the woods?" *Date? Boyfriend? Girlfriend?* Neither Cassie nor I had any concept of what she was talking about. We were just headed for the corral we were building so Betts could get off her horse and play when she came through the woods.

It wasn't long after that, Cassie became a beautiful girl and I was just another stinky boy. But eight years later, she was the only one who signed my yearbook with the word 'love.'

~~~~~

Back to Florida

IT TURNED OUT that Cassie and her husband lived in Orlando. We agreed to meet at the Strawberry Festival and it was great fun to get reacquainted. Her husband, Andy, was a nice guy, but quiet. He went to watch some Seminole dancers while Cassie and I walked around the fairgrounds catching up on everything that had happened since we last saw each other.

Her eyes got big when I gave her copies of my books. I'd had *Redtail* released as a paperback, but even though it sold well as an eBook, no one bought the paperback. I just used it as a promotional.

"It's got a different name than the others," she said, pointing out the author name. "Ari, what's going on? What kind of book is this? This couple on the cover is topless." She quickly tucked the book between two of the others, but she didn't offer to give it back.

"I've been writing a lot of erotica, Cassie. It's fun. People like it. It makes people feel good. I enjoy writing it. Please don't think ill of me. You might even enjoy it. Read it aloud with your husband," I suggested.

"There's more than this one?"

Well, it was a little like true confessions. Only I wasn't reading them, I was confessing. We stopped for a strawberry shortcake and coffee and I told her all about how I got started writing erotica and what I'd written. I had ten stories out by then. And then I told her about *Living Next Door to Heaven*. I was in the final formatting of the first few chapters and expected to start posting by mid-April.

"And I'm in it?" she demanded.

"Well, it's not like it's really you. No one would recognize you from the descriptions. I mean, I didn't even know you after freshman year. It's all pretty much made up. I just based a few characteristics that I remember from when we were little kids and let fantasies take over from there," I said. I'd never considered what would happen if one of my childhood friends got hold of the story and read it. I might have to change some names and places.

"Fantasies?" she said looking me in the eye. "Do we have sex?"

"Um… Not yet. And it's not us. For Pete's sake, Cassie. It's a story. There are scenes you might recognize. Places. But you won't recognize the character that started out as my best friend in kindergarten. I mean, really, the Cassie in the story is a late bloomer and hyper religious. You were a freshman cheerleader!"

"Four years," she sighed. She looked at me sternly. "If we have sex, it had better be damned good!" I think she meant in the story.

We rejoined her husband and then parted ways. I was going to go on to meet up with Writer Number Seven. I was enjoying meeting and connecting with other SOL writers and readers as I traveled. Cassie and I promised to meet at the reunion this summer in Indiana.

It was St. Patrick's Day and I was going to a ballgame in the evening. The Twins were playing the Tigers. It promised to be a good game—a preview of the season opener in Minneapolis. First, I planned to go out and look at the talent on the beach. A new crop had arrived over the weekend. They were always so bright and fresh at the beginning of the week. They started to look more sunburned and worn by the time they left on Saturday. There's a website where you can look up what colleges are going to what beaches during what weeks. Fort Myers Beach seemed to be the most popular place for the beach-goers this year. I was just going to watch. Really.

But first, I needed a green shirt. I had nothing green in my closet at all. I stopped at Walmart.

Walmart is one of the great contradictions in America today. I have friends who refer to it in Florida as going 'to the unhappiest place on earth.' I hate the fact that they drove so many small businesses out of business. The same way Barnes and Noble did. The same way Starbucks did. The same way Amazon did. I suppose that back at the turn of the twentieth century, people were complaining that Sears and Roebuck was driving the mom and pop mercantiles out of business. I hated that it happened, but it was reality.

I dislike just about everything about WallyWorld. Their politics stink. The way they treat people stinks. Their conservative social stances and the way they treat gays stink. Sadly, many of their customers stink.

But even bad people/organizations sometimes do good things.

I have stayed the night with my trailer parked in a Walmart parking lot during a rainstorm. I've bought emergency supplies at Walmart. I've gone to Walmart just to use the restroom. Walmart is one of the great constants of America. If you need something—food, clothing, camping gear, auto repair, a fuse for the trailer, the DVD of *Die Hard*— there's a Walmart within twenty miles. In this case, it was half a mile from my trailer and on the way to the beach. I bought a green Hawaiian shirt for five bucks. It was bright. In ten minutes I was changed and on my way to the beach. I guess my principles are a matter of convenience.

Nearly everything I wrote about in Brian's broadcast from the beach during spring break was something I saw there. Even the booth of 'Virgins till Marriage' with three of the most beautiful bikini-clad coeds I'd ever seen smiling and talking to each other. And yes, they had a little sign that said 'You break it, you bought it.' Brian was a far more reserved and upstanding young man than I am. I seriously considered making a purchase.

Instead, I took my beach chair and staked out a little space with my cooler and my book where I could watch the action. The fact that I was located just beyond a virtual campground of coeds was entirely coincidental. I don't spend a lot of time in the sun, so I'd chosen the only shady spot I could find. The dozen or so beauties were stretched out on their stomachs, their bikini tops all untied so that they could get unobstructed sun. I was just waiting for the moment when they all rolled over.

What I got was a rude awakening when one of the girls landed in my lap. I'd fallen asleep and missed the rollover, apparently. The girls were all up and playing with a Frisbee. A gust of wind off the Gulf had picked the disk up and directed it toward me. In her attempt to make the catch, the girl in my lap had tripped over my chair and fallen. I provided a nice soft landing. The padding she brought with her was softer than I was.

"Sorry," she said, wiggling around and trying to get up.

"Believe me; not a problem," I answered. "Most excitement I've had all day." She squirmed a little more and I was beginning to pay attention. One of her breasts was pressed directly onto my hand.

"At your age, it's probably the most excitement you've had in years," she giggled. *Oh, fuck you.* "Sorry. That was rude. You should turn your hand over if you really want excitement. I probably shouldn't have had two margaritas for lunch." I didn't care. She invited, I responded. My hand rolled over under her and firmly squeezed the breast pressed into it. The fabric had slipped a little, which was all that was necessary to ensure a hard little nipple was pressed into my hand. "I'm definitely gonna hafta get laid tonight. Thanks for the thrill." She pushed herself up and waved the Frisbee as I looked at the exposed nipple. She casually tugged her top over it and turned to rejoin the game. It moved off toward the water and I rearranged my package so it didn't look like a pennant was flying from a flagpole.

This day was a success already. But since the sun had moved enough that my shady spot was no longer shady, I decided to pack things back to my truck and find some food.

A lot of fast food places dotted the boardwalk, but I chose to walk a little farther downtown where the restaurants served real food. I'd just crossed the street when I encountered half a dozen girls headed my way. Bikinis and flip-flops. All of them were finishing ice cream cones. They must carry their money in their cleavage. The redhead that intercepted me was hiding her cleavage beneath a crop top that almost left the bottom of her boobs bare.

"I love that shirt!" she screamed. She wasted no time grabbing hold of it to test the fabric.

"Becky! You're assaulting a stranger again."

"But look at it. It's so silky. This is what I want. I'd wear this shirt every day. Where did you get it?" she asked me. "I've been looking everywhere."

"Oh!" I thought fast. "I tell you what. Why don't I trade you?" I started unbuttoning my shirt. She looked up into my eyes. Or as close as she could through both of our sunglasses. She pulled her glasses up and showed me the deepest green eyes I'd ever seen. I returned the favor and showed her my baby blues.

"Becky," one of her friends hissed. She scowled at the friend. The other five girls huffed and headed off without her. Becky pulled me into a narrow passage between two gift shops and grabbed the hem of her t-shirt.

"I'm almost as anxious to see you *in* this as you are to see me *out* of it," she whispered. I finished unbuttoning the shirt as she pulled hers off. I took my shirt off slowly and slipped it around her as she put her arms back for the sleeves. This had the pleasant side-effect of pushing her breasts into my chest. She shifted back and forth a bit, rubbing them against me. She leaned back a bit so I could finish pulling the shirt around her, slowly covering the sight of those beautiful breasts. "Better kiss 'em goodbye," she whispered.

I glanced back and saw no one staring at us, so I dipped my head to gently kiss each nipple before I pulled the shirt closed and began buttoning it. The backs of my hands rested against her soft bosom as my fingers worked the buttons.

"Here," she said. "You have to put this on." She handed me her crop top. This would be good. I managed to get it over my head. That was it. I'd just have to wear it around my neck. She ran her fingers up and down my bare chest.

"Nice," she breathed. "It's so different to see a man's chest instead of a boy's." It was nice to see her chest, too, with its hard nipples tenting out the thin fabric of my shirt.

"Would you like to see a baseball game tonight?" I blurted out. I'm not sure where that came from, but my hands were still on the buttons of the shirt as if trying to figure out which way they were going. She pushed forward and the nubs of her breasts were pushed into my hands.

"Who's playing?" she asked breathlessly.

"The Twins," I said as I squeezed again slightly. "Against the Tigers."

"Sounds like fun," she said. "You're not like an axe murderer, are you?"

"I'm nothing like an axe murderer at all."

"I can't really go like this. I'm staying at the Seashell on the left about three blocks that way. What time will you pick me up?" I released her breast and she sighed as I flicked my cell phone to see what time it was.

"It's two-ten. I'll pick you up at four. Is two hours enough time for you to get ready?"

"Yeah. I've had enough sun on the beach for today. I'm a redhead. Any more and I'll burn to a crisp. What do you drive?"

"Black Ford pickup. Washington plates."

"Washington? What are you doing clear down here?"

"I'm on spring break." We both laughed. "Don't change too much," I said, running my hand lightly over the silky fabric of the shirt. I didn't go directly for the nipples, staying just to the outside of her breasts.

"Right. I'll bring some sunblock. In case our seats are in the sun. But I've got to get back to my friends. They already think I'm crazy. I guess I am a little. I'll see you at four." She stood on tiptoes to give me a light little kiss on the lips with her hands still on my chest. "Mmm. Better kiss these goodbye," she said. My nipples were at about lip height for her and she added a little tongue to each kiss. "Thanks for the shirt. I'm Becky, by the way."

"I'm Aroslav."

"See you at four." She took off in the direction her friends had gone, leaving me staring after her. Just before she crossed the street she turned around and waved.

That was an experience.

I checked to make sure I still had my wallet.

I MOSTLY EXPECTED that she wouldn't show. It's one thing to be outrageous on the beach. It's quite another to actually get in the truck. Didn't your mother teach you not to get in a car with strangers?

I called the ballpark box office and ordered two tickets anyway. I could always scalp one at the gate at a discount. After I gave them my credit card, I headed back to the trailer to put some ballpark clothes on myself, lunch forgotten. I pulled Becky's little shirt off my neck. If she hadn't cut the ribbing around the neck off, I'd have torn it. As it was, though, I hung it neatly near my bed and… Yeah. I sniffed at it. Not that it did any good. There was a faint smell of suntan oil.

I shook my head at my own culpability and headed toward the rendezvous.

I WASN'T EXPECTING *FOUR GIRLS* to come bouncing out of the hotel when I pulled up.

"So, your name is Aroslav. Is that some kind of Muslim terrorist name?" the blonde who came up to me first asked. She had bigger boobs than Becky's substantial set and got right into my personal space with them so she could glare into my eyes.

"Bren! You promised to be nice!" Becky said. She pushed her friend aside and gave me a quick, and somewhat possessive, kiss on the cheek. "Ari, these are my friends. Brenda the Rude, Lisa the Flat, and Susan Anytime."

"Becky, that is so unkind," Lisa said. "Do you think I'm flat, Aroslav?" She pushed her chest out for me to examine. Smaller than her friends, but definitely not flat.

"I told them I was going to a ballgame and they all decided they want to *come*," she hissed. "Do you mind?"

"I only bought two tickets," I protested. What was I doing?

"Do you have the number?" Susan asked. She had her cell phone out. "We don't want to horn in on your date or make you pay for every-thing. We just don't want Becky the Reckless off with a stranger where none of us can get to her in an emergency."

I punched the redial button on my phone and handed it to her.

"When you get your ticket, punch your number in so I know how to get hold of you in an emergency." Inside of three minutes, Susan had connected and confirmed there were tickets available. She waved us all into the truck while she dug in her purse for a credit card. Becky slid into the front seat, but before I could close the door I held for her, Brenda shoved in beside her, moving Becky to the center. I was glad I'd taken a minute to clean out all the old coffee cups before I headed out.

I pulled away from the hotel and onto the highway. It isn't far from Fort Myers Beach to the Twins ballpark, but traffic over the bridge can be a bear and it usually takes as much as twenty minutes just to park. It was an early game tonight because the Tigers would have two hours on the bus after the game to get back to their home turf in Lakeland.

"Where are you ladies from?" I asked.

"University of Minnesota! Go Gophers!" they all shouted at once.

"Thank heavens! I was afraid I'd picked up a bunch of cheeseheads and would have to turn in my alumni card," I laughed.

"No way! You got your bachelor's from the U?" Becky asked. She had managed to wiggle up quite tightly against me and had her hand on my thigh.

"PhD," I corrected her. The girls all had a little exclamation to make about that. What a time that had been.

A Long Time Ago: Belly Dancer

THE THEATER DEPARTMENT didn't make a big deal about MAs and BAs. They expected you to pick up your degree at commencement, though most skipped the event and had it mailed to them. If you got a master's, you were on a PhD track. MFAs and PhDs were terminal degrees and had a special celebration at Rarig. I wrote about that in *Not This Time*.

Paula had gone to commencement and picked up her degree. I declined to attend. She got back, packed her bags in the new AMC Gremlin her daddy bought her, and gave me a quick peck on the cheek.

"Keep in touch," she said. Then she towed the U-Haul with all our meagre possessions—furniture, kitchenware, bedding, and records—to California. I attended our divorce decree a month later and the attorney forwarded her the papers so she could get her name changed back. She'd never wanted my name in the first place.

I sat in the empty apartment and started writing my first novel.

I gradually accumulated a few things over the next two years. Among them, lovers.

Like Isabel. Don't get her confused with Anabel. We never married. In fact, we barely got it all together. It was when I was invited to design *Kismet* for a local community theater. The reason Paula and I had chosen to go to Minneapolis for our graduate studies was that it was the second largest and fastest growing theater center in the country. We'd had an opportunity to go to New York, but as one of our theater directors had said, "That's like trying to get a last-minute ticket on the Titanic."

The problem with designing in Minneapolis was that you had to tech direct the show as well. In other words, you built it. We performed in the Hennepin Center for Performing Arts, which was really nothing but a big empty warehouse. I converted it into an Arabian fantasy. But building that show had me working around the clock for over a week. I was a wreck by the time we finally opened.

Being a wreck didn't mean that I didn't notice the belly dancers. There is an entire scene that is devoted to a bunch of women trying to impress the Prince into making them his wives. There was half a dozen

I would have added to my harem. The one that seemed most willing to be added was Isabel.

Isabel had a wardrobe malfunction, and I was the only tech person available to assist. I had been behind on getting the set up and ready. Paint was mostly dry when we opened. The Wazir's wife was still being stitched into her costume at the beginning of the second act. Poor Isabel had broken a snap on her rather delicate bra top.

I kept everything in my toolbox. Even a sewing kit. I only had black thread, but no one was going to notice that. The only problem was that I needed to sew a snap on and it was almost impossible to do with the bra top still on Isabel. She turned her back to me and whipped it off. I sewed. Once I was working, Isabel turned back to talk to me. She had one arm artfully concealing her nipples, but her breasts sort of bulged out on either side of it. Her very delicate and shapely navel was decorated with a cluster of rhinestones. Mmm. Dippin' Dots. Below that, her gauzy harem pants clearly exposed the bikini bottom under them.

"You're so nice to do this, Ari," Isabel said. "I know it's not part of your job, but everyone is so busy."

"Well, we can't have the most beautiful dancer in the cast risking undue exposure," I laughed.

"That kind of talk will get you in trouble," she responded.

"With whom?" I asked. "Have I offended you?"

"No. But your wife?"

"Past tense," I said.

"Oh. You're single?"

"Very." I grinned at her and handed her the top. She took it. With the hand that had been covering her breasts. Two very, very nice breasts with rapidly hardening dark nipples. Almost as rapidly hardening as my cock. She slipped her arms through the straps and carefully arranged her boobs so they were nearly overflowing the top.

"Will you fasten me?" she asked. I'd sewn the snap on. I'd better be able to fasten it. But I had to let my fingers slide in against her silky skin. I numbly got the damned snap fastened. "Thank you. I might need you to get me out of it after the show," she giggled.

She kind of looked toward the light booth from which I watched the show when she danced. The stupid Prince took a pass on her to move to the next dancer. I was not making that mistake.

The relieved cast headed for a downtown bar after the show ended. There are a lot of them along Hennepin Avenue. As long as you know which ones are gay bars and drag bars, you can have a great time in downtown Minneapolis. I'd even enjoyed the drag show at Augie's once. But this night, it was a quieter bar with very danceable music being provided by local band that no one had heard of.

Isabel took my hand and dragged me to the dance floor. That was no great task. I'd been in theater long enough to learn to dance. It didn't matter to Isabel. I moved around. She danced around me, against me. The harem pants that she now wore were opaque and the top was a halter. As she encouraged me to 'dance' with her, I felt nothing beneath either article of clothing.

I think I mentioned that bar in one of the *Model Student* books where Lissa and Tony danced at the racquetball nationals. It made a big impression on me.

Isabel and I didn't make love that night. We kissed deeply before we parted. She brought me her costume each night in the light booth so I could fasten her bra for her. She kissed me before she went on stage.

All that work for three nights and one matinee and I had to strike the set. I had a crew of volunteers who were impatient to get it over. This was no college production with forced student labor. The actors, dancers, musicians, and staff were gone to the cast party as soon as they had their costumes off. We hammered, hauled, and packed the set into a rental truck. The costumer had the costumes in her car to launder in the morning and wished me luck. I hoisted myself into the cab of the truck to drive to the storage facility where the theater kept its sets and found Isabel waiting in the cab.

"Fancy meeting you here," I said.

"Sorry I wasn't helping more," she said. "I helped on costumes but came out to wait for you when they left."

"I'm delighted to have your company." It wasn't legal, but she rode curled up on the seat hugging my arm. She stayed in the cab until we'd unloaded and stored the scenery. Then I drove the truck to the rental company and traded it for my car. It was two o'clock in the morning and Isabel had been asleep on the seat.

I didn't even ask her where she lived. I just went to my little apartment. She had a bag with her and I slung it over my shoulder before picking her up and carrying her into my apartment. She woke when I set her on her feet in my bedroom.

"Untie me?" she asked as she turned her back and lifted her hair. The halter tied behind her neck and behind her back. I released both. She kissed me. It could have been passionate if either of us had been less exhausted. We supported each other to the bathroom and she brushed her teeth while I showered. No way was I putting my filthy body into the bed with this beauty. When I came out, I found her in my bed. I spooned behind her naked body and she pulled my fingers to her lips before letting them rest on her breast. "In the morning," she whispered.

We were asleep in thirty seconds.

And in the morning—well, very late in the morning—Isabel danced for me. She didn't bother dressing, but came out of the bathroom with nothing on but finger cymbals and a veil over her face. I sat in the bed watching her undulating belly, shaking breasts, and shapely legs. She crawled up my body and hesitated long enough for me to lift her veil away from her face and kiss her. Then she settled immediately down on my cock and let it sink into her. She was exquisite. She kept up the belly dance moves as she was impaled on my cock. I stroked her breasts and vibrating stomach. I dipped a hand between us and positioned my fingers where her movements would stimulate her clit. She was lost in the world of her dance and I was lost in her.

When we came, she only paused momentarily and then began the rhythms again. And again.

I based Kate's dance scenes in *Triptych* on Isabel dancing for me.

That Sunday was worth having stayed at the U to complete my PhD.

~~~~~~

Back to Becky

When I was parked at Hammond Stadium, Susan handed my phone back to me.

"All our numbers are in your phone and we all have your number," she said. "Not going to interfere with you guys, but don't leave without us. We'll all sit in back on the way home. Brenda."

"If I hadn't pushed into the front, she'd have never sat in the middle," Brenda said. "I was just trying to help."

"Let's go," Lisa said. "You guys have fun." Becky's three friends piled out of the truck. I was reaching for the door, but Becky held me back.

"I need sunblock. Did you know that late afternoon and evening sun can be the most damaging? Especially to fair-skinned girls like me. I need you to help me apply the sunblock." Oh, hell yeah.

She gave me the bottle, slid over a little and lifted one shapely leg into my lap. I worked the sunblock into every not-so-square inch, front and back, right up to…

Damn it! When did those little gym shorts become something that girls wore out in public? Especially with nothing under them. Becky took a little of the lotion from my hands and started working it into her face. That was probably her most vulnerable part. To the sun. I just continued to work the lotion in all the way up to her crease. She sighed and switched legs. I repeated the action and she shifted her hips slightly when I reached her slit to rub up and down a bit.

"Becky, I have to ask you a couple questions," I said as I worked the lotion into the little crease between her puffy lips and that little hollow where her thigh ends. God, I love that spot.

"Go ahead, Ari," she sighed. I think she meant go ahead and ask the questions, but before I did, I lightly stroked up her bare pussy lips.

"Are you at least eighteen years old?" I asked. *Oh, please be eighteen!*

"I'm twenty-one. I'm a senior journalism major."

"Good." I breathed a sigh of relief. "Have you been drinking or doing any other drugs that could impair your judgment?"

"Not yet. I'm hoping you'll buy me a beer and some popcorn."

I moved to her arms and ran my fingers up under the sleeves of the best five-dollar shirt I'd ever owned. She reached up and unbuttoned it.

"This shirt probably doesn't have an SPF rating, so you'd better put lotion on all of me," she whispered, dropping the shirt to the seat. I glanced out the windows of the truck, expecting to see her girlfriends descending on us. There was no one near where we were parked, the traffic having moved to the rows farther out.

"Really?" I whispered.

"There's something you need to know about me, Ari," she said. Well, I'd already seen up her shorts, so she wasn't a male. I waited. "I don't tease. As soon as I decided to trade shirts with you this afternoon, my mind was made up to have sex with you tonight. The girls all tease me about being reckless because I make snap decisions about all kinds of things, but usually my decisions are right. I'd like to see the ballgame, but I want you to know that everything you see… everything you can touch… is going to be in your bed tonight. Am I clear?"

~~~

SOMEHOW, WE GOT into the stadium by the bottom of the first inning. Once inside, we were just a couple having a great time at America's second favorite pastime. And we were anticipating having a great time at the first, as well. The Twins beat the Tigers, who were already favored to win the pennant this year.

Becky sent a text message to her friends and they met us at the gate. They were all a little tipsy and giggly, but promised they weren't in danger of throwing up in the truck. They wanted to know if I'd take them to a club but I said I wasn't going to go out.

"We can drop you off," Becky said. "But you're on your own then."

"Are you really gonna?" Brenda asked. Becky scowled at her.

"You are so fucking lucky," Lisa moaned. "All I've had are drunk boys trying to paw me."

"Reap what you sow," Becky said. We'd had a beer, but it was apparent that we were the sober ones in the truck.

"Just take us to the hotel," Susan said. "If these two absolutely must get their twats stretched, I'll do it with Bob."

"Oh, Susan. We love you," Brenda said. She and Lisa sandwiched Susan between them for the rest of the ride to the hotel. Becky and I continued to my trailer.

"Where do you live when you aren't traveling in your trailer?" Becky asked after she'd done a quick survey of the tiny room. She tossed her overnight bag on the table and rummaged in it for her toothbrush. "Do you have toothpaste? I forgot mine."

"Sure. It's on the bathroom sink. I don't know where I'll live when I'm done traveling. I've only been in this for nine months."

"So this is it? This is your home?"

"WYSIWYG."

"Huh?"

"What you see is what you get. It's an old publishing term."

"What about a shower? Yours has… um… dirty underwear, two boxes of wine, and six gallons of bottled water."

"I got a good slot here at the park. The showers are just fifty feet up the road," I said. Reality was sinking in to Becky's cute little red head. I still had my keys in my hand. I figured she'd want to leave shortly.

"I didn't pick a rich, bestselling author, did I?" she sighed.

"Afraid not, honey. You got the one who lives in an attic smoking cigarettes and drinking scotch as he bleeds on the page. You want me to take you back to your hotel now?" I asked.

She came out of the tiny bathroom. How had I ever managed to convince Angie that living like this was fun? Angie was submissive. Becky liked to drive and take advantage. I figured she was just a little bit of a gold digger. I'd paid for our ballgame tickets, beers, and food so far. She had to see that she'd gotten everything from me that she could.

"Don't you want me to stay?" she asked.

"Of course I do."

"Then maybe you could help me out of this shirt. A guy gave it to me today just so it would keep sliding over my sensitive nipples keeping them hard all day. What kind of guy would do that? Huh?" I started unbuttoning the aloha shirt, pulling her closer to me, and letting the backs of my hands glide across her breasts as I worked the buttons.

"Probably the kind of guy who wants them nice and hard when he sucks and chews on them," I whispered. She put her arms around my neck and pressed her lips against mine as I filled my hands with her bared breasts.

I've had a few different kinds of breasts in my hands. Young ones and old ones. A reader once asked me to please put the bra sizes in for my characters in *Living Next Door to Heaven* so he'd know how big they were. Apparently, my descriptions of how they fit in my hands or mouth or how they compared with other women weren't enough for him. Well, I had yet to see Becky in a bra, so I had no idea what Walmart would say about her size. Large breasts tend to sag a bit, but there was a difference between whether the flesh that hung from a woman's chest felt full or not. If they were firm and hard, chances are they were augmented. Becky's didn't have that feeling. Everything here was natural, but they felt full. She hadn't worn a bra all day, but still they thrust out proudly. The areolae didn't cave inward from the pressure of gravity, but rounded out in a pleasant puff that you usually find on much smaller breasts. Her nipples were the classic pencil erasers and not big, fat, or long. And under my thumbs, I could tell they were very sensitive. Our kiss deepened.

"Undress, Ari," she whispered. "I told you, I don't tease."

Even here in an old people's RV park in Florida, I'd kept up with my normal practice of not wearing clothes in the trailer, so I had a hook on the bathroom door where my clothes were quickly hung. Becky was still wearing her little gym shorts and I skimmed them down over her round butt. She stepped out of them and stood with her feet more than shoulder width apart. She held my cock in her hand as I probed the dripping passage between her thighs.

"When were you last tested?" she asked. *Damn! I should have been asking that.*

"January, after my last lover left," I said. "And you?"

"You don't need to tell me about her. I was tested last week so I'd know I was clean when I got here. I've been looking, but I didn't find anyone until you," she said. We kissed again and I plunged two fingers deep inside her as she moaned. "I feel like we've been having foreplay all day. Let's go to bed, lover."

She gave my cock a squeeze and turned to face the bed. It's not like she had far to go. It's a total of eight feet from the bathroom door to the edge of the bed. But one of the things that she hadn't counted on was how high the bed was. There's storage under it, so even I have to focus on getting up into it. Becky wasn't as short as Angie, but when she walked right up to the edge of the bed, the top of the mattress was just above her mound.

"It's so high. Like a fairytale princess's bed," she giggled. I walked up behind her and reached around to hold her breasts as I nuzzled her neck and shoulders. "I don't know if I can climb all the way up there without a boost," she whispered. She bent over the bed, pulling me forward with my cock in her crack. Becky raised her left knee up to the bed and I slid down through her wetness. "Yeah," she whispered. "Find a way to boost me up back there."

The invitation was clear enough. I shifted my hips back a little and pushed forward, right into her welcoming snatch. She settled back against me and met each thrust as she bent forward over the bed. I still had her breasts in my hands, pinned against the mattress. I rolled her nipples between my fingers and she started bouncing back against me.

"Don't hold back," she said. "I want to feel it. I'm going to come. Come in me."

I didn't need more encouragement than that. Her sweet, round bottom cushioned my pelvis as I rammed forward and began to spray her insides.

"Oh god, yeah!" she cried out.

I could feel the vibration between her legs and realized she had a hand down there strumming her clit as she cried out. I collapsed forward, kissing her back and shoulders as we panted for our breath. She levered herself up with the knee on the mattress and I slipped out of her as she got all the way up onto the bed. I lightly bit her ass cheeks and watched our combined come run from her open pussy.

"I hope there's a lot more where that came from," she said as she rolled onto the bed and held out her arms for me.

WHEN I STUMBLED out of bed to make coffee in the morning, I figured my time with Becky was probably up. If the condition of my cock was any indication, she had to be seriously broken down there. She was the third lover on my journey, and prior to that, it had been a long, long time. Margaret and I made love once. By the time Angie and I made that step, we had only three days left together. I was unprepared for the athleticism and energy Becky showed in bed.

Once the ice had been broken, so to speak, Becky was voracious. If I tried to break off a kiss to catch my breath or add some variety to the action, she would clamp a hand on the back of my neck and keep me locked against her tongue. As soon as I'd begun to soften, her fingers and lips would be on my nipples, tugging them until I responded.

I felt a hand on my hip as I poured hot water over the coffee grounds and turned to greet her. I hadn't heard her get out of bed, and when I turned, I didn't see her. Instead, I felt my cock being inhaled into her mouth. She was on her knees next to me. I groaned. I hardened in her mouth and she began bouncing her face against my pubes, swallowing me as she fucked me into her face.

"God, Becky!" I moaned. My balls were aching to be released, though I knew there couldn't possibly be anything in them. "I was just going to ask if you wanted coffee. You don't have to be doing that!" She popped off my cock and grinned up at me.

"You've got a sex goddess less than half your age with your cock down her throat and you want to talk about coffee?" she asked. "I'll have a cup to wash down what you're about to give me."

I think she's a succubus. I was helpless to do anything but give her what she demanded. I felt everything contract and pulse, but I honestly wasn't sure if anything came out.

"Yum. I'll have more of that later, thank you," she said. I sagged against the counter. "You said coffee, didn't you?"

I poured her a cup and she sipped while I finally got my first cup poured and the taste in my mouth. There is absolutely nothing in the world that compares to the first cup of coffee in the morning. Or pot of coffee. Yeah. The first pot of coffee in the morning. And the second one. That's pretty damned good, too.

Why am I musing over the flavor of coffee when I have a sex goddess less than half my age impatiently waiting to get me back into bed and hard again?

I didn't get any writing done that day. I was sure my readers would understand.

WE DIDN'T SPEND all our time fucking. She still wanted to spend time at the beach each day. She collected her little suitcase from her hotel room and moved into the trailer with me. My phone buzzed about thirty times in the next fifteen minutes as her friends peppered me with questions. I agreed to bring Becky to one of the clubs that night.

The loud music and a couple margaritas were good for me. All four girls wanted to dance with me. Becky graciously shared. I had to use the restroom and a couple guys were coming out as I went in. One offered me a fist bump.

"Dude! Whatever you've got, man... Wow!"

"We won't horn in, but do you mind if we ask your ladies to dance with us?" the other said.

"They're the ones in control," I laughed. "Just be respectful, got it?" The guys nodded and made a beeline for my table as I went in to relieve myself.

When I got back to the table, Lisa was leaving it with another guy to hit the dance floor. Becky squealed and jumped into my arms. Susan and Brenda were already out with the guys I'd met coming out of the john.

"You got them guys!" Becky said. "You're so good! Now I have you all to myself."

"I didn't really do anything," I said.

"Those guys actually bowed before they asked us to dance," Becky said. "They said you told them it was okay to ask us to dance but that we were in control and they promised to be respectful. I think Susan left a wet spot on her chair. I know I'm dripping. Come on, Ari. Dance with me."

I danced. When I was finally too exhausted to go on, Becky polled her friends and they all told us they were fine and we could leave. I opened the passenger door for Becky and helped her up to the seat. She turned in place and spread her legs, showing me she had worn no panties under her little skirt.

"Eat me, Ari," she commanded. Faced with that succulent pussy, what could I do. She came twice as I stood beside the open door and plunged my face into her twat. Then she let me close the door and go drive.

~~~~~

IT WAS EVEN later when I woke up the next morning, still having written nothing the entire week. I considered writing about this experience and shrugged it off. I was known for writing stuff that could be believed if you were willing to stretch your imagination a little. No one's imagination stretched this far.

After Becky had her first cup of coffee, she was running faster than I did after a pot of it. She got me to finger her while she sucked me up again. I really didn't think she'd succeed, but holy shit, she was hot. Then reality crashed in. After she'd come on my fingers.

"I'm just a little sore down there," she said. I smiled. *A reprieve.*

"That's okay. We can give it a rest for a while," I said magnanimously.

"Good idea. You can fuck my butt." She bent over the bed, grabbed my bottle of lube from the headboard, and squirted it into her own asshole. "Oh! That's cold!" She reached back and grabbed my cock with a slippery hand and guided me to her anus.

"Oh, god!" I moaned as I sank into her. "This might take a while."

"Yeah! Do me," she said. "Do me for a long time."

THE AFTERNOON HELD more socialization. That meant meeting up with her girlfriends and their three new boyfriends at the beach, having dinner and drinks, dancing, fucking. Fortunately, I got a chance to sleep in the shade on the beach for a while as the others played. It happened that I was near the same group of nearly bare-ass girls I'd seen on Monday morning. I woke up to the feeling of a body descending on mine. I blinked my eyes open and found I was looking at the same brunette who had landed on me Monday. She squirmed around on me and jammed my hand into her bikini top. Yeah. That was a nice breast with its little hard point pressing into my palm.

"If I'd known what a stud you were on Monday, I'd have stayed in your lap," she said.

"I'm not, really."

"Like hell. The story is all over the beach. Even the guys talk about you like you're a legend. Do you have time to do me?"

"I… um…" There was a smack and a squeal. The brunette bounced up off me and began tucking her tits back into her top.

"Mine!" Becky snarled.

"Can't blame a girl for trying," brunette said. "Doesn't your pussy get tired?"

"When it does, he does my ass. Now look what you've done," Becky said, pointing at my slight bulge. "I'm going to have to go fuck him again. Come on, Ari." Becky grabbed my hand and basically dragged me to the truck.

⁓

"I DON'T THINK I can go again, Becky," I said Friday night. Let's see. If you added up the weekend with Angie and the night with her mother,

Margaret, and about the last seven years with Treasure, I'd had more sex this week than the total. I was sure I could last another seven years now.

"Uh-uh," she said. She bounced into the bathroom. "I have to leave for Minnesota tomorrow. I don't want to miss tonight." She came out of the bathroom rattling a bottle of pills. I groaned. Viagra. I'd asked my doctor for a prescription before I left on my road trip because, quite frankly, I wasn't sure the equipment worked any longer. She'd told me not to worry because it was far more likely to atrophy than to wear out. She gave me the prescription for four pills. A hundred fucking bucks. Literally. At that price, each pill should come with a pussy attached.

One of them was in my mouth and down my throat before I could protest.

Hell. Why would I protest. Becky was a sex doll. She not only was available for anything at any time, she was aggressively after it. I wondered exactly how many different sex acts we could have before the effects of the pill wore off. I was going to find out. My heart started to race as the pill took effect. I decided to catch up with it.

I picked up Becky and threw her on the bed, narrowly missing the stowage bin above the bed with her head. I pulled her feet around until her butt was on the edge of the bed, pushed her legs back until she was knees to nipples and dove in. I lapped her from bunghole to clit and back again until she was screaming. Then I stood and drove my cock into her sopping tunnel. I started pounding her.

～～

A Long Time Ago: Eat Me

THERE WAS NEVER a moment's doubt in my mind that Treasure was the love of my life. I was whipped from the first time she kissed me until long after we'd said goodbye. I still loved her as more than the mother of my daughter. But I remembered the very first time with her.

We'd been dating for a while. I'd started my publishing business and become acquainted with a lot of writers and editors in the area. When we first went out, we both tried to think of it as being a business date. Somewhere along the line, she'd changed clothes and we walked around Lake Calhoun in the moonlight.

We were still cautious. We did a lot of making out and petting, but we hadn't done the deed. We were heavily into it on my living room sofa one evening. It was getting late and she'd already said she needed to go home, but we were horizontal and neither of us was making any move to get up. She was wearing a red corduroy dress that night and my hand was well up under it. It took me all evening to work up the courage, but I scooted down and started kissing up the inside of her leg, edging closer and closer to her matching red panties. When I was near, I started down near her knee on the other leg and worked my way up again as she moaned. I hesitated just below her panty line. This was a big step for us.

"Don't think I don't *want* you to eat me," she whispered. Was that a double negative? When she raised her hips to give me clearance to pull her panties down, I no longer had any doubts. I'd worry about the stains on the sofa tomorrow.

"I loved licking your vagina," I whispered as I cuddled with her and she came down from three very fast and very hard orgasms.

"Pussy," she sighed. *Was she calling me that?*

"I never use slang for it," I said.

"When we are making love, I have a pussy and you have a cock and we fuck. They're all sexy words. They turn me on. Say it. What do I have?"

"A… uh… pussy," I stammered.

"What's this pushing out your pants?" she asked, grasping my erection.

"My penis… um… cock."

"And what are we going to do with your cock and my pussy?" she whispered against my lips.

"Fuck?"

"Yeah. Right now."

~~~~~

Back to Becky

YEARS LATER, WHEN I started writing erotica, I was still having trouble using the words. But right now, I was *fucking* Becky's tight little *cunt*.

She continued to scream so loudly that I thought the neighbors in the next trailer might come to pound on my door.

"Oh, god, Ari! You're killing me. Where did this come from? I've come six times and you haven't even come once yet. Let me suck you." Yeah, that's where I was headed next, only I squirted some lube between her breasts and started sliding my cock through the tunnel when I pushed them together. Becky took over pushing her tits together as I pumped between them and she captured the head of my cock in her mouth each time it came in reach. I'd hold at the peak and let her swish her magic tongue around the head for a few seconds, then retreat and push my way between her tits again. She'd almost calmed down when I started twisting and pinching her nipples.

I'd noticed during the week that she treated her own nipples much more aggressively than I did. I'd noted it when she was trying to tear mine off my chest. I like nipple play, but I wasn't sure I'd ever feel anything in my right nipple again after she was finished with it. When she touched it now, it was more irritating than sexy. But if she liked it, I was going to give it to her. I pulled them out away from her chest and pinched hard. She screamed again and I shoved my cock all the way back into her throat. She choked a bit as I withdrew.

"Yeah. Yeah. Give it to me. You're going to give it to me, aren't you, Ari?"

"Just like you want it, Beck. You turned my cock into iron with that damned pill. Now I'm going to shove it as deep in your ass as I can get it."

"Yes! Do it!"

I was slippery from having fucked her and sliding through the lube on her chest. Becky was producing so much lubricant that it had fully coated her ass. I put the head of my cock against her sphincter and shoved in. All the way. I swear, Becky's eyes crossed. And once I was all the way in, I treated her ass like a fucktoy. She panted. She screamed. She came.

And somewhere along the line, the Viagra gave out and I shot a load deep inside her. As I was coming, I pressed my thumb against her clit and bit a nipple.

Becky's scream was choked off and I looked up to see she'd passed out. *Hallelujah!*

I winced as my cock softened at last and I pulled it out of her ass. I rearranged us on the bed, lay down beside her, and passed out, too.

I TOOK ALL four girls to the airport Saturday morning. The group was subdued. I was guessing Becky and I might have gotten more sleep last night than any of the others, but we'd been so exhausted, physically and sexually, that we both still felt tired when we got up. For the first time since we'd met, my morning hadn't started with a blow job.

I took them to the departures curb and the other three girls got out and retrieved their roll-aboards from the back. Becky turned to me.

"Fucking best spring break ever," she whispered. "I don't know if my pussy or my ass is sorest. Or my throat from all the screaming. You're a fucking animal, Ari."

"Let's say it was self-defense and call it even," I laughed. She leaned into me and kissed me, her tongue automatically probing my mouth and her hand still clamped around the back of my head to prevent me from escaping.

"Don't forget you have my number in your phone," she said at last. "For when you come through Minnesota." She jumped out of the truck and grabbed her bag from the back. She limped after the other girls and turned to wave goodbye just before she went through the doors into the terminal.

I stopped to buy a bag of ice on the way back to my trailer.

5 For Whom the Belles Troll

5 April 2014

WHEN I left Fort Myers Beach, I camped in the Everglades for two weeks. The place was almost deserted since the season was technically over. It was more than thirty miles from the park entrance to the campground. I had to stop and take a picture at Rock Reef Pass, elevation 3'. I could always say that was the high point of my trip.

Electric service was still functional as were the restrooms and showers. I had to fill my water tank, though, so I could have water in the trailer.

That was when I discovered I had another problem. Somewhere along the way, my water pump had developed a crack and as soon as I turned it on, it started spewing water into my storage area under the bed. I didn't realize it until I saw water running out of the bottom of the trailer. Fortunately, everything in the storage bin was in plastic containers.

Fuck!

I'd paid for two weeks in this campsite, and even though that was only $150, breaking camp and towing the trailer to Homestead carried no assurance that I could find a replacement pump once I got there. It wasn't a complicated operation to replace it and I had the necessary tools, so when I went in for weekly supplies, I could shop around and do the install myself.

It was a big campground and there were only about six other RVs scattered around it. We waved and acknowledged each other's presence, but really didn't have much interaction. So, it was moderately irritating to get back from my unsuccessful trip to Homestead and discover a pop-up camper in the space next to mine.

Unlike Fort Myers, the campsites in the Everglades are a good fifty feet wide with grass and picnic tables and room to play. It wasn't really an imposition to have someone camped next to me and I let go of my irritation. Looking around the campground, I realized that the occupied sites, including mine, were the ones that had some shade. I could understand why the newcomers would want the site they chose.

I sat under my awning and had a beer and a cigar as the campers set up their pop-up. It was two women and a man. Looked like a fun party to have in that little camper. Then I realized the man was another woman, though a somewhat burly one. I figured that out while she was shooing the smallest of the three away from the camper and said, "We'll do it. Just relax." The banished woman sighed, looked over my direction and waved.

I waved back and motioned her to come on over. My first guess was that she was close to fifty, but she could have been thirty and had a hard life. She pulled a cigarette out of the pack she carried and asked for a light.

"They won't let me do *anything*!" she said. "They treat me like an old lady."

"Your kids?" I ventured.

"God, no! My girlfriends. Teach me to pick 'em so young. I'm Val," she said, sticking out her hand.

"I'm Aroslav," I responded. *Ah. Lesbians.* "Would you like a beer?"

"Thanks. You here all alone?"

"Yes. Just off seeing the world. In this instance, Florida." We chit-chatted while her girlfriends finished setting up the tent and got their refrigerator and lights plugged in. I had a little opportunity to assess my new companion.

She said she was thirty-seven years old and had a daughter who would be twenty in June. I was correct in assuming she'd had a hard life or simply lived hard. Her accent was consistent with her home in Knoxville, Tennessee. Her ex-husband had gone to jail five years ago for robbing a gas station.

"At least he was around long enough to teach the worst of the boys not to touch our daughter," Val said. "She's got even bigger tits than me, but she learned about rubbers before I did." I just sort of stared at her. That wasn't the kind of information you normally share with a stranger. But I soon discovered that Val had no filters.

"We're set up and Janna is cooking," the big girl in the group said. She'd come across the space between our trailers to tell Val when supper would be ready. I offered her a beer and she accepted, tilting her head back and draining the bottle in one long gulp. This was a very big girl. She was easily two inches taller than me and outweighed me by at least fifty pounds. And solid. I won't say she didn't have any fat on her, but if we went head to head in a wrestling match I didn't think I'd stand a chance. Back in my less socially conscious days, I would have called her a railroad dyke.

~~~~~

A Long Time Ago: Honorary Lesbian

BACK WHEN I was working on my PhD in playwriting—officially, dramatic theory—while trying to hammer out my first novel, I still had to earn a living. Paula's assessment was proving correct. I stood a *chance* of making money by designing and building sets. I'd taken my latest script to a startup theater on the east edge of St. Paul to meet with their artistic director. He'd nodded over the script and said it was interesting and funny, but he wasn't sure his group would be the right venue for a farce about an Indiana preacher. On the other hand, would I be interested in designing the theater's upcoming production of *The Crucible*?

I took the job after he promised that they had a crew that the stage manager had been cultivating. They liked to work together, but needed a pro to design and tech direct. An experienced crew? What a luxury!

Six women.

Donna, the stage manager, introduced me to my crew and I got a warm welcome when I showed them the designs. It turned out that the seven women, and a couple others I hadn't met, had formed their own little club to do theater tech. None of them other than Donna had any formal education in theater, but they had all met as volunteers for a show produced by the city's feminist theater group. Donna got them jobs. It was an unusual stage manager who could bring with her a full stage crew. Some women come together over coffee, books, social issues, or just for drinks. This crew had discovered they liked working backstage and it gave them plenty of opportunity to talk and have fun.

Two of the women were married. At least two and maybe more were gay. The youngest on the crew was nearly thirty and worked as an admin in a law firm. Ranging upward to about fifty years old, the women proved to be hard workers and one of the best tech crews I'd ever had.

"Theresa is mine," Donna whispered to me after the intros. "Don't touch. Take your pick of any of the others." Well, excluding the married ladies, that narrowed the field to three and none of them were flirty. We worked.

We got the show up and it was successful. It was one of the least stressful shows I'd ever designed and by the time we closed it, I'd been accepted as one of the girls. Mostly, unless I needed to give instructions to someone, I kept my mouth shut. You have no idea what women will say to each other when they forget a man is around.

There was the usual talk about offices, families, theater gossip, and television shows. But once we'd been working together for a while, conversations began to loosen up. The legal admin got some very explicit instructions on how to seduce the lawyer she'd become interested in. I mean, the ladies set up every detail for her, including telling her how she should dress and the best blowjob techniques when she got him alone. Some of those techniques were things I'd never experienced!

One day the conversation was about lesbian sex and what each of the women liked when having her pussy eaten. One of the married women, Mary, simply couldn't understand how a woman could put her face in another woman's pussy. It was gross. It happened, though, that she had been the one offering the most creative suggestions about blowjobs a few days earlier. Donna's girlfriend, Theresa, suddenly turned and looked at me.

"Are pussies gross, Ari?" she demanded. "Do you ever go down on a woman?"

"No, they aren't gross, Theresa," I said. "And yes, I go down. I'd have to say that I pretty much feel the same about eating pussy as you do."

"But what about queefs? Gross!" June said.

"I figure if I put the air in there, I can stand the vart. It's just an embarrassing noise, not a smell or taste." I said.

"Too bad you've got a dick. You could be a lesbian."

The night the show closed, of course, we had to strike the set and get it to storage. It was after midnight when Donna joined us and said she'd buy us a round at Screamers. I was all for a drink, and Mary had been casually bumping against me all evening.

"What about Ari?" Theresa asked.

"Oh," Donna said. Like the others, I think she'd forgotten I was male. She considered a minute.

"He's one of us," Mary said. Donna nodded.

"Ari, we want you to come with us. Screamers is a lesbian bar on 7th. There won't be any other men there at. If you want to come with us, you have to promise not to speak to anyone but us. You want a beer, ask one of us. Not all the women in the bar are lesbians, like Mary and Elizabeth and June, but they are all women. Just do like you usually do and make us all forget you're a man."

"I'll take care of him," Mary said. "Ari, ride with me. I don't want to stay out for more than one drink. Is that okay?"

"Fine," I said. I wasn't sure what I was getting into, but this was an adventure I wasn't going to miss.

Mostly, Screamers was just a neighborhood bar where a bunch of people went to hang out. Like Cheers, only for dykes. There was even the requisite number of Harleys in the parking lot. It was dimly lit and music was playing on a jukebox. It smelled a little like stale beer. The leather jacket crew were mostly sitting at the bar. There were a few women who were dressed to the nines and were obviously being hit on at every opportunity. They'd go dance with the woman who asked them, sometimes get into a little clinch, and then return to their table where they'd all make a big show out of kissing each other and then redoing their makeup.

"Lipstick dykes," Theresa muttered when we'd all packed into a tiny booth. I was smashed between her and Mary and was almost invisible. I hoped. "Order for us, Donna." Over the six weeks we'd been working together, it had become obvious to me that even though Donna was the stage manager and in charge on stage, in their personal relationship Theresa was the top. A waitress came to the table and Donna ordered eight Dos Equis. The waitress scanned the table quickly and paused when she saw me. I saw her eyebrow twitch, but she didn't say anything.

The conversation was lively around me, and filled with commentary on other bar patrons. I don't think men look at other men in a bar and talk about what they are wearing. I don't think they even talk about women in a bar like that. My experience was that most male conversation in a bar revolved around sports and, at most, which woman they'd fuck if given a chance. "I'd definitely do her." Most went home alone.

Not so in a lesbian bar. My companions had an opinion or information about everyone in the bar.

"She shaves her puss bare. But she never gets all the stubble. You can get serious rug burn on your face."

"She was in a really abusive relationship. Lila won't allow her ex in the bar anymore."

"I bet she squirts. You can tell by the way she's sitting. Look at her legs." *Really? You can tell if a woman is a squirter by looking at the way she sits?* I needed some more instruction. But I wasn't going to get it.

Four angry-looking women were headed toward our table.

"What's he doing in here?" the lead asked. I was toast.

There was suddenly a wall between me and the approaching women. A wall of six women who all slid out of the booth and stood between it and the rest of the bar. And it was obvious that these women were not taking shit from anyone. Only Mary stayed in the booth, gripping my arm so I wouldn't be tempted to interfere. *As if.*

"He's an honorary lesbian and he's ours," Theresa declared. "He's a better rug muncher than you, Karla."

"You're such a bitch, Theresa. You never complained when my tongue was in your crotch."

"I never dis a tongue on my clit, even if it isn't very good."

"You fucked her?" Donna growled.

"Drop it or you're all out of here," a voice came from behind them. I had no idea who it was, but I had to assume it was the bar owner, Lila. I could not see past the line of backsides that blocked my view.

"You shouldn't allow his kind in here," Karla said, but it was obvious she was backing off.

"It's a free country," Lila said. My protectors slid back into the booth around me and our waitress set a tray of beers on the table and beat a hasty retreat. A petite woman in high heels and a nice professional slacks suit stayed by the table. One glance at the baseball bat in her hand, however, told me that she was not a person I wanted to cross. "Drink up," she said. "Closing time is in an hour. You might not want to stay for last call." She looked meaningfully at me and I just nodded once. She returned to the bar.

"Well, that was exciting," Mary squeaked.

"You guys took a big risk protecting me," I said. "I should probably go."

"Not really," Theresa said. "Karla acts tough, but both her nipples are pierced and if you can grab hold of one and twist, she's on the floor begging to eat you. And you can't leave yet. You haven't had your beer. If you leave now, it will look like you're running away."

Yeah. Well. That would be true. Nonetheless, I drank my beer and everything seemed to return to normal.

"You fucked her?" Donna repeated.

"It was long before I found your silken tongue," Theresa said. She laid a very intense kiss on our stage manager.

When we were finished, Donna paid the tab and we left as a group. No one in the bar followed us and no one was waiting outside. I got into Mary's car and we left before the other women had gotten into their cars. I'd survived my first—and only—lesbian bar experience.

But my night wasn't over.

"SHOW ME YOUR apartment, Ari," Mary said when she pulled up to my door. It was nearly two a.m. and I was a little surprised, but invited her in.

"Would you like a sparkling water?" I asked. I didn't want to put her back on the road with another drink, but wanted to be hospitable. She accepted as she looked around.

"It's a little Spartan, isn't it?"

"I call this style 'early divorce'. It's something I just learned about and thought I'd try."

"Oh. I'm sorry, Ari." I turned toward her voice and she was in my arms with her lips on my lips and our tongues tangling. I was responding rapidly. "I'm ready," she whispered. "I've been ready ever since those bull dykes showed up at our table. Show me your pussy-licking skills, Ari."

"Mary," I gasped. "What about your husband? You aren't divorced, are you?"

"No. But whenever I go out with the girls, he expects that some lesbian will be licking me before the night is over."

"But I'm..."

"An honorary lesbian. Theresa said so. Do me, Ari. I'm dripping. Donna says my pussy is one of the sweetest she's ever tasted."

Well, I did have a bed. Or at least I had a large mattress on the floor. I led her in and started undressing her.

"I want to see more of this beautiful body than just your pussy," I said. "I want all of you."

"God! You are just like a lesbian," she said. We kept kissing and undressed each other. I'd always thought Mary was the cutest of the girls for all that she was at least ten years older than me. I knew she had two kids at home, too, but she'd taken extraordinary care of that body.

We got onto the bed and kept kissing. She stroked my cock a few times and I could feel her slick things up with my precome. I worked my way down her body and she spread her legs.

It wasn't as common back then for women to shave their pussies, but from the conversations I'd been privy to over the past few weeks, I discovered that it was a lot more common among women who planned to be eaten. A lot. Mary had a full bush down to where her slit began. Everything from that point down was smooth and bare. I parted those lips with my tongue and set about proving what a good lesbian I was.

"Turn around," she gasped after her first come. She was just as sweet as Donna had supposedly said. In fact, I wasn't sure but what she used some kind of flavoring down there. "I'm not going to leave you hanging, Ari. Let me do you while you give me another of those incredible comes."

In a few seconds, we were arranged in a sixty-nine and she was riding my face while she inhaled my cock. I tried to focus on her pussy, licking all the way up to her asshole and back to her clit. She shuddered through another orgasm before she really went to work on my cock.

"Oh, god," she murmured around the head of my cock as she kissed it and licked the shaft. "Eating pussy isn't so gross after all. It tastes just like my husband's cock." If that was what she needed to think, I was okay with it. She was the woman who had described blowjob techniques I had never experienced. Until tonight. She used her hands in concert with her mouth to both stroke and twist around my shaft. And when I was sure I wouldn't last any longer, she shoved a finger up my ass and I started spraying her tonsils. Rather than pulling back, she pushed her mouth down farther on my cock and I could feel her swallowing as I continued to pulse.

When my eyes uncrossed, she still held me in her mouth. I attacked her slit again and lashed her clit. It appeared she was just about ready for another good one, so I borrowed a page from her book and took my finger out of her pussy and shoved it in her ass. She screamed and squealed and bucked against my face until she'd finally had enough and rolled off me. My finger came out with a pop and she gasped again.

"Theresa is not going to believe this when I tell her," Mary said.

I guess that cemented my reputation as an honorary lesbian.

~~~

Back to The Everglades

"ARI, THIS IS Dolly. Dolly, this is Mr. Aroslav whose beer you just guzzled," Val said.

"I was hot," Dolly responded. She turned to me and offered a fist to bump. "Thanks for the beer. We just got ours on ice and it ain't cold yet."

"My pleasure, Dolly. Be sure to take one to Janna, too. Cook deserves to be treated nice," I said. Dolly grinned at me.

It's kind of a cliché to say a big woman has a really pretty face. As if the rest of her was an ugly mess. Well, Dolly did have a pretty face and there was really nothing wrong with the rest of her. I know that the tall women I usually write about are thin as a because… well, Carly. But even though Dolly was big around as well as tall, she wasn't an ugly woman at all. I supposed most men didn't give the giantess a second look, but that was their loss.

"You should see the slut," Dolly said, rolling her eyes. "As soon as I had the grill set up, she stripped down to her bikini and started dancing while she got the food ready. I think it's her bikini. Might just be her underwear. She has the sluttiest of both."

"Be nice, Dolly. You know she does it just for you," Val said. "Take off your shirt and show us *your* bikini."

"Aw, Val," Dolly said. She was blushing, but she pulled the sports jersey she was wearing over her head and off. Val definitely controlled her. It's a misconception to assume that a big woman—and I was face to face with a seriously big woman—necessarily has big breasts. I guessed that Dolly's bikini had less to cover than Val had. Val proved it by pulling off her shirt to show a bright yellow bikini as well. She stood on tiptoes and gave Dolly a kiss, tweaking a nipple as she did so. Dolly picked the smaller woman up and smashed her lips against hers. She set her down.

"Isn't she something?" Val said, turning back to me. She didn't seem to notice the tent in my pants, but I wasn't about to hide it. "I been trying to get her knocked up, but I can't find a guy who'll do her." Dolly turned crimson. You just don't think about a large lesbian being embarrassed. And the truth was, I liked her. She was big and, apparently, too much information was the standard for Val, but Dolly was a sweet girl. I estimated she was in her mid-twenties, though it was hard to tell. Her face looked so young.

"I'd do her," I said impulsively. "I couldn't knock her up because I got those parts disconnected years ago. We could practice, though. All night."

"Oh, gawd!" Dolly moaned. She turned to Val. "You are gonna get such a licking tonight." That image just burned itself into my brain.

"Hey you two sluts," called the bikini clad Janna from the front of their camper. "Dinner's ready. Get your asses over here." Janna wasn't a skinny girl, either, but she did have a skinny girl bikini on. It disappeared in some places. I handed Dolly a beer to take to Janna and she thanked me. Just before she left, Val gave my arm a squeeze, pushing her bosom into it.

"Thank you," she said. "I'm not really a lez, but those two girls suck clit like you would not believe."

~~~~~

THE WEEK IN the Everglades was peaceful. The ladies next door took off each morning to drive to one of the many beaches around Homestead and Miami. I went into town a couple of times because I had no Internet service out at the campground and I was trying to find a replacement water pump. It looked like I was going to be without water until I got north of Port St. Lucie. Oh well. There were showers in the restrooms just a couple hundred feet away, even if they were cold. I kept a bucket of water by the toilet for flushing and had bottled water for coffee. Everything else I cooked on the grill and ate off paper plates.

When they got back from their day's outing, if it wasn't late enough that I was in bed, Val would often stop over and either bring or accept a beer as she told me about their day.

"You have got to go to that beach, Ari," she enthused. "The tiniest bikinis I ever seen and the roundest asses. Every color you can think of.

Careless girls, too. One bitch parked her blanket right straight ahead of us and proceeded to bare her beaver while she laid in the sun. It was so hot out there, I *had* to offer to rub sunblock on it. It was already red and puffy."

"Sounds like a lesbian paradise," I laughed.

"Oh, there was plenty of guys if you swing that way. They sure were swinging!"

We compared notes on other parts of the park and other parks outside the 'Glades. I visited some of her recommendations. I tended to stay around camp most of the time, though. I was really getting into *Living Next Door to Heaven Part II: The Agreement.* I loved setting up some rules and then seeing how far the kids could push them without breaking them.

The morning I hitched up the trailer to leave, Dolly came to see if she could help. I thanked her, though there wasn't anything but power to disconnect. I did have leveling blocks to deal with and Dolly did a great job of directing me as I backed the hitch up under the tongue of the trailer. I figured I'd go say goodbye to the other two before I pulled out. Dolly held me back a moment.

"Did you mean it?" she asked.

"What?" I had no idea what she was talking about. We'd been camped next to each other for over a week and I'd even had the three of them over for dinner one night. When I make beans and rice, it always makes up a big batch.

"About... When you said you'd do me? Did you mean that?" I suddenly got the feeling that maybe Dolly wasn't a lesbian by choice. At least not first choice.

"Do you want to go inside the trailer and find out?" I said. She stared at the ground. "Dolly, you're a sweet woman. You are bigger than average, but that doesn't take away from you being a woman and yes, I find you desirable. Is that what you want?"

"No. Well, not really. I mean, I don't want to just go into your trailer and jump your bones. But, Ari, no guy has ever said anything like that to me. It's nice to know you meant it."

"That wasn't a particularly romantic way for me to tell you," I said.

"Wasn't romance. It was just sex. Still, it was nice to know."

I walked over to their camper with her and said my goodbyes. They'd decided to stay another week with the park almost empty. I was headed down to Key West just to get to Mile 0 of U.S. Route 1 and head north. Each of the ladies gave me a hug and a sweet little kiss. Dolly blushed fire engine red. Val wiggled her tits up against my chest and drove her tongue into my mouth.

"See you around, cowboy," she teased.

I got in the truck and pulled out of the campground.

KEY WEST IS basically an ugly tourist trap with a monument that says you are 70 miles from Cuba, and a beach that was one of the smallest I'd ever seen. I got my picture of Milepost 0 and a sticker for the back of my trailer, and headed north.

I found a nice little place on Long Key to camp and watched sunset and moonrise at the same time. I'd been clued in on a tiny restaurant reputed to have the best burgers in Florida out on Deer Key. I found it, as had enough other people to pack the place to overflowing. It was called the No Name Bar. The local ritual was to write your name on a dollar bill and staple it to a wall. The walls and ceiling were completely papered with one dollar bills.

After a couple days on the Keys, I decided to head north. The Keys were a bust as far as I was concerned and I'd read about a nudist park near the Georgia border that had a music festival coming up. I got a reservation there and was going to work my way slowly up Highway 1.

U.S. Highway 1 was six lanes wide coming out of Homestead, just another big highway lined with malls and auto dealers. I was already planning to leave it and find a backroad north instead. Somebody laid on their horn nearby and I looked out the side mirror. Down next to me was a gray Toyota wagon pulling a pop-up camper. Dolly was driving and had one arm out the window to wave at me. Val was in the backseat and had her head out the window yelling and waving. They peeled off into a shopping center and I edged over to the next entrance. They'd stopped in front of an auto parts store and I pulled into a space next to them. Dolly and Janna had the back of the wagon open and, after they waved at me, they headed for the store. Val came over to give me a hug.

"We blew a fuse in the car when we tried to plug the refrigerator into it," she said.

"I thought you were staying down there for another week," I said. I ruled out the idea that they were stalking me. There was no way they could know I would be heading out of the Keys two days after I got there.

"They mowed the whole campground this morning. Bugs came out of everywhere. You shoulda seen us swattin' and whackin' at each other. We closed up the camper and hitched up to get outa there. That's how we happened to plug the lights into the car with the refrigerator still connected. Boom!"

"So, you're just headed home?"

"We don't know where we're going. We'll just drive up here a way and find a campground near a beach. Must be one somewhere." The whole time Val was talking she was edging closer to me. I was up against the truck and she was a couple inches in front of me. "Where you goin' next?"

"I found a park up near Fort Lauderdale," I said. "Figure I'll spend a couple days there. Next weekend I plan to be at a nude park west of Jacksonville."

"I love nude! I never wear clothes at home. You should come visit me in Knoxville," she said. Well, she might not be the prettiest woman in the world, but she was certainly being one of the friendliest. I pulled out my cellphone.

"Give me your number and the rest of your name so I can give you a call when I get to the Smokies. I'll either stay in Gatlinburg or Pigeon Forge. That's not far." Under the pretense of looking over my hands as I thumbed in her phone number, Val closed the remaining distance between us and started rubbing her tits against the back of my hands. It was subtle at first, but soon became obvious that her nipples were hardening against my hands while I held the phone.

A Long Time Ago: Personal Space

AND THAT BRINGS me back to Joy.

Remember Joy? The judge's daughter who was way above my social class.

It was two weeks before high school graduation and Coach Hancock had come down hard on the seniors for goofing off in his government class. We were all squirrelly as hell and nobody was really concentrating on school. We'd already started partying and nearly every night we were out late playing games that mostly had to do with getting touchy-feely with classmates you figured you might not ever see again. Oh, the games all had 'science' behind them. We were developing trust with each other by having one person (strangely, always a girl) stand in the middle of a tight circle of guys sitting on the floor. She'd hold herself as stiffly as possible and then tilt until she fell backwards. The boy behind her would catch her falling body and toss it the other direction. Of course, there was a lot of catching her by the boobs and giving a little squeeze as we sent her on to the next guy until she'd start giggling and collapse instead of staying stiff. I'd wanted my hands on Shannon's boobs for three years and this was the only opportunity I'd gotten so far. But that's a different story.

The real story here is that we were staying out ridiculously late every night and sleeping through classes. Serious sleep deprivation. Coach Hancock said that since we couldn't focus on class, he was just going to assign us a paper to be turned in before the weekend and that anyone who didn't have it in would have to come to school during senior week when we all intended to be gone. He was a good guy, a six-six former marine sergeant who coached basketball, but he could be hard as nails if you disrespected him.

The assignment: *Research and describe a political geographic division within the state and tell how its boundaries were defined and what impact it has on state and local governance.* Well, smart person that I was, I chose to describe our judicial district. After all, we had a judge living right there in town and I figured I could just talk to her and get all the info I needed. So, I let the report go until Thursday because… parties. I was so sleep-deprived that it was all I could do to keep my eyes open as I walked down to the judge's house that evening. It was nearly nine o'clock, but over the past three years, I'd learned that she was a cool lady and people stopped in to see Joy all the time. All I really needed was a good map of the district and I'd fake the rest of it. There hadn't been an essay in three years that I'd received less than an A-minus on. I was a writer.

Joy answered the door when I rang.

She had a halter and a pair of shorts on. It looked like she was going to go out to a party tonight and I was going to be stuck in my room trying to stay awake while I typed up this stupid report. Blonde hair, sparkling white teeth, and deep blue eyes that I thought were a nice match for my own. Even though I wore glasses.

"Hi, Ari. What's up?" she asked when she opened the door.

"Oh, hi, Joy. I figured you'd be out already. I actually came to ask your mom a question."

"You working on Hancock's project?"

"Yeah."

"You're out of luck."

"What?"

"Mom and Dad went to a judicial conference in Washington, DC this week. They aren't home," she said. It took a moment for that to slip through the haze that lack of sleep and the presence of her breasts so nicely encased in that flimsy little halter had closed in over my mind. I think she noticed. She backed up a step and I wondered if I'd actually reached out to touch her. "What info are you looking for? Maybe I can get it."

"I just needed a map of her judicial district," I said.

"Oh, that's easy enough. It's the same as the county. Let me get a county map from her office. She has them lying all over everywhere." I watched her ass in those tight little short-shorts as she went into her mother's office. I followed and stood in the doorway. Joy was bent over a file drawer and I wanted nothing more than to slip up behind her and press my cock into that sweet round ass. I think she saw me.

She brought a folded map and handed it to me. Only she didn't let go. She held onto the map as I raised my hands to take it and opened it up to point out various features of the county as she moved closer. I tried to ask specific questions from my muddled brain. Not only was Joy close enough that I could feel her breath as she talked to me, I could feel her tits brushing against the backs of my hands as I held the map there. Her nipples were turning into hard points against me. I think I was a little short of oxygen when she pulled the map out of my hands and dropped it on the floor. I stood there looking at my hands touching her breasts, thinking in my irrational mind that she was going to hit me. Instead she kissed me.

"Ari," she said after a gentle brush of her lips. "When a girl shoves her breasts into your hands, it's okay to touch them." She kissed me again, and when I turned my palms to her breasts and started softly kneading them, the kiss intensified to something I was completely unprepared for. She had a hand on the back of my neck and moved me with her as she backed into the living room and we sank onto a sofa.

"God, Joy," I sighed. I couldn't think of anything else to say.

"Three years, Ari. Three years we've known each other and you never asked me out. Why?"

"You're always, so… your family is so much better than mine. I didn't figure you'd have anything to do with me."

"You're like third in our class," she said. "How can you be so stupid?"

"Joy, do you mean we'd…?"

"Oh, I doubt we'd ever have been boyfriend and girlfriend," she said. "But we'd have had a hell of a good time on a date."

"I really am stupid, aren't I?"

"I'm not going to fuck you, Ari. But you can touch me."

"Why? Are you a virgin, Joy?" I was lying half on top of her and had pushed the halter up so my hands were on her bare tits. I even had a condom in my wallet because… I was a senior. Who knew what might happen?

"You've got to be kidding. I wasn't a virgin when you met me three years ago. But you are. And fucking would mean something different to you than to me," she said. She untied the halter and tossed it aside. She pushed her hands between us and when she'd unbuttoned and unzipped her shorts she turned her hand over and started stroking my cock. "But we can touch. I don't think either of us would read too much into getting each other off. You've been getting Deb off, haven't you? And she's been doing you?"

"Oh, god! Deb!" I started to lever myself up off Joy. My girlfriend. I imagined this must be what it was like to be drunk.

"Suck my tits, Ari. Do you really think Deb isn't getting mauled by everyone she can this week? Don't worry. She still loves you. But we all want to have a little fun. Suck me, Ari. Get your fingers stinky."

Oh, fuck! I fell to those incredible tits that I'd been watching from afar for three years and feasted on them. And Joy wasn't idle. She got my shirt unbuttoned and scratched against my chest and my nipples with her nails, lightly stimulating them. That was like an electric connection straight to the tip of my cock. I slid a hand down her flat, smooth stomach. She didn't offer to push her shorts down, but she sucked her tummy in a little like that would make it easier to get my hand under the waistband of her panties.

Only there weren't any panties there. I slid right down her stomach and across her blonde pubic hair to her very wet snatch. I found her little nubbin and she jerked my head up to her mouth to kiss me while she squealed. I slid a finger into her wet warm depths. Her shorts weren't off, but my hand had pushed them down far enough that I could get into action.

"Oh, yeah. Right there. Deb taught you good. Rub that spot, Ari. You're going to make me… I'm going to come!" and she did. If she hadn't left her shorts on, she'd have left a huge wet spot on the sofa. She was panting and kissing me and rolling her hips on my hand. "One more. One more. Yes!" she cried. This one wasn't quite as juicy, but apparently, it made her too sensitive for me to keep going and she pulled my hand out of her pants and shoved my fingers in my mouth. "Suck those while I suck you," she said.

Joy started kissing her way down my body while her fingers unfastened my belt and my jeans. She paused to use her tongue on my hypersensitive nipples and I almost came in her hands. But Joy was going for the good stuff and shortly, she had my cock out of my pants and in her mouth.

My eyes crossed. I wished I was just a little less tired so I could really enjoy the sensation of having my cock sucked by fuckin' Joy the Judge's daughter. I came. I fountained and sprayed into her mouth and she gulped it down as fast as I could squirt it. And then she just held me in her mouth, swallowing and bathing my cock with her tongue as I softened. She gave me a couple final sucks and tucked me back into my jeans.

"Mmm. Feeling a guy come in my mouth is so good I don't want to let him go. You're not going to get hard again for another, though, are you?" she sighed. She kissed her way back up my chest and fastened her lips on mine, probing with her tongue. I'd never Frenched a girl who had just had my come in her mouth, but... *Fuck!* It was Joy and I knew I'd probably never have a chance like this again. I kissed her and got my hands on her perfectly gorgeous tits again. It was almost too much. I was struggling to keep my eyes open as we kissed because if I closed them, I'd go to sleep.

"You need to get home and finish that report, big guy," she said as she nibbled my ear. "I wish we'd have started this three years ago."

Back to Val

FEELING VAL'S NIPPLES hardening against the back of my fingers, I gave up all pretenses of trying to enter something in my phone. I spread my fingers slightly and scissor-pinched her nipples. She gasped and I think if we weren't out in a Walmart parking lot, she'd have done me right there.

"Got the fuse," Janna called as she and Dolly closed in on the car. Val looked up into my eyes.

"Call me from Pigeon Forge. I can be there in an hour."

I DECIDED RIGHT then to make a stop in the Smoky Mountains and reserved a slot in an RV park nearby. But first, I was headed to 'Barely Surviving', a music festival at a nudist park in Georgia. Despite considering myself a nudist in my home, I'd never actually been to a nudist park or an event that was nude. Except the Summer Solstice Parade in Fremont in Seattle. That was entertaining, but I was an observer, not a participant. My experience with public nudity was limited to the few days Angie and I spent at the Magic Circle in Quartzite where there were only two other couples. And to occasionally forgetting to put clothes on when I stepped out on my front porch in Seattle to get the morning newspaper.

My first experience made nudism a life choice. It would take me a while to figure out where nudist parks were located and how to reserve space for my trailer at them, but Barely Surviving was my kind of party. There were about a hundred people camped at the 'resort'. Apparently, it gets to use that word because it has a swimming pool. Aside from that, it's just a campground where people run around naked. There were trailers, motorhomes, and tents, organized with some sense of order and with enough space between the sites that you didn't feel like you were in your neighbor's bedroom all the time.

This festival had no underage kids at it. The owner explained that wasn't because of the nudity, but alcohol was allowed throughout the park and the authorities frowned on that. When the youngest at the park is twenty-one and the oldest is in his seventies, you can imagine the range of body types you can find. There weren't many singles, but people were all friendly and there were campfires, shared meals, bottles of Fireball, and a lot of good natured storytelling. And when the sun went down, the music went up.

And people danced.

It didn't make any difference whether a person was part of a couple or single, whether he or she was fit or fat. People got up and shook what they had. I had friends who posted memes on Facebook that said things like, "Every time I do laundry, I consider becoming a nudist. Then I look in the mirror." Well, here's a news flash: There are no mirrors. I spent the entire week thinking that I looked better than anyone else there. And I'd bet everyone there thought the same about themselves. There was no body shame and no embarrassment. And surprisingly, no erections.

Well, I did get started on a chub while I was dancing to 'Yesterday' with a single woman I'd been hanging out with. Nona was about fifty-five, but my best guess was that her breasts were only about twenty. She confirmed that later. She thought her husband would like something a little bigger and rounder, so she had them done about twenty years earlier. Then he up and died on her and she was really pissed about that.

She was a real southern belle, but as loopy as they come. She had the general life philosophy of an earth mother. She wanted natural everything—sea salt, organic vegetables, grass-fed beef—except her boobs. I really started getting interested in her when she started talking about her pagan celebrations and earth-based beliefs. But hidden beneath the surface of this aging hippie chick was the most conservative bitch I'd ever met. Obama was to blame for everything that was wrong in the world. Even the death of her husband. Gays should have no rights at all and gay marriage was an abomination. The whole liberal agenda was ruining America and she was ready to vote for the most outlandishly rightwing candidate for any office that she could find. And don't think you can take her guns away because she wasn't afraid to use them.

Okay. I have a lot of tolerance for people. I don't call that liberal or conservative. I call it live and let live. But you might have noticed from some of my stories that I tend to the left of center. I'm not afraid to call bullshit on my fellow liberals, though, any more than I am likely to ridicule science-denying conservatives. There is no global warming in Florida, but they are still seeking government aid and assistance because the water levels are rising and cutting into their beaches. But that's not because of global warming. God did it. And the government they want to be smaller should be providing aid because their tourist economy has been damaged.

Anyway, I was not going to contradict Nona as I walked her to her campsite, or get into an argument—especially when she was having me squeeze and examine her breasts to prove how natural they felt while she reamed my mouth with her tongue. In fact, her nipples seemed fine and stiffly welcoming of my caresses and kisses. When we hugged, a certain distance was enforced between our centers because we were held five inches apart by her boobs. They did not squish. They did not flatten. She could do jumping jacks and they would not jiggle. But I've fucked a plastic doll. I can get past inflated boobs.

Until…

"I told that other guy that's been sniffing around that it ain't gonna happen tonight," she said as we caught our breath and she caught my hand headed south. "I'm telling you the same thing. It ain't gonna happen. Unless you're ready for a lifelong commitment. My husband betrayed me. He was supposed to be my companion and take care of me for the rest of my life. In return for that I let him take me any way he wanted to, and I enjoyed it. I'd spread my legs whenever he was hard. I welcomed him in. But then he tricked me and died. Well, I'm not spreading these legs for anyone who isn't ready to take care of me for the rest of my life. I'm a lady, born and bred in the south. I deserve to be taken care of by a real man."

Holy fucking shit. I suddenly became a rantallion. I used that term in *Blackfeather*. When my heroine went back to the 1860s, I needed gutter talk and slang that was appropriate for the era. I found a document of Victorian slang euphemisms. It was particularly helpful to find a woman's genital region was called her privities. Well, a rantallion is one whose scrotum is so relaxed as to be longer than his penis, that is, whose shot pouch is longer that the barrel of his piece.

Who'd have thought there was a word for that? It made me wonder what kinds of slang we had today that made our language more colorful. I get so tired of referring to pussy, cunt, and twat. What happened to words like quim, muff, and madge? Or even 'old hat' (because it's frequently felt)? Oh. Like I said, my mind wanders and sometimes I have trouble finding it again.

There was a bit of a contest going on over whether my penis would shrink up into my gut before my balls found safety behind my liver. Regardless, there was no reason to continue my explorations south of the equator.

I'm fundamentally a cad. I wasn't going to do anything that implied that I was the caretaker that she should marry. But she'd already indicated that kissing her and squeezing those artificial boobs weren't activities that required a license, so I indulged myself one more time before saying good night and going back to my trailer to safely relieve a little pressure.

~~~~~

IT'S A LONG way through Georgia and the Carolinas. I got periodic texts from Val asking where I was and what I was doing. When was I coming to visit her? I'd often answer and ask a question but not hear back for several days.

I found another nudist park just south of Savannah and spent a week there, just because I wasn't ready to get dressed yet. I did take a day to go into the historic town, though, because a few years ago, I wrote two books at once during the month of November (NaNoWriMo). I always set myself new challenges for the novel-writing month. That time, I worked on one book over coffee in the mornings—a sequel to my mystery, *For Blood or Money*—and a second book while I was drinking wine in the evenings—*The Volunteer*. Vastly different books. One a mystery and the other very much literary fiction. They had nothing in common, except that one evening the two main characters met in a park in Savannah. Just in passing. The detective—a young woman disguised as an older woman with a limp—and the vagrant—a homeless man wandering from town to town looking for handouts.

The scene is very different depending on whose point of view.

I FOUND THE park and the bench where they met—all places that I'd researched and described, but had never seen in real life. I even bought a Savannah rose and kept it on the dash of my truck for months.

~~~~~

AND THAT BROUGHT me to Pigeon Forge, Tennessee.

I chuckled as I passed Dollywood. I remembered Kenny Rogers being asked on a talk show once, "You've worked with Dolly Parton a lot. Tell us, are they real?" Kenny shook his head sadly. "No. They're all wigs." Well, the Dolly I knew from the Everglades was all real; I'd seen enough evidence of that. Probably 200 pounds worth. And enough to know that, even though she was flattered by my comments, she had no real interest in a swinging dick.

Val, on the other hand, had made it clear that she was.

As soon as I got myself camped, I sent her a text message.

And heard nothing back. That wasn't unusual. I wasn't sure she even knew where her phone was most days. Her number had changed twice since I'd met her a couple months earlier.

The next day was gray and miserable. I stayed in my trailer and spent the day writing. I'd started posting *Living Next Door to Heaven* in April and the response was good. It didn't make any difference how people responded. I was committed to the project and was well into the writing of *Part III: Foolish Wisdom*. I was pumping out an unprecedented number of words each day and felt like I was draining them right out of my bloodstream.

The setting for LNDtH was based on my childhood home. Many of the characters had a basis in some little detail I remembered from that time—a name I particularly liked, a characteristic, a fantasy, or even just a hair color. But the only one I'd seen since my freshman year in high school was Cassie, and that was for an hour over a strawberry shortcake in Florida. Oh. I'll add that I'd seen Hannah. She came to my mother's funeral and gave me a sweet hug. Our parents had been very close. I hadn't seen her since sixth grade and I still had a crush on her. I made a bunch of shit up out of grade school memories and transposed people I'd met much later in life into that same story. I'm sorry to say that the Life of Aroslav wasn't as good as the Life of Brian. But I can dream, can't I?

The next day, I decided that, rain or no rain, I was going to drive up into Smoky Mountains National Park and walk along the Appalachian Trail. It was still pretty damp and I understood why the place was called the Smokies. They looked like they constantly had a shroud of smoke that turned them blue, even when you were right up in them. Nonetheless, they had a wild beauty that I loved.

I stepped out of the truck at one of the parking areas and took a walk along the Appalachian Trail. One of my nephews had walked the entire trail a few years back, and I was envious. I walked out a mile or so and then hiked back. When I got in the truck, I checked my phone, just to see if I had any messages, and discovered that I didn't have a signal. Of course, I wouldn't have one anyplace in the National Park. I continued my exploration and came out on the other side of the park.

As soon as I hit the little town on the south side, my phone chimed. I had a signal and I had a message from Val. "tried to cll u no answer. in pf anyway where u?" The message had been sent over an hour ago.

"Went to park. I'm an hour away. You still there?"

My daughter always makes fun of my text messages and Facebook posts because I talk in complete sentences, use capitals, and punctuate things. I guess that makes me an old fart. It had taken me a few minutes to figure out Val's message. No response. I turned toward the Interstate and headed back to Pigeon Forge.

My phone chimed again as I was coming to the long strip of restaurants and 'shows' that make up the town. Things like 'Noah's Flood. Experience the Biblical thrill!' I could imagine one that said, 'Crucifixion and Resurrection: Feel the nails like Jesus did.' Since I had been to the national park, I figured I'd leave the commercial district behind tomorrow.

"came bak at walmart"

I pulled to the side of the road and sent a message back. "Ten minutes away. Be there soon."

I was beginning to wonder about how much effort it was taking to hook up with Val, but I was also thinking of her hard nipples between my fingers. She wasn't the prettiest thing in the world. Her teeth were crooked, but it looked like she had them all. I'd seen plenty of women in the past couple months who didn't. She probably packed fifteen extra pounds on her short frame, but that had just made her feel squishy beneath my fingers. I was thinking all this as I pulled into the Walmart parking lot and spotted her standing by her car staring at her phone. No, not a beauty queen, but I was nobody's idea of a hunk.

"Hey," I said, stepping out of the truck.

"Hey. I'm hungry. I been trying to find you all afternoon."

That was abrupt, but I could understand. She gave me a quick hug and waited for me to open the door of the truck for her. I drove us across the street to Black Angus and we ate a big meal. With a bottle of wine.

I paid the tab and tried to figure out what I could cut out of my budget next week.

"Well, show me your trailer," she said. "Where you parked?" I took her to the trailer and let her inside. She was like a puppy, sniffing at everything and opening all the doors and drawers to look inside. She finally turned around, smashed her body up against mine and kissed me. "You want my clothes off or want to do it like this?" she asked.

It might have been better if I'd left her clothes on, but I like skin contact. Now that we were in the trailer, she seemed to be in a hurry. She got onto the bed and spread her legs. She was a little stubbly, but mostly shaved. I stuck my fingers in and she was plenty wet. Still, in the interest of primary research, I figured I'd get her revved by licking for a while. She grabbed me by the ears and hauled me up on top of her.

"I get licked. I don't get dicked. Put a raincoat on that sucker and shove it in!"

I certainly had no intentions of entering that cavern unprotected. I had condoms right next to the bed. I dressed and shoved.

"Yeah, baby. Give me that cock. Fuck! I haven't been fucked by a cock in a year. Fuck it! Oh gawd, yes." Her hips drove up to meet me like she was a pneumatic drill. She talked a steady stream of filth about fucking her cunt and biting her titties. As she got closer and closer, her accent became thicker and thicker until I could hardly understand her at all. I think I caught something about slamming that dog into this bitch. It could have been something completely different. It made no difference. She was coming and I was coming and that's all she wrote.

Literally.

As soon as I was out of her sopping cunt, she was out of bed and dressing.

"I gotta get home! I work in the morning and I'll be dead tired. Will you take me back to my car?" she asked. I pulled on my jeans and t-shirt and shoved my bare feet into my boots.

"Sure," I said. "I'm glad you came down. Sorry it was so rushed."

"Well, it cost me a bundle, too. You mind putting gas in my car?" That was a reasonable request, I suppose. She gathered up a bunch of toiletries and a candy bar in the convenience store and asked if I'd mind just adding those to the gas. The clerk already had it rung up and I'm just not the kind of guy that makes a big scene about things. She gave me a quick kiss at her car and jumped in to drive off. "See you this weekend, baby?" she said as she drove off. I didn't have time to answer. I looked at the receipt in my hands for $85. I hadn't known it was possible to spend that much at a convenience store gas station.

Early the next morning, I sent Val a text message after I got the trailer hitched and was relatively certain that she couldn't catch up with me.

"Driving up the Blue Ridge Parkway today. Headed on north. See you next time!"

I didn't get a response for several weeks. When she contacted me again, she was complaining about her miserable financial condition because of a doctor bill and wouldn't I send her money so she could come and join me on the road?

~~~~

A Long Time Ago: Succubus

WHEN ANABEL LEE and I got together, I was hopelessly in lust and would do anything for her that she asked. What she asked for was usually diamonds. Or a bigger house. Or a new car. Or art. Or clothes. Lots and lots of clothes. She was a user and I was an addict. She drove me into bankruptcy and I was still hanging on to her. Until Susie, her best friend, invited me out *to talk* one night. That talk ended up with a skinny dip in Lake Harriet. Oh, it was all innocent. I wasn't going to fuck Susie. If it had been Marla, that would have been different, but not Susie, even though the offer was clearly on the table. Or in the water. Still, I had no problems feeling up the offered bare tits and chewing on her nipples while we treaded water.

The next morning, Susie told Belle all about how I'd made a pass at her and it was all she could do to keep me from fucking her. Belle went ballistic. I think she'd been waiting for the opportunity and the more I thought back on it, the more I suspected that they had planned it all out together. I should have fucked the bitch. It really pissed me off.

Don't piss off an addict.

Belle came to my office and read me out loudly enough for my coworkers to hear. Then she stormed out. I went to my boss's office and told him I had to go take care of some personal business. Dan just shook his head. I don't think Belle was expecting me to catch a bus and follow her home. After all, she had our only car. I walked into the house to find her laughing with Susie in the living room.

"Pack your shit and get out of my house," I said. She looked up at me like I was an alien.

"Where am I supposed to go?" she asked. I almost pulled a Rhett Butler and said, 'Frankly, my dear, I don't give a damn.' I desisted.

"Why don't you get some good advice from your friend?" I asked, pointing at Susie. "I'm sure she's got room at *her* house. Just get the fuck out of mine."

I went back to work. I should have stayed and monitored the departure, but instead, I worked late and went out to dinner with

Marla. After dinner, we went out for a walk around Lake Calhoun and I ended up sprawled under a tree in the dark getting the best blowjob I'd had since high school. Belle gagged just licking my cock.

When I got back to the house, around ten p.m., it was empty. It hadn't taken her long to clear out everything she could carry. All the artwork was off the walls. All the dishes were out of the cupboards. All the books, magazines, and newspapers were gone. The bed was gone. The dining table was gone.

My office was untouched. In the living room, my stereo and CDs were untouched. In the kitchen, she'd left my coffee pot. Other than that, even the refrigerator was empty.

I about had my newly-divorced life back together six months later when she called me.

"Hey, Ari. How are you doing? Say, honey, I'm trying to get into a new apartment and I need a little cash for the deposit. Can you help me out, honey? I could come over for a while, you know."

I have absolutely no objections to any kind of sex if it's consensual. Non-consensual sex is not sex. It's rape. Rape is not about sex. It's not about a girl (or a boy) just asking for it because of the way she is dressed. It is a crime of power and violence. Don't give me any crap about it being non-consensual sex. RAPE. Call it by name.

As I was saying, I have absolutely no objections to any kind of sex, even when it's paid for if neither party is being coerced. Belle was a hell of a good lay when she was sane. But some pussies just aren't worth the price of admission.

"I think it's time you found someone else to mooch from, Belle," I said. "Don't call me again."

~~~~~

Back to Val

"I KNOW JUST what you mean," I texted Val. "I had a dental bill last month that just wiped me out! Hope you can get back on your feet. I'm thinking of you."

I never heard from her again.

6 Reunited Again

16 June 2014

B OSTON WAS one of those places that my sure sense of direction told me was in the East. It's funny how I never considered Florida, Georgia, the Carolinas or Virginia to be in the East, even though they all bordered the Atlantic. They were all the South, sadly lumped in with Alabama, Mississippi, Louisiana, and Tennessee. It wasn't until I got to Maryland and Washington, DC that I felt like I was in the East. Connecticut, Rhode Island, and Massachusetts embodied the very essence of East.

I'd driven up from the Delaware beaches—where I'd dipped my toes in the water of the third coast—north through New Jersey. Then I took a self-imposed detour, departing from the track of Highway 1 and staying well west of the Hudson River. I had no desire to visit New York City. People asked me on Facebook if I was going to go to Ground Zero and to send pictures of the memorial.

No.

I had no interest in seeing the place. I remembered in great detail the day of 9/11 and needed no pilgrimage to remind me. I remembered holding my little girl in my arms trying to explain to her what had happened and why everyone was so angry all the time. I had to explain to her that her little Muslim friend wasn't a terrorist. I wish I could find the words I used to comfort her now so that I could tell them to the nation.

There's a validity to remembering certain events to remind us not to let them happen again. Those who don't remember history are doomed to repeat it, so they say. But I'd seen plenty of evidence that the 'remembrance of our heritage' in the South wasn't to keep another civil war from breaking out, but to keep people reminded that they were part of a different country from the rest of the United States. They flew a different flag than the rest of the country, sometimes in addition to the American flag, but often by itself. The longest undefended international boundary in the world runs right through the middle of the USA. It starts on the Mason-Dixon Line. From what I'd seen throughout the South, we are still two different countries that share a government.

So, when it came to memorializing the Twin Towers attack, I couldn't see it as something that would heal our nation. The evidence is that it keeps alive the grievance, keeps the wound open. We don't want to heal. We want to hate. We will keep our hate alive by reminding people daily of what those bastards did to us. That's the only way we can justify sending ten thousand more Americans to their deaths in the Middle East so the three thousand in New York won't have died in vain. What the fuck kind of screwed up sense is that?

We'd rain death on one and a half million innocent people who had nothing to do with the attack on the Twin Towers. We'd make sure they kept their hatred alive as well.

I avoided New York City.

Instead, I immersed myself in the history of our country where pilgrims settled, where the Boston Tea Party was held, and where the Revolutionary War began. I toured old cemeteries, churches, markets, and the incredible park called the Boston Common and its adjacent Public Garden, where the Swan Boats famously ply the pond. And I sat outside a little tobacco shop and smoked a ten-dollar cigar while I watched people. Finally, I followed Massachusetts Route 2 along Commonwealth Avenue until it became U.S. Highway 20 at Boston University, a block away from Fenway Park.

A Long Time Ago: Eight-Tenths of a Mile

U.S. Highway 20 has always had a special place in my mind—maybe in my heart. It's the longest numbered highway in the United States at nearly 3,500 miles. It runs from Boston, Massachusetts to Newport,

Oregon. And it goes right through my hometown. Or it used to. Now there's a bypass.

When I was growing up, my address was Rural Route 2. That's it. City and State. With that address, the mail carrier could deliver our mail. He knew everyone who lived along that mail delivery route, often stopping to talk to folks and bringing Sears and Roebuck packages up to our door. I was sure he read all the picture postcards and knew everyone's business.

It was an address, but it wasn't a location. I couldn't invite a friend over to play and tell him to just come to Rural Route 2. The route covered about twenty miles. So, from the time I could talk, I was told that I lived eight-tenths of a mile north of U.S. 20 on Mosquito Road. I memorized it, recited it, and dreamed about it. I had a location.

Every day of my first fifteen years, it seemed, I crossed U.S. 20. It was on the way to school, to church, to groceries, to deliver my newspapers. No matter where I wanted to go, I either crossed U.S. 20 or traveled along it. My school was on U.S. 20. The church was half a mile off. Every day I'd look up or down the McKinley Highway and wonder where it went.

This summer, I decided to find out.

Back to Boston

I STOPPED FOR coffee at Starbucks, half a mile west from the terminus of U.S. 20. The mile markers on East-West U.S. Highways run from West to East. I briefly considered making a game of stopping at every Starbucks between Boston and Newport, but even I can't drink that much coffee. Or afford it. I had a great time on the journey, camping in the Berkshires, wandering along roads that twisted and turned through villages, and trying desperately to remember a poem I'd written years ago called "Eight-tenths of a mile off 20."

I took a week's detour north of Albany to visit a fan who invited me to use his RV pad for a week. It was a great treat to have some relaxed company. In the evenings we sat in front of a fire and smoked a cigar. I'd never been to Upstate New York, and had a completely relaxed time.

Along much of Scenic Highway 20, I saw signs that read 'No reservation. No separate nation.' It seemed funny to me, though, that when I passed through a corner of the Onondaga Nation south of Syracuse, none of the cars filling at the tax-free gas station seemed to be owned by natives. And I certainly availed myself of the four-dollar cigars at the tobacco shop—the same cigars I'd purchased for ten dollars in Boston.

YOU MIGHT BE wondering what I was doing for companionship during all this time. Well, it was true that the last time I'd had sex was in Pigeon Fucking Forge, Tennessee and I was a little gun shy, so to speak. I'd gone a lot longer than two or three months before. I figured that I could wait until I found something good.

I'd stopped at a strip club west of Boston and got a bit of a surprise. They didn't do lap dances and had no private dance room. It was all nude, but I noticed—Hey! I was paying attention!—that all the girls were completely shaved and absolutely sealed shut. I asked one of the girls about it. Even though they weren't allowed to touch a customer, they still came around and sat with you, hoping you'd tip them just for their gracious company.

"Seeing the slit is defined by our city council as artistic freedom. Exposing anything inside is considered pornography. Touching a customer is considered soliciting. We can have a private dance for you if we stay four feet away. And don't show our pussies. We have a wax we use to keep 'em closed."

I'll be damned.

Speaking of strippers, while I was camped at the north end of one of the Finger Lakes, I opened my email to find a message from Alice.

You remember Alice? Eighteen-year-old stripper with a wet pussy who wanted to *come* with me?

We *had*, on a few occasions. I liked the girl and she liked teasing me. We'd had phone sex once or twice and just seeing her email address in my inbox sent a little jolt of electricity down my spine to my balls.

A-ri,

God! You don't know how wet it makes me when I whisper your name. I do it while I'm fingering my clit and always end up sleeping in a wet spot. I have to be careful not to think of you when I'm on stage or the customers will get the wrong idea.

Guess what!

I graduated. I'm officially a student at the University now. Hot shit, huh? You know what you said about swinging back up to Montana when I graduated? How about it? Am I still on your list of favorite girls, Ari?

I know you're still out in New York because I read your Facebook post yesterday. I've got to say, you've been boring lately. You haven't sent me a juicy email since that college girl in Florida. What have you been doing? Honey, if you've got six months of come backed up when you get here, we'll never get out of bed! That's not a bad thought, is it?

How about you just park the trailer and fly up here for a booty break?

I know. You're on a mission to do that highway coast to coast. I looked on a map. That route goes right through Yellowstone National Park. I could join you there! I've never seen Old Faithful. Would you believe it?

Ari, I'm excited to join you for a week. But I'm a little scared, too. It's like I've been building this fantasy in my head about what being with you would be like. I'm afraid it's all just a fantasy and reality would suck. I've been following your trip long enough now to know that you aren't an axe murderer or anything. You're really a sweet guy. Maybe that's what I'm most scared of. I'm not like the kind of innocent babe you deserve. And I'm not submissive like that girl Angie. Or a sex-crazed maniac like the spring break babe. I'm pretty plain and ordinary except that about a million guys have seen my breasts and looked up my twat. No. Not that many, but some days it seems like it. I could have made a career out of being a training dummy for gynecology students.

Am I too... like... dirty for you, Ari?

I'm not expecting anything beyond a fun week when we get together. It's not like I'm trying to trap you or tie you down, you know. But I worry that I might not be what you expected.

I guess I'll never know if we don't get together. I'm ready and willing if you are. College classes start August 25th. Let me know.

Kisses,

Alice

I sent her an immediate note to meet me in Cody, Wyoming on August 16th. I might have to rush through a bit of the trip, but I wasn't going to pass up a week with Alice.

~~~~~

I STILL HAD seven weeks before that and in the middle of it was the class reunion for St. Joe Valley High, the school I never graduated from.

The class I graduated with at Tippecanoe Valley High School wouldn't be getting together again officially this year, but that didn't mean I couldn't take a little detour and see some old friends.

As I drove across Ohio, on what was absolutely the worst maintained portion of the entire route, the scenery started to look more and more familiar. By the time I crossed into Indiana, which happened to mean crossing under the toll road at the same time, I actually started singing 'Back Home Again in Indiana.'

I took a detour south to visit the Auburn-Cord-Duesenberg Museum in Auburn—fabulous cars of yesteryear's rich and famous in an Art Deco showroom—but I kept moving my campsite farther and farther west until I was camped at the lake where Jessica had proven so friendly. I spent an entire afternoon there watching the kids in the water. There were a few nice bikini bodies, mostly on the moms of kids who were in the water. It was pleasant, but no one really seemed to be having the fun that I remembered having.

I entertained nostalgic thoughts of buying the old homestead on Mosquito Road—now completely overgrown with trees—and setting up a parking slab, well, and septic where I could park the trailer for a couple summer months each year. There was a kind of romance to it as I thought about writing *Living Next Door to Heaven* and all the fun I'd had with the kids I grew up with. Sort of. It wasn't really them, of course. And Brian certainly wasn't me. I wasn't that smart. I wasn't that athletic. I certainly didn't have all those friends. Like Alice, I'd built a fantasy and reality fell far short.

A Long Time Ago: Unwanted Childhood

I WON'T SAY I had a miserable childhood. I'd have to say that, if anything, I was oblivious to my childhood. I'd blocked out all memories until I was fifteen, but when I started writing LNDtH, they started emerging, through a fantasy lens. Underneath it all, I was a lonely, insecure kid, just like any other kid. With the others on my section of Mosquito Road, I played softball in the summer, but we really didn't have much other contact. Carl had been my best friend, but most of what we did together was because our families were together or we were in church together. Cassie and I quit meeting in the woods and playing in the freshly plowed fields sometime before third grade. I don't know what happened. We just sort of went different ways.

I always liked redheaded Liz next door on the other side from Cassie, but about sixth grade she moved away and some people bought her house and planted all the field with blueberries.

And Hannah. Well, her dad was transferred after sixth grade. How far away didn't make a difference. I was twelve years old. I'd seen her at my mother's funeral fifteen years ago. She gave me a hug. Somewhere in my files, maybe buried beneath an old manuscript, I had her phone number. I'd had a severe crush on her in grade school. After she moved, I blew her a kiss out my window each night before I went to bed. For years.

Out of all the kids, I was the 'religious' one. At least that's the way it felt. I went to church on Sunday morning, Sunday evening, and Wednesday evening. And any other time something was happening at the church. Yes, I really did have a sixteen-year perfect attendance pin for Sunday School. And I won every 'sword drill' the Sunday School teachers could toss at us. I went to what I found out years later was a mainstream liberal church. I didn't know that. But I once visited a conservative Bible church with a cousin and they were all impressed that I could find verses or simply recite them from my Bible and that I could say the names of all the books of the Bible in order. I produced my first play in the sanctuary of our church for Easter when I was in seventh grade.

To cap off my feeling of being isolated and looked down upon, we were poor. When I think about the other families along Mosquito Road, I think we were all a little below median income. Of course, that wasn't even a word that was used back then. I keep trying to put it all in a better light, but I can't find kindling.

Things like my dad being on strike for several months a year when the union contract came up for renewal. Eating government surplus peanut butter, dried eggs, and cheese. Going to Chicago every other month to visit an aunt who worked for a soup company and gave us unlabeled cans. My dad taking a temporary job at a bakery and bringing home a sack of expired bread and sweet rolls twice a week. We'd rummage through the top third of the bag and stuff ourselves with the sweet things. The bottom two thirds of the bag were so smashed together that we dished it out to feed the dogs.

I knew my classmates avoided me. I suspected that I smelled bad. We didn't have indoor plumbing until I was in seventh grade. Taking a bath required pouring boiling water into a copper tub in the living room, near the stove. Before the plumbing was connected in our new indoor bathroom, I got to sleep in the bathtub.

When Mom got her teaching certificate and a job offer to teach second grade about fifty miles away, we moved. It was between my freshman and sophomore years in high school. I turned away from Mishawaka and swore I'd never go back. I even focused my mind on forgetting everything about my first fifteen years, and until I started writing *Living Next Door to Heaven*, I'd been successful.

Our old house was condemned and torn down the next year. It about killed my dad. He'd built it with his own hands and put every nail into the siding. It just wasn't very good.

~~~

Back to Indiana

WHY WAS I even considering buying the old homestead? The property I remembered as being all open fields with a little maple grove in the back connecting it to the other properties was all overgrown with trees. Big trees, eight or ten inches across. How could that be? Two new houses with long drives occupied the field where Cassie and I followed her father's plow and broke dirt clods with our toes. The apple trees my father planted were hidden among the hardwoods that had grown up around them. The huge oak trees where I played on a tire swing had been cut down to make way for the power lines that served the new houses. I took a video and sent it to my daughter and she reminded me I'd been gone for over forty years.

I drove down Mosquito Road and wondered where everyone I knew had gone. I knew Cassie lived in Florida. I'd heard Carl was in Detroit. I drove past his house and saw his older brother, Mitch, outside. For unknown reasons, I stopped and we chatted for a while.

Mitch, being four years older than any of the rest of us, hadn't been as central to the play group. But he'd turned out to be a jovial, if rather conservative, soul who recognized me right away. We talked for a couple of hours over coffee with his dad. He even called Betts and had me talk to her. She'd had a rough time over the past year with breast cancer, but she and her husband were still hanging in there. She said she was happy to hear from me. I tried calling Carl, but Mitch warned me that Carl didn't answer his phone if he didn't recognize who was calling. I sent a text message and a couple days later got a response that just said he couldn't make it to the reunion.

I gave Mitch my card and he said that I needed to drive down to his farm south of Bloomington and camp there. I promised to do that right after the reunion. He got a kick out of the fact that I wrote erotic romances and said he was going to read some of them. I never thought that he might read *Living Next Door to Heaven*.

One thing Betts said got to me. I asked her if she attended any SJV reunions.

"No. Why would I go back to see them? I never had any friends there. Nobody liked us, Ari. They still don't," she said.

Why? Why would I want to go back and live in a place where nobody liked me? Why was I even going to the reunion? What made me think I was the only one no one liked? Why was I romanticizing my childhood?

I wondered absently if Betts still remembered the two of us playing doctor and touching each other's privates.

I COULDN'T BELIEVE how nervous I was about going to a stupid reunion. I'd looked through that old yearbook and tried to identify people I might know. One image jumped out at me. Brenda—who I always considered to be a bubbly person, even though she wasn't one of the cheerleaders in real life—looked sad in her picture. Yes, she'd been an early bloomer and the fantasy of every boy in junior high. But in her freshman yearbook picture she just looked sad and maybe a little frightened. It's weird what you think you remember and something contradicts the memories. Perhaps she, too, made up stories about an idyllic youth in Indiana.

I went shopping and bought a pair of slacks and a shirt for the party. I had a nice sport coat that in my big business days I'd had tailored for myself in Singapore. I donned my plantation hat and decided

I looked as good as it was going to get. I was in town hours early and spent time at the Studebaker Museum wondering which of the cars my father had helped assemble. Finally, I walked to the banquet hall where the reunion was.

"Oh! You're Aroslav! I don't know if we ever met. I was from a different junior high than you, so we only overlapped for a year in high school. Welcome!" The speaker was our class representative, Sarah. She was nice and when she said she'd show me a table where I should sit, she wheeled herself ahead of me. A wheelchair? "Sorry I'm a little slow navigating through the crowd," Sarah said. "It's muscular dystrophy. I can still get up and walk a little, but I've put so much weight on that it hurts my legs. Look! There's Cassie!"

Indeed, Cassie Clinton Jones was standing by a table and waving at us. I looked around at the general condition of people at this reunion and Cassie looked spectacular. She'd chosen an off-the-shoulder party dress that made her look fifteen years younger than anyone else at the party.

"Ari! We saved you a seat with us," she said as she gave me a hug. She introduced me to the other eight at the table, three of whom were spouses to others. I didn't even recognize the names of the others who had supposedly been in my class. I looked around the room and saw a few people who I recognized vaguely, but wasn't sure who they were. Still, the party seemed to be a time where we were introducing ourselves. I handed out business cards with both author names on them. Some of these people would recognize the settings and a few might think they recognized someone I described, but they'd never really know. The fantasies were way too distant from the realities.

There was one guy I spotted and resolved to go visit with. Josh was sitting at a table with four couples and an empty chair. He looked alone. Like me.

There was dinner. There were drinks. And there was music. Some of the worst music I could remember from my school days. Cassie threw up her hands.

"Nobody is going to dance to any of this. We didn't dance to it when we were in school. I'll be right back," Cassie said as she headed toward the DJ. Cassie always had a strong personality. She was naturally a cheerleader. The next song the DJ played was a gentle ballad. Cassie was back at my side.

"Come on, Ari. Dance with me. We'll be teens for a while."

What she meant was that she'd wrap her arms around my neck and lay her head on my chest while I held her and we swayed to the music. Putting my arms around her, though, meant that I was holding her bare shoulder in my hand. It felt good. Really good.

"This is nice, Cassie. I don't think we ever got this close since second grade," I said.

"I used to hold your hand when we walked in the woods," she said. "Did I really hurt you, Ari? I cried when I read the scene in the woods."

"Oh, god, Cassie! Don't tell me you're reading that stuff. It's not real. It's just fantasy stuff," I said. I was a little panicked. Even my older sister had thought the things I wrote about were real. *As if.*

"I was just going to peek at it a little. I mean, it's not like I read erotic romances every day. Then you started posting that new story right after I saw you in Florida. It all seemed so familiar. So, I kept looking for new chapters. And then, there I was. I didn't recognize my character at all until Brian and Cassie started meeting in the woods to play. And suddenly I remembered you and I used to go play in the woods. Then in the story I ran away and Brian was really hurt and I was crying and I found so many memories just flooding out of my eyes. I remembered the last time we went walking in the woods. Remember those teens who saw us and called us boyfriend and girlfriend? You know, it took me a long time, but I finally figured out they'd been messing around and we interrupted them. But after that walk, I just never went back there with you again. We still played ball sometimes, but I didn't really do that very often. And I got to wondering if I really hurt you. I didn't mean to."

Wow! What a speech. The DJ went into another ballad and the dance floor was filling with couples. It was exactly the kind of music we needed. Cassie kept her arms wrapped around my neck, hugging her face to my shoulder.

"Cassie, we were eight or nine years old. I was becoming a stinky boy and you became... an even more beautiful and perfect girl. You were popular. I knew what I was. I didn't even become fully a human being until I was forty," I laughed. Cassie laughed, too.

"Silly. Nobody's human until they are at least forty. I'm so glad you let me rejoin the group. Who am I going to end up with? You? I'm dying to know." I considered and then nodded my head toward the table in the corner. Josh was sucking on a beer. It looked like everyone else at the table was on the dance floor. "Really? Josh? Hmm. He was always kind of geeky and quiet. Nice, I guess, but I never really knew him well in school. I hear his wife is really sick. Maybe dying."

"Damn. That's a shame. I'm going to talk to him. I just haven't gotten over there yet," I said.

"Ari, that reminds me of something. Please don't be offended."

"What?" I looked down at her and she raised her eyes to meet mine. I almost kissed her, but we were on a dance floor and even if no one remembered me, everyone knew Cassie.

"Uh... It wouldn't be a good idea for you to contact Hannah right now. She might think it was..."

"Oh, Cassie, please don't tell me Hannah has been reading *Heaven*. You didn't."

"She hasn't read it. But I sort of told her about it. She's still one of my best friends. I hated it when she left our school and moved to Angola."

"But she hasn't read it," I said, breathing a sigh of relief. I had no idea that a fifth and sixth grade crush could suddenly become such a devastatingly embarrassing thing at my age.

"No. But you know she always liked you. She told me she saw you at your mother's funeral. And I sort of told her that you'd written a part for her as a girlfriend of the hero in a story. I wasn't going to tell her that I'd read it because... I'm not that kind of woman, Ari. I have morals."

"Okay, so she already knew I had a crush on her in grade school. She isn't reading the story, so what's the big deal?"

"Her husband died last month," Cassie whispered. "I think Hannah would probably want to talk to you and maybe even see you sometime, but if you contact her now, so soon… She might think it was a little stalkerish."

"Shit. The poor thing. We're getting old, aren't we, Cassie?"

"Well he was a good bit older than us, but still, it was sudden and unexpected. He seemed to be in perfectly good health one day and the next he was dead. Both her parents died last year. I mean, they were in their nineties, but still. Both parents and her husband. Do you understand, Ari?"

"Of course I do, Cassie. It's not like Hannah and I are ever going to get together. I just feel bad for her. But I see what you mean about calling so soon out of the blue. I'll let it ride for a while."

"She's got a place not far from me in Florida. She's not full time, like me, but she spends a couple months there every winter. Maybe we'll all get together the next time you're down in Florida."

I sighed. The song ended and we went back to the table so Cassie could collect another dance partner. Poor Hannah. I decided to go say hi to Josh. We'd gone to different junior highs, but we'd had several classes together as freshmen. He and Carl got along great and the three of us did just about everything together that we could.

"Hey, Josh," I said, holding out my hand. "It's Aroslav." He looked at me blankly.

"I can't quite place you," he said. "Did we graduate the same year?"

"Well, we only really knew each other as freshmen. I moved away. You and Carl and I used to do all kinds of stuff." Josh kind of rocked in his chair and took another swig of beer.

"I kind of remember Carl. Sometimes we played cards in the cafeteria." He set the bottle down on the table. "Sorry I can't place you, Aroslav. I guess I'm too distracted. Marcie said I should come tonight, but I just want to go home and be with her. She'll miss it if I don't sing our song to her tonight. Excuse me." He got up and headed toward the door. I stared after him and then decided to go get another glass of wine. One of my two best friends as a freshman and he didn't remember me at all. It was too bad about his wife. I didn't get a chance to ask him what the problem was. This getting older sucks.

I did meet some other people I vaguely remembered. I even danced with a couple girls I remembered. Not enough to have made it into a story yet. I danced with Sarah. That was interesting. She just stood in front of her wheelchair while I held her hands and she bobbed back and forth a little. After that one song, she collapsed back into the chair.

"That was fun. I always loved to dance. I went to five proms! Just because boys who could dance asked me. You should have known me in high school, Ari. We'd have gotten along just great. I was kind of wild," Sarah said.

"Not Ari," Cassie laughed as she sidled up beside me. "He was perfect. He would never have done anything wild."

"Besides which," I said, "I was too low on the totem pole. You never would have noticed me. Nobody liked me."

"Ari! How can you say that?" Cassie said. "Okay. I know how you can say that, but it wasn't that nobody liked you. We were all a little afraid of you. We kind of hid everything from you."

"You thought I'd rat you out?" I asked. I'd done stupid things, but I'd never told on my friends.

"No! You wouldn't do that. It was more like we were afraid you'd disapprove. If you saw something that we did, we'd be too ashamed to go to school afterward. Do you see?" she asked.

"I was never a perfect little angel," I said, scoffing at her. "I got into just as much trouble as everyone else. I just wasn't around long enough to get caught."

"I bet I could have found his devilish side," Sarah laughed.

"I do, too," Cassie said. "Sarah, you have got to read his story about growing up here. It is just… Heavenly."

"I'm going to get such a reputation now," I said. "Among my two fans."

It was getting late and the party was beginning to break up.

"My feet are killing me," Cassie said as she took off her shoes. She was suddenly three inches shorter. I didn't remember her being that short, but I'd gotten most of my height when I was a junior. I'd always felt like a short little kid in school. Even though I was close to six feet now, I still felt like I looked up to everyone. When I finally got my driver's license my senior year, I'd told the clerk that I was five-eleven-and-a-half. He put down on my license that I was five-twelve. "Will you give me a lift to my hotel, Ari? It's over by the University." When anyone said 'university' in this area, they meant Notre Dame. I was parked almost a block away, but I offered to bring the truck around for her. She said she could walk a block if I'd let her lean on me. *Oh, hell yes.*

"Thank you for bringing me back into the story," she said once I'd helped her up into the cab of the truck. "Wow! This truck is as big inside as mine."

"You have a truck?"

"Motorhome. Class C. Built on an E-450."

"You didn't tell me that in Florida! Maybe we can meet up on the road sometime."

"I've been thinking of doing Quartzite for the big gathering in January."

"It's a blast."

"Are we going to have sex?"

I turned and looked at Cassie. Where the fuck did that come from? *Hell, yes, we could have sex.* I looked at her and still saw the fifteen-year-old I'd last seen getting off the bus next door to my house. I reached out and put an arm around her.

"Would you like to make love, Cassie?" I whispered as I moved in to kiss her.

She slapped me!

"Ari! I'm a married woman. What do you think I am?"

"But you just asked..."

"In the story, Ari. In the story." *Oh, fuck.*

"Oh. Sorry. I must have had more wine to drink than I thought. I didn't mean to offend you, Cassie." She reached out and I flinched a little as she stroked my cheek.

"Didn't mean to hit you so hard, Ari. You just surprised me. I know you must have the story all planned. I just want to know if there is going to be a hot sex scene in it that features Brian and Cassie, like the scenes in *Model Student.*"

"You read that, too?"

"I've read everything. Andy thinks our marriage has suddenly been revitalized. He's getting more sex now than he did when we were first married."

"Oh. Well, glad to be of help. I haven't gotten to the point of knowing who is going to have sex with whom. Nobody gets to have sex until they are seventeen."

"I didn't last nearly that long!"

"Maybe you can improve my sex life by telling me the story."

"I'm working on it. Tell me more."

"A few weeks ago, I wrote a scene about Brian and Cassie's first date. It was to be a couple days after your sixteenth birthday in January."

"My birthday is in June."

"It's not really you."

"Okay. What did we do on our date?" she asked. She'd taken my hand to keep me from sliding away from her and might have even slid a little closer to me after she'd soothed my cheek from the slap. My arm was still sort of around her shoulders and she didn't seem to mind, so I left it there.

"We went to dinner and a ballet."

"A ballet? On a first date? And you didn't get laid?"

"Cassie, what's got into you?" I laughed.

"About six margaritas," she sighed. "What else?"

"I introduced the 'kiss with promise,'" I said.

"What kind of promise?"

"The promise to kiss again."

"Wait a minute. They were all out at the lake and talking about kissing. I figured out the friendly kiss. We all do it all the time." She reached up and pecked my cheek. "The kiss with intent is pretty obvious. How is the kiss with promise different?"

"Well… It's soft and intimate, but not passionate," I said.

"Show me."

I looked at Cassie's face to make sure I wasn't about to get slapped again. Her eyes were closed and her lips slightly parted as she turned her face to me. I took a deep breath and kissed her.

It started with just a light brush of my lips against hers. She sighed. I paused as our lips touched again and pressed slightly into her. I brought my left hand to her cheek and stroked it softly as I gently squeezed her lips between my own. When I felt her tongue slip out to touch my lips, I pulled away. She leaned her head over on my shoulder and breathed deeply. The skin exposed by her off-the-shoulder dress was tantalizing. 'How many other women at our reunion had dared go braless?' I wondered.

"That was promising," she finally breathed. She hesitated, but then spoke again. "And exactly how does that differ from a kiss with intent? I'm sure I could feel your intentions. Naughty boy."

"Well, there's more passion…"

"Show me."

It started about the same as the first kiss, but this time, I touched Cassie's lips with my tongue and hers flicked out to meet it. I expected at any moment she would jerk back and say 'enough' but the kiss just deepened. My hand slipped from her cheek to her bare shoulder and I pulled her toward me as I gently stroked her skin. She made no move to break the kiss and, in fact, petted my cheek and head as we continued to explore each other's mouths. When my hand came across her bare shoulder to the front, she pushed away.

"Andy is going to get so fucked when I get back to Florida," she whispered. "I'd better go in while my virtue is still intact."

I scrambled out my door and around the truck to open hers, helping her down out of the cab. She leaned heavily against me as she directed me to her motel room. She got her keycard in the door and the green light went on. She pushed it open.

"Goodnight, Cassie," I said as I leaned in to kiss her again. She pushed me away.

"Ari! What are you doing?"

"I was just going to… uh… kiss you goodnight," I stumbled.

"You can't do that! I'm a married woman." She reached up and pecked me on the cheek. "There. Good night. I'll see you for brunch at eleven," she pointed at the restaurant next door that advertised Sunday brunch. She would? We were meeting in the morning? While I was still processing the information, she slipped into her room and closed the door.

I needed to get back to my trailer and rewrite that scene.

"ALL RIGHT. I want the rest of the cast list," Cassie said as we sat at the brunch table. I'd thought it was just going to be a normal brunch between old friends, but after we'd had a course of mimosas, she was right back on to the story. "Me, Hannah, Betts, Jessica, Liz. Those are easy. Carl, Josh, and Doug are easy. Who the heck are Whitney, Rhiannon, and Rose? Especially Rose! I'd almost have thought you were thinking of me when you wrote her with the cheerleader thing, but the size of her breasts obviously means you had someone else in mind. And Samantha. Who was the most beautiful woman in the world with no hair below her head? Give."

"Really, Cassie. Who doesn't want to make love to the most beautiful woman in the world? They're all just made up. I grabbed the fact we used to meet in the woods. Everything else is made up. I grabbed one little thing that happened with Jessica. Everything else is made up. It's the same with almost everyone. Rhiannon was a cute girl I met after I left St. Joe Valley. I never even dated her. Give me some credit for imagination."

"Oh, I do. I know we didn't do any of the things you wrote about, and I could only wish we'd had an agreement like the one you created.

I might have stayed a virgin longer. Maybe not. There were all those jocks," she said wistfully.

"They didn't seem to be buzzing around you last night like I expected," I said.

"They all had their wives with them. Andy gets off on the fact that Sarah and I were so wild in our teens. Most wives don't."

"Yeah. Well, you might have to learn to share with Sarah," I snickered. Cassie's eyes popped open as she stared at me.

"You're going to make me a lesbian?"

"And deprive all those guys of your favors?"

"But…"

"But you might have to share."

"All I can say is that you and I had better fuck in this story and it had better be as good as the scenes in *Model Student*." She looked at me intensely. "It's all we're going to have, Ari. Make it good."

We kept chatting and Cassie said she had some friends along my route across the country and she'd make sure I got introduced through Facebook. She admonished me to treat them well.

We parted with a hug and a friendly kiss and a promise to see each other in January at Quartzite. I neglected to tell her that I camped in the nudist area. I was sad when I got back to the trailer. The next day, I went to a picnic with cousins I hadn't seen in fifteen years and we laughed and talked about a hundred odd little events in our lives over the years. We told stories about growing up. We had a good time.

In the morning, I packed up and headed south. Mitch had promised me a place with peace and quiet on his farm for a few days, and I felt like I needed that. I had a lot to talk over with my characters and Cassie had gotten the conversation going.

They say that if you hear voices in your head and they are ignoring you, that you must be an author. If you hear voices and they are talking *to* you, you have a different kind of problem.

"Are you going to kill me, Ari?" she asked.

Kill her? How could I kill her? She was dead.

A Long Time Ago: The Most Beautiful Woman

I MET HER my junior year in college when she transferred in. Paula and I had become an institution with the expectation that we'd be married by graduation, even though our relationship was always on and off. But Samantha was the most beautiful creature I'd ever laid eyes on. And talented. She was an actress, of course. She absolutely dominated the stage at UIndy and we just knew she was going places. I wanted desperately to write the role that would win her a Tony. And she was versatile. She could play character roles as well as ingénues. We were cast together in a musical as the older parents of the young couple and got to sing a sweet duet together with a little waltz. She felt good in my arms.

"Haven't you suffered enough, Samantha?"

"You can't just let it go. It's been twenty years, Ari. You need to deal with it."

Twenty years? How can it have been so long?

Sam had a bright career ahead of her. Paula and I got married and moved to Minnesota to start our grad work. Sam headed straight for New York. Of course, she didn't land a leading role and make Broadway history. This isn't a fantasy story. Exactly. But she'd managed to start working in shows off off Broadway and became the only person I knew who had an Equity card and was earning money by acting. Not enough to live on, of course. She still had to hold down a day job, but her energy was indefatigable. Someone had stuffed a size twelve woman into a size 2 body. She dominated a room when she entered. People's heads just turned when she walked in. Like when that broker talks and people listen, rooms fell silent.

But all the time I knew her, she was also sweet and kind. She didn't seem to even realize how beautiful she was.

Well, I learned that wasn't completely true. It was a month before graduation that she came to me with an unusual request.

"Ari, I know it's not really your major thing, but I've seen some of the pictures you've taken of sets and productions and I was wondering if you'd take some pictures of me for my portfolio," she said.

"Sure, Sam. There's a lot of people with cameras that are probably better at it than I am. You sure you want me?" I asked.

"They know cameras, but you know lighting. It might sound silly, but you're really the only one I trust." It did sound a little silly. She'd been seeing Rick for most of the year and I knew he was as good a photographer as I was. He was a bit of a male prima donna, but he seemed to be smitten with Sam.

We arranged to have a photo session over the weekend in the rehearsal hall. There wouldn't be anyone around as our last show had closed. I'd been doing some work in the shop and rehearsal space to make sure it was clean and organized for the next tech director.

Rehearsal hall was all painted black and had a limited lighting set up. We did studio shows there as well as rehearsing. Studio shows were usually one acts that wouldn't draw an audience from outside the department. We could only seat about thirty. Most of the shows were done with minimal settings and lighting. Sometimes just with a few props.

In addition to acting, Samantha had done a lot of volunteer work in the costume shop. Everyone in our small department 'volunteered' in every aspect of every production. She'd selected a few costumes that she'd appeared in over the past two years and asked me to pull a few set props. She brought the camera and film and explained her concept for the shoot while we sipped a cup of coffee.

"I know I have nice color portraits in each of these costumes," she said. "But I want a set of art shots. I need to distinguish myself from the crowd when a director sees my portfolio. So, these will be in black and white." I nodded. It made sense. "Ari, do you know what I mean by art shots?" she asked.

"You mean interesting poses that might not have been actually part of a production but that show you in the best possible light," I said. I was confident that I knew what she wanted.

"Ari. Oh, god. Remember I said I trust you?" I nodded. "Some of them are going to be nude." I almost dropped the camera. "I want poses in costume, yes. But then I want artsy poses where I'm only partly in the costume or just looking at it or something. We'll work out the specifics as we go. I trust you to not tell anyone that you've taken a bunch of nude photos of me. I also trust you to tell me if a shot doesn't look right or if I'm not standing straight or if I'm showing too much of my Jill. I should have talked to you more about this before, but if you can't do it, I'm not going to do it at all."

"Samantha, how are you going to get them developed? Your pictures could end up anywhere."

"I have a friend with a dark room. He's agreed to do the processing and printing for me. He can't do the photography. He doesn't get around all that well," she said. "He's kind of old. My mother's uncle. But I can trust him."

"This might be hard," I said, "but I'll give it my best shot."

"I'm sure it will be hard, honey," she laughed. "But think of the images you'll have in your mind when you get yourself off tonight."

"You loved that day, didn't you?" she asked in my head.

"Every single minute of it. I fell in love with you that day."

"Ari, you fell in love with all of us."

The shoot was fun as well as serious. She was perfect. She was the first woman I'd ever seen who was shaved completely hairless. We didn't do spread beaver shots, so there was no gaping pussy, but there were a few that would clearly show the crease between her legs. We took photos that were clothed and photos as she stripped. I pulled out a fainting couch from the props room and she did poses that mimicked old paintings with drapes and a few props. I guess that's where the image of Tony's first painting of Melody came from in *Model Student.*

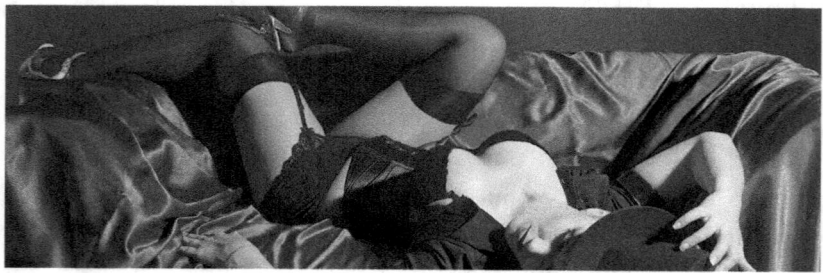

When we started, Sam had dressed in the dressing room and come to the stage area where I could set lights. By the time we finished, she was simply changing costumes right in front of me, asking me to fasten her up or to unzip her when the time came. And as I worked to manipulate the lights, she'd often just stand in the spot naked while I focused.

Just before Paula and I packed up to move to Minneapolis that summer, I had coffee with Samantha to say goodbye. She handed me an envelope.

"You probably want to keep these someplace secure," she said. "I don't want to create any problems for you and Paula, but you were so nice that I wanted you to have a few for yourself." I started to open the envelope but she stopped me. "You should do that in private, not at the Waffle House." I blushed.

I held her image in my mind as I described Samantha in LNDtH— the most beautiful woman in America.

"You still haven't dealt with it, Ari."

"I can't, Samantha. Please don't make me."

"You have to, sweetheart."

It was all so stupid. A misunderstanding. Mistaken identity. Some woman thought Sam was trying to steal her husband. She met her outside a theater stage door in Baltimore. One gunshot. Just one and she was gone. I was married to Treasure and we were expecting our child when I heard the news. Treasure put a comforting hand on my shoulder as I cried. She let me have my grief that I couldn't explain to her. I stayed up late that night, going through a storage box I had in the attic. I held the photos in my hands while I wept for Samantha.

How could I ever let that out in my story? I just wanted that beautiful, gentle creature forever in my arms. I wanted a happily ever after ending.

~~~

Back to Indiana

I STAYED CAMPED under an old sycamore tree on Mitch's farm for four days. I wrote and soothed myself. I took a field trip up to Bloomington and walked around the campus. I was particularly struck by a sculpture at the edge of Dunn Woods called *The Space Between*. I spent a long time sitting on a bench staring at it. I went to the library and was shown to a section of yearbooks with sports scores and team records. I knew now where the college years would take place in LNDtH. I didn't want to use UIndy for another novel setting. I'd already set *The Props Master 1: Ritual Reality* there. I photographed the pages of the yearbooks that had basketball and football scores and descriptions of the seasons. I went to the University archives section of the library and a very helpful archivist brought out the annual press kit for the women's and men's basketball teams for those years so I had the actual schedule, game times, scores, and players for all the games. I had a place for Lionel and for Whitney. Great!

MITCH AND I talked over dinner and drinks one night.

"I'm a farmer. I raise cattle. I read *Redtail* and I thought, 'I know these things. But I know Aroslav, too. How does *he* know these things?' When did you get so much experience on a ranch and raising cattle?"

"It's all research, Mitch. Did I tell you I called the School District Transportation Office up there to find out how long a bus ride it was for high schoolers from Centennial to the school in Laramie? Even found out about how many kids there were who made the trip. It's not just high school, but the junior high as well."

"Research. It was real enough. And horses! You didn't have horses. We had horses."

"I loved your horses! I got one when Treasure and I got married. She gave me a buckskin quarter horse for a wedding present," I said.

"Now that's fine gift. I tell you, those horses were a babe magnet. I got laid so many times in high school by taking a girl for a ride. It got to the point where I'd say something like, 'Dor and I are going for a ride,' and Dad would say, 'Oh no you aren't!' I think he discovered the secret." *Hmm. I had another scene to rewrite.*

"Well, I could imagine. Had they been my horses, my social life might have been better. Never figured out why Carl always seemed so out of it when it came to girls. He was a nice enough guy. I haven't talked to him since high school," I said.

"You're not likely to," Mitch said. He took a slug of his beer. "He still blames you for stealing his girlfriend."

"Stealing his what? Who?"

"Some girl named Georgia. None of us even knew he had a girlfriend. I mean they were in the youth group together, but I don't think he ever went out on a date. Man, did he cut loose in college. Still, he thinks you stole Georgia and he still holds a grudge."

Georgia. *Oh shit.*

A Long Time Ago: Georgia On My Mind

BEAR WITH ME. This is going to sound a little convoluted, but there's a point.

It started in biology when I was a senior in high school. Mrs. Adams began where most biology do, with one cell life forms. A cute girl in class that I'd lusted after for most of the past year answered an innocuous question by stating that all life started with single cell life forms, evolving from primeval muck.

"That's not right," Patty said. "God created each being. It says so in Genesis."

"Science is on my side," Deb answered. "Evolution is a proven process."

"Using the word 'proven' might be a bit of a stretch," Mrs. Adams said. "Evolution is a theory that we will not address in this class. Just as we will not address any theory of creation."

"It's not a theory," Patty insisted. "It's in the Bible."

"Lots of things in the Bible are metaphors," I said. "There are two completely different creation stories in the first two chapters of

Genesis. Evolution is not in conflict with religion. God just used that as a method."

"Mud," Patty said. "God created us from mud."

"I think that's just what Deb said," I answered. "She called it primeval muck."

"Class! Attention. This is not a subject we are debating on the first day of school," Mrs. Adams said.

"Could we debate it?" I asked. "Later?" Mrs. Adams thought about it a minute.

"If you have a solid presentation, I will allow each side one class period between Thanksgiving and Christmas to present their case. Patty? Will you accept leadership of the creation argument?"

"Against him? He can argue anything," Patty said.

"That's true," my friend Jon piped in. "He had Mrs. Streeter convinced that he was a recognized poet for speech contest."

"Hey! Thanks, friend," I said. "I know you haven't asked yet, but I accept the challenge to present the evolution side, Mrs. Adams."

"I want to help," Deb said.

Mrs. Adams put an end to the discussion and told us to pick our teams after class and to please pay attention while we discussed the difference between single cell animal life and single cell plant life. She also discussed the difficulties of classifying lifeforms.

And that was how I started dating Debra.

She was cute and fun and, aside from the fact that I couldn't even talk to her while she was eating, she was a great conversationalist. When Deb ate, she put all her concentration into it. She did the same the first time she gave me a blowjob.

But the upshot was that Jon and his girlfriend Carol joined Deb and me and the four of us put on a show. Jon and I both strummed guitars and Carol played piano. Deb owned, and had read, a copy of Darwin's *Origin of Species*. And that's what we called our little show. *Origin of Species: The musical.*

We combined a few show tunes, a hymn, and a skit about evolution. I'd read the script of *Inherit the Wind* and Jon and I reenacted Henry

Drummond's cross-examination of Matthew Harrison Brady. We ended the show by quoting the play. "You're absolutely right! God created man in his image. But you're looking for God too high up and too far away." I turned around and Deb shoved a big fistful of mud in my face.

Somehow, a photograph of that got into the weekly newspaper in our small town. With the caption, "Tippecanoe Valley Senior Defends Evolution." If you don't know small-town Indiana, you don't know what a controversy a statement like that could have. Indiana schools still teach creationism as fact and evolution as a theory. What I've painted in my stories as an idyllic, tolerant, community where everyone cares for everyone else is, in reality, an isolationist state where belief is far more important than truth. Our little town of Liberty—one of five towns in our school district needed to make a school big enough to qualify for tax dollars—had a population of 210 people. It had seven churches. That is an average of 30 men, women, and children per church. Two of the churches weren't large enough to hold 30 people. But all seven had sermons about creation and evolution on Sunday.

Our little drama group became much in demand. Rev. Dave had us perform at our little church on Sunday evening, but we had to do it in the church basement because the content might damage the holiness of the sanctuary. We played to a packed house, including fifteen very loud hecklers from the Bible Church. We got a call from a big church in Wabash and presented the musical there the next weekend. And so on.

Suddenly, our little drama troupe—the four of us—were being asked to perform *The Origin of Species: The Musical* almost every weekend. Many times, just for the youth group, but most of those were also attended by members of the church. And one of those weekend performances was at the very church that I left when we moved two and a half years earlier—where Carl was the president of the youth fellowship.

We went. We performed. We were asked a lot of questions by people and generally adored. There were cookies and cocoa after the performance and shuffleboard. Don't ask. There was a shuffleboard court painted on the cement in the basement and kids liked to play— or pretend to play.

And there was Georgia. Georgia attached herself to my right side when she was unable to dislodge Deb from my left. She wanted to know all about how *I* developed the show, wrote the script and music, and produced it. I am not sure she realized that there were three other people on stage. And I didn't really notice she was cutting everyone else out because I was a freshly minted eighteen-year-old, and of course it was all me that did the show.

Now, Georgia was a junior. We were seniors. She was sixteen. I was eighteen. And, she was damned cute. Skinnier than Debra. I've mentioned how Deb enjoyed food. Not that Deb was fat, but she had curves. Georgia's curves were far subtler. I figured that in a few years, she could be a real beauty, but right now, she was cute. She gave me a hug before we left for the hour-long drive home.

Jon was driving and Deb and I were in the back seat.

"You have an admirer," Deb laughed. She didn't seem offended by the attention I'd received from another girl. "Did she give you her panties?"

"Deb! What do you mean?"

"If you'd sung another song, she'd have thrown them on stage for you," she laughed. "'What inspired you, Ari?' 'How did you come up with that song, Ari?' 'Was it hard to learn to play guitar, Ari?' 'You're so creative, Ari!' I bet she's home rubbing one off, right this minute while she sighs your name."

"She didn't. She wouldn't. Was she really like that?" I stammered.

"Oh, geez, Ari. Even I could smell her," Carol laughed from the front seat. She turned to look at us and found Deb and I kissing. "If she'd done that to Jon, I'd have strangled her with her own panties."

"What's it like to be a rock star, Ari?" Jon asked. They were all teasing, even though Deb was teasing down between my legs with her fingers while they all tossed barbs at me.

"Boy, if I'd realized how girls were going to throw themselves at me when I wrote this, I'd have thought twice about having a girlfriend with me all the time," I said. I pinched Deb's nipple and she gasped.

"Yeah, but then you'd be constantly wondering if you'd make it with one of them instead of being assured of a blowjob on the way home."

"You what?" Jon exclaimed. "In the car? While I'm driving." Deb had me unzipped and was fishing in my pants even though Carol was watching over the back of the seat.

"Don't worry, Jon," she said. "I'll describe it all to you and then do a replay after we ditch them. She's got his cock out now." Jon moaned. "Keep your eyes on the road!"

Deb and I had fooled around a lot, touching and kissing, but it was the first time she gave me a blowjob. It set a new standard for the back seat of Jon's car. I had my hand under her shirt diddling her nipples the whole time.

"I bet she calls you," Deb said, popping off my cock before I popped. "You should definitely do her."

"I have all I need right here," I sighed. Deb kissed me and went back to sucking.

It was only a week until Georgia called me. There was a Valentine Dance at her school and she wanted to know if I'd take her. I almost said no, but then what Deb said slipped into my mind. My entire freshman year in high school, I'd tried unsuccessfully to get a date to a school dance. It would be like returning victorious.

Deb reiterated that I should go.

"You should go and give her the time of her life. We're young and we haven't decided to spend our lives together," Deb said. "You should totally have some other experiences. Only don't fuck her. Anything we've done together, you can do with her, but nothing else. Is that fair?"

"I should be taking you out for Valentine's Day," I weakly protested.

"I think Carol and I will give Jon a little thrill." *Oh shit!* I could only imagine. But fair was fair. I called Georgia and told her I'd take her.

The dance wasn't formal, but I wore a suit. I had a nice corsage for Georgia. She wore a strapless party dress that stopped about mid-thigh. Since it only started about six inches below her neck, the dress itself didn't cover all that much. She giggled as I pinned the corsage on. My fingers were against something very soft.

And modest. I said she wasn't as curvy as Deb. She had very nicely shaped small breasts. They were soft when I held her in my arms at the dance. I honestly don't remember seeing anyone else I knew. I guess everyone changed over the past two-and-a-half years.

Georgia was still in full hero-worship mode and I fell for it. We left the dance just before midnight and I took her home. We sat in the drive kissing until her mother flicked the porch lights.

"You can come in," Georgia said. "Mom said we could make out in the living room if we wanted. I just need to be inside by midnight to meet curfew."

I didn't have a curfew, and even though it was an hour drive home for me, I could stay out all night if I wanted. I went in the house with Georgia. We sat on the living room sofa with a dim lamp on and kissed. And kissed. I started to move a hand over her breast and she wiggled around a little, but eventually let me gently squeeze her.

Apparently, strapless gowns don't depend on the breasts to hold them up. This one had a wire or plastic framework that held it in place. Which meant that it wasn't tight against her breasts either. From my angle, looking down to kiss her, I suddenly realized I could see right down the front of the dress. Those perfectly shaped little breasts were capped with delicious-looking reddish nipples that I wanted to suck as soon as I saw them. I returned to the kiss with vigor and my hand moved up off the fabric and then back down beneath it.

"Oh! Ari! You shouldn't," Georgia said. "I shouldn't let you." She was squirming around as if she was going to push my hand away, but the squirming opened the gap between her breast and the dress further and my hand slipped down to cup that sweet tit in my palm. Georgia squeaked and slammed her mouth against mine, sucking my tongue in and making me believe she would have me for a late dinner. I pinched her little nipple and I think she came.

That was the only conclusion I could draw. After she panted and squeaked into my mouth she struggled away and stood up. She was panting and squeezing her eyes shut and open again. I wondered if it was the first time she'd had an orgasm. It really didn't seem like it was me she was startled by.

"You… uh… you need to go now," she said. "I can't take you to bed with Mom in the next room. Oh, my god! That's all I'm going to think of for the rest of the night. Go quick, Ari. Oh wow! I think I love you."

If there were ever words to make me go quick, those would do. I grabbed my jacket and headed for the door. Georgia caught me there and slammed her mouth into mine again. I was eighteen and had no practical sense at all, except that Deb had given me permission to do anything with Georgia that I'd done with her. As I bent down to kiss Georgia, I reached my hand down and slid it under her skirt and up the back of her leg to cup her butt and squeeze her close to me. She gasped and pushed me out the door.

"Wait!" she said as I was turning to leave. I looked at her. Her hands went under her skirt and came out sliding her panties down her legs. "Here!" she said. She threw them at me and closed the door. It was like I got hit in the face with a wet washcloth.

Very fragrant.

I went home with a raging hard-on and a pair of panties held against my face. When I got home, I lay with the panties on my pillow while I rubbed off a giant-size come.

~~~~~

Back to Indiana

"I HAD NO idea she was Carl's girlfriend," I said.

"I'm not sure *she* had any idea," Mitch agreed.

"Well, if it's any consolation, he dodged a bullet on that one. She was a stalker. She actually followed me to college," I said. "The dorm monitor was a friend and during an inspection found her mirror covered with photos of me and hearts drawn in lipstick. It took another crazy woman to resolve the problem. It was damned frightening."

"Life is strange," Mitch mused. "I'd suggest to him that he read *Living Next Door to Heaven*, but he really doesn't have much sense of humor. He's a real liberal."

"Well we have that in common. You ever hear anything from Jessica?"

"Oh yeah. She and her husband were up to visit about four years ago. It was while my wife was still alive. She is just as much a tease now as she was when we were kids."

"I should have used a different name in the story."

"The story? You mean the Jessica in that story is *our* Jessica? You're kidding. She's pretty, but she was never going to be a model. She teaches math at a school in Western Kentucky. When she came to Purdue, we finally made it a few times," Mitch said. "She liked sex almost as much as me."

"I wish I'd been a couple years older," I sighed.

"Even when she and Brett were here to visit, she was jumping on my lap and rubbing my shoulders. At one point, she leaned down and whispered in my ear, 'It's a good thing Brett and Jane are here or we'd be naked.' She's still a good looking woman, too. I'd never have thought that was who was in the book, though. Heaven? Well, I guess I could see it. I'd still get naked with her, just for fun."

〜〰〰⌒

I HITCHED THE rig and headed north back to U.S. 20 and my continued trip west the next morning. I camped at Indiana Dunes State Park for a couple days and was amazed that even in August, Lake Michigan could freeze your feet in a half-mile walk along the beach. But I'd dipped my toes on the North coast.

I wrote furiously. I had new scenes to include in the book. I went back and added a scene about Elaine and Brian spending a day at the beach. I had plenty of experience with that. And then suddenly Nicki popped up in the story. That's the way my brain works. The way my head works. Get reminded of Georgia the stalker and crazy Nicki makes an appearance in my daydreams. As I headed West for my rendezvous with Alice, Nicki became the focus of a whole subplot in *Living Next Door to Heaven*.

I was going to have to do some more thinking about Nicki.

Later.

7 Buffaloed

2 August 2014

EVERY DAY was taking me closer to the nineteen-year-old stripper, Alice. There's no fool like an old fool. I was sure I was the King of Fools. I was amazed at what an important focus of my journey Alice had become, but I was determined to enjoy every day for itself. That included meeting my old friend Stan at Brookfield Zoo in Chicago. He was one of the younger guys I'd worked with a few years ago, and I'd been a mentor in the office. We walked around the zoo and I got the scoop on the fact that he had fallen in love and that he was in training to become an EMT. I figured he'd be good at it.

"How did you meet Roberta?" I asked.

"Gaming. We were at a LARP in Arkansas and kind of fell in love while hunting a magic ruby," he said.

"What is a LARP?" I asked.

"Live action role playing. It's a game. We have a big one in Wisconsin about every two years. Takes a week. I'm a game master for a weekend LARP that I host in downtown Chicago twice a year," he explained. "You should try it. I bet you'd be good."

"Sounds interesting, but I can't imagine it."

～～～

I TOOK ANOTHER detour south of the highway in eastern Nebraska. Not terribly far, but I met a fan in Fremont. That was quite a trip for me since I'd chosen Fremont out of thin air as Tony's hometown in *Model Student*. Bob showed me some of the places that I'd written about—not terribly accurately. He pointed out one gravel road to me that was just west of town.

"I figure Tony lived about a mile or two down that road," Bob said. "Heck, when the story came out and Tony visited his parents out here,

I drove up and down nearly every road out here trying to figure out which one was his."

"It's fiction, Bob."

"Oh, I know that. I eventually realized that the location wasn't a real spot, but you wouldn't believe the number of old farmsteads out here that match what you described. It was fun to just imagine that I might bump into Tony and Lissa and Melody and Kate and Wendy as I was walking down the street. I even joined the Y to try to get fit," he laughed. "Not like I actually expected to see them there. But it was a motivator. Might not look like it, but I've lost forty pounds."

Another unexpected result of writing erotic fiction.

⌒⌒⌒

WHEN I GOT to Wyoming, I still had a few days left before I was supposed to meet Alice. As much as I wanted to hurry things up, I knew that getting to Yellowstone a week early wouldn't mean seeing her a week early. And there was something else about Wyoming.

Redtail.

I'd never been to Laramie, Wyoming. But I'd written an entire book set there. Like I told Mitch: Research.

⌒⌒⌒

Not So Long Ago: An Erotic Paranormal Romance Western Mystery

A FEW YEARS ago, *The Gutenberg Rubric* won an award. I received almost as much money from the award as I did from sales the next year. Don't let anyone tell you selling books is profitable. It's a good thing that's not why I do it. But I did start to get more involved with the writers' association and ended up volunteering to help with the annual literary contest.

That help included getting together with the other category chairpersons to sort competition entries and distribute them to the various readers. It was a social event for those of us who were volunteers. Most of us were writers and when writers get together, they talk and tell stories.

One of the topics that came up was genres. We were separating the manuscripts into categories. Occasionally, we would make a joke about someone's title and say something like, "Sounds like sci fi instead of romance."

That led to a discussion on genres and genre-mashing which led me to jokingly say, "I think next year I'll write an erotic paranormal romance western mystery."

Never joke with the universe.

I'd no more than said it than I knew what the basic concept of the story was. I just needed a place for it to happen and a cast of characters.

Enter Laramie Wyoming Bell.

I'd spent a summer at a college prep school in Colorado at the urging of Joy. I probably mentioned it before. Joy didn't spend any time urging me to go, but she went to a college prep school in the East in the summer and she was the coolest, so I figured that's what I needed to do. I found one with a playwriting course and enrolled.

Of course, playwriting wasn't the only thing offered and there were about 150 students enrolled for the summer. You couldn't possibly know and talk to all of them. That was the summer of Sue and hiking and getting lost in the desert. One of the other students—I'm sure she was a senior, or maybe even a grad—was a regal dirty blonde whose very presence would make me choke up. I wasn't in her presence much, but I knew who she was.

She was Laramie Wyoming Bell.

I never spoke to her all summer long. I just admired her. I admired the way she walked, what she looked like at the pool, and the way she handled her horse in the arena. She didn't seem stuck up or anything, and didn't flaunt her beauty, but she just carried herself like a queen.

The story I heard was that she was some Cheyenne mucky-muck's daughter. As soon as I'd thought of setting *Redtail* in Wyoming, I thought of Laramie.

~~~~

Back to Laramie

I SPENT THREE days in the wind, camped at Laramie. I drove out to Centennial and fell in love with the Bear Claw Café. I talked with folks there and gave them a copy of *Redtail* to share around. It was the only one of my erotic adventures I'd had made into a paperback at the time.

I took a day to walk back and forth across the campus of the University of Wyoming and promptly became a Cowboys fan. Not Dallas. The *real* Cowboys of UWyo. While I was there, I stopped in the library to see where you could get a view across campus from the upper stories. And that took me to the rare books section and the University's historical archives. I gave the librarian my card and told her that I'd written a book set in Laramie, some of it back in the 1880s. She asked for the name of the book and I had to tell her that it was published under a different author name. She tapped a few keys on her keyboard and said, "Oh, yes. We have a copy. Ordered it as soon as it came out. I haven't read it, but I will. Are you thinking of doing a sequel?"

I hadn't been, but now I was. I left Laramie and started north toward Cody with the idea for *Blackfeather* brewing in my head.

~~~

I CAMPED AT Wapiti, just at the eastern edge of Yellowstone. I spent my first night cleaning the trailer from top to bottom and the next morning went back into Cody for supplies. I was as nervous as a teenager getting ready for his first date. When my phone chimed, I almost dropped it.

"Ari, are you here?"

"I'm here, darlin'. Here being in Cody. Where can I meet you?" I said.

"I'm stopped at the tourist info on the west edge of town. How soon, Ari? How soon can I see you?" she said.

"I'm at the grocery store. I'll be there as soon as I finish checking out. Can't wait to see you, babe." Oh, that was suave. 'Babe'? What kind of cool dude was I supposed to be? I finished paying for the groceries and headed toward the tourist info center across from the Buffalo Bill Museum. After I parked, I stepped out of the truck and looked around nervously. I wasn't sure what to expect. I didn't even know what Alice drove.

"I'd recognize that big black truck anywhere," her voice said from behind me. I turned. She wrapped her arms around me and brought her lips to mine. "Kiss me, Ari. I've been waiting a fucking year for this."

Alice was beautiful. I've described her. She's tall and in her cowboy boots, she had to bend her head to meet my lips. When we broke, I tried to keep my eyes focused on hers. But… She had a western chambray shirt on—mostly. The sleeves had been torn off completely and instead of snapping it closed she had it tied beneath her unencumbered breasts. She wore cutoff shorts that were long enough to cover her butt ledge, but left the pockets hanging down below the ragged fringe. From there, her smooth bare legs extended down and into the tops of her bright red cowboy boots. I tilted my head under her cowboy hat and welcomed her lips again.

The skin at her waist was so smooth and the kiss so warm and welcoming that I was afraid we might get arrested if we let it go any further.

"Wow! God, Ari! Maybe we should do something to cool off and get used to each other before we get closed in a small space together. We might never come out otherwise," she said. I shifted and stuck a hand in my pocket to move my hard-on to a more comfortable position. "Keep that thing handy. We'll need it later," she whispered.

After a few minutes' debate, we decided to just go across the street to the Buffalo Bill Museum. It was cool and we spent a long time in the Smithsonian Firearms exhibit. I discovered Alice knew a lot more about firearms than I did, though I did find an example of the Smith & Wessons that Cole used. When I told Alice that I needed to find a good example of an 1860s revolver that a woman could easily handle, she found the Colt Navy that I'd ultimately include in *Blackfeather*.

"Did Buffalo Bill really live here?" she asked as we went through the historical section about 'Buffalo Bill's Wild West and Congress of Rough Riders of the World.'

"Oh, yes. The town is named after him. A number of years ago, on my first trip through, I stayed at a ranch out west of here that was still owned by one of his descendants." I didn't say how long ago. It was before my daughter was born and Alice was younger. I didn't want to dwell on that.

I asked her if she wanted to stay in town for dinner or go out to the campground and grill the steaks I'd purchased and put in my cooler before I met her. She got quiet and then said that she'd like to have the steak. She also said that she'd follow me out to the campground in her own car. I figured she'd drive out. I can't imagine what had to be going through a teenager's mind as she followed an old man to a remote campsite to spend a week with him. We'd had several phone chats over the past year—some pretty explicit. But it was different being face-to-face.

She pulled in behind the trailer when I pointed it out to her and I pulled the truck in front of it. I didn't want her to have the impression that I was blocking off her escape route. Or mine.

I unlocked the trailer and took the cooler inside to put things in the fridge. I turned around to find her just inside the doorway sort of peeking at the layout. She seemed nervous.

"Ari," she said, backing out of the trailer as I came toward her. We stepped outside.

· "What is it, hon?"

"I know the rules, but could we not get naked right away? Do you mind?"

"Alice, you know I made that rule up just for Angie. I'm not going to make you be naked all the time. In fact, I'm not even ready to be inside the trailer. It's hot in there. There are no RV hookups out here, so no air conditioning. It's cooler outside. Let me light a fire and we'll sit out where it's comfortable and look at the flames," I said.

"Oh, Ari. It's not that I'm not *interested* and excited. But... I just don't want to feel like a stripper. Do you understand?" she asked. Yeah. I could see that.

I got the firewood out of the back of the truck and Alice helped get it started. We used a match, but I kind of felt she was hot enough to start a fire just by touching it. I pulled a can of sparkling water out of the cooler for each of us and we sat in front of the fire just getting reacquainted. I really *did* understand how she felt. It wasn't just an empathic understanding. I was more than twice her age—I wasn't saying how much more—and this was significantly different than either Angie or Becky. I had already grown to care for Alice through our correspondence and occasional phone calls. I wanted whatever we were going to do to work for us and be something—I didn't know what—something that was more than a weeklong fling.

~~~~~

A Long Time Ago: Canoe Camp

I'D BEEN DOING an internship at what the churches called 'Summer Institute' after I graduated from high school. I assisted the director of theater at the institute in whatever stuff he needed to have done. High school students cycled in and out of the institute for a week at a time with a different group each week. There's another story there for later. We got to the end of the last week of the institute and the conference director of camping came running into the theater calling for me. I got off my ladder and joined him.

"Ari, we've got a situation. I know you'd normally be taking a vacation now so you're fresh before classes start in a couple of weeks, but one of my counselors for the junior high camp just went into the hospital to have his appendix removed. I hate to ask this, but could you do a week of rough camping with these kids? You'd have an experienced co-counselor. And I know you've done primitive camping before," he said. He'd rushed all the way through the speech and I was thinking I could do that. He looked desperate. But what was I going to do otherwise? Deb had moved out east almost as soon as we graduated and started with a summer session at Wellesley. My parents had moved again to help get my baby sister into a better school system, so there was no home where I knew people. I said sure.

I swung by my parents' house long enough to change from theater gear to camping gear and Sunday at noon, I pulled into the camp.

I met my co-counselor, Ruth, as soon as I checked in. *Oh. My.* What do I know? Maybe I was just eighteen and horny. Deb and I had to part before we ever got around to consummating our love affair. We both knew we'd never get around to it now. The graduation blowjob was the last of the relationship. *Damn, I miss her.*

Ruth was as short as Deb but at least twenty pounds lighter. Everywhere except in her boobs. Those were tucked neatly into a lifeguard-style one-piece swimsuit. She wore a pair of shorts over this. She had short blonde hair in what I'd almost have called a man-cut if it weren't for the bangs. The sides were trimmed up over her ears.

"Thank god you got here before the urchins," Ruth said. "And thank you for coming to our rescue this week. I about died when Rob took sick Thursday and we had to get him out of here in an ambulance."

"Nice to meet you," I said. "I'm Ari."

"Oh. Sorry. I'm Ruth. Rob and I have worked this camp all summer, so we really knew everything about each other. You and I are going to have to learn as we go. How are your canoe skills?" she asked. *Canoe? No one said anything about a canoe.*

"Well, I can paddle, but most of my rough camping has been on land. I'm good at that," I said.

"If you can make a fire with wet wood and no matches we'll be fine. Last week we got rained on and had to depend on a single burner camp stove for two days. I was sure that was what triggered Rob getting sick, but they told me it was his appendix," she said.

She grabbed a backpack and I shouldered mine as she led me down to the shore. She tossed hers down and I put mine beside it. "Let's go up to the lodge and cart our supplies down. We've got five girls and three boys this week. That works out well. When there is an even number, they tend to pair up and then you end up chasing them all over the woods. We'll have five canoes. Can you handle a canoe by yourself? I never trust the supplies to a camper on the first day out. It's better if you and I each paddle a canoe loaded with packs and supplies. We'll put the three boys in a canoe and split the five girls between the other two canoes. Tomorrow we'll have more time on the lake for training."

"I'll try not to let you down," I said. I grabbed up the packs that contained food while she dragged a tarp with tents on it. We packed the counselor canoes as we got better acquainted. She told me what her signals were for both time on the water and time in camp. I could see she was as well-organized for the canoe camp as I had been with the theater institute and I just followed her lead and agreed to everything. She'd done all this before.

At two o'clock, the campers started arriving and by three o'clock, we had all our eight in their swimming suits and down by the canoes for orientation. I could see trouble forming right away. Three of the girls were in two piece suits and one of those definitely counted as a bikini. The boys practically had their tongues hanging out. Ruth was cool. She handed out camp t-shirts to everyone and told them to put them on before they got sunburned. She had gym shorts that would fit each of the girls and told them that the canoes had aluminum seats that had been sitting in the sun. They would have blisters on their butts if they didn't cover them. The boys were disappointed to see the flesh disappear, but I figured we hadn't seen the end of it. These were kids between twelve and fourteen. There would be hormones.

Ruth explained the rules. Everyone got their lifejackets on and we launched our canoes. The first thing the boys did was roll their canoe. I was glad Ruth and I had the supplies. It was five o'clock by the time we made camp—only about half a mile from the lodge beach.

This was where I excelled. We had tents set up, sleeping bags unrolled, and a fire burning by five-thirty. We started having fun.

Of course, the kids wanted to stay up late on their first night at camp, but when I let the fire die and then poured water on the coals, they all got the message and went to bed. We had two girls' tents on one side and one boys' tent on the other. Ruth's and my tent was in the middle. I was surprised when I found out we were sharing a tent.

"It's a safety thing," Ruth said. "Not only do we have to keep the boys and girls separated like their parents expect, but we can't risk being alone with a camper. Having a camper accuse one of us of improper behavior toward them would end the entire program, even if we managed to avoid prosecution."

Shit! I did not like the sound of that at all. And I really didn't mind sharing a tent with Ruth. I was getting my sleeping bag rolled out, figuring I'd probably lie on top of it since it was still hot out. At least we didn't have hiking boots to stow. We only had our water shoes. I turned to ask Ruth if we had a tent check for the kids planned and found her topless. I stared. Ruth caught me.

"Oh. Sorry. Go ahead and look. I bared 'em, you stared 'em. I'm so used to tenting with Rob that I didn't think about how it might look to you. I sleep in a t-shirt and panties. Believe me, you'll want to be in something besides your swim trunks when you bed down." She pulled a t-shirt on and then pulled her suit the rest of the way off. It wasn't like she was showing me her slit or anything, and it was dark so I couldn't even tell the color of the little tuft of hair I saw, but just the fact that we were in a small tent meant that we weren't going to hide much from each other. She put her panties on and stretched out on her sleeping bag.

What the hell? I pulled off my trunks and put a pair of cutoff sweats on that I sometimes slept in if there was a reason. I hadn't had to all summer, but I figured I'd need to jump out of bed in the middle of the night if anything happened and it was better not to run around camp naked.

Ruth sighed.

"You take the boys' side and I'll take the girls' side. Just a quick reminder to them to take a buddy and their toilet paper if they need to get up in the night," she said. She crawled out the tent flap and I followed, close behind her shapely rear. We went to our charges' tents and quietly spoke the instructions. They all murmured their assent and I figured the guys, at least, were asleep before I finished my own trip to the latrine. I went back into the tent where Ruth was already stretched out on her sleeping bag.

"You didn't take a buddy to the latrine," she laughed softly.

"Oh. I... Um..."

"I'm teasing, Ari. Get some sleep. We'll be up with the sun. If it gets cold during the night, you might wake up to find me cuddled up next to you. Try not to grope too much. We're adults and we've got eight little responsibilities asleep outside," she said.

"I think we'll have a good time this week, Ruth. I'm glad I agreed to come along," I said. I was more tired than I realized and was off to sleep in minutes.

I did wake up to find Ruth cuddled against me and pulled a light-weight blanket over us. Then I went back to sleep until daybreak brightened the tent and I heard Ruth moving outside. She was already dressed in her swimsuit.

We had a great week. We spent most of Monday on the lake teaching the kids how to recover if their canoe was swamped, how to get into a canoe from the water without tipping it over, how to paddle and jay-stroke. We were less rushed and the campfire included storytelling and singing. We paddled to our rendezvous with the truck on Tuesday and were taken to the Pigeon River. We were on the river for three days, moving our camp and just having a blast. We were taken back to the lake on Friday and camped back at our base, then packed everything Saturday morning, policed the campground, and paddled back to the lodge. At one o'clock, after the only meal we ate at the lodge, parents arrived to retrieve their tanned and tired kids. I grabbed my pack and piled it into the back of the car.

"Can I get a lift to Fort Wayne?" Ruth called.

"Sure. It's a little car, but there's plenty of room." Ruth didn't have much. She'd been at the camp for eight weeks and only had one backpack. "Boy, you sure pack light," I laughed.

"A couple swimsuits and some panties don't take much room. It's not like I could get up every morning and rush into the bathroom to put on a ton of makeup. So, are you headed for school now?" she asked.

"Orientation starts Thursday. I'll check into the dorm on Wednesday. It's kind of exciting," I said.

"You'll love college. I've got another year, but I'm taking a break before I finish."

"Really? You'll stop right before you graduate? Isn't that kind of risky?"

"I can take a break year without triggering repayment of student loans," Ruth said. "It's a special program that continues to list me as enrolled while I'm doing a field practicum. If I wait till after I graduate, I have to start repaying loans."

"What are you going to do?"

"Backpack around the world."

"No way! By yourself?"

"I'm starting off with a girlfriend on Labor Day. We'll fly to New Zealand first, but then we're heading to Australia and from there to India. She can only go until Christmas, so I hope to have made enough contacts and friends to plan my next stage from there. I'm used to living out of a backpack," she said.

"It's just…" I thought about the kind of an adventure I could have hiking around the world. "I want to do that," I said firmly. Yeah. I wanted to backpack around the world. I'd do it with Ruth if there was an invite.

"Ari, you've got to make a big decision in your life. You've got to decide if you really want to *do* that, or if you want to *dream* about doing it. It's not an easy thing to be on your own and alone. Believe me," she said. I'd lose track of that advice in the future, but eventually, I'd decide if I was a doer or a dreamer.

"I guess I'll get a year of college under my belt first. I sure had fun with you this week, Ruth."

"I loved working with you and having you sing in the evening and tell stories. The kids loved you. And I appreciate that you were respectful. It was kind of nice to wake up in your arms when it got cold at night," she laughed. "Even with you hand on my tit and your cock rubbing my ass." That had been an embarrassing morning, but Ruth had laughed it off and told me I could expect the same treatment. "Ari, under different circumstances, if we got together without the responsibility of all those kids, I might have been interested in… you know… in finding out if we were more compatible. Me being a little older and ready to run off around the world doesn't make it an option. Not to mention that you've got your own adventure ahead of you in college this fall. Maybe our paths will cross again someday. But even if they don't, know that you made a friend this week. I'll always cherish that."

～～⌒

Back to Alice

ALICE AND I talked. Oh, I still appreciated looking at her tall slender body, and she didn't object to my eyes straying into her cleavage, but we really did talk. You might assume that an older guy doesn't have much he can talk about with a young woman. I mean, what do we have in common? But Alice wasn't into pop culture, so I didn't have to listen to her rave about some boy band or actors I'd never heard of. Her tastes in music, because of her profession, tended to be things with a strong, driving, and sensuous beat.

She dug right in to help prepare vegetables to grill with the steak and was suitably impressed with my method of grilling corn on the cob. I don't husk it and try to clean the silk out or wrap it in tin foil. I toss it on the grill still sealed in its natural husk. When it is done, I cut off the stalk end and grip it with my Ove-Glove. Then I can just shake the corn right out of the husk, silk and all. Alice got into it and I scooped butter off her chin that had run from the corn. The steaks were perfect. I had zucchini on the grill, seasoned with Italian herbs and covered with Parmesan cheese. I poured wine from a box and she laughed, asking what vintage it was. It wasn't legal for her to have alcohol. Technically, I didn't think it was legal to have it in the National Forest, even though they never object to having it in your RV.

Mostly, our conversations were philosophical. That seemed to cut across the age difference like a knife.

"I'm not into Christianity," she said. "Too much condemnation. Same with all the religions. Muslims don't recognize Jews as the chosen people. Jews don't recognize Jesus as messiah. Protestants don't recognize the Pope as the head of the church. Baptists don't recognize each other when they come to Roxie's Foxes." I laughed at her. She had the kind of worldly sense of humor that I'd always enjoyed. "Can I sit on your lap, Ari?" she asked out of the blue. Well, the one luxury that I've carried with me on this trip has been my oversized camp chair. I've even slept in it overnight and Angie and I used to cuddle in it while we were together. I opened my arms and Alice flowed into them. She kicked her boots off and curled up in my lap.

Alice is as tall as I am. It was easy to think of a couple of the tall girls that I'd written about. I wondered why I named them all Whitney. But the one thing that impressed me most, was Alice's ability to curl up in a little ball in my lap. She was like having a kitten. A very sexy, silky smooth kitten.

She didn't wiggle around or make like she was doing a lap dance. We didn't kiss. I just held her in my arms and enjoyed her closeness as we kept talking.

"I think life is about seeking enlightenment," she said. "You need to 'know thyself', as it says at the Temple of Apollo. Self-knowledge."

"I don't know," I said. "I've met myself. I wasn't that impressed."

"I was."

"I'm so glad," I whispered. I pressed my face into her hair and just inhaled. I gave her a little squeeze. "The concept of self-enlightenment has always impressed me as being a little… masturbatory."

"Ari!" Alice giggled in my lap. "What do you mean?"

"Think of it. It's focusing on yourself. What's in you? It's a solo endeavor. I like masturbation as much as any other guy. I'm alone most of the time. I'm experienced at it. It feels good. But it doesn't make babies. It doesn't even connect me with another person. It's all in my head."

"And in your balls," Alice laughed.

"Yeah. The thing is that for a lot of people, making love continues to be an act of masturbation because they are focused inside. A true narcissist can make love to a woman and hate every bone in her body except his own. Seeking self-enlightenment is similarly focused inside."

"So, you think we should seek enlightenment through other people?" she asked.

"I'm not sure *enlightenment* is that important. Why do you want to become enlightened?"

"To have peace."

"Why? What's so important about having peace?"

"To be a better person."

"Why? What makes you want to be a better person?"

"Because I believe we are here for more than our own pleasure. I believe we are here to improve humanity."

"Presto! You're enlightened," I laughed.

"What?"

"When you get down to the statement that starts 'I believe,' you are down to your true faith. Now enlightenment is no longer about having peace. It is about making the world a better place. Your self-enlightenment is no longer focused inside you. You aren't masturbating any longer."

Alice snuggled in my lap and we watched the fire as it burned down. The sun had set. Occasionally, she would giggle a little and whisper "Masturbation." Later she'd find something completely different to be amused about and whisper "Lap dances." She wasn't really talking to me. We were just enjoying being close to each other. I could sit in front of the fire like this all night with her in my arms. The problem with that, of course, was that the fire was dying and to build it up again, we'd have to get up. When the sun had gone down, the temperature had started to drop as well. The elevation was over 6,000 feet, and even though it was eighty-five degrees during the day, it still got into the fifties at night.

"I'm cold," she said, curling into an even tighter ball. I had her bare legs beneath one arm and the other was wrapped around her back where the shirt rode well up above her waistband. Of course, my first reaction was to rub that exposed skin to improve the circulation and warm her up. "Um… that's nice, Ari, but I think I need to go in and warm up." We laughed.

I picked her up as we got out of the chair because she'd taken her boots off, and carried her to the door of the trailer. Once it was open, I set her inside, thankful once again that the trailer was built low and I didn't have to lift her too high.

"I'll get your boots and put out the fire," I said. "If it's cooled down enough in the trailer, turn off the fan over the bed. We can probably sleep with the windows still open." I pointed out the bathroom and the bottles of drinking water, and left to douse the fire. When I was sure the embers were dead and had checked to make sure we hadn't left any food scraps around, I grabbed her boots and went into the trailer. "I think it might get chilly tonight," I said. "Might even rain by the smell of it." My folk wisdom and weather sense faltered when I saw Alice. She stood by the table with her suitcase open on the bench seat. She was setting her toothbrush and toothpaste on the table.

And she was naked.

"Alice? I said you didn't have to get naked, honey."

"I said I didn't want to feel like a stripper, Ari," she smiled. "Not that I didn't want to be naked with you." She gave me a soft kiss. "I'm going to brush my teeth. Take your clothes off and get ready for bed, baby."

A tear was leaking out of my right eye and I wiped it away. She was just so damned beautiful. I considered taking a little blue pill and rejected the idea. What would happen would happen. I grabbed my toothbrush and used the kitchen sink. I folded my clothes as I took them off and stuck them in the closet. I'd show Alice the empty drawer for her things in the morning. The bed suddenly looked awfully small. It wasn't like I hadn't slept with anyone in this bed before. But I just hoped she'd be comfortable and debated whether we should each use a blanket folded in half for extra warmth, or if we should stack the two blankets to cover us both. I was second guessing everything and finally just threw myself down on the bed and stretched out where I usually did, slightly right of center.

When I realized that, I snorted at myself thinking that I should be slightly left of center to be true to myself. Then I muttered "masturbation" just as the bathroom door opened and Alice crossed the four steps to the edge of the bed. I started to get up to give her room and she pushed me down with one hand as she crawled into the bed and over me, pausing long enough to give me a kiss and then slide down onto the mattress beside me. Mostly beside me. Her left arm draped over my chest and her left leg twined with mine.

"Even cuddled together, we're going to need a blanket," she sighed. I hugged her and then lifted enough to tug one of my two blankets up from the foot of the bed to cover us.

"There's another where this one came from if we need it," I whispered. I flicked off the light and Alice kissed my chest before wiggling up to reach my lips. We had a long, sensuous, but not overly passionate kiss.

"I'm going to love sleeping with you," she said around a yawn.

I kissed her head and held her in my arms as we went to sleep.

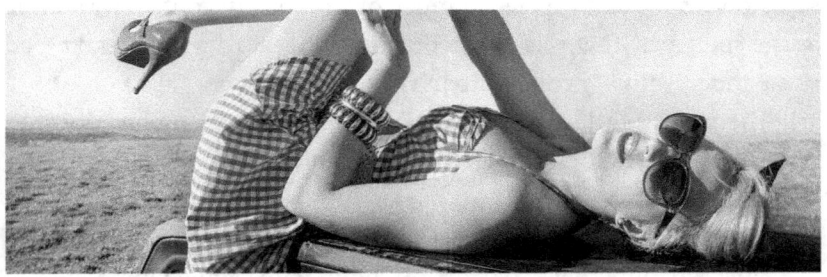

MY EYES POPPED open at five just like always. It no longer seemed to make any difference what time zone I was in. I woke up at five every morning. It was different today, though. Today, I didn't want to get out of bed. I didn't want to make coffee. I didn't want to write. I just wanted to lie here with this beautiful creature in my arms. Ultimately, my bladder won out and I slipped out of the bed and out of her arms. Alice rolled over away from me and stayed asleep. Much though I regretted it, I pulled the blanket up over her bare ass. To keep her warm.

After I came out of the bathroom, I set water on the stove to boil and prepared my coffee pot. While I waited, I opened my computer and realized I was out of range for my cellular hotspot. No bars. I started typing, just jotting down some ideas and then working on a scene. It was the first time I'd ever written a scene where two guys were involved with two girls all together at the same time. Carl, Brenda, Louise, and Brian. I kept dragging out the writing. I normally could write three or four thousand words a day without a problem. But I kept pausing in the middle of hot sex scenes and putting the computer aside. I kind of felt that if I dragged out writing the scene, the characters would enjoy it longer.

Brenda's incredibly flexible legs spread so wide that I sank another inch into her and we drove each other into an ecstasy of come that lasted most of the night.

I stopped there and let them enjoy their 'ecstasy of come' while I made coffee. When it was done, I filled the thermos—no microwave to heat cold coffee when dry camped—took my cup back to bed with me, and propped the laptop on my knees. The slight movement of the bed must have triggered a subliminal message in Alice's brain as she rolled back toward me and wiggled as much of her body in contact with mine as she could get. That was distracting. I read what I'd written and typed one handed with my coffee cup in the other.

There was a little nip at my elbow as I typed and I looked down to see Alice, still with her eyes closed, but smiling.

"Is there coffee for me?"

"Sure is," I said. "I'll get you a cup."

"Just stay put. I have to pee. I can pour coffee while I'm up."

"If you say so," I said. I pulled the laptop back out of the way and held my coffee cup aside so she didn't bump it as she crawled over me to get out of bed. Bits of her scraped against bits of me as she moved and I watched with pleasure as she minced four steps to the bathroom.

I looked at what I'd written, saved it, and closed the laptop. In a couple of minutes, the toilet flushed. Water ran. Alice came out of the bathroom.

"I honestly don't think I can shower in there," she said. "Even alone. And certainly not with you."

"We'll find a way. There's an outdoor shower, too."

"Ooo, kinky. Cups?" I pointed to the cabinet and she opened it and found a coffee mug. She didn't have to reach up very high, but just lifting her arms above her shoulders did wonderful things for her profile. She poured her coffee and turned. "Milk in the fridge?"

"Bought a little carton of half and half for you. It's in the door."

"You'll make me fat." I didn't think there was much chance of that. I set my coffee cup down on the headboard where there's a shelf and took her cup so she could crawl over me to get back in bed. This time she paused, stretched out on top of me, and kissed me. So dreamy. She propped herself up on a pillow and leaned into my outstretched left arm. When she was settled, I brought her coffee to her with my right hand and reached back to get my own.

"Good morning, sweetheart," I said. She smiled over the rim of her cup and took a sip of the coffee.

"There is nothing like the first sip of coffee in the morning," she sighed. "And coffee covers up morning breath." She lifted her lips and gave me a light kiss. "Did you get a lot of writing done?"

"Not really. I just wanted to lie here and hold you."

"Okay. I could get used to this life."

~~~~

A Long Time Ago: Morning Coffee

I KNOW I keep interrupting and you want me to get on with the sex with Alice, but I told you at the outset, my mind tends to wander. And sitting in bed with an arm wrapped around the bare shoulders of an incredible girl who was not being shy about expressing her pleasure as we talked and sipped our coffee, reminded me of a very happy time.

I was happily married for 20 years. Out of 31 years of marriage to three different women, that's not a bad percentage. Treasure was... my treasure, and most of those happy years were with her.

In the early years of our marriage, I struggled with getting out of bed. For the first time in my life, it seemed, I had a reason not to. From the time I was twelve and started delivering newspapers on that miserable route in Northern Indiana, I've been an early riser. Yeah, Brian got that from me. Even when I went to college and started working late nights on stage, I'd wake up at five o'clock in the morning. I'd roll out of bed, plug in my coffee pot—an old electric percolator—and by the time I'd get back from the dormitory bathroom, I could pour my first cup of the day and hit the books. My first class during freshman year was biology with Dr. Dennis at 7:30 a.m. That's when I'd go back to sleep.

But waking up next to Treasure at five in the morning was different. I didn't want to get out of bed. We never slept with clothes on, even after Maddie was born. Waking up with the love of my life naked beside me was like having a bed magnet.

Eventually, of course, I did get up because I couldn't lie awake forever, waiting for her to wake up. I'd get the morning newspaper and make coffee. About six-thirty, I'd steam some milk, pour her coffee in it, and take it to Treasure in bed. That's how she woke up in the mornings for the better part of twenty-five years. On Sunday mornings, I'd bring the newspaper and settle back into the bed with her, laughing at the comics, reading book reviews to each other, exclaiming over heartbreaking news stories. Occasionally, we'd manage to have a little loving time before Maddie woke up demanding breakfast and attention.

I continued to bring her coffee in bed right up until the day I moved out.

Just writing about those sublime moments continues to bring tears to my eyes.

~~~

Back to Alice

"THERE ISN'T A sound but the two of us breathing and talking."

"And the rain," I said. Alice was lying quietly listening to the silence of our retreat when I heard the first patters of rain sweeping down out of the mountains. The wind picked up and my little trailer rocked. I had the stabilizers extended and the awning most of the way in, so it didn't concern me.

"Are we safe?" Alice asked, hugging me. The raindrops hit the roof, starting as a hiss as the smaller drops reached us and then like drumbeats when the big drops hit. I set my empty cup aside and held her in my arms, rocking slightly.

"Safe and sound. The trailer stayed anchored firmly in Laramie. I've never camped anyplace that was so constantly windy." She handed me her cup and I set it aside while she wrapped her arms around me. It was an 'all's right with the world' moment. We slid down in the bed a little farther and pulled up the blanket.

Mostly, I'd been letting Alice take the lead so I wasn't pushing her, but looking at her dark brown, almost black, eyes, I was just drawn to her and had to kiss her.

It was the right thing to do. The kisses started softly and steadily intensified. Our tongues joined our lips and we spent time exploring each other. Until the previous day, Alice and I had only kissed in the middle of an orgasm in a strip club. As intense as that was, it wasn't particularly memorable. We'd almost started at that level in the parking lot yesterday before we pulled back to learn how to be together before we were having sex.

Our kisses this morning were like starting new. We had to explore and find out what each other liked. How we liked to kiss. Where we liked to be touched. What we tasted like and sounded like and felt like. There's no way to get to know a woman quite like kissing her. Alice wasn't aggressive, meaning being on the attack as I withdrew, but didn't retreat when I approached. She was more than welcoming, participating in the dance with her whole body moving against mine.

We explored each other with our hands, starting like most new lovers by touching hair and faces. Then shoulders and backs. Then I had my hand on her butt as she moved closer to me.

"Ari, I know you make a big thing in your story about being clear when attention is being invited. Don't be afraid to touch me, lover. I want to explore all of you, and I want you to discover all of me," she whispered. Our next kiss intensified and in the process, we found each other's nipples.

"What do you like, Alice?" I asked as I pressed a thumb against her hardening nipple.

"Mmm. I like them touched and kissed and sucked. But not too rough. I don't like to have my titties pinched. A soft touch just connects all the erogenous points of my body. My lips, my nipples, my pussy, and even my toes. But rough play just hurts them," she said, demonstrating the way she liked to be touched by caressing and kissing my own nipples. Yes, I could understand exactly where she was coming from. I hated having my nipples twisted or my cock gripped in a hand like a vise. But this little play was delightful.

I scooted down a little so I could kiss across her shoulders and around her breasts.

Breasts are one of the miracles of the human race. Stop and think of it. On most mammals, the teats and nipples are purely functional. This is how babies get food. That's cool, but I don't know of any other species in which breasts play such a strong role in the attraction of male to female. Or even female to female. You can say that it is because we cover them up and sexualize them that they are so attractive, but even in cultures that have less concern for clothing than in the West, breasts still play an important part in sexual stimulation. For a straight male with even passably working equipment, a woman's breast is a source of limitless fascination. Maybe it's that way for other women as well. I imagine that if I were a woman I would stand in front of a mirror all day just staring at my breasts. Well, that's a guy talking.

A woman can wear the tiniest, skimpy bikini, showing her entire breast except the dark center, and men will pant, hoping for a slip of that fabric that will expose the nipple. I tent my pants just lying back and thinking about caressing a tender breast in the palm of my hand.

There is nothing remarkably different in the physical sensation of squeezing a woman's soft butt and squeezing her soft breast. Some guys can't even tell the difference by touch. There was a scene in the movie *Summer of '42* in which the boy thought he'd set a record for holding a girl's breast in his hand until his friend told him that he'd been holding her arm. But when you have a breast laid bare for your enjoyment, resting in the palm of your hand, there is no feeling that is quite the same.

Alice's breasts, as I'd noticed in my first contact over a year earlier, were larger than my one-time lover Carly's. They had a beautiful soft roundness that begged to be caressed exactly the way she said she liked. They were small enough that there was no sag when she stood, and no noticeable flattening when she lay down. And unlike the common way oafs describe breasts in sex stories, these weren't two half oranges planted on a flat surface. They weren't half globes or melons. They rose in a gentle slope that you could almost detect starting just below her collar bone and after they peaked, tapering off just above her last rib. While I could kiss her breastbone between the two hillocks, it was a valley that smoothly transitioned from one breast to the other.

I honestly don't know—and I've been searching my memories— where I first began to love small areolae and nipples. Maybe that was part of the legacy of playing doctor with Betts. I have absolutely nothing against huge dark circles with fat, long nipples in the center, but I adore a nipple and surrounding area that is so near the same color as the breast that it appears translucent. I love a small nipple in the center that stiffens and swells enough to tongue and lave with attention. Alice's nipples were like that. The transition from her breast to her areolae was almost more of texture, with light little bumps in it, than of color. The nipple, just a little larger than a boy's, was perfect for sucking on and responded by swelling and stiffening just enough to remind me of licking a woman's clitoris.

For her part, Alice was expressing her enjoyment of my attention with little moans and with feather-light strokes along the length of my cock.

I raised my head again to kiss her and Alice wrapped strong arms around me, rolling to her back and pulling me with her.

And then a miracle occurred.

As we continued to kiss, seemingly without moving and without being guided and without jabbing at her, I simply glided into her wet folds and into her vagina.

I had planned—inasmuch as one ever plans in these situations—to continue down her body until I could use my tongue to satisfy her. But instead, my cock had effortlessly slid into her. And we both froze there. The feeling was so sensually overwhelming that I couldn't separate the regions of my body that were responding to her. She'd described the connection between her nipples and lips and clit and even toes. I could understand in that instant exactly what she meant. Even the base of my spine was tingling.

"I'm sorry, Alice," I said, starting to withdraw. "I didn't mean..." She clamped her hands around my butt and pulled me tighter.

"Don't apologize. Oh, god, Ari! This is what we both wanted. And we're here. You weren't even fully hard! I can feel you stiffening inside me. It's... so incredible," Alice said. She kissed me again until she broke to gasp for air.

"I don't think... I feel like a teenager... I don't think I can hold off, Alice."

"Don't! Don't wait. Come in me. Fill me. I think I'm going to... I've never had an orgasm from intercourse and I'm... Come in me, Ari. I'm going to... Oh, god, Ari!"

We hadn't moved since she stopped me from pulling out. I was simply buried deeply inside her and my penis pulsed as my soul rushed into her waiting vagina. She gripped me as she came. Her legs eventually relaxed which resulted in me dipping even farther into her depths as we both gasped again.

I was lost. I opened my eyes, not even realizing I had them squeezed tightly shut. She was looking up at me, tears flowing down her cheeks. Her dark eyes flashed at me and she pulled me to her for another kiss. I was, sadly, softening in her, but even as my cock slipped from her hot depths, I felt residual charges of electricity jolting through me.

"What did you do to me?" she whispered. "Ari, I'm never going to be the same."

IT RAINED MOST of the day. That was a good enough excuse for us to just stay in bed. It doesn't mean that we were fucking the entire time, but we certainly didn't jump out of bed and get dressed. Under the best of circumstances, it takes me a while to recover from a good come and be ready to go again. When my entire essence had been drained from my body, it was certainly going to take a little longer. After we kissed and held each other for a while, I got up and made breakfast. Alice cut up the melon that I'd purchased, so we each had a thick slice of bacon, scrambled eggs, and honeydew. I tossed towels on the bench seat at the table and Alice laughed about needing something to catch the drips. I knew she'd caught the first several in her hand on the way to the bathroom, but between her juices and my leavings, she was still dripping.

We went back to bed.

We read for a while, she had a Kindle and had downloaded Jay Cantrell's *Daze in the Valley* from SOL. Occasionally, she'd nudge me and read a scene or a speech out loud. We'd giggle a little and kiss, then go back to reading. Eventually, we both fell asleep again, listening to the rain on my fiberglass roof.

WE WOKE UP face-to-face and sleepily smooched. She squeezed and I felt her pussy muscles clamp down on my cock.

"How did we do that?" she asked. We'd been sleeping on our sides, holding each other face-to-face, but we hadn't been fucking when we went to sleep. Still we woke up with my cock deep inside her.

"I don't know how, but I like it."

"It's like our parts are just drawn together. Make love to me, Ari."

I was happy to oblige. Our first time, neither of us had moved much once I'd been fully inserted. The initial feelings had been so intense that we came without any other stimulation. This time, I pulled back and pushed in again slowly. She pushed forward to meet my stroke. Perhaps it wasn't as intense as our first coupling, but I could still feel the residual shocks charging down my spine like I'd been struck by lightning. We rocked slowly together and continued our early explorations of each other with kisses, light touches, a grasp of buttock or breast. We looked into each other's eyes as we made love and when we came, we kissed through the entire orgasm, trying to be joined in every possible way at once.

WE DIDN'T STAY in bed making love all week. The next day was sunny and we headed into Yellowstone to see Old Faithful. In addition to being an awesome sight, we took some funny pictures that made it look like she was mad and the geyser was spouting out of her pretty head. We hiked along a trail near the visitor center, walking hand-in-hand and enjoying the peace.

"Ari?" she whispered. "What's that?"

I glanced to my left where she was looking. A bull elk, about twenty feet off the path in the shade of interlocking trees, was quietly watching us as we passed. I kept Alice moving. Beside the bull were three cows and two calves.

"I think we should just keep going," I whispered.

"Shouldn't we go back?"

"This trail is a loop. We should just keep going." We didn't rush, but I kept Alice moving.

I have a lot of respect for animals—especially wild animals. I'd seen a video of a bull elk jamming his antlers right through the side of a car it thought was invading its territory. I did not want to give it the impression we were considering bedding down where he was. We were a good fifty yards down the path before we started to breathe easy again.

Of course, people are idiots. On the northern side of the lake as we drove back toward our campsite late in the afternoon, traffic was stopped for the herd of buffalo that was blocking the road. People were getting out of their cars and approaching the two ton beasts to take selfies with them. A sixteen-year-old had been gored by a bison just this spring. Witnesses had said he was about three feet away from the huge animal taking a selfie.

We waited in the line of cars, getting out and sitting on the hood of the truck to take our pictures. It was after dark by the time we got back to camp.

A Long Time Ago: Yes I Will Yes

I won a contest my senior year in high school. It didn't surprise me. I'd won lots of contests. When I was a paper carrier, I won all sorts of contests. That dude ranch that Brian kept visiting? Yeah. I went there a bunch of times. I won trips to baseball games in Chicago, the State Fair in Indianapolis, and once I even won a four-day cruise to Nassau in the Bahamas. That's a story I'll have to tell you sometime. Fifteen years old with seven other paper carriers and two circulation managers on a cruise to paradise. Toss in appendicitis. That wasn't this trip.

The prize was a theater tour in New York City. It was a mixed group of seventeen- and eighteen-year-old boys and girls. What could possibly go wrong? We'd been selected through the state speech contest and were sponsored by the regional theater in Indianapolis. I'd never be able to find the hotel we stayed at if I went back there. It was cheap and we were assigned to dormitory-style rooms with four single beds and a bath in each one. I'm sure they figured that keeping us bunched up like that would make it harder for us to have a boy slip into a girl's room or vice versa. And it did. We were good kids. Which didn't mean there was no fooling around. We just didn't sleep together.

There was a total of thirty-two students and eight adults that boarded a charter bus in Indianapolis at nine at night on Thursday. Officially, we all had Friday and Monday off school. We'd arrive in New York by noon on Friday and get settled in our hotel, do a little touring of Broadway, including a backstage tour of The Lyceum Theater and then attend *Zalmen or the Madness of God* Friday night after dinner. We'd see a total of four shows and then Monday we'd be back on the bus headed for Indiana. None of us would be worth shit in school on Tuesday.

First, there was the fourteen-hour bus ride from Indianapolis to New York City. We boarded the bus and did our best to grab seats so we could sleep on the way. That was the intent. I grabbed a seat and propped my pillow against the window. There weren't enough seats for everyone to have one, but I was surprised when a girl I didn't know plopped down next to me.

"You look like you've got a comfortable shoulder. Can I sleep with you?" she said as she pulled her pillow between us.

"I usually like to know the names of the girls I sleep with," I laughed.

"Allison," she said, offering her hand. I took it lightly.

"Aroslav."

"I know. I saw you do your one-man rendition of *A Midsummer Night's Dream* at state finals."

"You were there? Wait. You did that incredible interpretation of Molly Bloom from *Ulysses*."

"That was me."

"Inspired. I will never hear the word 'yes' again in the same way."

"I borrowed it. Saw Siobhan McKenna do it in London a couple of years ago. I've been working on it ever since. They wouldn't let me do it naked, though."

"They… You… What?"

"Well, maybe not completely naked, but someday I want to do the whole thing instead of just the four-minute cut and I want to do it lying in bed like Molly would be, examining her breasts and trying to figure out why men are so fascinated with them. Don't you think that would be cool?" she asked.

"The idea is… fascinating," I said weakly.

"Well, now we can sleep together while crossing state lines. You can put your arm around me. It will be more comfortable."

For whom? She pushed her pillow up against me and I let my arm fall to her shoulder as I pushed her pillow down and out of my face. We shifted a little so we were both lying back and got comfortable. Except my hand was dangling down over her shoulder and I knew it was just an inch or so from her breast.

Apparently, Allison knew about it, too, because before she went to sleep, she took hold of my hand and held it for the rest of the night, sort of between her breasts.

New York was great. *Zalmen* was heavy. I'd read some of Elie Wiesel's work when I went out to Colorado a couple years previously, so I was kind of expecting the dark cry of despair. Like a lot of our group, though, I had a hard time staying awake through the second act.

Saturday afternoon, we scored a bonus. Those of us who were over eighteen could buy tickets to a matinee of *Oh! Calcutta!* It had recently been revived and we couldn't wait to see it. Of course, the big draw was that it included full nudity, but the music was damned good, too. And it was funny. And they were naked.

The second act started with a filmed segment where the actors were all dancing around nude. Allison had been holding my hand all through the show and leaned over to whisper in my ear.

"You can put your arm around me." I obliged, placing my hand on her shoulder and pulling her toward me more firmly. That apparently wasn't what she had in mind. She leaned forward a little and pulled my arm behind her back and my hand under her arm. By the time the scene 'One on One' began, she'd pulled my hand far enough forward to cup her breast. It was a nice breast to cup. It was also then that I realized she wasn't wearing a bra. It was *really* nice. I petted and squeezed her breast through the entire act and when I lagged, she shifted a bit and made sure her breast was moving against my hand.

During the finale, there were supposedly comments being received from the audience. The whole cast was standing around nude on stage, taking comments. "How come none of the guys have hard-ons?" one questioner asked. Allison leaned up to my ear and licked it. *Shit!*

"Do you have a hard-on?" she asked. *No shit, Sherlock!* I couldn't care less about the naked actors. I had an incredible tit in my hand. She didn't give me a chance to respond. "I have a hard-on. Feel it under your fingers?" I let my fingers glide across the curvature of her breast and tweak her nipple a little. She gasped. "Yes," she whispered. She put her hand on my chest and continued to whisper in my ear as the audience began to applaud for the curtain call. I couldn't move and she practically crawled into my lap. "His heart was going like mad and yes I said yes I will Yes." I turned my head and we kissed. Yes.

That night we saw *Porgy and Bess* at the Uris Theater. I love that music! Unfortunately, when we got our tickets, one of the kids who hadn't been with us at *Oh! Calcutta!* had the ticket for the seat between us and refused to move. We were late getting into the show and ended up sitting a seat away from each other with the smug little pug between us. When he asked where we'd been while the rest of them had been to see *Fiddler on the Roof*, Allison answered with the words *"O quel cul t'as!"* which is French for "What an asshole you are!" she told me later.

On Sunday, we were allowed time to go get our own lunch and explore as long as we were in a group of four or more. We met Bert and Frankie, another couple who had hit it off during the trip. We had a nice late lunch at a genuine New York Deli in the Theater District. Allison kept stroking up and down my thigh with her left hand while we ate. I had a raging hard-on, but she never quite touched it. We got to the Circle in the Square Theater in plenty of time to make sure we had seats together after we'd wandered up and down Broadway,

Forty-Second Street, and Seventh Avenue. The big treat of the trip was to see Tennessee Williams' *The Night of the Iguana* with Richard Chamberlain.

Indiana Rep wanted to impress upon us that theater was serious business and between *Zalmen* and *Iguana*, I guess they succeeded in getting their point across. Frankly, I found *Iguana* an easy show to love with my arm wrapped around Allison, once again playing with her nipples as she stroked my thigh. This time, about every third or fourth stroke, she'd glide her fingers up the full length of my cock. I was erect through the entire play.

I was looking forward to the bus ride home on Monday morning. I figured we'd cuddle up in our seat again and this time, the petting, at least, would be serious. Of course, we didn't get to do that for the whole fourteen hours back to Indy. It was daylight for the first eight hours and people were raucous. We joined in the card games and even charades, played in the aisle of the bus.

It got dark soon after we crossed into Ohio, though, and people started to settle down. Allison slid into the seat beside me and reached up to turn off our overhead light. Just that movement, though, set her breasts in motion in such a way as to let me know she'd somehow lost her bra. We shifted ourselves around this time so that she was lying back across my lap with our pillows under her. We had one of the light bus blankets over us. As soon as we started to kiss, Allison guided my hand under her sweater and I felt the luscious flesh of her tits in my hand. She shifted enough that she could stroke my continued erection.

It took nearly two hours of kissing and whispering before I got my hand beneath her waistband and into her pussy.

"You've got to kiss me really tight, Ari," she said. "Because when you get me off, I'm going to scream. Do it. You've got the spot, right there. Just a little more. I've been waiting all weekend for this." True to her word, she ramped up for an ear-splitting scream that was *almost* completely muffled by my having our lips sealed together and my tongue halfway down her throat. She didn't get my cock out of my pants, but she turned her head enough that she could nibble at my jeans from my balls all the way up to the crown. She had it in her mouth, jeans and all, when I came.

"Why me?" I whispered as we calmed down and just continued to make out in the quiet darkness of the bus. "Why did you choose me, Allison?"

"I'm going to need a first act before I do my Molly Bloom one day," she whispered back. "You'll write it for me, won't you, Ari?"

"Of course I will, darling. Of course I will."

〜〜〜

Back to Alice

"WHY ME?" I whispered late the night before Alice left to return to school. We'd made love for hours, it seemed, and she'd fallen asleep in my arms. I lay awake most of the night with the same questions going through my mind.

"Too much mental masturbation," Alice whispered without opening her eyes. I hadn't thought she was awake.

"Go back to sleep, love," I said as I petted her hair. So pretty. So young.

"You're tormenting yourself, Ari," she said, her eyes flicking open. "Call it Karma and I'm the punishment for your wicked ways."

"I'm glad I lived such a bad life. What would my reward have been if I'd been good?"

"A frigid virgin. You'd keep each other pure." She giggled softly.

"It doesn't answer the question," I said after a while. "You're nineteen. Why are you even interested in an old fart like me? Even as a diversion? You have to want someone closer to your own age."

"Ari, love, I don't know. I don't know why I find you attractive. Maybe it's just the stability of having someone older."

"Stability? I'm one step above living in a white van down by the river," I laughed.

"Yeah. I guess I have to scratch that off my list." She wiggled herself closer, if possible. We hadn't spent all our time making love this week, but we'd spent a good share. "Please don't take this wrong, Ari, but I love you."

"How could I possibly take that wrong?"

"I'm not making a life commitment to you. I love you, but I don't know what's going to happen tomorrow. Maybe you'll become impotent and there will be no reason to have me."

"Thanks. Alice, I…"

"I know, Ari. You love me, too. But you aren't making a commitment. I'm a freshman in college. You are living the life of my dreams. When I'm ready to live that life, you might be done with it and want to hide in a cabin in Montana for the rest of your life. Which, by the way, isn't an unattractive prospect. But the thing is we don't know."

She kissed me again and we hugged each other close. Her kisses just did something to me. I placed my finger against her lips to keep her from responding until I was finished.

"I love you, Alice. I wanted you to hear that from my lips so you weren't just assuming it was true. Now you know it. I love you and no matter where our paths lead or when they cross, I will always wish you the best of all possible worlds." I kissed her again.

"Then write me more stories. Call me in the middle of cold and snowy Montana nights and make me come with your voice. And…" she shifted only slightly and gasped as I slid into her yet again. "And make love to me again, darling."

"Aren't you too sore by now?"

"I don't care. I just want to feel it again. I'll take another week off work so I don't have a swollen pussy when I dance."

We made love. The rest of the night.

⌒⌒

I WATCHED HER as she left, choosing to let her go before I could get the trailer hitched and be tempted to follow her. An hour later, I pulled out of the campground and resumed my journey westward.

8 White Line Fever

14 September 2014

I MADE it to the Pacific Ocean the second week of September and spent a couple days camped at Newport. I'd made my lifelong fantasy trip across the country on U.S. 20. I needed to decide what to do next. I headed north on the Pacific Coast Highway, slowly making my way back to Seattle. I spent a weekend in the Siuslaw National Forest campground about a mile from the beach and since I was feeling a little isolated ever since Alice left, I decided to go to Church on Sunday.

I do that every so often. I'm terrible at bars. If you are a man in a bar by himself, you are obviously either a drunk or on the prowl. I suppose it is different for women, though they'll say they just went out to have a drink and a little fun. The truth is women never go to a bar alone. If you happen to be one of the guys who goes to the bar alone on the prowl, you not only have to compete with the other guys who are on the prowl, you have to separate a prospect from her herd and then try to speak cleverly at a volume she can hear over the music and shouting at the ballgame on the big screen TV.

Tom Twain had me edit his book *The Real Man's Sex Book*. I admit that he was a lot more successful at picking up women than I was. He'd never been married. He did a lot of traveling around the world and seemed to have a successful engagement with a woman in every port of call. He had advice on picking a girl out of the crowd.

"Pick up the wingman," he said. "First, she isn't as pretty as the main target at the table. Usually, she's a little hungry for attention. Her friend, the pretty one, always has guys trying to get her to dance, buy her drinks, feel her up. So, chat the wingman up. Make wry comments about the way guys are falling over her friend and how well she's putting them in their place. And then slip in that you think those guys are missing the opportunity to get to know someone really sweet by wasting their time on her friend instead of her."

Tom swears that this has gotten him laid every time he's tried it. It's also left a few very startled and suddenly alone debs in bars abandoned by their wingman.

Me, I find that getting laid is only part of the attraction. I don't mind that part, for sure, but I just like to talk to people and if the person happens to be a nice or pretty woman (not necessarily both) it just ups the enjoyment. Churches are a great place to meet people. A single man of an appropriate age, who is intelligent and enjoys good conversation over coffee after church, becomes a target for eligible women and/or their mothers.

So, I went to the Unitarian Church that weekend because Unitarian Universalists tend to have a very liberal outlook on life, relationships, and politics. I remember the first time I went to a Unitarian Church after having been disillusioned by the Methodists who refused to ordain gay ministers. Rev. Barbara, the minister at the UU Church, who was also obviously gay, had greeted me after the service and listened to my complaints.

"Well, Ari, you know what they say about Unitarianism. It's the halfway point on the slippery slope from Methodism to Golf." I don't play golf, so I figure I reached the bottom of the slope on a free fall.

Oh, yes, I was telling about the service at the UU Church near the beach in Oregon. The speaker for the day was a woman who worked in social services and counseling. She talked about dealing with depression. I was dealing with that.

It wasn't that I was particularly depressed. Having Alice for that wonderful week together and then being three weeks on the road alone with my thoughts and my characters, certainly left me with a wistful feeling. But overall, I was excited about what was brewing in my head. I was thinking I'd write a sequel to *Redtail*. I'd always planned on that being a one-off, but since I visited Laramie and Centennial, Wyoming, I'd become enthused about going back.

The depression I was dealing with was Hannah's. LNDtH was only posting around chapter fifty, but I was writing Chapter 107. Hannah was dealing with her guilt and depression and Brian was struggling to 'fix' it. The speaker started talking about developing our own 'mental health first aid kits.' Brilliant! What would I put in my own mental health first aid kit. Besides a condom. And a Viagra. Some people joked that their kits were filled with chocolate. But the speaker was talking about having things like a CD with a piece of music that always makes you happy, an uplifting poem, a baby picture of your child, or a ribbon you won at the 4H Fair. It was to be filled with things that would remind you that life is fundamentally good, even if you are having a bad day, and that you are fundamentally a good person, even if you don't feel like it.

'The Kit' was born. It would be months before I wrote the chapter it appeared in and a year before it posted, but the first—very first—image in my mind of my kit was of walking into the trailer and finding Alice standing naked in a box marked, 'Mental Health Kit.'

Some old guy, who said he planned to write the story of his life because it had been very interesting, monopolized my time during after church. I was afraid that I would hear the entire story before I could get out for lunch. I didn't care, though. I had a new idea.

I KEPT GOING north without anything significant other than the thousands of words I was writing. I would be finished with the writing of *Living Next Door to Heaven: The Rock* before November and able to focus NaNoWriMo on my *Redtail* sequel. I was still struggling trying to find a title, but it would come.

I did have a little surprise when I went to explore Tillamook, the home of Oregon's premier cheese. I turned into the Tillamook Creamery, only to discover that I'd misread the sign and it was the Tillamook Crematory. Tillamook Dairy was a couple miles farther on.

I got to Seattle in time for the various poke and prod appointments that men of a certain age need annually. Doctor, dentist, eye doctor, accountant, lawyer, and daughter.

Maddie and I have always had a great relationship, even though neither one of us is good at sending regular messages to the other or picking up the damned phone. Nonetheless, as soon as we meet at Red Robin and start consuming a burger and beer, our literary conversation is likely to go all over the charts. God help the person who overhears.

"Dad, I need to kill a guy with something in an artist's studio. It has to be something the artist would normally be handling every day so that everyone would expect her fingerprints on it. What's sharp enough? And should I stab him in the heart or in the neck?"

We hammered that issue out for a good long while and I caught a couple raised eyebrows as our server came by with more fries.

"So, I'm thinking that the brother and sister are close to each other and would be totally in love if it weren't for the fact that they are related and society says no," I said. "But the characters they are sent back in time to occupy have fallen in love with each other independently. Now, brother and sister are riding in the heads of these two lovers as they consummate their marriage. Are they committing incest?"

"You're going to torture your characters again, aren't you, Dad? I love it!"

Well, you get the way our conversations go.

Maddie and I agreed long ago that it wasn't appropriate for her to read her father's porn. But we're happy to discuss the characters and plot twists. When she found out that I intended to write my *Redtail* sequel from the perspective of the girl involved, she said I needed help.

"Those librarians in Laramie said they'd help, didn't they?" she asked.

"Yes, but the issues I'm having with this are scarcely historical details. I'd come off as an old pervert if I started asking college women if they'd ever had sex with their brother."

"So, get someone else to ask the questions."

What questions? We worked out an entire interview questionnaire that would help me think and talk like a ranch girl in Wyoming.

Like Mitch when he wanted to know how I knew so much about ranching and cattle in *Redtail*, many of my readers have asked how I know certain things. Many have also pointed out mistakes that I've made. A few have been surprised to find out I was a man instead of a woman and have asked how I write women so well. One email I got said, "If you are a man, you know women better than most women do!" I wrote back, "If you are a woman, I take that as a compliment."

Here's the basic truth. Research. I'd never been to Wyoming when I wrote *Redtail*. I filled notebooks full of descriptions I found, dates of railroad construction, homesteading, legends of old Laramie, wildlife behavior, how many bales of hay it takes to winter beef cattle, and the difference between the amount paid per pound for a cow versus a steer. I looked up unsolved robberies and missing money to locate actual scenes where all clues disappeared.

By the time I left Seattle and worked my way back east to Laramie, I had a three-page interview questionnaire and a plan for research at the University Library.

The questionnaire was to get discussions started, not to get a bunch of yes or no answers. So, the forty bullets each contained several questions. Some of it was simply to get context and to listen to how the women sounded. Other parts were to get some explicit information from young women that they would not normally share with an older guy—or any guy for that matter.

1. *What type of music do you enjoy and listen to? Who are your favorite artists? What are your favorite songs? Is it different if you are dancing instead of listening?*

2. *Where do you go to dance? What kind of music is played? With whom do you dance? Are there school dances? Name the top three places for nightlife.*

3. *Do you ride (horses)? Were you raised with them nearby? Where do you like to ride? Describe the training your horse received.*

Those were pretty innocuous as a warmup for the interview.

6. *Describe high school dating. What do you define as dating and is it common? When did you begin? What did you do on a date? Were there social pressures surrounding dating? What were your favorite places or activities for a date? Did*

*you become serious with a person you were dating? How
quickly? Are you still seeing your high school sweetheart?*

7. *How does college dating differ from high school dating? Is it
easier to find a date? Do you have a 'steady' that you date?
Are you engaged?*

Of course, the really interesting stuff came later in the interviews.
I could only hope that the interview would get this far.

24. *Are you sexually active? When did you begin? How do
you reconcile your sexual behavior with your religious
beliefs if any? Do you consider yourself to be permanently
monogamous, serial monogamous, pluralist, polyamorous?
Is sex important in a relationship? Do you have experience
with same-sex relations? How did it work out? Do you
have favorite sex acts? Absolute sexual no-nos?*

25. *Are sex and love always together for you? What are your
views on sex outside of relationships?*

26. *What is your opinion of romance? Is it important to you?
Do you want a permanent long-term relationship (as in
husband or wife)? How soon?*

27. *Do you have siblings? Same sex or opposite sex? Are you
close? What do you love about your brother/sister? What
do you hate? Do you think it is okay for siblings to be sexually attracted to each other—regardless if they ever act on
that attraction?*

I had high hopes for my research trip to Laramie, but few expec-
tations. However, when I sent a copy of the questionnaire to Alice to
get her opinion, she sent back nearly twenty pages of detailed answers,
some of which we used for phone sex. I'm still pulling gems out of that
little document.

~~~~~~

IT WAS WINDY in Laramie. Most people had already pulled out of the
KOA campground, but they still had a section for winter campers that
had power and insulated water pipes. I was warned to disconnect my
hose at night. There was no way I'd be able to use my awning without

turning my trailer into a kite. Every time I tried to cook on my gas grill, the wind blew out the flame. I would be cooking inside the trailer for my two weeks in Laramie.

"You know how Laramie was founded?" the campground host asked me. I'd told her that I was in town doing research for my novel.

"I've read about the coming of the railroad," I answered.

"Well, that's only part of the story. The first settlers were headed to California. They came over the ridge of the mountains there to the east of us and got hit by this wind. As soon as they got to the river here, they decided to make camp and hunker down to wait out the wind before they continued," she said.

"Oh." I'd never heard that story. I guess it made sense as being how the Union Pacific decided on this location for their station.

"Yeah. They're still down there," she deadpanned.

I'd been had.

～～～

MY FIRST RESEARCH stop was at the Union Pacific Station Museum. I got lucky. The museum is run by volunteers and is normally only open by appointment. I happened to pull into the parking lot about six blocks from where the original station had been just as a volunteer was opening the door to do some maintenance. He let me in to tour the exhibits, which included a variety of information about the creation of Laramie City, Wyoming.

The Union Pacific had vast land grants along the route from Chicago to Promontory Summit where it met up with the Central Pacific Railroad and the famous golden spike was driven. The land was much, much more than the right of way for the tracks. It included land for stations, water and coal depots, forest land for ties, gravel pits, and even towns. The UP began selling lots at one of the major termini for the railroad in April of 1868 and in two weeks Laramie City had 5,000 residents. The railroad arrived on May 9. On May 10, hundreds more people, goods, and supplies arrived on the first train. Laramie City was the staging point for the construction of the long grade that moved the rails over the Rocky Mountains.

I'd found the perfect place for my characters to come to their climax, so to speak.

There were still a number of the original or restored storefronts and businesses in Laramie, including the first building made of brick and a few facades saloons and brothels. Brothels were a big business in Laramie. They were still legal until the 1960s when the City finally did away with them. Some of the most colorful characters of the 1860s were associated in one way or another with the brothels, which included most of the music halls and bars in town. Some were no more than tents with a line of workers waiting outside to get their shot at one of the prostitutes.

It was when I got to the Coe Library at the University of Wyoming the next day, though, that I started on the true road to discovery, and the nature of my research changed.

"MAY I HELP you with something today?" the librarian in the rare books room asked. She was a nice woman in a business suit sitting at the first desk. I guessed that she was about thirty—one of the professionals and probably not a student. Though she had no trace of accent, I'd met enough people of Mexican descent since I got to Laramie that I recognized her Latino heritage.

"Hi. My name is Aroslav. I'm doing some research."

"The author," the librarian said. "It's a pleasure to meet you. I read *Redtail* after your last visit."

"Really?"

"Yes. We had a lottery and I lost." She had a bright smile when she said that and I hoped she was joking.

"Uh…"

"We knew from the listing on Amazon and what you told Ms. Cooper when you were here that it was a dirty book and I volunteered to read and review it before the pure eyes of any of my colleagues were forced on it."

"I hope you didn't consider it dirty or offensive," I said.

"Anything that says erotic is assumed to be pornographic until proven otherwise. We order copies of everything that we discover has mention of Laramie or historical Wyoming in it. There are some sexy scenes in the book, but nothing that made me masturbate. Not everyone in the department has read it," she said. "By the way, I'm Aubrey Diaz. How can we help your research? Are you writing a sequel?"

"As a matter of fact, I am. Since I wrote the first book without ever having visited Laramie, I thought that I'd spend a couple of weeks doing research before I started this one. I'm jumping back a few years in the time travel sequences for this one and my characters will arrive about the same time that the railroad does," I said. "I'll see if I can heat up the sex scenes for you and make them more satisfying."

"Oh, it's not as if I wouldn't have done Cole if I'd met him in a study room," Aubrey laughed. "I can see already that you are going to make me a character in your next book."

"How can you see that? I only have a rudimentary sketch of what will happen in this book," I said.

~~~~~

IN FACT, I'D only figured out the title and the role of the raven while I was in Seattle. My editor, Jay, had looked at my potential titles which included "Wapiti", "Bugle", and "Chogan" and shook his head.

"What are these?" he asked.

"Well, *Redtail* refers to a type of hawk. He's the catalyst for Cole's time travel. I'm not settled on the catalyst for this one. The first two refer to elk and the third one is the Algonquin word for raven. I'd prefer something to do with a raven, but there's no reason to have Algonquin language in Wyoming. Unfortunately, the Cheyenne word is *kohkahycumest*."

"Redtail is also a descriptive term. Why don't you think of something distinctive about the animal and use that? Like if it was an elk, you could call it Elevenpoint."

Brilliant. This is why we have story consultants and editors.

Blackfeather.

~~~~

"I'm psychic," Aubrey said. I looked at her. "Seriously. My mother was a Mexican spirit reader. I'll read your cards, your tea leaves, your palm, or your fortune. Oh. Sorry, you don't have much of a fortune, do you?"

"You pegged that part right," I said. "And I think you are right. You just got a role in the book. How would you like to be a sixteen-year-old virgin selected for the sex-act that starts the time travel?"

"I wasn't a sixteen-year-old virgin even when I was sixteen. It sounds like fun! Now let's get the rest of your research underway."

I started describing the basics of what I planned and Aubrey started bringing me resources. They were spread out over two tables with my laptop open on one and resource books next to it. Aubrey spread out original plat maps and directories so I could take pictures of them on the other table. Nice, short, tight skirt.

I didn't stop for lunch and worked until the special collections room was ready to close. I had enough historical data collected to keep me sifting through things for days. Aubrey brought me a history of Laramie City written in 1875 that said,

> of those [5,000 residents], a thousand were strong, earnest, daring men, ready to face any danger or ready to undertake any perilous task if they could, in any honorable way, better their fortunes. Another thousand were ready to adopt any policy, honorable or otherwise, so that they got money, and ran no great risks. The balance, with the exception of a few good and noble women, were made up of gamblers, thieves, highwaymen, robbers, cut-throats, garroters, prostitutes, and their necessary companions, who made their living by preying upon the poor laborers who, as soon as their month's wages were in their pockets, would

rush into town from the road and timber, and sport while
there was a penny left.

I packed up my dead computer, dead cell phone, and dead camera. Everything needed to be recharged, including me.

"Aubrey, you've been so much help today, I don't know how to thank you. May I buy you dinner?" I said.

"I knew you were going to ask that, so I cleared my calendar," she said. "Let's go to Rosie's. Tomorrow is the border war and you'll see lots of students there. Probably Pistol Pete and the Cheerleaders, too."

Maybe she *was* psychic. Maybe I'd get lucky, too. That skirt... When she'd been leaning over the table in front of me spreading out maps, I'd had some distinctly pornographic thoughts about her bending over.

"I know what you're thinking," Aubrey said. "And the answer is definitely... maybe."

I might have found a woman crazier than me.

You'd think I'd have learned my lesson about crazy women when I found Belle wandering around the house in the middle of the night with a butcher knife. Even neurotic Paula who couldn't go to sleep at night if she had to get up in the morning. Once when Treasure had gotten testy over something and I responded calmly, she laughed that she needed to write a thank you note to Paula and Belle for making her look normal. Then there was the groupie, Jodie. Or Becky in Florida, or the nudist Nona, or Val the leech in Tennessee. I'd had experience with crazy.

Or Georgia. Remember her? None of them could compete with Nicki, though. Which was worse, the sickness or the cure?

~~~

A Long Time Ago: Stalker

"You are in so much shit!" Nicki said as she approached me in my workshop. As a sophomore, I'd been given a work study grant to put in ten hours a week in the theater scene shop. Carlos, who took care of the school stage at Ben Davis, had been hired to design the shows, but I was his assistant technical director, so I had a lot of work to do on the fall production of *Hamlet.*

"Are you on my crew today, Nicki?" I asked. That was about the only thing I could guess that might be deep shit. I liked Nicki, but she scared the bejeezus out of me. She was just... batshit crazy.

"No. I just came over to inform you about your troubles and wait to watch you explain it to Paula," she laughed. Nicki's laugh never sounded funny. It was the kind of laugh you expect the psycho in a horror movie to have, only it wasn't fake. It was the simple enjoyment of something purely evil. Paula and I were still kind of feeling our way around a relationship. We were sort of boyfriend/girlfriend and sort of not. We didn't go out. We just hung out together on campus most of the time. Who had money to go out?

"How about just telling me what kind of trouble I'm in," I sighed.

"You have a secret admirer. Or maybe she's not a secret to you and you've just been hiding her from the rest of us," Nicki said.

"How do you know this?"

"I saw your picture on her mirror during dorm inspection." The color drained from my face. I sat down.

"Maybe she is on a freshman scavenger hunt," I suggested. "They have those for orientation, don't they?"

I didn't doubt that Nicki had seen a picture if there was one. She was the freshman dorm monitor. That was a sophomore who could act as a big sister to the freshmen and perform the duty of room inspections once a week. Personally, I believe Nicki got the job because it included a private room and there was not a woman on campus who would share with her. She'd gone through four roommates during our freshman year. The last one had withdrawn from school three weeks before finals. Apparently, she was flunking out, but rumors had it that she simply couldn't stay three more weeks in a room with Nicki.

"Mmm. It's not just one picture," Nicki continued. "I recognized you right away, so I investigated carefully. There's a newspaper article that looks to be about three or four years old with a picture of you getting mud in the face and a description of your musical based on *Origin of Species*. I didn't know you did that! Nice notices. There was a prom picture and a series of you onstage. Couldn't tell the production. And she cut your photo out of the yearbook. Who cuts up a yearbook?" Nicki asked.

I was wracking my brain trying to come up with an answer. Prom? Had Deb transferred? If so, Paula and I probably wouldn't last the month. But Deb wouldn't be housed in the freshman dorm.

"She has lipstick hearts and kisses all over her mirror with 'Mrs. Aroslav' and 'I ♥ Ari' written on it."

"My god! Who is this crazy woman?"

"Her name's Georgia."

It's a good thing I was sitting down. Georgia, the crazy girl who gave me her panties after the Valentine's Day Dance my senior year. The last time I'd seen her, she had found out I was assisting at the Summer Theater Institute and had enrolled for a week. She'd popped up near me every time I turned around. I don't think she ever attended any of her own classes that week. I kept sneaking around the campus trying not to run into her. The last night, she'd shown up at my dorm room and knocked. We didn't have peepholes or anything like that. I just opened the door and she pushed her way in. She was wearing a diaphanous gown that showed clearly there was nothing beneath it.

I thought Georgia was seriously cute. I'd spent an entire evening staring down her dress at her tits and finally managed to get hold of one of them. They were just about perfect. But she was also scary. For three weeks after that date, I received a card from her in the mail every day. Some of them were expensive cards. They all had hearts, or messages like "Love is running your fingers over the cracks in someone's heart and soul while looking into their eyes with a smile that says 'I'm staying.'" Where do people find these things? She started calling once a week until my mother asked her to stop. I thought it was funny at first. Deb even thought it was funny and wanted to act out what I'd done with Georgia. Then it got spooky and then stalkerish.

She stood in the middle of my room at Institute and dropped the gown, confirming my notion there was nothing under it.

"Take me. I want you, Ari. I can't stand waiting any longer. We'll have such beautiful children together."

Oh, fucking shit!

"No! You've got to get dressed, Georgia. You have to leave. I've got a girlfriend. This room is monitored. I have to get up in the morning. You have to go!"

It was so painful to do that! Those little titties… I couldn't take my eyes off them the whole time she was there. They were so perfect, I just wanted to suck on those little nipples! But coming to my room naked? Have my children?

I'd waited until I thought it was safe, packed an overnight bag and ran for my car. I drove the seventy-five miles home, snuck into the house, and slept on the sofa. I didn't really have a room in this house because my folks had just moved there with my baby sister when I left for college. I had my sleeping bag with me and Mom found me there in the morning.

Now Georgia had followed me to college? *Just shoot me!*

Why did such perfect little titties have to be attached to someone so creepy?

"Nicki, you have a master key, right?" I moaned.

"I am not going to let you into her room so you can have your wicked way with her. You want in the girls' dorm, you come to *my* room."

"That's not what I was thinking. I was wondering if you could go in late tonight and sort of smother her in her sleep," I groaned. "Or me. I'll give you the key to my room and you can sneak in and smother me."

Nicki seemed to consider it a minute.

"I was kidding, Nicki. I was kidding!"

"Oh, don't worry. I'm not really a serial killer. But I might be able to classify this as 'just cause'. Well, I could do you if you promise to fuck me before I kill you. I hear that men have an incredible orgasm while they are suffocating," she said.

"Nicki, please. This is serious. I need to stop this. She can't just follow me around for the rest of my life. I'll have to talk to her," I complained.

"I'll figure out something for you, but you'll owe me big time."

"No violence. You know how I feel about violence," I said.

"Yeah, yeah. Like I'd go to prison for you. Ha!"

Nicki stood to leave and I looked at her tattered black jeans, t-shirt, and camo jacket. Her hair this week was black on one side and purple on the other. I couldn't leave well enough alone.

"Nicki, what color is your hair really?" I asked. She turned to face me. She popped open the top button on her jeans.

"If you really want to know, bring your face over here and take a really close look."

"Nicki! Stop! Geez you're weird!"

"Don't you want to get in my panties, Ari?"

"I'm afraid of what I'd find."

"I am NOT a boy!"

"I know what to do with a dick. I'm afraid you might have teeth down there."

"Nobody will say things like that when I'm rich and famous," she snarled.

"How are you going to become rich and famous?" I asked.

"Paranormal research," she answered. Suddenly, I'd unleashed a demon. She got a brown envelope from her satchel and approached me, ignoring the fact that her jeans were coming unzipped now that the top button was open. She apparently didn't wear underwear, because there were light brown hairs peeking out of the fly. "I finally got the photo I've been waiting for. I set a time-lapse camera with long exposures that I layered one on top of the other when I printed this image. Girls have been telling stories about the basement of the dorm being haunted for years. Would you believe that two years ago, a girl claimed the ghost got her pregnant? I captured the ghost. Look at this!" She triumphantly showed me the photo that showed a rather blurry black and white image of the common room in the basement of the dorm. There was a bright spot on the left edge of the picture.

"Where's the ghost?" I asked.

"There! There!" she practically screamed, pointing at the bright spot. "You can see eyes in the center." I examined the photo more closely.

"Nicki, I think that's the reflection of the exit light in the window," I said.

"You'll see. When I've refined the processing and push the film a little more, everyone will be able to tell that I've caught the specter. You'll see," she muttered as she stuffed the photo back in the folder and left. *Oh, crap! That makes two crazy women to deal with.*

That was the least of my worries, as it turned out. Two days later, posters started appearing around campus. That's not unusual, especially in mid-September. Classes were electing officers and since our school didn't have a Greek Council, we elected a typical student council. There were always posters up for the student offices. They didn't usually have *my* picture on them, though. I was walking to the cafeteria with Paula and *she* spotted it.

"So, I'm not enough? You have to date all the girls on campus?" she yelled at me. She stomped off. I read the poster.

"Aroslav for Campus Boyfriend. Heck with the rest, Date the best!"

Not only was there a poster; no, there were lots of posters. Everywhere the campus candidates had put posters, my face showed up. And there were stickers, too. "I ♥ Ari." I saw one on a girl's backpack. This was not good. In my first class, six girls turned around to look at me and held up their notebooks. They all had stickers that said, "Future Mrs. Aroslav!" It lost a little something with the black lipstick print, but I couldn't expect Nicki to spring for color stickers. I couldn't believe she'd paid what must have been a fortune for stickers and posters. I knew her parents were rich, but this was ridiculous.

I dragged myself into lunch with people I'd never met slapping me on the back and telling me I had their vote. Girls were coming up to kiss me on the cheek and say, "Will you be my boyfriend next?" Nicki had put together a whole fake campaign so that Georgia's little mirror display looked like she was just copying everyone else on campus.

Paula came up to me as a cute girl from my sociology class was giving me a hip check and dragged me away to a table.

"Okay. I got that it was a joke. Nicki explained everything. You are a bastard!" she said.

"It's not my fault, Paula. Really."

"You've never fucked her, have you?" she said flatly.

"No! I escaped."

"Then tonight you come to my room and demonstrate every single thing you've done with the little bitch. Every. Thing." Paula left. That, at least, wasn't a bad prospect. In fact, it was reminiscent of Deb. I'd never slid my hand into Paula's shirt to squeeze her bare breasts, nor had I seen her naked.

The campaign settled down when a guy who was well-liked and very popular was also nominated for the position of Campus Boyfriend, though his posters weren't as classy as mine. I heard that Georgia withdrew from school. Neither my name nor the other guy's actually appeared on the ballot.

I felt bad, but if the only reason Georgia came to this college was to trap me, we were both much better off with her going elsewhere. Cute little titties and all.

But one day, I was going to have to deal with Nicki.

Back to Laramie

Rosie's Cantina was just what Aubrey had promised. We drove separately so she could go home and change clothes before she met me. I wandered around downtown to scope out what happened on Friday nights. Things were lively. I spotted the Coal Creek Coffee Company and couldn't help but stop in to get a quick cup. Good espresso, even though prices on everything were a dollar more a cup than most places. They called my usual 'shot in the dark' a 'turbo.' Every coffee shop has its own term for adding a shot of espresso to a cup of coffee.

When I got to Rosie's, I had to wait for a table. There was no sign of Aubrey yet. The promised cheerleaders, however, were bouncing around in their little short skirts and crop tops. If I recalled the pictures I'd seen, this wasn't an official uniform for games. There were NCAA rules regarding cheer uniforms just like there were for sports uniforms. These, I assumed, must be a special edition for, let's say, lifting people's spirits the night before a game.

Pictures seemed to be the order of the day. For a dollar, a cheerleader would pose with a fan. I was told the money was being collected as part of their big charity drive. It was a well-established menu card. For five dollars, the cheerleader would sit on your lap for the photo. Multiple cheerleaders at once, multiple dollars.

As soon as I was seated, a very cute little redhead cheerleader rushed to my table and asked if I'd like to support their charity by having a picture. I told her my cell phone was dead, but I'd make a donation. I intended to pull out a single, but realized I'd laid a ten on the table for her. She pushed my legs apart and sat on my knee.

"Darla! Snap the pic!" she called, waving her phone. My hand automatically went to her waist to steady her on my knee as she leaned in and planted a kiss on my cheek. That was a very silky smooth, and bare waist. She stayed put while Darla handed back the phone. "I'm Reba," my cheerleader said. "What's your number? I'll send you the pic." I gave her my cell number and she sent me the photo. "Now you'll have my number, too." She leaned in close to my ear. It was a little difficult to hear what she was saying over the noise in the room. But I got the message. "I know older guys sometimes have needs that aren't being met at home," she whispered. "Sometimes I have needs that I can't afford and a couple hundred extra spending money comes in handy. Call me." She kissed me on the cheek again and slipped away.

I was a little dazed when I looked up and saw Aubrey grinning at me.

"You didn't waste any time. You've got lipstick on your face," she laughed.

"I guess the donations are for a good cause," I said lamely.

"Things get crazy the night before the Border War," Aubrey laughed. "It's a good opportunity to raise money for the cause. This is Mandy. Mandy, meet Aroslav." A woman stepped around Aubrey and scanned me from head to foot. I guess it was a woman. The left side of her head was… not quite shaved, but the dark hair was no longer than my beard. The hair on the right side was blonde with purple streaks and hung to her shoulder. She had multiple piercings in the visible ear, one through her nose, and when she finally spoke, I caught a glimpse of a stud piercing her tongue. "Be polite, Mandy," Aubrey admonished. Mandy sighed and held out her hand.

"Nice to meet you, Mr. Aroslav," she said.

"It's a pleasure to meet you, Mandy," I said, recovering my sense of equilibrium. I wasn't expecting Aubrey to bring a chaperone. I wondered what kind of relationship she had with the much younger woman. "We can wedge another chair in here at the table. I'm starving. I hope you two are hungry."

The waitress came to take drink orders and carded Mandy when she ordered a beer. Apparently, she passed as the drinks were on the table and we'd ordered a double rack of ribs to share among us. Aubrey played the part of a chipper and lively hostess, a stark contrast to Mandy's almost sullen quiet.

I discovered Mandy was a sociology major in her last year. When she spoke, I was fascinated by the flashes of the silver stud in her mouth. She was a good bit taller than Aubrey, but not as tall as me.

It wasn't as if Aubrey was using Mandy as an excuse not to be friendly to me, either. We got messy because there just isn't a good way to eat ribs without using your fingers.

"I'm going to have to go wash up before I can put my hands on the steering wheel," I laughed. "This sauce is great."

"I can help," Aubrey said. She grabbed my right hand and started licking my fingers.

"Slut," Mandy muttered. Aubrey grinned at her and reached out to dip her own fingers in barbecue sauce. She offered her hand to Mandy and while she licked my fingers, Mandy licked Aubrey's. I was feeling how constricted my jeans were.

I love my 501s. They're good-looking blue jeans and probably Levi's best. But I once read a comment that compared them to a cheap hotel. There's no ballroom.

"You've been watching my clit-flicker all through dinner," Mandy said to me. She locked her eyes on mine and I discovered I couldn't pull my gaze away. Deep, purple eyes.

"Your what?"

Mandy answered my question by sticking her tongue out and wagging it so the stud clacked against her teeth. She looked over at Aubrey.

"You sure?" she asked.

"Please?" Aubrey said. Mandy returned her gaze to me.

"My girlfriend wants to play with you," she said. "There's just one problem with that."

"What's that?" I asked. "I don't want to create problems for you."

"Oh, it's no problem for me. It might be for you, though," Mandy said. Her whole demeanor had changed once the finger licking started. "You see, you can only get to little Miss Diaz's tight little pussy through me. You got it in you, cowboy?" I breathed out, not knowing how exactly to respond. "Better yet, can you get it in me?"

AFTER A VERY small amount of debating and a few barbecue flavored kisses beside my truck, the two women decided to ride with me and go to the trailer rather than either of their apartments. Even though they considered themselves a couple, they didn't live together and they had kept their relationship secretive.

"This is so cute," Aubrey said when we were inside. The wind was whipping up a storm outside and I wouldn't be too surprised if there was some snow by morning.

"Make yourselves at home," I said. "I need to go out and disconnect the water line so the hose doesn't freeze tonight."

"We won't have water?" Mandy asked.

"We'll have water," I said. "It will be through the internal tanks and pump, though. Not from outside."

I went out and did the work. It only took about three minutes to disconnect and drain the hose. That was enough time for Mandy and Aubrey to get naked and into my bed.

When I'd started fantasizing about Aubrey bent naked over the edge of my bed this afternoon, I'd never considered the possibility of a two-for-one. I stripped as I watched the two of them kissing and loving on each other in my bed. The view that was exposed to me was Mandy's back. Hardware wasn't the only addition to Mandy's body. The artwork on her back was incredible. She had a rose tattoo. I don't mean a single long stem rose discreetly displayed on her shoulder blade. This was an entire rose bush that ran from her shoulder and the base of her neck down the left side of her back and wrapping around to her stomach. I counted five large blossoms and many, many thorns. It covered about two-thirds of the width of her admittedly slender back. It was breathtaking.

Aubrey looked over Mandy's shoulder at me as I stripped.

"See anything you like, cowboy?" she giggled. Mandy had her face buried in Aubrey's shoulder. The roses were turning red.

"I don't think I've ever seen two more beautiful women together," I said. I brushed the length of Mandy's torso from her neck to her butt as I leaned over her to kiss Aubrey.

"After reading your descriptions of Mary Beth, Ashley, and Cole together, I decided it was my duty to get you a better education about how two women and a man work together," Aubrey said. "In the interest of being a good research assistant," she giggled. Mandy playfully slapped at her and then turned her head to look at me.

"You don't think I'm too much of a freak?" she asked.

"Mandy, you are beautiful, and this artwork is nothing short of gorgeous." The younger woman rolled slowly toward me, still held in Aubrey's arms, until I could see her breasts and the roots of the rose bush wrapping around her stomach. Her navel was pierced. I leaned over her and brushed her nipple with my lips before raising my face to hers for a deep, sensuous kiss. I felt Aubrey take my hand and guide it to her own skin as I kissed her girlfriend. Aubrey rolled slightly away from me, exposing her breasts to my eyes and questing hands as I reached across Mandy to kiss her. I started to get into the bed, too, but was prevented by Mandy pushing her butt out to the edge so there was no room for me.

"Just stay there for now, Aroslav," she whispered. "Touch all you want, but let us get things started before you try to jump in." With that, she pulled Aubrey's face to hers and kissed her deeply while she fondled the Latina's breasts and stomach. Her hand disappeared between them as I reached out to explore Mandy's curves and trace her artwork with my fingers. That pleased her greatly. Her hips moved forward and I saw that she and Aubrey were slowly humping each other's thighs.

"He has nice hands, Aubs. Strong fingers, but gentle," Mandy whispered. Aubrey moaned. "He's stroking my ass, but he's not digging between my cheeks. Oh, god! He found that spot on the side that always makes me wiggle. Right below my hipbone. Did you feel how much juice leaked out of my pussy against your leg?"

"Is he hard, Mandy?" Aubrey gasped. Mandy's hand snaked around behind her and I made sure she found my cock on the first try. She stroked it and squeezed a few drops of precome onto her fingers.

"Really hard. Taste. Does he taste good off my fingers?"

"Ye-es," Aubrey whined.

"Will you eat his come out of my pussy?"

"YES!" Aubrey arched her back and shook as she came from Mandy's expert manipulation. "Is he? Is he going to fuck you, baby?"

"Soon. We need to get things lined up. Come on. I know what you want between your legs. Scoot around." Mandy dropped down off the bed and turned to kiss me deeply. "Next time you kiss me, I'll be covered in Aubrey's come. Better give her a quick kiss, too. And I just know you're dying to squeeze those sweet boobs."

"You're psychic, too?" I asked.

"You think I need to be psychic to see you looking at her fat nipples and just know you want to squeeze them?" she asked. I leaned over her side to kiss Aubrey. Aubrey latched onto my lips and clung to me as she kissed until she suddenly gasped and jerked away. I saw Mandy twisting a nipple. I squeezed Aubrey's other boob and Mandy worked her way between us.

"He's going to watch now. He'll watch while my long pink tongue parts your pussy lips to lick you," Mandy said to Aubrey. She turned toward me and gave me another light kiss. "Go easy, cowboy. I don't do guys very often. Treat my pussy nicely."

Mandy turned away from me and bent over the bed far enough that she could put her head between Aubrey's legs and open her older girlfriend's lower lips with her tongue. I watched as I continued to rub Mandy's back and slid my hands around to caress her slightly more modest breasts.

"He's rubbing me, Aubrey. He's touching my tits," Mandy managed a running narration as she continued to lick at Aubrey's slit. "He knows... knows how to treat a girl's nipples. I can feel him behind me. He's so hard. He's leaking all over my ass. You'll have to make sure you get every drop with your tongue, girlfriend. Ah-um... He's rubbing his cock up and down my ass crack. You think he wants to poke in my pooper? Maybe some time, but not before he fucks my tight little pussy. Mmm! Do you feel that? That's my leg pushing up against yours on the bed. He... he put my leg up there. Oh, Aubrey. That means my pussy is wide OH! Open. Oh. Aubs he licked my slit. All the way from button to butt. I... He's... might make me come before he... Yes!"

I licked Mandy as she kept up a running commentary and had her first orgasm. I could hear her licking change as she started beating a tattoo on Aubrey's clit with her tongue-stud. Aubrey screeched and I stood to line myself up with Mandy's wide-open pussy.

"He's doing it, Aubs. He's pushing that big fat cock up into my little tiny hole. It's so tight. He's almost all the way in. Oh, no! There's more. He's still pushing in. Can you feel my finger up inside you, baby? He's so much deeper than that. I don't think I can take any more. This is his big long cock coming right out of my mouth into your pussy. Feel it? He's fucking you right through me!"

I'd bottomed out long before Mandy's narration ended. But seeing her mouth engulf Aubrey's pussy each time I bounced against her butt and drove into her was incredible. And what she said about being tight and wet was completely true. I wasn't sure how long I'd last like this.

Aubrey's feet came up to wrap around Mandy's back and I caught hold of them to start licking her toes. She squealed again.

"He's licking my toes while he's fucking us," Aubrey screamed. "Fuck me. Fuck me. Fuck me!"

With Aubrey's feet over my shoulders, I hunched down against Mandy's back, hugging that rose bush. My hands slid under her to squeeze her breasts again and keep going up to her neck and then under her chin. I found her hand busy plunging in and out of Aubrey as she flicked her clit with that stud. I managed to wiggle a finger into Aubrey's hole with Mandy's and started sawing in and out with the motion of my hips. Both women were shaking and I was vibrating against Mandy's ass. When Aubrey reached up and twisted her own nipples, the scream that issued from her mouth was met with my bellow as my come rocketed out of my cock. Mandy's whine was somewhat muffled in Aubrey's pussy.

Long after I'd come, my hips convulsively rocked up against Mandy. As long as I could stay hard, I wanted to stay in. Mandy seemed happy to have me there as she pushed back against me and I kissed her rose tattoo. Mandy was wiping her entire face through Aubrey's pussy. Eventually I slid out of Mandy and our combined fluids began running out of her.

"I've got a creamy center, Aubrey," Mandy said. "Let me up on the bed and you can have your little treat." The two girls worked around so that Mandy was lying on her back and Aubrey was going to work on her come-filled crotch. Mandy turned her head and kissed me, smearing Aubrey's juices all over my face. Then she dropped her head slightly and sucked my limp cock into her mouth. I began to harden as Mandy moaned with Aubrey's ministrations. When she called out her next orgasm, she almost swallowed me. I responded to her sucking and hardened rapidly. Mandy came again.

"I'm ready," Aubrey said. "Is Ari ready?"

"Are you ready to fuck my little Mexican girlfriend, Ari?" Mandy asked. "I know how juicy she is. She's going to slide down this pole as easily as my mouth does." She demonstrated and I moaned. We shuffled around and I lay on my back. Aubrey crawled up from my feet and straddled me. For the first time since we left the library, I focused all my attention on Aubrey as she slicked my cock with her pussy juices and bent forward to kiss me.

She had brown eyes with little gold flecks in them. I'd only known one other woman with eyes like that.

And she was a witch.

～～～

A Long Time Ago: Initiation

I DIDN'T BECOME a pagan overnight. I'd been raised in the church. It was true that I had a perfect attendance Sunday School pin that had bars for sixteen years. I was a true believer. I thought all my grade school and high school classmates hated me because I was the religious kid. Yes, I knew that Hannah and Cassie and Carl all went to the same church I did, but I was the religious one. I was going to write Christian plays. Even in grad school, I was focused on discovering the dramatic structure of a Bible book. Religious drama was one of the things that had drawn Paula and me together.

My mother warned me, all the way back when I got my Bible at confirmation when I was twelve, that too much studying of it would damage my faith. I later wondered if she was warning me or encouraging me. She was right. The more I studied, the less faith I had. The more remote that God became. In theater, people are likely to experiment with anything. There were people doing Feldenkrais exercises, people smoking dope, people studying Buddhism, people who lived only for sex. Some things were even taught as ways to make characters more real—the Stanislavski method.

Paula had become upset with an actor in a one-act she was directing. "Phil, why don't you know the part yet?" she demanded the last week of rehearsals.

"I'm still looking for the effervescence of the character," he responded.

"Learn the damn lines. Then you can look for tiny bubbles," she shot back.

For my part, I learned creative visualization. I learned to relax and to create things so real in my mind that they became real in my life. Richard Bach. Read *Jonathan Livingston Seagull* and *Illusions:*

Adventures of a Reluctant Messiah. Shakti Gawain's *Creative Visualization: Use the Power of Your Imagination to Create What You Want in Your Life.* You get the idea.

And then there was the witch.

Her name was Judith, and I don't know if I found her eyes more bewitching or her tits. I'm sure she'd waited on me at the Uptown Bar and Grill on numerous occasions before I ever got my eyes up far enough to meet hers.

A bunch of guys got together every Friday night to play cards in the basement of a local cigar store. I went every week. Jim would let me fill my pipe from one of the tobacco canisters if I was short of money. There were some hard times back then. I had a five-dollar limit when we started playing and stuck to it rigidly. At a nickel a chip I could usually play the whole evening. And if I won five dollars, I'd stop at the Uptown on the way home to have a burger and a beer at a quarter after midnight.

Judith was the waitress. And looking at her boobs in the tight little t-shirt she wore in the bar was all the entertainment I needed for hours. I was sure she wore a bra because I could see the outline of the straps over her shoulders. But it must have been one of those that were just thin nylon or something, because I could also see the clear outline of her constantly hard nipples.

I took a book in on a Sunday afternoon once, during the time between Paula and Belle. Figured I'd just watch a football game or whatever was on the big screen while I drank a beer. I was spaced out.

"You know you can use that power for more than attracting money," Judith said as she set my beer down. I was reading Gawain's book yet again. That's when I looked up into her eyes. So dark brown they were almost black with little gold flecks in them. "Like you can improve your relationships, attract sexual energy, or just become one with the earth around you. Read this book and let me know what you think." The book she handed me was Starhawk's *The Spiral Dance.*

I'd already begun writing *Behind the Ivory Veil*, but I knew that I was missing the catalyst that would bring Rebecca to Greece. How would I connect what she was studying in Edinburgh with the mythology of the Metéora? In *The Spiral Dance*, I found the rituals that would permeate *The Props Master* series, and that would gradually become the guidelines for my life.

But it didn't happen all at once.

I'd collected works on Greek, Roman, Norse, and Celtic mythology when I wrote my thesis. I'd read the *The Chronicles of the Deryni* by Katherine Kurtz and was fascinated by the weaving together of magic and Catholicism. My dissertation dealing with oral versus written traditions and focusing on the ballad dance had gotten me started on my book. But now I added other books, in addition to my own copy of Starhawk. *Ritual Magic, Practical Witchcraft, Candle-burning Rituals, The White Goddess.* Over the years, the simple rituals and oneness with the earth displaced the judgmental hierarchy of western Judeo-Christian-Islamic religion.

Belle and I managed three years together before the spectacular conclusion of our relationship. When it imploded, I found myself once again sitting alone at the Uptown staring into Judith's headlights. Then I lifted my eyes to hers.

"It's your birthday, isn't it," she said. I nodded. "Why are you here alone?" I explained my sad story. "Shit. You do have some lousy luck, don't you?" She slid into the bench on the opposite side of the booth. "How long have you been practicing the pagan rituals now, Ari?"

"About five years now, I guess."

"Have you ever been initiated?"

"Just the ritual in Starhawk's book. I've been a solitary," I said.

"You have a robe?" I nodded. "All your tools?" I nodded again. "Wear it and bring your tools. I'll pick you up at seven tonight. Ari, you'll still be a solitary when we're finished, but you'll know." I looked into those gold-flecked eyes and nodded.

I'm not going to go into all my initiation ritual. It was very personal. We wore robes to the clearing where we gathered wood for a fire and she prepared the space. There's places where you can do that in Minnesota. When she shed her robe and directed me to do the same, I got to see those firm, tight orbs just as she viewed my staff. And orbs they were. I'd have sworn they were fake if it weren't for the fact that I later got to test them. From the moment she challenged me at the edge of the circle with the point of her knife held at my chest until the last embers of the fire had died and the circle was released, I was in her power.

"Know that it is better to fall upon my knife and die than to enter the presence of the dread mighty ones with fear in your heart," she said.

"I come with perfect love and perfect trust," I answered.

We spoke ritual words. We broke bread and drank wine. We danced around and around the circle. We spread our robes on the ground and made love.

I won't try to convince you that there were visible walls of flame rising from our cone of power, but I could feel it. And when I came in her, with her, it might have been the only time in my life that instead of feeling drained by sex, I felt filled.

We were never lovers again, though I invited her to my next Solstice Celebration. We had come together in my initiation. She was my high priestess.

Back to Aubrey and Mandy

WHEN AUBREY KISSED me, she slid forward and then back to take my cock inside her. It was no slow, sawing insertion as I'd had with Mandy. Not that Aubrey jammed herself down on me, but once she started down, she just kept going until we couldn't go any farther.

Aubrey had a way of just doing pelvic thrusts, rocking forward and back, while we kissed, that gave all the stimulation we needed. I was soon in the same rhythm, just rocking my pelvis back until we almost disconnected and then forward until we were completely joined. Every single thrust stimulated the entire length of my cock and the entire depth of her pussy.

And we didn't come.

I can't even say we made love, though fucking sounds so limited to describe the next twenty minutes of kissing and rocking in and out. Nor was Mandy idle, though she did not try to incite us with her commentary as she had when I'd taken her from behind. She lay with us and petted us. She joined in our kisses. I learned a lot about three-way kissing that night.

Eventually, Aubrey started to shift.

"I can feel it," she said. "It's going to be so good. In a few minutes, you are going to spray more come into my *coño* than you thought you had in your body. It's time to get into position."

'Into position' involved me sitting up and leaning against the several pillows I keep stacked on my bed. I do half my writing in bed, propped up on pillows. Aubrey turned to face away from me and reinserted my cock where it would do us the most good. She leaned back against me and pulled my hands around to play with her breasts as she exposed her neck for me to kiss.

When Mandy started at my balls and licked all the way to Aubrey's clit, I almost lost it. We paused and settled back into a slow and gentle rhythm again. Mandy would wait until I was almost out of Aubrey before she licked up the entire length of my cock. Then, as I pushed back into Aubrey, Mandy would tap our lover's clit with her stud. When I was all the way in, she would lick my balls and suck them into her mouth, tapping softly with the hardware in her mouth.

Aubrey's breath was coming in long, drawn-out moans. I realized I was harmonizing with her. And, indeed, it was just a few minutes—never having changed the pace or rhythm—that we came.

Years of habit had trained me to drive deep and hold while I came. Aubrey and Mandy enforced maintaining the rhythm—though with a few stutters—throughout our orgasm. It made it seem like it went on forever. The stimulation of pulling out of Aubrey as I came and having Mandy lick the length of my cock as I pressed back in, still jetting, was fucking unbelievable. When Aubrey pressed down to hold us together in the aftershocks, Mandy kept gently bathing my balls and Aubrey's pussy with her tongue. It could have been irritating, but it was just enough stimulation to slow my softening and let us stay joined that much longer.

And when I finally flopped out, Mandy was there to catch the residue with her tongue and suck our combined fluids off my flaccid cock. Aubrey lay back against me with her hands on mine cupping her breasts.

"I knew that would be spectacular," she breathed.

"You've done it before like that?" I asked.

"No. I'm psychic," she said.

~~~~~~

OUR FRIDAY NIGHT fun lasted most of the night. I wasn't always involved. Mandy and Aubrey were good together. They liked to have fun, but they were kind and considerate lovers to each other. When I was no more than a limp noodle, it was fun to be beside them while they made love.

Even these two voracious lovers, though, had to take a break on Saturday afternoon to go into town and watch the Border War, UWyo's annual clash with Colorado State University. The game this year was at Colorado, so we went back to Rosie's Cantina and managed to get three seats at the long bar. We had beer and later we had fries. Finally, we had big bowls of chili. It looked good until about the middle of the third quarter and then the Cowboys started to slip and the Colorado Rams edged them out.

I took a selfie of the three of us in the bar with my recharged cell phone. Aubrey took charge of the phone to send the picture to her and to Mandy and to see that I had their numbers in my directory. Aubrey, of course, discovered the photo of Reba.

"Uh-oh," she said. "Have you called her, Ari?"

"Uh… no. Should I?"

"Not if you ever want in this pussy again. How much did she say she'd charge you?" she demanded.

"Is this like a thing with the cheerleaders?" I asked, avoiding her question.

"No. Just with her. No one has proven that she solicits. No guys will testify. Don't get me wrong. I don't blame them. A couple hundred and you get to stick it to a nineteen-year-old cheerleader? Even if you decide not to, you don't want to spoil it for anyone else. Besides, *you'd* be the one in the spotlight if you brought accusations."

"I see no reason to call her. There is nothing she has that the two beautiful women who spent the night in my bed last night don't have double of," I said. I had *thought* about calling her.

"Good answer," Aubrey said. "I'll leave you the picture because she's good masturbation material for man or woman. But I'm deleting her contact info."

We walked out of the cantina with several slightly pissed and pissed off fans grousing about the game.

"Too bad the team lost," I said. I was becoming rather fond of UWyo.

"Probably for the best," Mandy said. "There won't be as many jailed or injured."

"What?"

"Well, if the home team loses, it can be kind of hard on the visitors," Aubrey said. "It might not mean that you get beat up, but the police might just suspect that you were drinking and pull you over, just because you have out-of-state plates. The home fans on both sides of the border are pretty enthusiastic about their teams."

"Well, I'm glad we were right here in Laramie," I said. "Uh… I didn't actually make an official invitation, but it is Saturday night and I'd love it if you joined me again."

Mandy and Aubrey held a whispered conversation. Then Aubrey pushed Mandy toward me.

"Ari? Is the invitation only open for *both* of us?" she asked. She was looking down and I thought she might be blushing.

"Of course, you are both welcome," I said. "Oh. But if only one of you can or wants to come tonight, that's okay, too. Is everything okay between you? I don't want to create any problems for the two of you. You are way too sweet."

"It's okay," Aubrey sighed. "We'd each like to spend one-on-one time with you, though. I don't work on Mondays. Mandy has class. So, it makes sense that tonight is her night and I get Sunday. If you'd like to be alone with each of us, that is."

"I'd love time with each of you," I said. "I'm here for another week, though. I hope we'll all be together again. I really like both of you."

"I knew you would," Aubrey said. She winked at me. She didn't need to be psychic to figure that out.

9 Blackfeather

24 October 2014

WE DROPPED off Aubrey at her apartment after sizzling kisses for each of us. Mandy stayed in the center seat with her head on my shoulder. The sun was just about to touch the mountains in the west.

"It's early," she said. "Why don't you drive me up to the pass? I'll show you a couple things about the area you're writing about." It sounded like a good idea to me, so I gladly drove the twenty-five miles out to Centennial and then four more miles to the top of the pass. When we got to the top, we could still see the sun, just touching the horizon.

"A day with two sunsets," I said. "What could be more perfect?" I snapped a picture of the dipping sun and then slid back into the driver's seat. I started the truck, but Mandy pulled my face to hers for a questing kiss. Each touch of her lips felt as though she was searching for something. I wondered what.

"Drive back a mile and then turn in toward the ski lodge," Mandy directed as I turned the truck around. It was a nice-looking lodge, but it was deserted. "Snow will fly in a week or two. The only people around right now are those who are grooming the slopes. If there's no snow by Thanksgiving, they'll start making snow. Forecasts are that it will snow by next week, though."

I pulled into a remote area of the parking lot and turned the lights off. Mandy was in perfect synch as she melted into my arms and my kiss. Her tongue stud tapped against my teeth a few times as we kissed. She pulled her shirt out of her jeans and pushed my hand under it against her smooth bare tummy. I took the hint and climbed higher until I was holding her breast and rubbing her tender nubbin with my thumb. Mandy was panting and I decided I wanted to get her back to the trailer *now*. I dropped my hand, caressing her tummy as I went. She sucked her stomach in so that there was room for my hand to slip under the waistband of her jeans. I could only reach the top of her slit but Mandy was squirming all over.

I finally withdrew, debating over whether I should unfasten her jeans and try again. She shoved her shirttail back into her pants and took two deep breaths, which she blew out almost like a long distance runner.

"Let's stop at the Beartree for a beer on the way home," she said brightly.

"Okay." *Anything you say, honey.*

On Saturday night, the Beartree Tavern and Cafe had live music. It was country music, and very danceable. A few people stared at Mandy's hair and piercings, but once we had our beer, we headed straight for the dance floor. I might not be the greatest dancer, but I learned to two-step by dancing with my baby daughter to K.D. Lang's "Big Boned Girl." Mandy was a great partner and once we'd had a dance, we were just another couple in the bar. The place was incredibly friendly. We both ordered Cokes after our beer.

"Good," the waitress said. "We want folks to have fun, but if you have to drive back to Laramie, we don't want you to only get part way."

"How'd you know we were going back to Laramie?" I asked.

"I read your book," she grinned. "After you were here a couple of months ago and gave me a copy. We just want you to be safe and write us into the next one!"

While I was there, I found out all about the Centennial Uptown Breakdown or CUB that had taken place over Labor Day. The waitress's attitude and the concept of a big dance outside combined to give me an idea for a scene in *Blackfeather*. After a few more dances, Mandy just led me out the door and back to the truck.

"Thank you for doing something special with me," she said. "Aubrey and I hardly ever go out. We just find a place to get together and fuck. Laramie is the most liberal place in Wyoming, but it still isn't that friendly to gays and lesbians."

What a cultural contradiction. Laramie was the first place in America to give women the right to vote. It was the first place to ever seat a woman on a jury. There was a sign on Second Avenue that said, "Wyoming: Where women make the laws and men break them." To think that this bastion of freedom in the 'Equal Rights State' was still narrow-minded when it came to homosexuals and bisexuals was just hard to grasp.

I broke one of my own rules and put my arm around Mandy as I drove back to the campground one-handed.

I KICKED OFF my boots when we got back to the trailer and hung my hat. I know I'm a drugstore cowboy, but the only thing I could do to blend in more in a truly western state is to wear a gun. And I could be approved for one here in twenty-four hours. The only reason it would take that long is because I'm from out of state.

Television distorts our sense of the world. When I was growing up, I thought of Tombstone and El Paso as being the West. "Wyatt Earp, Wyatt Earp. Brave, courageous, and bold…"

But when I traveled across the country this summer, I discovered the real Old West was in Nebraska, the Dakotas, Colorado, Wyoming, and Montana. This is where cowboys head for the bar at night, driving a mud-caked Jeep Wrangler with a winch on the front to pull a tree out of the road after a flood. Or they might have done the job with a rope attached to their saddle horns. Some of these guys still live in the saddle and that hardware on their hip is just another tool of the trade.

Mandy had her shoes off and was sitting tailor fashion on the bed. She hadn't undressed, so I kept my clothes on.

"Want anything?" I asked.

"Got one of those bubbly water things?" she asked. I grabbed a La Croix out of the fridge and handed her one. I popped one for myself, too. It was very refreshing.

"Do you, like, pick up girls everywhere you go?" she asked.

"No," I said. I edged myself up onto the bed and sat facing her. "I'm not averse to it, but when it happens, it usually comes as a surprise."

"You're good looking enough," she said.

"Thanks. But you forgot to add 'for an old guy'. It's not a problem with looks or being friendly," I said. "It's mostly timing. I've been traveling. Usually not more than two weeks in one location and then on to the next. It takes time to build up to a relationship. You just can't rush these things."

"Unless you happen on a couple of sluts who'll do you for the thrill and let you go. You got laid by two girls and propositioned by another in twenty-four hours."

"Is that how you think of yourself, Mandy?" I asked. "Are you a slut who just did me for the thrill of it?"

"No. I did you for Aubrey. I'd do anything for Aubrey," she whispered.

"We're alone tonight," I said. "You don't have to do anything for anyone."

"But…" she said looking at me plaintively. "But what if I want to?"

"Is that what's worrying you?" I asked.

"I liked it. I mean, I liked it when we were with Aubs. I don't know if I'll like it without her."

"Are you a lesbian or are you bi?" I asked.

"What's the difference?"

"If you are a lesbian, your sexual preference is women. Period. You might consent to being fucked by a man, but it would be to either hide that you are a lesbian, or to please your bi lover. You'd never willingly just choose to be with a man."

"But if I'm bi, I'm a lesbian with a woman and hetero with a man?"

"No. Let me put it this way. If you were H2O, you might be steam or water or ice. But no matter which form you took, you'd still be H2O. Bisexual people don't change their sexual preference based on who they are with. They are always bi," I said.

"So, if I like being with a man and I like being with a woman, but I'd prefer a woman?"

"Does it make a difference if a man likes women, but prefers his wife?"

"That's like what it's supposed to be!"

I just grinned at her. She finally smiled.

"So, I don't have to worry that I can't have Aubrey if I like having sex with you?" she asked. I nodded. "I liked kissing you. Can we kiss some more?"

We scooted around on the bed so we were in a good position for kissing and let nature take its course. The course nature chose was to have us both get naked and enjoy moving together until we were too exhausted to keep going. I liked this tattooed and pierced young woman. A lot.

And I liked her lover just as much.

We got together for Sunday brunch at the trailer. I grilled during a lull in the wind that let me keep the grill lit long enough to cook steaks. I had tomatoes that I sliced in half and covered with salt, pepper, and parmesan cheese to grill as well. Aubrey was kind enough to bring a salad.

She approached her lover cautiously, as if to discover if things had changed. The kiss Mandy gave her reassured her.

~~~

MY ONE-ON-ONE TIME with Aubrey was a little strange, but then… Aubrey. She took me on a guided walking tour of Laramie after Mandy had excused herself to go study. Aubrey pointed out various historical markers in town and went on to explain how distorted the legend had become over time. The Bucket of Blood Saloon where the chief gang was 'arrested' was probably a place called Belle's. I thought that was kind of funny, but didn't explain it to Aubrey. History says that the night the vigilantes cleaned up the town was a fiasco and that most of the outlaws fled town when an excited mob member fired off his gun too soon. The story says that the gunfire at Belle's was so heavy that the air was blue with smoke from the gun powder and that an uncountable number of shots were fired. Yet the only casualty was the piano player. Sounds like a battle between Luke Skywalker and the Stormtroopers.

Laramie, Wyoming of 1868 was an incredible place.

~~~~~

AUBREY WAS AMAZINGLY different than Mandy, not only in body, but in attitude. Aubrey barely topped five feet tall and had some serious curves. Not overweight, by any stretch of the imagination, but a narrow waist with a butt that was large and round. Her breasts were large and round, too, but not oversized for her frame. She would never win a thigh-gap contest, but she could create a space between them that was completely adequate to welcome me.

She showed me all this within a minute of getting back to my trailer. Aubrey had none of Mandy's hesitancy. Her clothes came off as soon as we were inside and she'd confirmed that my space heater was sufficient to warm us up. I have a gas furnace in the trailer, but when I'm running it, it always seems to run out of gas in the middle of the night. I've had to get up at three o'clock in the morning to switch tanks entirely too often. When I'm camped where I have power, my little ceramic space heater keeps the tiny space toasty warm with no difficulty. And it was already in the forties outside.

Aubrey crawled onto my bed and wiggled her butt at me as I undressed. Then she sat cross-legged at the foot of the bed and grabbed my lap desk. She pointed to the head of the bed and told me to sit. She put a deck of tarot cards on the desk between us and told me to shuffle them and mix them up any way I wanted to.

I took my time. Sitting in front of a naked woman who faced me cross-legged was an experience to be savored. When Aubrey realized where I was staring, she started vamping and making the most of it and shifted to a Yoga pose with the soles of her feet together and her knees as far apart as possible. The flower of her sex opened in front of me as she blithely exposed herself.

"If you play your cards right, you can get a lot closer look," she laughed. "But no touching until I've done your reading. I don't want to get my cards sticky."

When I'd sufficiently shuffled the cards, Aubrey laid them out in a cross pattern and started turning them over. Tarot is one of the things I've often thought I *should* learn, but have never taken the time. I know there are numbered cards in four suits—cups, wands, pentacles, and swords—and that there are a bunch of major arcana of which I don't comprehend the hierarchy at all. All the stories that use cards seem to focus on the Fool and the Hanged Man. James Bond, anyone?

I have no idea what the cards were, but Aubrey wove a tale around them that had enough truth in it that I could readily identify parts of my life. It doesn't take much of a psychic to tell me that I face a long journey on which I am healing from a deep emotional wound and will be helped along by four types of women, none of whom would be my life mate. But Aubrey was so good at weaving her story that I found myself mesmerized by her words as much as by the winking eye of her pussy—or *coño*, as she called it.

I heard her sniff and looked up into her gold-flecked eyes. They were moist. She gathered up the cards and wrapped them in a silk cloth. She hopped off the bed and put the bundle in her purse on the way to the bathroom. I stowed my desk and figured the weird stuff was over, so I rearranged pillows and blankets so we could cuddle up together. It seemed like she'd ended the reading kind of abruptly and there was no real conclusion. It bothered me and I was relieved that she was still naked when she came out of the bathroom. I was afraid she had seen something that made her want to leave.

"The space heater doesn't heat the bathroom all that well," she said as she cuddled into my arms. I pulled the blanket up over us and we kissed, her lush curves molding to my body. "I just want to ravish you and fuck until I can't walk any longer," she sighed. "My *coño* is dripping and ready for your hard cock. But…"

Oh, shit! I could hear the words in my head. *Could we just cuddle?* Of course, we can, sweetheart.

"I need to finish your reading before we lose ourselves in carnal lust," she giggled.

"I thought we were finished. You put the cards away. What now? Reading my palm?" I laughed. I didn't intend to make fun of her, but there are certain kinds of woo-woo that I find too uncomfortable to explain.

~~~~~~

A Long Time Ago: Tealeaves

I WAS EXPLORING relationships. Belle was gone. I'd met several women after Judith initiated me who seemed to be uncommonly interested in me. Maybe I'd just never noticed their interest before.

One of those women was Treasure.

We knew each other professionally. We had mutual clients for different aspects of projects. She focused on editing and I focused on design. Of course, Belle had bankrupted me and my business when she left, but I still had clients and was getting a little revenue. I was just going to have to sell my house before the bank took it. Treasure and I had gone out once and agreed that we had fun and should do it again. Neither of us could decide whether that one time was a date or a business meeting. I think we both wrote it off our taxes. I liked her. A lot.

Another of the women was one of my clients, Olivia. Olivia represented a company that was currently responsible for about sixty percent of our publishing revenue. It was probably stupid to get involved with her, but she'd indicated that she was interested, so I invited her out. As it happened, I had to be out of the house Sunday for the Realtor to have an open house, so Olivia and I used the opportunity to get to know each other. We had lunch, went for a long walk around the lake, and eventually wandered down Lake Street to an odd little shop called Sunsight. Turned out it was one of those woo-woo shops. Olivia wanted to have her cards read and I waited patiently. She came out of the reading a little glazed about half an hour later.

"My reader said we should have our tea leaves read by Aura," Olivia said. "Will you do it?" Frankly, I'd been thinking about 'doing it' all afternoon. Olivia was a little quirky, but she was quite pretty and had been holding my hand or hugging my arm all afternoon. I agreed to the tealeaf reading.

Aura emerged from behind a curtain to bring us each a cup of tea. She was what I'd expect from a commercial enterprise like a bookstore. She was older—probably in her sixties—and wore a long skirt, white blouse, and had a scarf tied around her head. A regular gypsy.

We drank the tea until there was just a bit of liquid with the remaining leaves floating in it. A woman came out of Aura's curtained cubicle.

"Thank you! Thank you so much, Aura," the woman said as she hugged the gypsy. "I'm so relieved. You are wonderful." The woman turned and saw our teacups. "You'll love her. She's so wonderful." That was her recommendation, apparently, as she hurried down the stairs and out the front door of the bookstore.

"Well! One at a time or together?" Aura asked as she approached us. I was about to say that Olivia could go first, but she beat me to the draw.

"Together!"

We carried our cups into the cubicle and set them on the table where Aura pointed. As we sat, Aura peered from one cup to the other and back. Then she picked up Olivia's cup, swirled the leaves and started talking. It was kind of the usual drivel about how there were many questions in her mind that only time could answer. That things were going well at work and she would prosper. That relationships were the thing that was most prevalent on her mind and that she had to be patient. You could sit in front of just about anyone with a little rudimentary skill and give the same speech.

Then she turned to my cup.

"Chaos and uncertainty," she started. "You are on a path to recovery from an emotional and financial disaster. You have a lot of doubt about your future. You don't have much faith in people, but don't let that dampen your willingness to take a risk. Especially a risk on love. There is a woman emerging from your leaves. You know her professionally and have worked closely with each other." I glanced toward Olivia and she was practically squirming in her seat. "This woman holds the key to much of your future. She holds happiness and sorrow, but if you ignore this opportunity, you will miss the best that life can offer you. This is a truly great love." Aura looked up from the cup and into my eyes. Then she looked at Olivia. She reached out to take Olivia's hand between her own and said softly, "I'm sorry, dear. It's not you."

You would think that would be a major wet towel to throw on a date. Olivia, however, was not to be deterred. She continued to hold my hand and, as we walked through the shops in Uptown, she welcomed my arm around her. We had dinner at Figlio's and a glass of wine to cap off the evening, then walked the few blocks to my dark and quiet home. I'd find out tomorrow whether there had been any activity during the open house. Maybe I'd be rid of this monstrosity soon. Regardless, the evening was shaping up to be quite promising.

I put a fake log in the fireplace and lit it. I didn't have much in the way of furniture after Belle had stripped the house, but the real estate agent had put together a nice little loveseat setting in front of the fireplace as staging. Olivia and I settled into the loveseat and into each other. I heard the phone ring and ignored it. There was a voice on the answering machine, but I figured it was just the Realtor and I'd check the message later. Olivia and I were progressing toward some serious making out and I was thinking this could be the best night I'd had since my initiation in the woods.

The phone rang again and we ignored it.

Olivia had already welcomed my hand to her breast as we kissed and made no complaints as I began to unbutton her blouse. I trailed kisses down her neck and onto her chest as I uncovered her lacy pink bra. I love front-catch bras. A quick flick and I was feasting on Olivia's rosy nipples.

The phone rang again and I could hear what sounded like an angry voice.

"You'd better find out what's so important or we're never going to get any peace," Olivia said. "Someone sounds angry."

I gave her nipples one more suck and reluctantly went to the kitchen to check the answering machine. The phone rang again and I snatched it off the cradle.

"What?" I snapped.

"Where have you been. We need you," Dan shouted at me. *At the office? What the fuck?*

"I worked eighty hours this week, Dan. I told you I was taking the day off. I've been out."

"Well, we need you to come in. This project is all screwed up."

"You've got John and Darcy. What can't they handle?"

"They can't solve it. You set the project up. They can't figure out what went wrong."

"All they had to do was press start and feed the damn paper in the slot," I snarled. "Even John and Darcy couldn't mess that up."

"Darcy found a typo as the pages were coming out of the printer, so she canceled the print and fixed it. Then she couldn't get the print to restart. You have to come out and fix it. We promised this project to GenSys at eight a.m."

"Yeah and who did that?" I groused. "I'm busy."

"This is your job, Ari. If you still want to have it tomorrow, get in here and fix this." Dan slammed down the phone and I slammed down the phone.

"God damned fucker!" Dan was my best friend and I'd negotiated to have him hired as my boss after my bankruptcy. *But damn it!* I turned to go back to Olivia and she was standing in the doorway. She was finishing buttoning her blouse. "Olivia…"

"I know. I could hear most of it. You've got clients, Ari. I'd probably be the same way if it was my project. Would you like me to drop you off at your office?"

"Thank you, Olivia. I was… This was nice… I'm sorry about what Aura said this afternoon. I think we could…" *Could what?* I was horny as hell, but I certainly wasn't ready to declare my undying love. I'd love to continue sucking her tits and bury myself in her pussy. But I had no pretenses that she was what I wanted as a wife.

"Ari," she said as she hugged me and placed a light kiss on my lips, "I can be, will be, anything you want or need. I don't care what the tea leaves said. I could be the one. Just say the word."

I couldn't say the word that night. I went in to find the entire project had been fucked up. The typo had caused a change in page breaks and there were widows and orphans through the next ten pages. The first print order was stuck in the spooler blocking the next print order—*What the fuck?* She'd sent it to print how many more times? It made no difference. I needed to flush the spooler and restart all the systems. Then I'd have to babysit the machine as I hand-fed the heavy-weight glossy stock into it one sheet at a time.

GenSys was a demanding client and I worked 110 hours that week making their emergency changes to content and design. Two more nights after Sunday, I just never went home. Darcy was all apologetic for messing up the project and my date. She asked if a blowjob would help, but when I started to unzip my pants in the middle of the office, she screamed and ran to the break room. Not that I wouldn't fuck Darcy. She'd certainly shown she was a fuck-up.

Sunday, I slept late and didn't want to get out of bed, even when the real estate agent showed up for the afternoon open house. I scrambled around stuffing dirty clothes in the back of my closet and trying to smooth out my matted hair so I could go out. I'd made a date with Treasure two weeks earlier and we were supposed to meet for brunch at Becky's Cafeteria. The only reason it had been Olivia last week and not Treasure was because Treasure was out of town.

I felt like crap and believed I looked even worse, but I couldn't help but smile when I saw her. The kiss on the cheek she gave me in greeting was new. We hadn't reached the point of even being that familiar with each other.

I'll cut to the chase since you are probably getting tired of this story, there being only interrupted sex in it. Treasure and I ended up at the same bookstore that afternoon that Olivia and I had been at the previous week. We were laughing at some of the book titles we saw and wandered upstairs.

"Oh, let's have our tea leaves read," she laughed. "That will be fun."

I was a little less enthused, but agreed and Aura brought us tea. We talked about our week at work, what kind of clients we were dealing with, and how tired we both were. Aura collected our teacups and seated us in her little cubicle. Once again, she started to read Treasure's leaves, but kept turning to my cup.

"Are you married?" she asked suddenly. We both laughed and shook our heads. We'd just started dating, really. "Then what are you doing in his cup?" She proceeded to tell us that life was going to have some significant challenges for us, but we had a strong future intertwined together. She could see a farm on an island and a ring. And a big move. "The move will be very good for both of you."

We left that reading a little stunned. Each time we looked at each other, we giggled a little and blushed. Somewhere along the line, Treasure took my hand as we walked. We'd started something, even though we were both going to approach it cautiously. We'd both recently come out of bad relationships and were determined to go slow and meet other people.

Somehow, though, I never got around to dating Olivia again. Treasure and I were married a year later. She was the love of my life.

Back to Aubrey

"Ari, you may never heal," Aubrey said. "I'm so sorry, honey. That's why I had to get up and go to the bathroom. I didn't know how to tell you what I saw. So, I'll just say it. Each time you start to heal, you tear off a new part of yourself to give to someone else. When that doesn't work out, you are left with a hole. But it is so important for you to keep doing that because you are healing others." I looked at her and could only think, 'This girl is crazy. Let it go.'

"Well, that explains it then," I chuckled.

"It's not easy, Ari. It won't get easier by denying it. Tell me that even while you have my naked body in your arms right now and even though you know that in just a few minutes I'm going to welcome your hard cock into my wet pussy... Tell me even now that you aren't thinking a little bit of Mandy. That you aren't yearning for her to be here with us."

I couldn't tell her that. It was true. Even when Aubrey was walking toward me from the bathroom I'd thought of how much fun I'd had with Mandy and hoped she was doing okay alone tonight.

"You felt the same way about me last night," Aubrey continued. I nodded. That was true, too. "You fall in love with everyone. And when you are in love, you are vulnerable. So even if you are the one who ends things, you end up wounded. But the people you touch are always better for it. You are sad because Mandy is not in your arms with me tonight. But Mandy... I could tell when I kissed her that Mandy is better than she was a few days ago, before we met you. She doesn't have that much experience sexually. She loves to talk dirty and it just gives me such a charge, but you were only her second man. And you healed, in one night, damage from the first man that she's carried for four years. Don't stop falling in love, Ari. Fall in love with me, too. Love me."

~~~~~~

THE LAST WEEK of October was full of research and sex. Aubrey and I spent most of Monday experimenting with 'things I've never done.' It seemed that we both had quite a list of things we'd never done, and a couple of the things were going to stay on it. I told Aubrey in no uncertain terms that I would watch her pee in the toilet and she could watch me if she wanted, but if she tried to pee on me, I would throw her bodily out of the trailer and lock the door—no matter what time it was or how cold it was or how naked she was.

"I'm not really *interested* in it," she explained. "It's just on my list of things I've never done. How about with me on my back with my head over the edge of the bed and you fucking my mouth?" The woman was certifiably crazy. It took exactly one thrust and she sat straight up and yelled, "If you ever do that again, I'll bite it off!" I held onto my gut where she'd punched me and promised that she didn't need to worry about it.

On the other hand, when I fucked her ass, I might have been a little more rigorous than was strictly called for. It was on her list, not mine. My list included a standing 69. She was small enough and light enough that I could hold her upside down while she fellated me and I ate her out. For about three minutes. Then I fell back on the bed and she crawled off. We both just lay there and cuddled for half an hour before either of us were ready to look at the list again. I flat-out refused to hit her or choke her. When I surprised her with an ice cube on her clit as she was coming, though, she screamed so loud and so long that she passed out. *Damn! It really did work!*

I met Mandy after her last class on Tuesday and she gave me a tour of the campus from a student perspective. That included going to each of her classrooms as she told me her class schedule. I met the director of the MFA program in Creative Writing. He downloaded *Redtail* to his Kindle while we were talking.

Mandy arranged a tour of a house on sorority row under condition that it remain anonymous. Five young women met me at a table in their kitchen and laughed and blushed for forty-five minutes as I asked them questions from my research questionnaire. I got some usable answers.

Mandy and I held hands as we went to the student union for dinner and I watched people wandering in and out, grabbing food from the half-dozen vendors there. A young woman walked past and then turned around to talk to us. It took me a minute to recognize her.

"I didn't know I had competition. I'd have discounted the price. Still available if you want something other than a freak," she said. It was Reba the cheerleader whore. Mandy was ready to jump up and start a fight and barely restrained herself when I laid a hand on hers.

"Honey, you couldn't compete with Mandy if you were giving it away," I said.

"Fuck you!" the cheerleader said loudly enough to be heard at surrounding tables. People stared at us as Reba stalked away. I glanced at the nearest table, filled with young men and women in camo fatigues.

"I'm too expensive for her," I said as I shrugged. They stared at me for a minute and then broke out laughing. Mandy and I decided it was time to leave. We spent a quiet night as she studied and I wrote, and then just cuddled up to me as we went to sleep.

Friday night was HalloNaNoWeen. It was a tradition I'd started in Seattle years ago, and this was the second year I wouldn't be there to participate. So, I joined the NaNoWriMo group for Wyoming Elsewhere and invited local writers to join me to kick off the month of November.

I suppose that I need to explain HalloNaNoWeen.

A Few Years Ago: HalloNaNoWeen

I'D STARTED MY participation in National Novel Writing Month (NaNoWriMo) ten years before. I'd just gotten into blogging, and the folks at Blogger decided they'd sponsor NaNoBlogMo. Blog your novel during November. I said, "Sure. What the heck?" I was a lot more reserved with my language back then. The novel is still up, though I've lost my password and can't correct it and all the picture links have broken. What a surprise! It's a story about small town Indiana called Willow Mills. It doesn't have any sex in it. I didn't write *that* kind of stuff. I was a serious author and this was literary fiction.

I didn't know that NaNoWriMo had forums. The next year, though, I met some other people who were participating and they told me about it. It was cool. "I'm going to go to the 24-hour Starbucks on Halloween night and start writing at midnight. Anyone who wants to can join me." It was a great idea and several people agreed that they'd join me. Only we had a storm that night. All the power in the area went out and they closed at eleven. I tried to get word out that I'd be at Denny's instead, but no one else showed up.

The next year I put out the message that the people at Denny's had been nice and thought it was a great idea. So, I invited people to join me there for the kickoff at midnight on Halloween. I dubbed the event HalloNaNoWeen. A dozen people joined me and we had a blast getting our novels kicked off. The next year there were forty people and Denny's put out a call for more wait staff. Without intending it, I had become the host for the annual NaNoWriMo kickoff event:

HalloNaNoWeen. My last year hosting it, Denny's closed the restaurant to all but our group and nearly 200 writers showed up.

~~~

Back to Laramie

IN LARAMIE, THERE were two other writers. We sat in a booth at Shari's, the only all-night restaurant in town, and laughed at each other's costumes and novel ideas. We stayed there until a little after two in the morning meaning that I was there late enough to join my hometown event via Twitter.

> *"Who are you?"*
> *Of all the things that I imagined and all the things Pa had told me, I never expected the girl into whose eyes I was looking to say that.*
> *I never expected her to say anything. I tried to pull back, but she kept me trapped there. I tried to take control, but she held firm.*
> *"Somehow you've managed to get inside me. You could at least tell me your name."*

I'd begun writing *Blackfeather*.

Although I was bursting with words for the novel, I made time to play with Aubrey and Mandy most of Saturday night. There was a lot of emotion built up among us and I orgasms brought on more tears than usual—both from the women and from me.

"Remember, Ari," Aubrey admonished me just before we parted on Sunday afternoon, "keep slathering your left arm with sunblock or you'll get trucker's skin cancer. You need to take care of this arm. Try wearing long sleeves on your left side and driving gloves. It's in the cards."

The woman was crazy, but just as she'd said in my reading, I'd fallen in love with her, too.

Monday morning, I was on the road headed south, hoping to beat winter to New Mexico.

~~~

NORMALLY, I AVOID interstate highways. They are made for people with a destination. When I'm on one, I'm looking for the first exit that will lead to a more interesting route. But I wanted to get south before weather closed me in and decided to take the most direct route to New Mexico, Interstate 25.

My *Blackfeather* characters began talking to me north of Fort Collins and kept up a non-stop chatter. I could barely complete a 200-mile drive without pulling over to write. But as they yammered, they started pointing the old raven out to me. He was a sentinel along the highway. "He's watching out for you, Ari." At least once in every five miles, I would see a raven sitting beside the highway. He was always facing away. He was rapidly becoming my totem. And he symbolized creativity.

The campgrounds along I-25 south through Colorado were semi-closed for the season. You could still camp if you filled out a registration and dropped the fee in the box at the gate. But there was no one on duty, the camp store was closed, and I saw a total of two other people when I stopped. I fixed myself a can of soup for dinner and got four thousand more words written on the story.

SOUTH OF PUEBLO, I cut off the interstate for a couple of days to go see the Capulin Volcano that Angie and I had missed when we were caught in a snowstorm in Taos the year before. I missed that girl. We'd only been lovers for a few days out of less than four months we were together, but it was her simple charm—and nude body—that I missed as a traveling companion. We kept in touch by email and Facebook, but I decided to give her a call after I'd made the hike up and around the volcano's crater.

"Uncle Ari! I haven't talked to you since you were someplace in Wyoming with that sweetheart Alice. I'd love to meet her sometime. Where are you now?" she asked when I connected with her.

"Remember when we were going to go across the pass to see the volcano but got snowed on?" I said. "I just walked around the crater. Saw half a dozen mule deer right on the path about twenty feet ahead of me."

"How cool! I wish I was there."

"How are you doing, Pudding? Is school going okay?"

"Yeah. I'm almost finished with my coursework and will start my thesis in January. I'm going to push to graduate in the spring. I've been getting some classroom time as a substitute teacher this fall."

"That's great, Angie. I'm heading south for Ruidoso again so I can write in front of the fireplace."

"You scared me so much when you showed me a separate room. God, Ari, those were some good times."

"Want to join me for Thanksgiving?" I asked.

"Oh. Um… Ari, please don't be upset. I've kind of… well, I'm seeing this guy. I mean, he's not just a guy. He's really nice. And I think… I love him," she whispered.

"Angie, that's wonderful. You know I want you to be happy. Tell me all about your Prince Charming," I said.

It was true. I did just want her to be happy and neither of us had any commitment to the other after she left last Christmas. Once I got her talking, Angie just bubbled about her guy. Even taking into account the love-blind newness of her relationship, I could tell he was a good man. Angie had left the bulk of her submissiveness behind and Adam treated her like a princess. He was a structural engineer and worked on bridges for the county. He had a lot of respect for teachers and was very supportive in her drive to finish her master's and start teaching full time.

I was happy for Angie. We wished each other well and disconnected. *There went another little piece of my heart.*

I PARKED THE trailer at a place in Alamogordo and loaded all my supplies, clothes, and liquor into the truck. I connected electricity and set the thermostat at fifty-five. It was likely to get cold and I didn't want to risk the trailer freezing, even down at the lower elevation of Alamogordo. I'd booked two weeks in the condo and didn't plan to do anything other than write. I'd contacted several other writers in both Alamogordo and Ruidoso and figured there would be a few sessions where we all got together. For eleven months of the year, writing is a solitary endeavor for me. One month a year, it is a social event.

I was sitting at Sacred Grounds on Friday afternoon the fourteenth when I typed the words THE END on my first draft of *Blackfeather*. It had taken me two weeks to write the 77,000-word story. I was pleased with it, but Jay had made me promise to send it to him before I put it into the cycle of posting on SOL or made an eBook out of it. I had the notion that this was a story I'd submit for contest, so I wasn't rushing it into posting. Part IV of *Living Next Door to Heaven: Deadly Chemistry*, had just begun posting. I'd finished Part V: *The Rock* and it was in the hands of my editors. I'd been pushing myself to make sure I finished each part of LNDtH before it started posting. I'd recently added Floyd to my editorial team and I was getting used to cycling each chapter through three editors instead of just two. It was a good addition and he was catching inconsistencies in sequence that I'd been missing.

Since I'd finished *Blackfeather*, I decided that after the weekend, I'd start *Part VI: El Rancho del Corazón*. But there was the matter of the weekend to deal with.

~~~~~

I MET HARRIET at church. When I'm hanging around a place for a while, like I was in in Ruidoso, I often drop in at the local Unitarian Church to meet people and socialize. High hopes.

The church happened to have an early Thanksgiving carry-in dinner after the service. As a visitor, I was invited to join them. There were a couple hundred people there and the church committee had supplied turkeys, dressing, and potatoes. The (primarily) ladies of the congregation supplied salads, side vegetables, cranberry sauce, and pies. Lots of pies. I filled a good-sized paper plate and picked up a cup of coffee, then started looking for a place to sit. A nice-looking lady was sitting alone at one of the long tables and I asked if I could join her. I was welcome. And so were the other six, somewhat older, unattached ladies that came to join us. It was unfortunate that I wasn't going to be in Ruidoso long enough to spend time with each of them. Maybe next time.

Harriet was German and a widow. She'd been married, I discovered, to an English actor who had been active on the stage in the rather spectacular theater that Ruidoso boasts. She lived in Michigan during warm weather, but wintered in Ruidoso. That might seem strange. Most of us old folks go someplace warm in the winter. Don't let the words 'New Mexico' fool you into thinking it's warm there. Ruidoso is a ski resort town. And Harriet loved to ski. She was about the cutest 75-year-old ski bunny on the slopes.

Of course, if you've ever seen me on skis, you'd know I wasn't going to meet her up there. I never got past the stage of using edgy-wedgies to tie the toes of my skis together so I could snowplow down the bunny slope. I've had many a good time at ski resorts, though, sitting in the lodge drinking hot cocoa laced with schnapps and playing cribbage with all contenders. If there's a fire in the fireplace, so much the better.

Since I had initially begun my dinner conversation with Harriet, and in the interest of not appearing to be a cad, I focused on her through most of the meal. And on the pies. I believe that each of the ladies at the table had brought a pie and I was obliged to sample each of them. Three pumpkin, two apple, a strawberry/rhubarb, and a mincemeat. I have never figured out what kind of meat mincemeat is. A little sweet and a little savory. By the end of the meal I could scarcely move. I was thankful that Harriet had brought the strawberry/rhubarb so I could praise it highly. It's one of my all-time favorites.

Most of the writers I'd been meeting over coffee were a good bit younger and prettier than the old dolls here at church, but they were all married with children. I made arrangements to meet Harriet a couple times that week and we got along well. She was funny and entertaining.

And insane.

I sure can pick them. I'd just finished writing the first chapter of *El Rancho del Corazón* that started with Brian and Hannah in bed, basking in the glow of finally making love. It was too bad I'd be leaving in a couple days. I liked Ruidoso. Harriet and I were having coffee on Friday when she pulled a vial of her husband's ashes from her pocket.

"I always carry a little bit of him with me. He likes to ski. I talk to him and ask his advice. He said you were a nice guy."

Thank you, dead husband. Well, I suppose it wasn't so terrible. Angelina Jolie carried a vial of what's-his-name's blood around. It could be weirder.

It was.

"Arthur was always surrounded by young women. He was very handsome, and actors are like that. Of course, you older gentlemen always need to have a young woman around to get it up. But sometimes we can slip in and use the erection before she gets to it," she said casually.

I begged to differ with her. I don't think we older gentlemen need a *younger* woman to get it up. We need an *interested* woman. Treasure could have had it anytime she wanted if she'd had any interest in it at all. Well, you know that story. I didn't like to think of that because I was still—would probably always be—in love with Treasure. We older gentlemen appreciate younger women because they always seem to be interested, even if they aren't interested in *us* per se. Aubrey and Mandy had certainly been interested. My protests fell on deaf ears.

"I still have his last come in the freezer." *Say what?* "Two weeks before he died. I spit it into a baggie and put it in the freezer for safe-keeping." I know I have a reputation for writing fiction, but guys, some things you can*not* make up.

Harriet declined to kiss me goodbye because she was afraid she'd like it too much and then I'd leave. I was afraid my tongue would end up in the freezer in a baggie labeled 'last kiss'.

Saturday morning, I checked out of my condo and headed back to my trailer in Alamogordo. I spent Thanksgiving with friends in the Gila Mountains west of Silver City. I brought all the food to their little cabin and they cooked it.

I also brought bourbon and Samuel and I spent a long night in front of the fire swapping stories and sippin' liquor.

～～～～

"I READ THAT book you sent, *The Gutenberg Rubric*. It's good," Samuel said. He'd told me a bunch of his experiences as a screen writer, but those are his stories to tell and I'm not going to try to repeat them. "Why aren't you published through a big publisher? Isn't self-publishing kind of a stigma? Even though you have a company with a different name, I know you own the company."

"Well, several years ago, a couple buddies and I decided to go into the publishing business. We had the unique concept of having everyday readers go through our slush pile and rate the manuscripts we received. If the manuscript achieved a hundred points from the ratings, we'd work with the author to get it edited and ready to publish. If all worked out well, we'd publish the book at our expense and split the profits with the author."

"Sounds like an interesting concept. What happened?"

"Well, we were successful with our first book. It was good. It got rated highly. And we published it. We didn't want to be a publisher with just one title, so each of the partners contributed what he considered his best work. We edited the books as carefully for each other as we did for our clients and when we released the book and hit Amazon, we had four titles in the market. None of our books did as well as the one we published for our new author, but we were putting all our marketing efforts into his book, so that was understandable. Unfortunately, his was the only other book we published."

"Why? Didn't you get submissions?" Samuel asked.

"Yes, but most were the bottom of the slush pile. They didn't even achieve thirty point ratings. And authors were trying to game the system by getting all their friends to go online and rate their book so they could get a contract. Our black box for computing the scores, though, dropped the rating of any reviewer who just gave a score and didn't leave a review of the manuscript. There were two notable exceptions that hit our criteria. The first read well. We allowed authors to upload the first 5,000 words of their manuscript and that's what was rated. Unfortunately, when we got the whole manuscript in, we discovered that the first 5,000 words of her book were the only part that was semi-literate. It was such a disaster that we sent it back and told her to cut 20,000 words from her 115,000-word book and to decide what her POV would be and what the point of the story was before we looked at it again. It was harsh and Jay wrote about ten pages of very specific critique, but we never heard from her again."

"I've never figured out how publishers and agents could decide what to publish based on the first ten pages," Samuel said.

"Sometimes it's easy," I laughed. "The second story that topped our ratings was good. It was a thriller and there were a few places where the pace lagged and at one point the hero was saved by a miraculous rescue that was unbelievable. But overall it was a solid, publishable story. The author took our comments, did the work we suggested, and submitted it to an independent agent who got him a publishing contract with a mainstream publisher."

"So, he used you to improve his manuscript without having to pay anything and then sold it to someone else? Well, that sucks," Samuel said. "Sounds like Hollywood."

"Yeah, my partners were discouraged and ultimately I took over the remaining assets of the business and restarted it as my own. An agent I knew sent me a manuscript and asked me if I could publish it and do it fast because the author was dying. It was a good manuscript, but needed editing badly. I took it on and had it edited and released as a paperback, hardcover, and eBook in forty-five days. He died three months later and sales died with him. I got a couple more manuscripts that I could share the cost of publishing for a share of the profit. And then I thought, if I'm publishing all these other authors' books, why shouldn't I publish my own? My first new release was a book of fairy tales, essentially, but not for children. Think Grimm's, not Disney. Then *The Gutenberg Rubric* won an award and I went on tour with it."

"Did you ever think about getting an agent yourself?"

A Long Time Ago: Agency

I WAS PLEASED with *Behind the Ivory Veil* after I'd rewritten it ten times. Life was good. Of course, I had to have a regular job in a small business publishing company to pay my mortgage, but Treasure and I were making progress toward a life together and I'd proposed to her on her birthday. I was still waiting for her answer, but I was a patient man.

That's when I got the response back from Elizabeth Hanley, an agent with one of the top houses in New York. I'd sent queries and excerpts to nearly every agent listed in the *Writer's Guide*. I'd been systematic about it, sending off three every week. I was the proverbial author who could paper a wall with rejection slips. But Hanley liked it.

> *This is a fresh concept. Your synopsis shows that you know where the story is going and we have a real upsurge in urban fantasy hitting the market. Good work.*
> *Now the bad news. Your manuscript isn't ready to publish. Starting a thrilling fantasy novel with a professor lecturing to himself in the desert just doesn't cut it. You need to bring the action forward. Your first paragraph should grab the reader and hold him. I believe that the pagan rituals later in the book add just enough suspense to carry the work to the end, but you need to get to me on the first page.*
> *I want to see this manuscript again. Soon. If you decide to take my advice, send me the first fifty pages after you've rewritten it. And for Pete's sake, have someone proofread it!*
> *Elizabeth Hanley*

I was ecstatic. I took vacation time from my job and locked myself in a room for a week to do the rewrite. I could see what Hanley meant and was determined to get it right. Treasure read and edited what I wrote, and unlike Belle who laughed at it, Treasure helped me get it right. I packaged it up and sent it off to the agent with a note thanking her for her advice and encouraging her to tell me anything else that needed to be fixed.

The next week, Treasure said 'Yes.'

I didn't hear from Hanley.

In fact, four months later when Treasure and I were married, I still hadn't heard from the agent.

It was Christmas, eight months after my submission, that I got a package in the mail from the agency. It contained my manuscript and a short note.

> *Dear Author,*
>
> *We are sorry to tell you that agent Elizabeth Hanley passed away in September after a long fight with cancer. Our office has been reeling with the loss, but we are attempting to contact all the authors with whom she was working to return their materials. We are sorry it has taken so long to contact you, but this has been a very difficult time for us. If you are missing materials that you sent to Elizabeth, please let us know and we will attempt to locate them. We here at the agency wish you the very best of luck in the future.*

Fuck!

Back to New Mexico

I SLEPT IN the greenhouse room at Samuel and Candace's mountain home and woke up in the middle of the night with light in my eyes. It took a while for me to realize it was starlight. The stars were that bright up there. I watched them turn their course through the sky. It seems their path never ends. Maybe mine doesn't either.

It's Not About the Destination

5 December 2014

I'D BEEN in my little travel trailer for seventeen months and the year was drawing to a close. I camped after Thanksgiving down south of Tucson where I had absolutely no cell coverage and no Internet. I needed time to contemplate the lint in my navel and decide what I was going to do next. What had I accomplished when I 'hit the road, Jack'?

I'd traveled 38,000 miles through thirty-six states and up into one Canadian province. I'd been to national parks and monuments, and some of the most beautiful and romantic places in the U.S. Most of them alone. In the not-alone times, I'd had seven lovers ranging in age from nineteen to fifty-five. But most of them had been for only a night or two.

What was the point?

～～～

A Year and a Half Ago: It's About the Journey

I REMEMBER THE first night I moved into my trailer. Maddie came out of the house in her pajamas and robe with fluffy slippers and knocked on the door. It was easy. For a few days, until I got the trailer stocked and everything moved into it, it was parked in the carport. She brought hot cocoa packets and a carton of milk. The first thing I'd moved into the trailer was my coffee mugs.

"So, Dad," she began. She was using her most mature voice—the voice of reason. "What's your goal? Are you out to discover yourself? Do you have a quest to see all the states? The National Parks? Old girl-friends?" We laughed. I pulled a bottle of crème de menthe out of the drawer that I'd designated as my liquor cabinet, although there was only a bottle of wine and half a bottle of scotch in it with the liqueur. I poured a little into each of our mugs with the cocoa.

"Well, sweetie, I don't have a goal, I guess."

"Not going off to get in touch with your inner being or something? What's the point?"

"It's not about the destination. It's about the journey," I sighed. "You don't always need a goal. It isn't about getting from point A to point B. It's about seeing what's along the way. When I pull out of the driveway on August first, I'm not even positive what direction I'm going."

"I'm going with you."

"Um…"

"I'm not going to let you just take off with no idea where you are headed until I know you are okay out there. I'll take a week off work and fly back here from wherever we end up." She was determined, and it wasn't a bad prospect, either. I didn't want her to feel deserted and I didn't want her to be worried.

"In a week, we might still be in the State of Washington and I can just drive you home."

"Whatever. Maybe I can catch a train."

We sipped our cocoa in silence for a minute, no thought of talking about our writing. Most of our conversations were filled with creative stuff. She talked to her mother about boyfriends, money, and jobs.

"You know, you can come and visit me, too. In fact, since I'm on the road and have no destination, pick a place where you'd like to meet and I'll park there. Someplace you've never been," I suggested.

"Really? Florida? Get out of Seattle in the winter?" We laughed at her sudden burst of enthusiasm. "That will be cool. It will help me figure out if it's what I want to do. I've got a little savings. I've got a car. I've got camping gear. Maybe I'll just quit my job next summer and leave," she said. I shuddered.

Never let it be said that parents don't influence their children.

Back to Tucson

I NEEDED SUPPLIES, so I went into Tucson and stopped at Starbucks first thing. As soon as I had my computer connected to the Internet, I checked my email.

Ari! Guess what! I miss you!
I'm almost finished with my first semester. Can you believe
it? Well, I just realized that second semester doesn't start
until the third week of January.
Ari, could I visit you at Quartzite? It would be so cool to
not be the only one naked. Besides, I really want to see the
expression on Cassie's face when I walk out of your trailer
in nothing but my flip-flops and a smile.
I'm sending you a picture of what I'll look like except I
couldn't find my flip-flops so all I've got on is the smile.
What do you think, Ari? Do you want to see me again?
Love and kisses,
Alice

WANT TO SEE her? Hell, yeah! A little break with Alice would be a great way to end the year. I shot back an email and told her to make her flight plans to come to me. Eighteen months in a sixteen-foot trailer would be worth everything to spend three weeks with Alice. I'd been a lot of places and experienced a lot of things this year-and-a-half, but if anyone asked what the best part of the journey was so far, the answer was Alice.

That will be a good place to start the next volume of *Wonders of My World*. Right after I decide what to do with the rest of my life.

In the meantime, I have a photo I'm just going to keep staring at.